THE
SPIRIT WASTES

THE
SPIRIT WASTES

P.R. BREWER

First paperback edition 2023

Cover design by James T. Egan of Bookfly Design
Layout by Bodie D. Dykstra of BD Book Design
Map by Sarah Waites of Illustrated Page Design

ISBN 978-1-7354440-2-4 (paperback)
ISBN 978-1-7354440-3-1 (ebook)

Published by Lockegee Books
Newark, Delaware

www.prbrewer.com

For Barbara

THE WASTES
SYLVANIA
STEAMBOAT GRAVEYARD
SUNKEN TOWN
RUSTED TOWN
THE BLUEGRASS
THE HOLLOWS
THE TIDELANDS
GHOST CITY
RIP
RUINED TOWN
PINNACLE
THIRTEEN POINT
GARDINEL
BALD MT
THE PENNYROYAL
N
THE CUMBERLANDS
RAM'S HORN

PROLOGUE

THE NIGHT OF THE GREAT WAKENING
143 Years, 11 Moons, and 23 Days Ago

JESSIE WAS PLAYING HER FIDDLE WHEN THE NIGHT OUTSIDE HER window turned green. Blood rushed to her head, as if she'd hung upside down from a tree, and a faint whisper fluttered in her ears. The pattern on the wrinkled wallpaper seemed to swirl hypnotically.

She set down her bow and rubbed her eyes. Now the sky was black and full of stars again.

"Did y'all see that?" she called out, but nobody answered. No surprise there. Mom and Dad were downstairs listening to President La Follette drone away on the radio. If Jessie bugged them with her wild fancies, they'd scoff and tell her to go to bed. Her sister was rehearsing lines for the school performance of *Thirteenth Night*, and her brother must be caught up in a Juliette Verne novel or an issue of *Eerie Tales* magazine.

Time to get back to practicing. Her fingers were sore, but she'd play them bloody to win a prize at the Sorghum County Fair. And to show up Mildred Fannin, who always looked down her nose at Jessie's wormy old fiddle. Mildred owned a violin with aluminum strings and took paid lessons with a music professor.

Jessie played a few scales, but the notes came out all wrong. Not wolf tones; more like a dissonant harmony. She retuned her strings and tried again, but this time the notes sounded even stranger. She plucked a string in frustration and then almost dropped her bow.

A ball of green light was floating just beyond her window.

Clutching her fiddle and bow, Jessie crept up to the pane. The light was the size of her fist and the shade of a glowworm. Was it swamp gas? Or a ghost? Or some weird sort of lightning?

She touched the glass. With a soft trill, the light drifted closer.

"You stay right there," Jessie told it. On fire with curiosity, she ran down the stairs and toward the front door.

Her mother scowled at her from the sofa. "Where are you going?"

"I thought I'd practice in the hayloft," Jessie said. "So's not to bother you with my caterwauling." That's what Mom and Dad called her playing. But maybe they'd be proud if she snagged the blue ribbon at the fair.

Her parents turned back to their crystal radio. "We'd sure appreciate the quiet," said her father. "The signal's been fuzzy this evening."

"Don't stay up too late," said her mother. "You're cleaning the coop first thing in the morning."

Jessie started to argue but then thought better of it. "I'll be back soon," she mumbled as she crossed the threshold to the porch.

This was the first night of spring, but the air was still freezing outside. Jessie wished she'd stopped to put on her coat.

Behind her, trees rustled on the dark hills. Down the hollow, a gold glow lit the way to town and the school she walked to five days a week.

Jessie was sure the green light would be gone by the time she turned the corner. But no, the odd little bogey was levitating next to the clothesline.

"Where'd you come from?" she asked it. "The sky? Or the swamp? Or the grave?"

The ball of light circled her and made a quavering noise. Did it like music, then? Jessie put her fiddle to her chin and set to playing "Fire on the Mountain." Like before, the notes sounded off, as if she'd tuned the strings to a key that had never existed.

The green light darted into the woods.

"Wait up," she shouted. "I didn't mean to scare you away." But the thing had already vanished. So, that's how it was. Everyone hated her playing—her parents, Mildred Fannin, and even the mysterious bogey.

Jessie slouched back toward the house. As she climbed the steps to the porch, a bad smell brought her up short: a lightning bug stink, but stronger. She leaned on the railing and sniffed.

Then the house caved in with a crash.

The next thing Jessie knew, she was flat on her belly and half buried in chunks of the roof. Her mouth tasted of blood, but she still had a grip on her bow. When she crawled out from under the wreckage, she saw her fiddle lying in the grass. Pale green rays washed over the yard, as if cast by an emerald moon.

Trying not to cry from the pain in her ribs, Jessie rolled onto her back and looked up at the thing that had flattened her home. A tower of light stood above her, as silent as a stone monolith. Long streamers twined down from its spire.

Jessie instinctively lunged for her fiddle. The monster swayed overhead and stretched out its shimmering garlands. It was fixing to kill her, and she was helpless to stop it.

Or was she?

The little bogey had fled when she'd played it her out-of-tune music. Maybe this monster would, too.

She raised her fiddle and scraped its strings seven times with her bow.

PART ONE

THE VOICE FROM FAR AWAY

Fall 2nd, Year 143 AW (After Wakening)

Dear Zora,

It was a blessing to see you again after so many years. I've always been proud of you—not that I claim any credit for what you've done—and I've missed you every day I've been gone. No hill or hollow has felt like home since I left.

I'm glad you had the chance to meet Quinn and launch your spirit-chasing venture with him. I was wrong to keep y'all in the dark and wrong to drop out of sight with no explanation. I'm sorry for all the pain my mistakes have caused.

Now that your mom and Quinn's mom are here, I ought to be on my way. I don't imagine they want me around, and I can't say I rightly blame them. I left the spirit-shooter you gave me; I'm done traveling by night, so you may be needing it more than I will. The wagon is yours and Quinn's to keep (by the way, I like the new paint job). Take care of Undine and Ursula; they're the finest horses I've ever met. And good luck working on your inventions. I don't follow the science behind them, but I know they—and you—saved us all from the harbinger.

I'll write you every moon, and you can visit me once your mom ungrounds you. If you're curious, I'll tell you about the time she ran away from home just like you.

Until then,

Your loving father

*One other thing: I've been thinking on your theory that the Wakenings rewrote the laws of nature. Nevan McBrain (may he rest in peace) once loaned me a handwritten book that set out the same notion—*Observations on Arcane Astronomy *by Henrietta Fleming. He'd found the musty thing on one of his treks in the Wastes, somewhere along the route to the Bluegrass. In a mansion on a horse farm devoured by kudzu, if I recall correctly. I reckon the book's at the bottom of the lake with old Nevan now, but I read it cover to cover before I gave it back to him. I couldn't tell whether the writer was more scientist or sorcerer; her notions of cosmic strings and convergences made my head spin. Even so, one bit stuck in my mind—a note in green ink on the final page:*

THE KEY TO THE GATE LIES UNDER THE CASTLE ON THE AZURE DOWNS. FOLLOW THE SIGN OF THE GOAT TO PASS BELOW BUT BEWARE THE RIFTS IF YOU CHERISH YOUR SOUL.

You're smarter than me, so maybe you can decipher that.

1

ZORA PULLED HER GOGGLES DOWN OVER HER EYES AND SWEPT the wagon's blue searchlight across the darkness. The beam revealed snow-dusted silos and scarecrows in empty fields, but no sign of any spirits. Ahead of her, the dirt road wound toward the woods beyond Lightning Bug Hollow.

A little ways longer, and she'd see whether her new weapon could stop the biggest spirit in these parts: the elemental known as Old Smoky.

Zora shivered as a blast of wind cut through her wool coat and canvas overalls. Her fingers felt frozen around the reins. Beside her, Paige zipped up the aviator's jacket she'd inherited from her great-great-grandma Zhu.

Another gust roared through the narrow valley, whipping Zora's hair sideways. By now, her neighbors would be snug inside their little houses. Above the hilltops, the stars were already shining. She could make out her favorite constellation—the Hunter— along with the Seven Siblings and, just faintly, the Twins.

"Trot," she told Tycho, and the mule plodded a bit faster.

"Feels grand to be back in the field," said Paige. The apprentice Spotter's short black hair stuck out from beneath a cap that made her look like an old-time biplane pilot. "I was getting cabin fever something fierce from all the studying at my boss's lodge."

Zora nodded. "This is the first time Mom's let me leave home without her since last fall." Stuck in her lab for almost six moons, with a half-moon to go until she turned sixteen. Until she was free to wander the Hollows and fight spirits again. "I had to swear we'd be back by midnight."

The wagon rattled past barns painted with Sylvanian hex signs: hearts for love, rosettes for luck, and stars to ward off danger. Hooey for the superstitious. Zora never trusted in chance, and she counted on her own devices to keep herself safe.

She didn't believe in love-charms, either.

"Any roamers stray through here lately?" asked Paige.

"Not even a boge. It's been quiet spirit weather all season."

"So, no target practice yet with your thingamajig." The apprentice let the silence linger, and then she smiled. "This'll be good for a thrill."

Tycho snorted when they came to the sign for Hildy's Inn. The neon letters cast a halo of light around the tin-roofed building. "No stopping," Zora told the mule. "But I'll give you a lump of sugar when we get home." She leaned closer to Paige and lowered her voice. "He's a fine mule, but I miss the horses." And her big brother. Quinn was probably chasing down some rare type of spirit tonight.

Paige reached into her backpack. "I have a surprise for you." She held up a reddish-brown hat with long tassels on either side. "The yarn matches your hair."

"Did you knit that yourself?"

"Hardly. I couldn't stitch a seam if my life depended on it.

My mom made this to thank you for saving the Hollows. The tassels were my idea, though. I like your hair down, but the pictures in the papers made the old pigtails part of your—what do you call it?—public image." Paige handed her the hat. "And now I can still call you Foxtails."

Zora took the reins in one hand and tried on the hat. "Don't get modest on me. We saved the Hollows *together*. Me, you, Quinn, and Signe."

She steered Tycho to the right, and they left the sign's glow for the forest. Branches stretched toward her with frost-tipped needles, blocking her view of the stars.

A half dozen bends, and Zora caught a flash of spirit-shine in the pines up ahead. With a soft beep, an orange bulb lit up on the sensor band strapped to her wrist. Paige drew the banisher Zora had built her: a squat pistol with a brass grip and a glass barrel. A second alarm sounded when Tycho crossed the covered bridge, and the beeping kept up until all ten bulbs on the wrist-watcher had come to life.

The roots of Zora's teeth twinged.

The final bend led to another sign—not a neon one this time, but a wooden board on a pair of stakes. It bore the image of a skull rendered in luminous paint. Zora had added the reflective tape that warned *KEEP AWAY—ELEMENTAL*.

The mule halted well short of the sign. A clearing lay beyond, and at its center stood a shack engulfed in the brilliant green phosphorescence of the elemental. The spirit's tendrils billowed above the ash that ringed the foundations, coiled around the weathered siding, and reached toward the sky from the holes in the roof. Fragments of glass glinted in the corners of the windows.

The elemental seemed riled up tonight. If Zora didn't know better, she would've sworn it had been expecting them.

"Big, ain't it?" whispered Paige.

"It's small for an elemental." Not half as large as the pair Zora had faced last year and pint-sized next to the ones lurking in the Wastes, but still strong enough to turn a human or a mule to dust within seconds. "We call it Old Smoky. It rose the night of the Great Wakening, and it's dwelled here ever since." For a hundred forty-four years, minus seven days. "That ruin used to be a station agent's house." She pointed to the west. "The railroad ran all the way to the Bluegrass. If this new weapon works, maybe someday we'll clear a path along the tracks and follow them down to what's left of the cities. I can salvage spare parts, and you can search for lost treasures while Quinn and Signe raid the libraries."

"Sounds funner than proofreading my boss's spirit guide."

Zora grabbed her crutches from the footboard and lowered herself to the ground. Her boots crunched against the ice as she scanned for roamers with the illuminator strapped to her arm.

Paige hopped down and hitched Tycho to a rusted post by the road. "Still packing your hidden rocket?"

"Right here." Zora lifted one of her bronze-shafted crutches. "I'm always ready for the spirits." Never mind that her stomach was churning or that she could taste bile in her throat. The elemental was an earthbound spirit. It might give them a touch of vertigo at this range, but it couldn't hurt them if they stayed outside its sway.

Tycho whimpered as a breeze from the ruin brought a scent like rotten mushrooms. The forest around them was silent and still. Neither bear nor outlaw would dare visit here by night.

Zora circled to the back of the wagon and inspected the cargo in the hay: a glass tube like the one in Paige's banisher-pistol, but as long and as thick as a log. "Haul it over there. And be careful not to crack it."

Paige hefted the tube in both hands, lugged it to the edge of the road, and gently laid it on the ground. "I recognize this. You swiped it from Evelyn Fontaine's mansion."

"Confiscated it," corrected Zora. "She didn't deserve it, not after the things she did." Like trying to steal Zora's inventions and plotting to sell out everyone in the Hollows.

Paige fetched the other parts from the wagon and mounted the tube on a tripod. Then Zora fixed a silver arc ladder to the tube's front and a copper coil to its back. At the turn of a dial, the device buzzed like a hive of electric bees.

"You say that spirit's been here going on a century and a half." Paige raised a scuffed-up pair of binoculars to her eyes and surveyed the ruin. "It's weird to think how we're fixing to zap it away."

"Legend says the station agent's family was asleep when the Wakening started. None of my neighbors would step in that shack if you paid them a hundred bits, but I searched it a few moons ago." By daylight, with Mom hovering over her while the elemental slumbered beneath the ground. "I had to see for myself."

"Find anything?"

"An empty cradle in the bedroom." Zora aimed the banisher-cannon at the shack. "I don't feel too sappy about saying goodbye to Old Smoky."

She pressed a button on the coil. Argon lightning crackled inside the glass tube, and sparks leaped along the arc ladder.

An instant later, a violet ray shot from the cannon toward the spirit. The aura around the ruin flared even brighter as a rumble pulsed in her eardrums. Paige grimaced and lowered her binoculars.

Zora twisted the dial to give the cannon more power. Something ripped underground—something thick and dense, like an anchor chain—and then a blast of force threw her backward onto the hard earth.

For a moment, she was too dazed to do anything except look up at the Dog Star and try to catch her breath. Next to her, Paige muttered words she surely hadn't learned from her studies with Darius Epps.

When slush began seeping through Zora's overalls, she mustered the will to push herself to her feet. The spirit had vanished, leaving the shack half hidden in shadow. Every bulb on her wrist-watcher was dark, and the pain in her molars had faded. The banisher-cannon lay next to her, tipped over but unbroken. The night was quiet except for the howl of the wind.

She brushed the snow from her coat and laughed. "So long, Old Smoky. And say hi to your friends when I—"

The wrist-watcher beeped. Emerald specks flickered in the gloom of the shack, and a wave of dizziness swept over Zora.

"Well, crap," said Paige.

Green vapors rose from the ash, growing until they shrouded the ruin once more. The elemental swayed its tendrils lazily, as if to taunt Zora.

"I'll find a way to knock you back to your world," she shouted, but the threat came out sounding pitiful. The spirit couldn't understand what she was saying, anyway.

Paige patted Zora's shoulder. "I know you will."

"Right." Zora plucked the arc ladder from the cannon. "Let's pack up this junk and go home."

♈

"It's so aggravating," Zora said as they left Hildy's Inn. "My rifles and grenades can handle most types of spirits, but they won't cut it against the likes of hounts and spires. Without a way to beat those, we'll never retake the Wastes. Or learn whether anyone's survived outside the Hollows."

Paige sipped the apple cider she'd bought from Hildy. "What about those sound-shooters you were making?"

"My sonic weapons don't work at all. I can't even budge one tiny wisp with my prototypes." The fiddler girl from the ballads had dispelled mammoth-sized spirits with her music, but Zora's experiments with string vibrations kept failing. Now the cannon was a bust, too. "I guess I'll be spending more time in my lab."

Far to the west, a beacon blinked from the tower where the Rangers kept vigil over the borders. From that high up, they'd see the spirit-aurora that hung over the Bluegrass. The foragers who ventured down there to find gold bits or century-old bottles of bourbon described it as a land of blighted pastures and crumbling manors.

"Your mom seemed keen on shooing us away," said Paige.

"I think she only allowed this outing so she could spend the evening alone with your boss." Mr. Epps was wise and kind, not to mention the best Spotter alive in the Hollows, but watching Mom fall for someone felt strange.

"Lucky for us." Paige gave her a sly smile. "Speaking of courting, did anyone catch your eye at the Winter Fair?"

"Nope." Zora did her best to sound nonchalant. "Lots of boys wanted to know how we stopped the new Wakening, or if they could fire one of my banishers, but none of them asked me to dance." She shuffled her boots against the footboard. Nerve damage or no, she could cut a few moves. "Did you find yourself a girlfriend at the lodge?"

"No such luck. There were ten apprentice Spotters in my wing, all of us spending our first fall away from our folks. But two had boyfriends back home, another pair bunked up together right away, one was a real loner—pretty common for Spotters—and the rest, well, they just weren't right for me." Paige fell silent as the wagon rolled by zigzag fences and frozen ponds. "I wish your brother and his honey-pie were here," she said at last. "Heard from them lately, or are they too busy canoodling to write?"

"They both sent me letters after the solstice. Quinn was planning to call on Dad"—saying that still felt strange, too, after their father's eight-year disappearance, but they'd started patching things up with him—"and then head to your old stomping grounds to see his mom." Ms. Prosser was so different from Zora's mother: grave instead of scrappy, handier with a scalpel than a soldering iron. "Signe's visiting her family, too. She said the new parasol I made her was *exquisite*." Zora was bragging now, but she'd spent days on end crafting the gadgets in the handle and giving the canopy one of those spiderweb patterns Signe adored.

Paige guzzled the rest of her cider and crumpled the paper cup. "Did y'all figure out how those eyes of hers scare away spirits?"

"We ran some tests, but I'm still sorting out the paraphysics. Of course, she has her own peculiar notions about it."

"Unlike you."

"Unlike me," Zora said with mock gravity. "Her theories are all about fate and mystic forces. Mine are one hundred percent scientific."

They passed the sign that read *FIONA COLDIRON & DAUGHTER—ENGINEERS*, and Zora drove the wagon through the violet beams of her spirit-proof fence. Tycho quickened his pace—anxious for his treat, no doubt—and the familiar smell of corn diesel filled the air.

A small herd of goats greeted Zora at the barn, bleating and rubbing their heads against her. She scratched their necks and checked the generator clanking away in the corner. Running the electricity all night took plenty of ethanol, but she could buy barrels of the stuff thanks to the deals she'd struck with Mack-anical Wares and Kirk's Iron Works. And she slept sounder with the fence up, even if the harbinger couldn't return for another lifetime or so.

Tycho brayed impatiently as Paige undid his harness. Zora fed him his sugar and sat at her workbench to update her log-book. *Date: Winter 83, 143 AW. Banisher-cannon test #1. Subject: Elemental outside Lightning Bug Hollow. Ectospectral frequency set at 10^{14} cycles per second, etheric modulation at 2.3. Target exhibited initial vaporization before rematerializing and I'm so tired of this place but I promised Mom I wouldn't run away again if anyone finds this message it means I've died from boredom please carry on my work and tell Quinn to bury me with my banisher-pistol.*

She quit writing and peeked at the compact on the work-bench. The new hat looked sharp, though it didn't cover the welt a flying rivet had left on her pasty, freckled forehead.

Once Paige finished unloading the wagon, the two of them

walked down the blue-lit path to the house. Zora banged the screen door as she went in—loudly enough to be heard over the mandolin jangling on the radio—and led the way to the living room.

Zora's mom and Darius Epps were snuggled up on the sofa, with her head resting on his shoulder. They both sat up when they saw Zora. Her mom brushed back her orange and white hair, and the Spotter adjusted his owlish glasses.

Zora plunked herself into the floral print armchair by the fireplace. If she threw copper sulfate on those flames, they'd burn green like the spirit beneath the ruin. Give her a bucket of water, and she could douse them in a heartbeat. Too bad Old Smoky wasn't so easy to snuff.

"You're back sooner than I expected," said her mom. "I figured you'd spend a while at Hildy's blowing off steam."

"Did your apparatus vanquish the elemental?" Mr. Epps asked in his deep, booming voice. He'd grown a winter beard, a full one with grizzled curls.

Zora shook her head. "I need to try it on a spirit that isn't quite so big, like the landwight in the abandoned mine down the road." But Mom looked ready to object, so Zora backed off. "Maybe this spring. Did you finish writing your book?"

"Indeed," said Mr. Epps. "Signe Janasdottir persuaded her parents to print it with twenty color plates depicting the most striking varieties of waterbound spirits."

"Good for her," said Zora. "I can't wait to read it."

"I shall be delighted to deliver a copy for your birthday."

"Darius was just telling me how he photographed the spirit in the Big Lake," added Zora's mom.

Paige made a sour face. She was seventeen and past being

grounded by her mother—unlike Zora—but her boss had suspended her from the field for sneaking off to help rescue Quinn from a cult of spirit-worshippers.

"The first recorded snapshot of a leviathan," said Mr. Epps. "I used a waterproof camera that we liberated from Evelyn Fontaine." As he spoke the Spiritist priest's name, a shadow of unease stole into the room. "Have the Rangers found any trace of her whereabouts?"

Zora leaned toward the fire. "Not since the fall equinox."

"None of the followers she left behind knew why she made off for the Wastes," said Zora's mom. "And they talked when they realized she'd tricked them."

A burst of static from the radio made Zora start. The music went tinny and then stopped. After a second of dead air, a distorted voice spoke a string of unintelligible words. Feedback shrilled from the speaker, and the voice said something like *loom*—or maybe *doom*—before dissolving into white noise.

Zora hurried over to the radio, but the music resumed as she reached for the antenna. *This is a land of constant sorrow*, a woman sang in a mournful alto. *We've seen trouble all our days.*

"That was bizarre," said Paige. "Some sort of pirate station?"

Zora fiddled with the dial, searching for the distorted voice. "Could be interference from a shortwave transmitter."

Her mom looked thoughtful. "Or a stray signal bouncing off the atmosphere."

Zora gave up on finding the voice and turned the dial back to the Limestone Knob station. *In these Wastes, I'm cursed to ramble*, the singer wailed.

Zora closed her eyes, and the scene from her nightmare played out in her memory. She was alone in a desolate valley, surrounded by mountains taller than any she'd seen in real life. The ground lay blanketed in snow.

I have no one to help me now.

Sleet stung her cheeks, yet the sky was clear and starry. As she stood petrified, a green tint bled from the horizon and soaked the landscape.

You may bury me in some deep valley . . .

She flicked off the radio.

Paige gave her a sideways glance. "You okay, Foxtails? You look a mite pale."

"Just a spot of déjà vu," said Zora. Which was true, in a way.

From there, the conversation turned to the laying of the new Trans-Hollow rail line and the campaign for the open Judgeship and the latest misadventures of a roving hex-chanter they all knew. Zora leaned back in her armchair and listened to the others talk as the logs in the fireplace burned down to embers.

Around half past ten, Mr. Epps rose to bid them good-night, pleading weariness from his journey. He'd rolled up his sleeves—a first for him, at least in Zora's presence—and she caught herself staring at a tattoo of a hex sign on his forearm. It was a triple star inked in black and purple on his dark brown skin.

"Ah," said Mr. Epps. "You've never seen this symbol of my youthful folly, have you? I had it done when I was your age."

Zora looked up into his eyes. Way up—he would've towered over her even if she weren't sitting down. "I always figured you spent your teenage years holed up in a dusty attic with a stack of spirit guides."

"I dabbled in all manner of enchantments before I divined that my calling in life was to monitor the spirits. I looked beyond the path set before me and conjured up a new vision of myself." He gave a slight bow and departed for the guest bedroom, ducking his head along the way to avoid the hanging lamp.

"I know that little speech by heart," said Paige. "Mind if I grab the leftover chicken in your icebox?" She tromped off toward the kitchen without waiting for an answer.

Zora and her mom watched each other across the coffee table. A pendulum ticked slowly inside the grandmother clock, and the wires from the eaves hummed in the gathering gale.

"So," Zora said. "How was your evening with Mr. Epps?"

"He tells fascinating stories." Zora's mom wrapped a wedding ring quilt around her shoulders. "And he's a good listener. Not like—oh, not like any of the other men who've courted me over the years."

"I'm happy for you." Now that she'd said it, Zora realized she meant it. Mom deserved a fresh start after raising such an ornery daughter by herself. Especially seeing as how Zora planned to hightail it out of Lightning Bug Hollow at the first opportunity.

"Fox-Kit, I can tell you have something else on your mind."

Zora took a deep breath. "I've stuck to your rules, so how about letting me leave a half- moon early?"

"You mean now?"

"The Hollows are safe. No one's seen any of the nastier roamers since the fall equinox, and it's not like an earthbound or waterbound can sneak up on me so long as I have my sensors."

Her mom frowned. "We agreed you'd wait till you turned sixteen."

"Mr. Epps is taking Paige on his next expedition." Zora was

trying hard not to whine, but she couldn't help it. "Quinn's spent the past two seasons hunting spirits without me."

"They're of age, and you're not."

"I'm not a little girl hiding under her bed anymore. I know what I'm doing."

"That's precisely the attitude that scares me. There's so much about the spirits we still don't understand." Her mom raised her voice a notch. "Not even you."

"I understood enough to keep them from destroying the Hollows," snapped Zora.

Paige had just stepped out of the kitchen with a drumstick in one hand and a hunk of cornbread in the other. She turned right back around without a word.

Zora's mom took off her copper-framed glasses and pinched the bridge of her nose. "Yes, and I know I can't keep you cooped up here forever. Just give me a little more time before you fly away. We can work on your cannon together while you wait."

Zora sighed but then nodded. "I could use your help." She hesitated, feeling awkward. "I get how much it hurt you when Dad ran off. I promise I'll always come back."

"I believe you." Her mom came over and stroked Zora's hair. "And now I think it's past my bedtime."

"We should clear out anyway so Paige can take the sofa." Zora was grateful for the company, but the one-story house seemed more cramped than ever with a pair of guests staying over. At least Paige could fall asleep anywhere, be it a chair, a floor, or a patch of ground. Spotters learned to rough it when they tracked spirits by night in the wild.

Once she'd laid out a blanket and pillow, Zora trudged to her own bedroom, navigated the piles of clothes to the bed, and sat down to take off her boots. Her tumble at the shack had bent the steel strut on her right ankle brace. That would need fixing tomorrow.

She unstrapped her braces and changed into her flannel pajamas. Outside the window, a point of light flickered in the west—the evening star or a giant airbound spirit floating high in the ionosphere.

Zora switched off her bedside lamp, pulled the down-filled counterpane up to her chin, and began composing a mental list of tests to run. Anything to keep her mind off the nightmare. If she didn't dwell on it, maybe it wouldn't come again.

But of course it did.

The ceiling stretched out into a canopy of night sky. Stars blinked to life like winter solstice lights, and black peaks rose from the earth to encircle her.

Zora was in the Wastes. She knew it, though she'd never set foot here in waking life. She'd only seen the fringes of these barrens from the hills by her grandparents' farm. And from the summit of Clack Mountain, where Evelyn Fontaine's ancestors had built their mansion above a coal mine.

A greenish spiral took shape in the darkness, and an inhuman voice whispered in her mind. *I shall see you despair, little one.*

"You can't frighten me," Zora said. She'd banished this monster, the one spirit that could summon and command all the others. The harbinger, Nevan McBrain had named it. The Voice of the Spirits, its human worshipers called it. "We beat you."

Time and space entangle you yet.

"You can't come back." The snowy earth shook beneath her bare feet, like it always did in this dream. "Not till the stars line up again."

Look upon what lies in wait for you.

Foxfire glimmered above the mountains, and Zora glimpsed a vast shape between the peaks. She trembled as it thundered toward her. "I sealed your gateway."

Other threads entwine your world to mine.

Zora's blood went icy. She should've woken by now. This part of the nightmare was new. "What do you mean?" she shouted. "What threads?"

The thing behind the mountains drew nearer. Its footfalls echoed across the valley, and its aura lit the horizon like a green dawn. Another moment, and it would clear the final ridge . . .

That was when Zora jerked awake, drenched in sweat despite the chill in the air. She stayed up until sunrise before finally falling asleep.

♈

A knock broke through Zora's hibernation. She rolled over to face her windup clock. Almost noon. "Too early," she grumbled.

Zora's mom opened the door and poked her head into the room. "Come quick. We have a visitor."

Zora followed her, still shoeless and wearing her pajamas. Paige was standing by the hutch, and Mr. Epps had taken his favorite spot on the sofa. They were both watching the baby-faced man by the doorway.

"Ms. Zora." Ranger Emerson Tate doffed his cap and smoothed the wrinkles in his olive uniform. "Sorry to disturb your nap. The captain sent me with a message from the Judges."

Zora's chest tightened. Emerson seemed as calm as ever, but

he only showed up when there was trouble. "Is Evelyn Fontaine back?" she asked.

"Or the harbinger?" said Paige.

"No," said the Ranger. "We heard a radio signal from beyond the Hollows. There's folks alive out there, deep in the heart of the Wastes."

2

QUINN CREPT ALONG THE SIDE OF THE CLIFF WITH HIS BANISHER pointed straight ahead. To his right, the icicles of a frozen waterfall hung down like stalactites in a cave. To his left, the ground ended at a steep drop into Red River Gorge. Between the white of the waterfall and the black of the chasm ran the narrow trail to Sky Bridge.

If the locals were right, that's where he'd find the spirit. And if they were wrong, he'd just wasted an hour slogging through the darkness.

As Quinn picked his way across the rocks, he warmed himself with a fantasy of cruising down to the Delta on a Coal Age steamboat. Signe was at the bow, looking out over the broad, muddy river. Paige had both hands on the wheel, and Zora was barking orders to the engine room through a speaking tube. When they made it to the sea, maybe they'd sail a ship to the ancient docks of the Tidelands or the sandy isles farther south or one of those distant shores on his creased and yellowed map of the Olden World. Anywhere would do, so long as it lay beyond the barrens that hemmed in the Hollows.

A slip on a patch of black ice cut short Quinn's reverie and sent him sliding toward the rim of the gorge. His boots launched a small avalanche of stones over the edge, but he caught his footing in time to keep himself from plunging after them. Far below, faint splashes echoed from the void.

His heart pounding, he leaned against the cliff to steady himself. A swim in the Red River was the last thing he wanted on a night like this. His toes had gone numb already, and the cold was leaching through his buckskin jacket. He should've stuck to the road home instead of chasing this roamer by himself.

But the children at the trading post had looked up at him with wide eyes, and their parents had watched him with hopeful faces, and now here he was.

Quinn rounded a curve in the cliff, and a rock arch loomed before him. Even the library in Hoary Hollow would've fit beneath that sandstone vault. It was Sky Bridge, all right.

He raised his banisher, keeping one hand on the chrome grip and the other on the long glass barrel. When he swept the sapphire tracer beam along the arch, the sensors pinged twice. A pair of orange dots lit up on the banisher's stock, and a muffled sound drifted down from the murk. At first, Quinn took it for a sob—the cry of a lost child or one of the ghosts from his grandmother's tales. Then he heard it again and knew that no human, living or dead, could ever have made that noise.

He aimed the banisher at the source of the sound, and a cloudy form glimmered in the beam like fluorescent ink suspended in water. The spirit was as wide as a headstone and smelled of grave dust.

Quinn kept his weapon trained on the thing as he wracked his memories of Nevan McBrain's *Field Guide*. Was it an indrid?

No, those were smaller and wandered in flocks. A jarmara? Wrong shape, wrong sound. But what about an umbra?

That was it. *Umbras are solitary roamers with dim auras,* the Spotter had written in his book. *I have sighted them only on the darkest of nights. Though the umbra's cry is haunting, this spirit poses no threat to beast or human.*

Quinn holstered the banisher over his shoulder, pulled off his goggles, and retrieved the camera from his backpack. Whenever he and Signe found a harmless roamer, they took pictures of it and logged its location. She herded the more dangerous ones toward the Wastes, and he banished any that went berserk.

The umbra mewled like a squonk in a sack. Without the blue beam and his cobalt-lensed goggles, Quinn had to strain to see the spirit's green aura. He snapped three photos of it, put the camera away, and turned to retrace his path along the gorge.

By the time he arrived back at the ramshackle trading post, its windows were already dark. He plugged in his weapon's battery and swung by the stable to check on Ursula and Undine. Then he inspected the wagon, from the selenium cells on the roof panels to the spokes of the wooden wheels. If Evelyn Fontaine still had spies lurking in the Hollows, they'd recognize it even without the letters on its side spelling out *COLDIRON & PROSSER VENTURES.*

No sign of any booby traps or spirit-lures, so Quinn went inside the wagon and fired up the stove. The petals on the rosette-faced clock pointed to half past midnight. His bunk was a mess of quilts and lumpy pillows. The other bunk—Zora's— had lain empty all winter.

Tracking down spirits wasn't as much fun without his little sister.

Quinn stretched out on his bed and leafed through a stack of letters. Old Woman Calvert had written to tell him that her grandkids were catching bluegill in the oxbow where he'd banished a kelpie. Sammie Stegall had scrawled a picture of her new elemental-free home. And Lurana Underwood, presently residing at the Hollows Reformatory Farm, had penned a lengthy apology for helping the Spiritists offer him as a sacrifice on the night of the fall equinox.

The final letter was from Quinn and Zora's father. Like the others he'd sent these past two seasons, it detailed a few of the journeys he'd taken during his long absence from their lives. A voyage with Nevan McBrain to track the harbinger in the Near Wastes. Trips to sift through the relics at the scavenger stalls in the markets. And an expedition to the Ruined Town to search for records of a professor named Maxwell Doran. At the bottom of the page, Dad had scribbled a postscript:

I sure appreciate you calling on me. Watch out for hounts and any of that antlered woman's followers who got away. Say hey to Signe for me, and tell Zora she's welcome to drop by whenever her mom says it's OK.

Quinn folded the letter and tucked it away with the others. Seeing his father had stirred up all his old bitterness at the man's vanishing act, but at least the visit had gone better than the one last summer. This time, Quinn had said goodbye instead of stealing away in the dead of night.

To distract himself, he flipped to page one of *Carson van Patten and the Case of the Missing Geologist*. Signe had given him the entire set of van Patten novels as a winter solstice present. The two of them had finished the first book together, cuddled up beneath a comforter as he read to her by candlelight.

One more half-moon, and he'd see her again. Then they'd meet up with Zora and get back to hunting spirits as a team.

A barn owl screeched in the distance. Quinn set down the book and peered out the round window by his bunk, but a layer of fern frost obscured the world beyond the panes.

He closed his eyes and fell into a dreamless sleep.

♈

A day and a half later, Quinn stood before the white columns and red brick wings of the Prosser funeral parlor. The weathervane creaked above the rooftop, and the empty porch swing swayed in the breeze. Farther up the slope, the lichen-stained markers of the family graveyard jutted out from the brown grass.

After a season of wandering the Hollows, he'd finally come home to rest for a spell.

Quinn untangled his windblown hair before mounting the steps to the porch. A bell chimed as he opened the door, and a young woman in a drab suit stepped out of the office. Claire Zhu had the same black hair and sharp chin as Paige but none of her big sister's restlessness. When Paige had dragged him to go sneaking aboard the Floating Tavern or spelunking down the Haunted Sinkhole, Claire had stayed home and honed her taxidermy skills on the corpses of squirrels and possums. She'd jumped at the chance to take his place as assistant undertaker.

"Hail," Claire proclaimed in her froggy voice. "The mighty hunter returns to his humble roots, as dashing as ever—if a tad scruffy. How goes the spirit-busting racket?"

Quinn let her teasing roll off him. "Slow, lately. How's business?"

"Blooming like daisies. It's a shame your half-sister couldn't make it. I'm dying to meet the famous Gadgeteer Girl of Lightning Bug Hollow."

"You'll get your chance soon. I hear Zora's raring to chase spirits again."

"And where's your sweetheart?"

"Signe went to see her folks." He looked around the foyer where he'd spent so many days sitting with the dead and listening to sad ballads on the phonograph and pining after Paige Zhu. Before he'd set out on his own. Before he'd met Signe.

Claire dropped her sardonic air. "She was spooky. I liked her."

An empty casket lay on a bier in the alcove, bathed by the amber glow from the chandelier. "Is Mom around?"

"In the embalming room, with a new body. This one died under mysterious circumstances. The Rangers brought him in yesterday." Claire straightened her necktie and set to polishing the casket.

Quinn made his way to the back of the parlor, past the tintype portraits of his mortician forebearers. The business had stayed in the family for six generations counting Mom, but he'd broken that chain.

Cool air rolled over him when he entered the embalming room. Black curtains blotted out the noon sun, and bare bulbs cast a harsh light on the steel table. His mother was leaning over a cadaver and washing its face. The gray hairs in her braid had multiplied since his last visit.

She brushed her gloves against her leather apron and glanced up at Quinn. A mask hid the lower half of her face, but he could tell she was smiling by the wrinkles around her eyes.

"Welcome home," she said. "Mind giving me a hand?"

Quinn donned his old apron and joined her beside the table. He swallowed hard when he caught a good look at the body. He'd worked on hundreds of cadavers, but never one so strangely altered. Green veins showed beneath the dead man's skin, and his shaggy hair was a vivid shade of chartreuse.

The room suddenly felt even colder.

"He used to be blond," said Quinn's mom. "And that's not all." She pulled back one of the corpse's eyelids to reveal an emerald iris. "His eyes were originally blue. Ever run across a spirit that could do this?"

Quinn examined the dead man's fingernails. Sure enough, the moons had a greenish tint. "Last summer." Just thinking about it made his throat go tight. One of Evelyn Fontaine's followers had sold Signe a parasol with a spirit-lure hidden in the handle, and the beacon had drawn a spire from the Wastes to strike her down. Quinn would never forget the sight of her lying sprawled on the grass, as motionless as the corpse on the table. "When Signe almost died from spirit-sickness."

His mother stuffed padding in the dead man's mouth and sewed shut his jaw. "Did the Rangers ever catch the woman who planted the lure?"

"She vamoosed on the night of the equinox, just like Evelyn Fontaine. The Rangers never even found out her name. I asked Dad if he knew her from his days as a huckster, but he didn't recognize the sketch on the wanted poster." Quinn brought his mother an embalming pump with a chrome flywheel and a clockwork motor.

"How is he?" Her voice stayed level as she slid a tube into

the dead man's jugular. The blood came out a muddy green instead of red.

"Partway toward pulling himself back together, though he says he's done peddling tonics and cure-alls. He's staying on the old Moss family farm to grow hemp for the folks from the railroad. They need diesel for their locomotives." The final drops of the dead man's blood dribbled into the glass bottle. "He cut his beard and hair, too."

"You could use a trim and a shave yourself." Quinn's mother smiled and tilted her head toward the counter. "Could you bring me the formaldehyde?"

He fetched a beaker labeled CH_2O *Solution* and watched her pump the fluid into the dead man's arteries. "Who was he?"

"A moonshiner by the name of Del Burnett. A pair of Rangers patrolling the eastern border found him in a ditch beside Feather Crown Pike." She poked a silver trocar into the late Mr. Burnett's abdomen to drain his organs. "A long way from the Wastes for a spire to stray."

Unless someone—or something—had summoned it there. "Did the Rangers find anything else?" asked Quinn.

"Nothing but a few jugs of stump hole whiskey. His pockets were empty."

"I should send a message to Zora and Signe and Paige. Just in case this wasn't a random attack." Maybe Mr. Burnett had built a still in the Border Hollows, away from the watchful eyes of the Rangers, and a spire had followed him home from a bootlegging run. A bad turn of fortune for a reckless moonshiner but no cause for a broader alarm. Then again, maybe Evelyn Fontaine had returned to take her revenge. Or maybe the harbinger had found a path back from its world to this one.

"I'll have Claire hire a courier. You must be tired after so much traveling."

She was right. Quinn felt weary down to his bones from riding on bumpy roads and trekking down deserted trails. Sooner or later, every one of those paths wound its way back to the same hills and valleys. His father had spent half a lifetime crisscrossing the Hollows, but Quinn kept catching himself in daydreams about lost cities and endless oceans.

"I hope Signe can visit again," his mother went on. She'd ditched her notions of matching him up with Paige and taken a shine to Signe instead. "Next time I'll teach her how to sew a coffin quilt."

"I'll ask her." The thought buoyed him. Better to long for someone a few hollows away than for phantoms of far-off places he'd never see.

His mother paused in shaving the dead man's stubble. "Come to think of it, a courier came by with a letter for you."

"Not another invitation from Evelyn Fontaine, I hope." He wouldn't play hount-bait for that double-crosser again.

"No, this one's from the Judges. I left it in your bedroom. You can read it while I wrap up here, and then we'll eat dinner."

"I'll fry us some kilt lettuce," said Quinn. "I miss cooking in a real kitchen." His mother nodded and began powdering the dead man's face.

The narrow back stairs led Quinn to his old room. The inside was a dusty museum of childhood artifacts. Cardboard record sleeves lined the baseboards, and the shelves sagged beneath the weight of old books stacked to the ceiling. A framed photograph from his ninth birthday hung above the dresser. Dad was flashing a broad grin, the one he'd used to hawk his elixirs.

Mom wore a glum expression, as if she'd cottoned onto his two-timing ways. The shy-looking boy between them had his father's snub nose but his mother's dark hair.

Quinn found the letter on a pile of pulp magazines with lurid covers. *To Quinn Prosser, care of Anne Prosser,* read the ornate script on the envelope. *From the Assembled Judges of the Grand Court.* He broke the wax seal and skimmed past the formal pufferies until he came to a part that made his mouth go sandpapery.

A citizen of the Hollows has discovered a radio signal from a small band of survivors in the Sounding Gap. The roamers of the Wastes besiege them, and we ask for your aid in a rescue mission.

He finished reading the letter, took his atlas down from the shelf, and started studying the map of Old Appalachia. So much for his visit home; tomorrow morning, he'd be on the road again.

♈

Quinn roused himself from bed as a gray dawn broke above the rounded peaks of the eastern ridge. His mother and Claire were waiting for him at the stable with somber looks on their faces. He helped them load the moonshiner's casket onto the family hearse and then hitched Ursula and Undine to the wagon. The chestnut mares pawed the ground, eager to go.

Quinn's mother handed him a tin pail. "I made you your favorites. Grits for breakfast and chicken dumplings for dinner, plus a few jars of chow-chow and shuck beans for the road. I put some leftover stack cake in there, too." Her voice cracked, and she hugged him tightly. "I'm sad to see you go."

"I wish I could stay longer." He felt a little choked up himself. Mom almost never broke her steady graveside manner like this.

"Tell my sister hi for me." Claire gave him a wool scarf with blue and purple stripes. "My mom knit this for you. I hope it keeps you warm where you're headed."

Quinn thanked her and climbed onto the wagon's seat. "Walk on," he told the horses, and they set off through the frost-coated pastures of Cascade Hollow. Claire and his mother followed in the hearse but turned north at the mouth of the valley. He waved to them before they passed from sight behind the white trunks of the beeches.

With a three-day ride ahead and only a pair of draft horses for company, Quinn had plenty of time to mull over the dangers of the expedition. How did the Judges expect the rescue party to cross the Cumberlands? An overland journey would take them through mountains full of hounts and spires and worse. A boat might make it up the Moonbow River as far as the falls, but giant alties swam in those waters. And no one had flown over the Wastes since the fiery crash of the airship *Sheltowee*.

He was stumped, but maybe Zora could find a way.

When twilight fell, Quinn stopped at a crossroads tavern lit by gold lanterns hung from its balconies. He brushed his hair down over his eyes and wrapped his new scarf around his mouth, but a team of scrappers at the bar pegged him straightaway as the Spirit-Shooter Kid. They bought him a glass of cider and shouted drunken toasts while he ate his fresh-caught walleye by the hearth. Afterward, he gave the wagon its nightly once-over and made sure the grenades were fully charged. Then he settled under the covers to read more about Carson van

Patten's search for a woman possessed by the soul of a wicked coal baron.

The next morning, he took the road that skirted the shore of the Big Lake. High above him, the tower of the Ranger headquarters crowned the taller of the Twin Knobs. Down the slope, slate-gray waves splashed against the rocks of the coves. Farther out, the water rippled around the brim of Witch's Hat Island. Somewhere in those depths lay the bones of Nevan McBrain, the Spotter who'd foretold a new Wakening. And below slept the spirit he hadn't seen coming—the leviathan Quinn had been helpless to stop.

Ursula whinnied, and Undine flicked her ears forward. "Ho," he called out. The wagon shuddered to a halt at the side of the road.

The wind died down, and a spell of silence fell over the woods. Quinn held his breath until the drumming of hoofbeats broke the quiet. One horse, approaching swiftly. Meltwater dripped from the trees and landed on Quinn's cheeks, but he kept his eyes fixed on the bend ahead.

A black thoroughbred tore around the curve at a full gallop. The horse's coat shone with sweat, and its mouth dripped with foam. The woman on its back had a crop in her hand and a bandana around her face. Her hair was dark red beneath her derby hat. She whipped her horse, and it charged past the wagon in a spray of mud. Undine tossed her mane with a furious snort. The rider turned her head to glare at Quinn, and then she was gone.

Grinding his teeth, Quinn hopped down to unhitch Ursula and Undine. As they grazed on the sparse grass, he rubbed their withers to soothe his anger. Who would hit a horse like that?

A chill gripped the back of his neck. The rider had the sharp-eyed gaze of the Spiritist spy who'd disguised herself as a parasol huckster. The hair was the wrong color, but maybe she'd hennaed it after slipping away in the chaos of the equinox. He pictured her wearing a garish peddler jacket instead of a riding coat.

It was the same woman, for sure.

Quinn reharnessed the horses in a rush. Ursula and Undine were too slow to catch a thoroughbred, but he'd send word to Captain Flores when they reached a Ranger post: *Look out for a fast-riding Spiritist.* He set their pace at a trot and flicked on the radio to listen for news of trouble. The station was playing a song about lonesome scenes of winter and frozen, scornful hearts. The music didn't lift his mood a whit.

They rolled into the next village beneath a darkening sky. To Quinn's surprise, the main square was bustling with life. Children threw snowballs and skated figure eights while their elders huddled around bonfires and sipped from steaming mugs. At the near end of the square, a woman on a ladder looped fairy lights around a maypole. At the far end, a girl on a stage played a steel-strung fiddle and tapped her toes. Her spectators hooted when a prop spirit made of green fabric floated up behind her on wires.

The folk of the village were holding a festival, and it was a perfect target for a Spiritist ambush.

Quinn ducked inside the wagon, grabbed his banisher, and hooked a few of the amethyst-tiled grenades to his bandolier. Then he jumped down from the seat and scanned for roamers. Clear so far, but the sun had set not long ago.

The girl with the fiddle spun around and scraped out a flurry of dissonant notes. The green prop fluttered away to cheers from the audience.

Where would the cultist hide a spirit-lure? Quinn wove through the crowd as he surveyed the square's perimeter. The pavilion? Too open. The courthouse clock tower? Too high up from the revelers. The antennae on the roofs of the shops? That's where Lurana Underwood had set her beacons last summer.

A stray snowball whizzed past Quinn, startling him into raising his banisher. Two young women near the pavilion glanced his way and whispered to one another.

"Look, Dad!" A towheaded boy pointed straight at Quinn. "That's the spirit-hunter from the papers!"

Now everyone was staring at him and the weapon in his hands. The skaters stopped in their tracks, and the girl on the stage lowered her bow. A middle-aged man in a raccoon coat stepped forward. "Howdy there," he said. "You're *the* Quinn Prosser?"

"Evening, y'all." Quinn looked past the crowd, up to the woman on the ladder. She was still trimming the maypole, with her back turned toward him. Were there lures in the fairy lights? "Sorry for crashing your shindig," he added.

The man in the raccoon coat cocked his head. "Say, are we in for some spirit weather?"

"I don't—" Quinn stumbled over his words. "There's no need to panic." A murmur ran through the crowd, and he silently cursed himself. The fairy lights on the maypole flickered to life in pink and teal. "Stay calm while I finish a quick sweep of the—"

The banisher's sensors pinged five times. The girl on the stage shrieked and dropped her fiddle. Onlookers gasped as glowing yellow filaments sprouted from the shadows behind her. Quinn's skin prickled, and a moldy scent wafted over the square.

"What in the Wastes is that?" bellowed the man in the raccoon coat.

The girl on the stage stood silhouetted against a shining backdrop. With her bow quivering in her hand, she took one tentative step to the left. The spirit undulated like a curtain of hair, each strand ablaze with its own sulfurous light.

It was a snarlyyow. Quinn had never fought one, but he'd seen pictures in the *Field Guide*. The touch of those filaments would burn worse than battery acid.

The spirit snatched the fiddle and waved it in the air. The girl bolted from the stage, screaming, while the spectators surged toward the opposite end of the square. A flying snowball hit the snarlyyow and vaporized in a puff of yellow smoke. The woman on the ladder toppled into a haystack. Quinn barreled toward the stage, only to collide with the man in the raccoon coat.

Howling as if in rage, the spirit smashed the fiddle to splinters. The snowball-throwers abandoned their forts, and the skaters staggered away on their blades.

"Good luck, young feller," said the man in the raccoon coat. Then he turned tail and fled toward the courthouse.

The tide of spectators flowed past Quinn, leaving him alone with the snarlyyow. It twisted its strands around the prop spirit and yanked, snapping the wires from their rigging.

He strode toward the stage with his banisher held high. The rigging crashed to the ground, and the clock tower bell clanged out an alarm. The snarlyyow ripped bolts of green cloth from the prop, like a child tearing the wrapping from a present.

Quinn drew a bead on his target and fired a ray that sliced through the spirit's filaments. The snarlyyow gave another howl, even longer and eerier than the first one. Quinn fired again, cutting away more of the writhing yellow curtain.

Cresting like a wave, the spirit poured over the stage's apron. As the threads streamed toward Quinn, he unhooked a grenade from his bandolier. One more chance before the snarlyyow was upon him.

He lobbed the device toward the oncoming spirit. The grenade exploded in a bloom of violet energy, and a charnel stench filled his nostrils. Covering his mouth with his scarf, he ran past the fading tatters of the snarlyyow and leaped onto the stage.

When Quinn split the prop spirit's papier-mâché heart, he found what he'd expected: a tiny device with a helix-shaped bulb. The beacon flashed crimson, and he shattered it against the wooden stage.

But he also found a surprise hidden under the lure. The envelope was cucumber-colored and bore a seal in the shape of an antlered woman. Quinn knew that symbol. He tore open the envelope, then read the note inside with rising fury. And fear, too.

Dear Mr. Prosser,

No doubt you recognize my handiwork. You must pardon my emissary's crude method of delivery, but I wished to make certain I had your fullest attention; I knew you would never pass up the chance to play hero to a village in need. I cordially invite you, your talented sweetheart, and your brilliant half-sister to my new lodgings. Details about the time and place of our reunion shall be forthcoming. We have old memories to revisit and new opportunities to discuss.

I look forward to seeing you again.

Affectionately yours,

Evelyn Fontaine

3

SIGNE TOOK OFF HER GLASSES, AND THE WORDS WENT BLURRY. *Proceed with all due haste to Hot Springs Hollow,* the Judges had written. Well, at least she'd see Quinn sooner than planned. And she'd get a chance to soak in the Bubbling Cauldron before risking her hide in the Wastes.

She squinted at the mirror on the chiffonier. A reflection with pale skin and long, snowy hair squinted back at her.

Signe put on her glasses, and the world turned clear again. The lenses cast a blue shade across her vision, but she was used to that. She stuffed her warmest dresses and a few gothic novels in her trunk, wrapped a spiderweb shawl around her shoulders, and marched downstairs to face her family.

They were waiting for her at the long dining room table. Mamma and Pabbi, dour-faced as always, had taken their chairs at the ends. Her three older brothers sat on one bench, her three older sisters on the other. All of them had sandy hair and ruddy cheeks. Not like Signe, the seventh child who always stuck out from her family.

"How kind of you to finally join us," said Mamma as

she ladled out the lamb stew. "What do the Judges want with you now?"

"Assistance on a mission of mercy." Signe sat facing away from the glare of the sun. "They picked up a distress call from the Far Wastes."

Everyone stared at her, shocked. Then her siblings all began talking at once.

"Are they sure it's real? Maybe it's one of those phantom signals."

"Or a fraud. Like that hoax back in the twenties."

"No word from out there since the Lesser Wakening. Not a peep for, what, sixty-six years?"

"Sure, that's what the Judges tell us. But we had a client at the print house—"

"The one who claimed he'd heard a secret radio transmitter?"

"Right, him. He paid us to publish his book. What was it called, again?"

"*Revelations from the Veiled Realm.*"

That title sounded intriguing. Signe resolved to take a side trip to the library on her way to Hot Springs Hollow.

"Who sent this distress signal?" asked Mamma.

"The last survivors of a town named Ram's Horn," Signe said. "Out in the Sounding Gap."

Pabbi cleared his throat. "You're not going there yourself, are you?"

"It's my calling." Signe looked down at her beets and turnips so she wouldn't see her siblings roll their eyes. "I'm sure Quinn will go, too."

"How would you get past the spirits of the Wastes?" asked Pabbi.

Signe shrugged and ate a bite of roasted turnip. "I expect we'll work out a plan." Though the question vexed her, too. "Maybe Zora can build a tunnel-digging mole ship or a—"

"Stay here, with us," said Mamma. "Let the Rangers and Spotters and Judges handle this problem. If you care about Quinn, ask him to stay, too. Write a book together about how to chase spirits, and we'll print it. You could even launch your own school."

Signe let herself imagine that. No more long trips on a hard wagon seat, no more nighttime vigils in briar-filled forests. No more staking her life on a talent no one could explain, not even her. Just a safe, cozy routine and the blessing of her parents.

Her siblings watched her with fretful expressions. "We'd love to have you back home," said Pabbi.

Signe steeled herself and shook her head. "I think the universe chose me to do this."

"Don't count too much on your sweetheart's aim or his sister's inventions," said Mamma. "Or your vision, either, however you came by it."

Which reminded Signe of a question she'd been meaning to ask. "Now that you mention it, Zora has a theory about my spirit-sight. She thinks some sort of event—a kirlian anomaly, she called it—altered my eyes before I was born. Did anything unusual happen back then?"

Her father blinked, and her mother hesitated. "Not when I was pregnant with you," said Mamma.

"She was home the whole time," Pabbi said. "The doctor told her to stay in bed. It was touch and go for a while. We were afraid we'd lose you."

"We still are," Mamma added softly. "Your friend's theory must be wrong."

Signe could tell they were hiding something. All those years of wondering, and maybe her parents had held the key all along.

Mamma sighed and rested her chin on her hands. "You've always followed your own star, and I don't suppose we'll ever change that. When do you plan on leaving?"

Signe studied the symbols on the heirloom tapestry behind her mother. Three sigils from an ancient grimoire: one for opening hills, one for crossing rivers, and one for laying ghosts to rest. "As soon as we're done here."

Everyone ate slowly, but dinnertime still flew on by.

Afterward, Signe cornered her father alone in the barn as he was fetching her horse. Pabbi's eyes were shadowed, and his face was lined with worry. She'd seen that same look on the day she'd left home nine moons ago.

"Tell me the part you left out," she said. "I deserve to know the whole story."

"Nothing happened while we were expecting you." He put a bit in Fylgja's mouth. "But the year before that . . ."

Signe forced herself to stay calm. "Was it a spirit?"

"I don't know." He glanced toward the loft, as if his memories lay buried up there in the hay. "Your mother and I had gone to the market to deliver some posters. On our way back through the woods, the horses got spooked. Then the sun went dim, and the sky went gloomy. I remember smelling ozone in the air and thinking a storm was ready to break."

The wind moaned through the gaps in the planks. A tremor ran along Signe's spine, and she hugged herself to keep warm.

"As it got darker," Pabbi went on, "a blue glow appeared all around us. It covered the ground like kudzu and crept up the wagon to your mother and me. We panicked at first, but the thing didn't hurt us."

More and more peculiar. Spirits were always green or yellow or somewhere in between. "What sort of blue?"

"The color of indigo ink. When the glow touched us, everything dark turned light and everything light turned dark, like we were trapped in a photo negative. Sparks danced around the trees and the horses and us." Pabbi got a faraway look in his eyes. "A strange feeling came over me, as if I'd fallen into a dream. Or another world."

Signe brushed Fylgja's mane as she puzzled over her father's story. Had he and Mamma come across a new sort of spirit? Or something completely different?

Pabbi coughed in embarrassment. "After a few minutes, the sun came back out and the glow faded away. We went home, told the local Ranger, and sent letters to the Spotters we've published, but none of them could explain it. We had our hands full once you came along, so we left it at that."

"Exactly when did this happen?" asked Signe.

"I forget the date, but you could find it in a minute with an old almanac," said Pabbi. "Look for the solar eclipse in spring 125."

She picked up her parasol and pointed it at him. "You could've told me this a long time ago. Like when I first discovered my spirit-sight." At the age of twelve, she'd spotted a flock of sylphs drifting high on the thermals beneath a blood moon, invisible to all eyes but hers. No one had believed her at the time.

Fylgja gave a low, comforting nicker, but Pabbi just stood there with his hands in his pockets. "Your head was already stuffed with notions about destiny and whatnot. Your mother and I wanted to help keep your feet on the ground. You didn't need to know, anyway. You didn't even exist when we came across that glowing whatever-it-was."

"Did you ever think maybe it changed you and Mamma?" asked Signe. "Did you ever wonder if you passed that change along to me?" She flicked open her parasol to shield her sun-shy eyes and led Fylgja out of the barn.

Pabbi followed, but he didn't answer.

Everyone else had gathered around her wagon. She'd bought it last spring with her savings and painted it white, black, and purple. It fit only one bed and a snug built-in booth, but it felt more like home than the six-gabled house she was leaving.

Signe's siblings talked over each other as they mobbed her.

"We stocked your cupboards with food."

"And loaded your trunk in the back."

"Keep an eye out for spirits."

"And an ear out for mysterious signals."

"We worry about you, baby sister."

Mamma and Pabbi came over to her, and in the bright sunlight, they looked older than she'd remembered. Pabbi gave her a stiff pat on the back, and Mamma kissed her on both cheeks.

"I'll see you again this spring," Signe told them. "I promise." Then she dipped her parasol, vaulted onto the wagon, and told Fylgja to walk.

Soon she was alone among the dazzling white hills.

♈

Signe's shadow had turned long and gaunt by the time she crossed the toll bridge. Below her, a sleek brown otter split the surface of the river, raised its head like a periscope, and sank back under the murky water. For a moment, she was mesmerized by the eddies of the current.

Stifling a yawn, she tossed a copper half-bit to the tollkeeper and urged Fylgja forward.

On the other side of the river, Signe saw a man walking up ahead with a bucket in his hand and a dip net on his shoulder. As the wagon caught up with him, he broke into a gap-toothed grin. "You look mighty familiar," he said. "Are you the spirit-seer?"

"I am." She gripped the reins tighter. Most strangers who hailed her just wanted to talk about spirits they'd sighted, but she'd learned to stay on guard for Evelyn Fontaine's moles.

"My wife was right." The man quickened his pace to keep up with the wagon. "She said a traveler in black would bring us good luck." Water sloshed from the bucket onto his trousers, and he winced. "I'm Finley Boyd, and I sure could use your help."

"Let me guess." Signe pulled on the reins, and Fylgja stopped shy of a fork in the road. "A roamer strayed onto your farm, and you want me to shoo it away from your cows."

"Close," said Finley. "But the farm is for catfish and bass, and instead of one roamer, it's a shoal of waterbounds. Take care of them however you please, and we'll pay you twenty bits. My wife will tell your fortune, too—her name's Cassie, and she's a card-reader."

Despite her drowsiness, Signe was tempted. "Where's your farm?"

"Thataway." The man pointed his net to the left.

She turned off the main pike and followed him to a flat, open stretch by the river. As they drew closer, Signe could make out nine square ponds in a grid of earth dikes. Skinny herons stalked the banks, and olive-brown fish drifted beneath the films of ice. The road ended at a cabin squatting on four wooden stilts.

The front door swung open to reveal a moonfaced woman in a calico dress. "Who's our visitor there?" she called down from the cabin's deck.

"The answer to our troubles," Finley said. "The spirit-seer herself!"

Signe couldn't resist playing the part. With a flourish of her parasol, she swept down from the wagon and curtsied to them. "And you, ma'am, must be the clairvoyant."

The woman beamed. "Ain't you a vision. Call me Cassie, and bless you for coming. Those spirits are plaguing our brood-stock. They showed up six days ago, blooming like algae and roiling the water."

"Can you describe them?" Signe asked.

"All we see is pale green lights under the ice. And we hear these weird hissing sounds."

Not kelpies, then. Or welkies or nixies. But that left plenty of other possibilities.

"We're afraid to go too close when it's night," said Finley.

"Where do you get your water?" Signe strolled over to the dikes for a better look, and the herons flapped away to a chorus of squawks. In the closest pond, a dead catfish with pockmarks on its white belly was floating upside down against the ice.

"We pump it in from upriver," said Finley. "The pipes have screens to keep our fish in and everything else out."

"Those wouldn't stop spirits. And where does the water go?"

"Down there." He gestured toward the riverbank.

The last of the daylight was fading swiftly. The spirits might appear any minute now. "Can you open the drains?" Signe asked.

"Sure thing." Finley twisted an iron handwheel at the end of the nearest pond. "That's a steady flow. Now for the rest." He set out along the dikes, loosening the other valves until he'd worked his way back to her.

"You should wait at your house," Signe told him. "I'll let you know when it's safe."

Once he'd left, with Fylgja in tow, she took out the goggles Zora had made her and pulled them down around her neck. The western sky turned red, then purple, then black. The evening star rose, and the temperature dropped. She listened for the spirits, but all she could hear was the rush of water draining from the ponds.

Signe's eyelids grew heavy, and her chin drooped, and a soft, warm wooziness settled over her thoughts. As she stood entranced, a voice murmured from far below.

See what was and is and will be.

Rows of crystalline trees sprouted from the center pond, and the ice on the others flowed upward to form castles with rime-fringed turrets. The dikes had become alleys paved with white bricks. The scene looked strange yet vaguely familiar. Had she seen it in a picture book about an enchanted palace where time stood frozen?

No, it was from a photograph of the college in the Ruined Town. She was in a quadrangle, flanked by icy replicas of long-abandoned halls and laboratories.

Deliver me from here, pleaded the voice.

A figure emerged from the shadows beyond the quad. Blue

coals burned in its eye sockets, and a pair of horns curled out from its forehead. Signe backed away, pushing through her sluggishness until she bumped against something behind her and lost her balance. Bracing herself with her parasol, she glanced over her shoulder into the depths of a well. The water at the bottom spun in a whirlpool of darkness.

Save me from this abyss.

Signe opened her eyes, and the scene blinked out of existence. The quad was gone, and so was the figure. The gray planes of the ponds stretched away from her in every direction.

She paced along the dikes to rouse herself. Perhaps she'd drifted off there. Or perhaps she'd seen a premonition. The Coldirons scoffed at such things, and her own family did, too, but Mr. Epps had said that brushes with spirits could give people glimpses of the future. Hadn't she dreamed about a green maypole a few nights before the spire had almost killed her? And hadn't Quinn told her about his nightmare of a deer with bloody human hands—

A loud crack made Signe jump, and cold water splashed on the hem of her dress. She turned just in time to see a ray of molten light plunge through a hole in the ice. As the spirit traced a whorl beneath the frozen crust, other lights appeared under the surface to form a pattern of intersecting swirls. Whishing sounds rose and fell in time with their pirouettes.

So, a school of tangies had strayed in from the river. To the fish-farmers—or anyone else in the Hollows—the spirits would be nothing more than faint greenish streaks, but to her eyes, they were brilliant ribbons of opal and jade.

"You're beautiful, in your own way," Signe told the tangies.

"But you don't belong here." She had no idea if they could comprehend her; still, it was worth a try.

Ice shattered again as one of the spirits shot up from the pond on the other side of the dike. A jet of foul-smelling water spattered Signe's sleeve, and she clenched her jaw. Too close—the tangie's aura had come within an arm's length of lashing her. It was time to shepherd these waterbounds to the river.

Signe dashed to the near end of the dike, dodging more leaping tangies along the way. Once she'd caught her breath, she took off her glasses and put on her goggles. The tint of the world shifted from light blue to deep indigo.

"Swim along now." She fixed her gaze on the closest pond, and the tangies darted away—not along graceful parabolas but in straight lines toward the valve. They gurgled and gyrated around the drain as the pressure sucked them down.

Signe let herself bask in a moment of self-satisfaction, and then she tramped along the dikes to clear the other ponds. When she'd driven the last of the tangies into the pipes with her stare, she put her glasses back on and ran to the bank where the water spilled into the river. The spirits were flowing downstream in a whirling current of iridescence.

"You can follow the river all the way to the Wastes," she shouted after them.

The breeze picked up, and Signe caught a whiff of pond scum. She flicked at her dress, but the muck didn't come off, so she gave up, closed the drains, and made her way back to the cabin.

The fish-farmers were watching her from the deck's railing. Finley waved her up the ladder to the front door, and Cassie ushered her inside. Signe's glasses fogged over as her hosts led her to a low-lit room.

She wiped the mist from her lenses. Burgundy velvet draped the walls, and black candles burned on the mantle. The scents of stoneroot and ginseng overpowered the stink on her clothes. "The spirits won't trouble you again," she told her hosts.

"We saw the whole thing." Cassie guided her to a wicker chair at a small round table and took the opposite seat. "I knew you'd succeed."

"It's a gift to help others." Signe tried to sound modest.

"And now let's see what the future holds for our brave young seer." Cassie shuffled a deck of gilt-edged cards while Finley stood beside her with a solemn expression.

"What are those?" Signe was enthralled. She'd played with planchets and talking boards at slumber parties and visited palmists at fairs, but she'd never had her fortune told from a deck.

"My own special hex cards. I'll deal you five." Cassie turned over the top card and smiled down at a heart surrounded by tulips. "The Wilkhommen. You'll see your true love soon."

Signe liked the sound of that. No doubt Quinn was on his way to Hot Springs Hollow by now. "Go on."

The candles flickered as the fortuneteller dealt the second card. It showed a triangle pointing upward, cut crosswise by a line. "The Zephyr. You'll travel like the wind."

From Hot Springs Hollow to the Sounding Gap, Signe presumed. But how?

The third card showed a pair of songbirds—one right-side up, one upside down. "The Distelfinks," said the fortuneteller. "They'll bring you luck, but also danger."

Signe shuddered when she saw the next card. It depicted a spiral in a sky full of stars. Cassie seemed perplexed, but she'd never seen the harbinger with her own eyes. Not like Signe.

Having her fortune told didn't seem so fun anymore.

"The Skywheel," said Cassie. "Its presence in this sequence is an enigma."

The final card showed a coffin on a railcar. The fortuneteller exchanged a glance with her husband. "The Black Train can mean many things," she said. "But always a transition of sorts."

Signe took that for pure sugarcoating. The coffin must be an omen of death. But perhaps her siblings and Zora were right, and hex signs meant nothing at all.

"Thank you for the reading," Signe said. "By the way, the spirits doused me with your—ah—fragrant pondwater. Do you have a hot shower I can use?"

♈

They didn't, and so Signe wound up feeling positively grungy when she arrived at the Hoary Library the next afternoon. Still, the sight of the grand limestone building brightened her mood right away. It was her favorite place in the Hollows, and the Judges could wait while she did her research.

She deposited Fylgja at the stable and traipsed up the steps to the library. The double doors opened into a foyer with a high tin ceiling and leaded windows. Motes of dust floated in the sunbeams like wisps swarming up from a sinkhole. The musty smell of old paper brought back memories of browsing the shelves with Quinn on a drizzly fall day.

Signe flipped through the card catalog before setting out to search for two books. She found one in the maze of first-floor stacks and the other up three flights of stairs. Then she ensconced herself in a nook and took her magnifying glass from its case.

Holding the lens up to the *Hollows Almanac,* she pored over astronomical charts until she spotted the entry that matched Pabbi's tale. *Spring 42, 125: Partial eclipse of the sun.* She wrote a note in her sloppy cursive: *ECLIPSE = INDIGO GLOW = SPIRIT-VISION?*

A scuffing sound came from the stacks. "Hello?" Signe called out. The noise ceased abruptly. She craned her neck to look down the long rows of shelves. Nothing there—not a librarian or a ghost or a rat.

Signe shook off a pang of foreboding and leafed through the book she'd learned about from her siblings: *Revelations from the Veiled Realm* by Ulysses V. Bell. It rambled on about signals from a station that called itself Peryton One. The author's transcriptions read like nonsense to her, but she jotted them down in her journal. *Autumn 61, 114: The doe is in the second house; the stag and the hart have followed the tracks,* went one. *Autumn 63, 114: The stag and the hart lie slain, but the doe lives on to avenge them,* read another. Could that be a Spiritist code?

A long gap followed, broken by three final signals. *Autumn 63, 140: Unravel the loom's pattern. Winter 35, 140: Track the professor's trail. Spring 11, 141: Find the fiddler's songbook.* If the fiddler was the girl from the legends, then who was the professor? And what was the loom?

Signe's eyes stung from reading too much fine print, but she had one task left to complete. Ignoring the throb in her temple, she took the steep, twisting stairs to the basement and rifled through box after box of brittle old newspapers. First, the stuffy

Gazette; then the fire-breathing *Herald*; and, finally, the disreputable *Sun*. She stopped at a story from spring '25: *SOLAR SHROUD SUMMONS CERULEAN SPECTRE.*

Logan Rayburn of Sodium Lick reports that he sighted a phantasmal blue light spreading over his meadow by the dark of the recent eclipse. He dashed for his barn, but the azure apparition enveloped him, too. "I've had spirits graze me," he told us. "But this thing felt different, like it was sweeping me clear out of the here and now."

That echoed her father's description of his own uncanny experience. Had the eclipse opened a door to a world beyond humans and spirits?

We asked Nevan McBrain, the most renowned Spotter in the Hollows, for comment, but he said he had "no time to talk to you yammering turkey vultures."

Poor Mr. McBrain. An unpleasant man, but he hadn't deserved such a horrible fate. She read on:

Mr. Rayburn's tale has a curious postscript. He made another discovery come nightfall: the patch of yalleries in his meadow had vanished! The little earthbound spirits first appeared there on the night of the Lesser Wakening, nearly 48 years ago . . .

Signe couldn't make out the rest—not because the print was too faded or tiny but because tears had clouded her vision. She'd come one step closer to finding the source of her gift.

She was sure of it.

4

ZORA WATCHED OUT THE WINDOW AS THE GIANT HEMLOCKS AND sycamores rushed past her. She still felt queasy from the motion, but she was glad to be riding this shiny new train. The Hollows had a working railroad again for the first time in five generations, and she was here to see it.

Her breath steamed the glass, blocking her view of the woods. She wrote her name on the pane with her finger and drew fox ears on top of the O. "I've never traveled this fast in my life," she said.

Viola Mack and Kirk Slocum both puffed up at that. The two merchants sat across from her, decked out in their winter finery: a suede duster and cloche hat for her, a felt cap and tweed jacket for him.

"It's so *delightful* to show you our progress," said Ms. Mack. "All powered by our hemp diesel engine."

"We're extending the line this spring." Mr. Slocum spread his hands wide apart. "Out past the route you helped blaze."

Zora wiped the pane with her sleeve. "I remember climbing that big mound of earth over there." She and Quinn had spent a warm summer night clearing the forest of spirits. "But so much has changed since then."

Her mother frowned. "I'm still sore you went tangling with orbs."

Zora looked away toward the fallen tree trunks and the pits in the ground and the thickets of rhododendron. Signe had burst a boiler over that escapade, too. She'd marked a safe path through the spirits, only for Zora to follow her trail and hunt down every orb in the woods. Back then, they'd been rivals, not friends.

"I've observed six varieties of orbs on my journeys," said Mr. Epps. "From a safe distance, of course. They're fearsome but quite fascinating. The largest ones tend to be solitary, whereas the smaller types cluster in—"

"Not the time for a spiritology lesson." Zora's mom shook her head at him fondly.

"Ah, yes. Force of habit."

Zora decided she needed some air. "I'm going to check out the rest of the train. Maybe I'll visit the caboose and pester the crew."

She swayed down the aisle as the floor lurched beneath her and the passengers gawked from their seats. She passed a thin man with a green-tinged scar on his brow. A woman swathed in a pink feather boa. Two chipmunk-faced girls and their father. Were any of them Spiritist spies?

Zora took a deep breath and crossed to the dining car.

"Over here." Paige had parked herself in an oak-paneled booth.

Zora squeezed in next to her, opposite Emerson Tate and a raffish man with a banjo. "Howdy, Ms. Zora," said the Ranger. "Allow me to introduce Bela Holcomb."

"I recognize you." She shook Mr. Holcomb's hand. He had long, black-painted nails and callused fingertips. "What brings you this way?"

"A show at the Grand Courthouse, plus a chance to ride the rails with the Ranger I'm courting." He tuned a string. "I'm always on the road, and so is Emerson."

"I saw you play last summer," Zora said.

"And she's heard that song you wrote about her," Paige interjected. Zora elbowed her before she could say more. The lyrics to "The Ballad of Calamity Coldiron" were full of embroideries about Zora's heroics and brazen lies about her "auburn-tressed beauty."

Mr. Holcomb inclined his head. "Emerson's told me all about you."

"Oh, I could fill in some colorful details," Paige said. "But Foxtails has sworn me to secrecy."

She was stretching the truth about that. The only skeleton in Zora's closet was one night of underage drinking at the instigation of a certain apprentice. Her headache the next morning had killed her taste for stump hole whiskey. "Let's talk about the expedition," she said. "Can you tell us more about who sent the signal? Or how we'll be crossing the Wastes?"

Paige brandished a hushpuppy reddened with ketchup. "Spill it."

"You'll hear the full story when we meet with the Judges." The Ranger lowered his voice. "Until then, we should keep quiet about our plans. Evelyn Fontaine has always had ears everywhere."

"How about I play them a tune?" Mr. Holcomb strummed his banjo and launched into a song about a black train and a lady filled with worldly pride. As he finished the final verse, the locomotive whistled a long, doleful note. The brakes screeched, and the wheels clacked to a halt at the end of the line.

A battalion of blue-jacketed stewards sprang into action. One hauled Zora's trunks to the platform, while others unloaded her crates from the back of the train. Ms. Mack and Mr. Slocum fussed over her all the way to the mud-wagon they'd summoned for the final leg of the journey.

"It's always a kick doing business with you," said Mr. Slocum.

"Safe travels wherever you go," added Ms. Mack.

Zora took one last look at the train's glossy black cars and jet-colored engine before climbing into the coach.

♈

"Welcome to Hot Springs Hollow." Signe swished her parasol like a carnival barker's cane. Her charcoal blouse and long ruffled skirt made Zora feel even plainer than usual.

But forget that. Their old team was almost complete, with only one missing piece.

"Nice umbrella," Zora said as she stepped from the wagon onto the grounds of a timber frame lodge.

Signe smiled. "Your craftwork is magnificent. Practical but elegant, with a pair of surprises tucked inside."

"I have a surprise for you, too, Fairy Eyes." Paige gave Signe a pair of plum-colored gloves. "My mom knit them. I told her you liked purple stuff."

"Is Quinn here yet?" Zora asked.

Signe's tranquil facade slipped for a moment. "He sent word he'd run into a snag and wouldn't arrive till tomorrow."

"What kind of . . ." Zora began, but Captain Sylvia Flores motioned for silence. The Ranger commander wore an eight-pointed badge on her uniform, and her cap had gold braid on its brim. Zora had seen her smile exactly once.

"Thank you for coming." The captain nodded to Zora and her traveling companions. "Officer Tate, fine work delivering them safely. Take their bags to the lodge and stow their gear in the armory."

Emerson hurried off to follow his orders. The banjoist winked and trailed him at a leisurely pace.

"Mr. Epps and Ms. Coldiron the Elder," the captain went on, "please come with me to the station. The rest of you, take it easy this evening." Zora felt peeved at not being invited to the grown-ups' table with her mom and Paige's boss, but she persevered in holding her tongue.

"Hi," said the third member of their welcoming party, a girl who'd hung back until now. She was around Zora's age, with mouse-brown hair and a rabbity smile. "I'm Abigail Putnam. I volunteered to show you around."

Zora figured she must be on staff at the lodge. "Which way to the Cauldrons? I've always wanted to see them."

"Follow me!" The girl set off toward a white stucco building topped by a green copper dome. "I must say, it's an honor to meet you. I admire your work so much."

Zora would never, ever tire of people telling her that. Hot Springs Hollow's hospitality lived up to its reputation so far.

"Quinn and I visited here last fall," said Signe. "For a spell of recuperation."

Paige gave her a jab on the shoulder. "Did y'all take a romantic midnight dip in the springs?"

Abigail's eyes widened, but Signe didn't so much as blink. "Only he and I and the stars know the truth about that," she said placidly. "Good luck asking the constellations."

Zora silently thanked the stars for that uninformative answer. Watching everyone pair off was starting to annoy her. Her brother and Signe, her mother and Mr. Epps, Emerson Tate and his troubadour.

Abigail led them into a wing of the bathhouse and flung open a cedarwood closet. "Let's find bathing suits for y'all."

Zora took one with a high neckline and trunks that came down to her knees. Their guide picked a suit with a similar cut, but Paige's one-piece was a fair sight more daring. Signe had brought her own outfit, of course: a swim-dress with black and white stripes.

Zora ducked into a changing room. She reemerged feeling chilly and a little self-conscious.

"Now to the Bubbling Cauldron!" Abigail promenaded past a row of mineral spas as Zora followed and tried to keep her rubber crutch-tips from slipping on the wet marble floor. An archway brought them to a mist-shrouded spring that smelled faintly of brimstone.

Zora walked up to the edge and dipped her toes in the water. It was almost too hot to bear. Still, better to boil than stand here freezing her tail. She closed her eyes and eased herself into the spring. The knots in her shoulders dissolved, and the weight on her spine melted away. A schematic of crystals and coils took shape on the backs of her eyelids: a new design for the banisher-cannon. Old Smoky would be in for a rematch once she made it back to Lightning Bug Hollow.

Paige suddenly laughed. "We're like these monkeys I saw in

an old magazine photo. They were up to their necks in a spring, same as us." She slicked her hair into spikes with her fingers. "On second thought, were they macaques? That's going to haunt me till I look it up."

"Isn't the Cauldron more relaxing than any bath you've ever taken?" said Signe.

Zora nodded. Now if only their guide would get lost so the three of them could swap stories about their adventures.

As if she'd sensed Zora's thoughts, Abigail clambered out of the spring. "Pardon me, but I should be going," the girl chirped. "I'll see you at the big meeting tomorrow."

"You will?" Zora hadn't reckoned on that.

"Why, sure. Didn't they tell you? I'm the radio operator who discovered the signal."

♈

Zora was brushing her teeth and Paige was tying her boots when someone knocked twice on their door. They both rushed to open it.

Quinn smiled at them from the hallway, looking as doe-eyed as ever. His dark hair was tousled, and his trousers had mud on their cuffs. Behind him stood Signe, wearing a flowy black dress and her serenest expression.

Zora leaned against her brother. "Took you long enough."

"I missed you, too." He wrapped his arms around her shoulders, and the world felt a little safer.

"Hey, Pine-Box." Paige slapped Quinn on the back. "The whole gang's together at last."

"Not to hurry you," said Signe, "but the meeting is about to begin." She and Quinn held hands as they led the way through the lodge's hallways.

Zora kept pace beside Paige. "What did you think of Abigail?"

"That girl sure is a big fan of yours. Maybe you've found yourself a new lab assistant."

"I might've misjudged her," Zora admitted. "Like I did with Signe at first. I'll try to be nice to the new kid—even if I'm jealous of her for finding the signal."

Her heartbeat sped up as they entered a room with a kaleidoscope skylight. At the head of a table sat three stern-faced Judges, all dressed in identical robes. Captain Flores stood to one side, flanked by Emerson and a stout man with a neatly waxed mustache. Zora took a seat between her mother and Quinn, while Paige plopped down next to Mr. Epps.

"We have gathered in response to a momentous event," intoned the Chief Judge. "The discovery of a radio message from beyond the Hollows. Proceed with your account, Ms. Putnam."

Abigail fumbled with a fancy phonograph set. "I—I heard the signal twelve days ago." Her hands shook as she started the turntable spinning. "I work with radios. I build them and fix them and listen to them every free minute I get. I was scanning the shortwave band late at night when I came across this and caught it down in wax with my Scully lathe."

She lowered the needle onto a record. It popped and crackled for a few revolutions, and then a soft tenor spoke from the phonograph's horn:

. . . all gone except me, my sister, and the children. The power won't last much longer, and the spirits are gathering outside the walls. If you can hear me, please help us. We're at Ram's Horn, in the Sounding Gap. The coordinates are 37.15 north, 82.63 west.

The speaker gasped and then shouted:

The hounts are back. I can't stay here—

The voice cut off in mid-sentence, leaving only the sound of the crackling. Zora looked at her brother, and he looked back at her. The hount they'd run into last summer had come within a glowing whisker of killing them both.

"I missed recording the first part," said Abigail. "The signal caught me off guard. I heard something about the Stars of the Ram and the Mark of the—the Syzygy, whatever those mean."

Mr. Epps underlined a pair of words on his notes. "The voice said *spirits* and *hounts*. If the people of Ram's Horn use the same nomenclature as us, then they must have had contact with the Hollows at some point since the Great Wakening."

"No word on sick or injured survivors?" asked a woman who was clearly a doctor, what with her black bag and white linen smock.

"I'm afraid not."

"Did the message mention a loom?" Zora asked.

Signe gave her a sharp glance. "Or a trail or a songbook?"

The radio operator shook her head. She looked even more flustered now. Zora figured the girl must have a bad case of stage fright.

"Did the signal ever come back?" asked Zora's mother.

"Not anywhere on the high-frequency band," said Abigail. "I sent word to the Rangers first thing in the morning and helped them set up a listening station. We've heard nothing but static since then. No response to our own signals, either."

Zora's mother folded her arms. "Which means they may already be dead."

"Unfortunately true," said the Chief Judge.

Quinn raised his hand. "How do we know the signal isn't a fake? Or a trap?"

"We don't," said the Judge. "But we've decided to answer the call, nonetheless. Captain, the floor is yours."

Captain Flores unrolled a topographical map and jabbed her baton at its center. "We're here." She swept the baton past green blobs and blue squiggles to an X in the southeastern corner. "And those coordinates are all the way down there. The route is impassable by horse, let alone wagon. It's a seven-day journey on foot, not counting delays from bad weather. Then a trip back with children of unknown age and condition, through terrain crawling with spirits."

Zora's stomach sank. She'd trained all winter to keep up her strength, but she could never hike that far through the Wastes. She doubted anyone could.

"What about taking a boat up the Moonbow River?" asked Paige.

"You know better than me what an altie could do to a paddlewheel steamer." Captain Flores tapped her baton on one of the squiggles. "There's no way around these falls, anyhow."

"So, what in the Wastes *is* the plan?"

"That's where my old friend Walter Vandy comes in." Captain Flores nodded at the man with the mustache, who grinned and bowed in return.

So *that* was Barnstormer Vandy? Zora had read about his flight over the Pass and seen his photographs of the glow from the Ruined Town. He was short—not much taller than Zora herself—with silvery pomaded hair. His trousers were flared at the thigh, and his jacket had fur on its collar.

"You may know of me as a balloonist," said Mr. Vandy. "But

we can't just drift on a breeze to the Sounding Gap." He chuckled. "Hot air balloons go where the wind blows them, whether you like it or not."

Captain Flores drummed her fingers against the table with ill-concealed impatience.

"Now for the good news." Mr. Vandy stepped up to a sheet-covered easel. "I've spent the past few years designing this project." He started to pull back the sheet but then held up a finger instead. "I call it the *Reynardine*, after my favorite—"

"Get on with it, Walter," said Captain Flores.

"Okay, okay." Mr. Vandy whipped off the sheet to reveal a blueprint of a zeppelin. The airship had a gondola under its keel, fins on its rear, and propellers along its sides. "I built the hull's frame with duralumin girders, and the envelope is varnished linen. It has ten gas cells plus condensers to catch water vapor."

Zora stared at the blueprint in awe. She felt a stab of longing to see the real thing. No, to *fly* it. And yet it had one obvious flaw.

Her mom beat her to the punch. "What if the hydrogen in your airship ignites? It only took one bolide to bring down the *Sheltowee*."

"I guarantee *my* ship won't catch fire." Mr. Vandy paused for dramatic effect. "I've filled the *Reynardine* with helium gas."

"Helium?" Zora sputtered. "Where in the Hollows did you find enough?"

"One of the springs here gives off bubbles full of the stuff." Mr. Vandy stuck a thumb toward a window overlooking the Cauldrons. "That's why I built my secret hangar just yonder."

Quinn raised his hand again. "Your ship sounds grand, sir, but a cloudbuster could knock it right out of the sky."

Mr. Vandy remained unruffled. "And *that's* why we plan on flying by day. The *Reynardine* can make the journey with sunlight to spare. Though we should arm my ship with some of your weapons"—he aimed his fingers at Zora like they were pistols—"just in case we cross paths with an airbound. As soon as that's done, we'll be ready to sail. We'll be there and back before the spring equinox."

Zora had already picked a spot at the rear of the gondola to mount her redesigned cannon. She could add banishers to the platform on top and a cargo of bombs to drop from the bay.

"On the topic of spirits," said the Chief Judge, "we've asked our most eminent Spotter to provide his thoughts."

Mr. Epps placed a cellophane overlay on top of the map. It showed a web of ether fields and ley lines stretching out from the Hollows. "Great peril awaits in the Wastes," he boomed. "Elementals have ravaged the valleys, and leviathans dwell in the deeps of the lakes. Hounts and spires prowl what remains of the forests. Our flight path will cross a front of derechos—cloudbusters, in common parlance." He pointed to the mountains surrounding Ram's Horn. "Worse still, the titans themselves roam the peaks of the Cumberlands."

Abigail blanched, as if she'd heard the banshee from Quinn's campfire stories. "I—I thought those were legends."

"Far from it," said Mr. Epps. "Though few humans have sighted one and survived."

Zora had seen a titan, but only from afar through a rift in the sky. And in her nightmares ever since.

"It's an unparalleled opportunity for a Spotter," Mr. Epps continued. "We could surpass Clementine Geller's survey of the Pennyroyal or Nevan McBrain's trek to . . ." He reined in his enthusiasm. "We shall face grave hazards, particularly when we reach the gap."

"That will be the tricky part," Mr. Vandy agreed, with less of his earlier swagger. "There won't be a mooring mast waiting for us, and we won't arrive till late in the day. We'll need a safe place for the ship—and ourselves—while we wait out the night."

"Please weigh the risks before you commit to this task," said the Chief Judge. Zora considered for a split second and then made up her mind.

Captain Flores squared her shoulders. "I'll lead the mission myself, with Officer Tate as my second. Mr. Vandy and his crew have offered to fly us. Doctor Caudill, would you serve as our medic?"

"I'll go wherever I'm needed," said the woman in white.

The captain turned to Mr. Epps. "We'd appreciate your expertise."

"I've dedicated my life to observing rare and unknown varieties of spirits," he said. "I could hardly decline your invitation. My apprentice may come as well, if she wishes."

Paige held up a fist. "I'm ready to see what all's out there."

"Mr. Prosser?" asked the captain. "And Ms. Janasdottir? Your talents could come in handy."

"I feel called to do this," Signe said without hesitation.

Quinn answered more slowly. "I won't turn my back on people in trouble."

"Count me in, too," Zora said. "I'll show those hounts what my inventions can do."

"And me," Abigail chimed in, to Zora's surprise. "I want to meet who's on the other end of the signal I found."

But Captain Flores shook her head. "You two are not yet of age. We can't bring you with us, but we could use your help here in the Hollows."

"You'll need an engineer who can fix my inventions," Zora persisted.

"That's why we've asked your mother to join the mission," said the captain.

Zora gritted her teeth. They must've settled this yesterday during their private council. Everyone who mattered would be going without her: her brother, her friends, and even her mom.

"With all due respect, Captain," said Quinn, "I'd feel safer with Zora aboard."

Signe nodded. "Her skills have saved our lives more than once."

"She's the brains of our team," Paige said.

Zora's hopes rose for a second, but Captain Flores shot them back down. "I respect your loyalty to young Ms. Coldiron, but I can't risk her life on this mission. Nor yours, either," she told Abigail before the girl could open her mouth. "I'm asking you to fit the airship with weapons and a two-way radio. Once we're underway, you can use Ms. Putnam's transmitter to advise us."

Zora pictured her brother and friends soaring over the mountains while she was grounded back here in the Hollows. But they needed her help, even if she couldn't join them. "I'll do it," she said.

"Same here." Abigail didn't sound any happier than Zora felt.

"I'm grateful to both of you," said Captain Flores. "One more thing. The Spiritists have poked their snouts back out of the ground."

Zora bit down hard on her lip. That couldn't be a coincidence.

"I found this." Quinn held up a smushed device with the telltale design of a spirit-lure. "After I blasted a snarlyyow that went on a rampage. I also found an invitation from Evelyn Fontaine to visit her new hideaway."

"Did Antler Woman include directions?" asked Zora. If she couldn't go on the mission, maybe she could track down that fake priest and show her who was smarter.

"Not this time." Quinn set the device on the table and touched Signe's arm. "I saw the woman who delivered the message. She's the one who sold you the tampered parasol."

Signe scrunched up her face, and Paige's expression turned fierce.

"I've stationed a team of Rangers to guard the airship," said Captain Flores. "And I've sent patrols to search for our Spiritist emissary." She looked around the table. "The timing of this attack strikes me as suspicious. Keep our mission a secret from anyone who's not in this room."

The three robed magistrates rose from their chairs. "The folk of Ram's Horn await our help," said the Chief Judge. "Captain Flores will lead you to the hangar. The expedition leaves at the break of dawn tomorrow."

As everyone filed out of the room, Zora grabbed her mother's sleeve. "Hold up a second." Quinn lingered at the doorway, but Zora waved him away.

"I'm sorry I couldn't tell you before," said her mother. "I know this must be hard for you."

"Was it the captain's idea or yours?"

"We made the decision together."

Zora struggled for words. "Mom, you could *die* on that trip. And I won't be there to help you."

"Yes," her mother said softly. "I know what it's like to wait and to worry. But if the worst happens, you'll still be alive. That's what matters the most."

Zora looked up at the rainbow skylight. "Let's make sure that zeppelin is armed to the gills. Or the gas valves or whatever." She tried to smile, but her heart felt denser than gold—let alone air.

5

THE AIRSHIP WAS EVEN BIGGER THAN QUINN HAD IMAGINED. IT stretched the length of a seven-car train, and a pair of showboats would have fit side by side in its shadow. The sight of it floating over the hollow filled him with wonder and dread. Come tomorrow, the *Reynardine* would be taking him into the unknown.

The wagon's wheels clattered over a pothole. "It's like old times," he told Zora. "Busting our tailbones to help folks in danger."

"Ursula and Undine seemed happy to see me," she said.

"They've pined for you all winter long," Quinn said. The horses had nuzzled her like a lost foal.

"I'll take good care of them while you're away." Zora tugged on the tassels of her fox-colored hat. She'd put on a stoic expression, but the waver in her voice gave her away.

As the horses clomped down toward the valley, a sharp whistle came from above. A young woman perched on a branch was pointing a rifle straight at them. Her clothes blended in so well with the bark that she was almost invisible. Her gun was the kind that could take down a deer—or a person.

Quinn froze until he saw the eight-pointed badge on her

shirt. She fixed him with a piercing stare and lowered her rifle. "You're clear to pass."

"She was giving you the eye," Zora said once the young Ranger was out of earshot.

Quinn pretended not to follow his sister's drift. "Isn't that her job as a sentry?"

Zora threw up her hands. "You're as clueless as I remembered. At least those radio dramas about us haven't gone to your head."

"I'd rather listen to Signe tell bedtime stories." She loved to spin tales about trolls under trestles and krakens in sinkholes and secret towns that only appeared once every seventeen years. *I come from a long line of elves,* she'd said one night after staring down a tailypo the size of a bear. *Huldufolk blood flows in my veins.* Then she'd burst out giggling and rubbed her nose against his.

"I approve," said Zora. "Maybe my nieces and nephews will have spirit-sight."

"Let's not jump too far ahead." Quinn had no idea how he felt about raising children, but he did know one thing: he'd never leave a son or daughter behind like his own father had. Not to stop a spirit. Not to keep a secret. Not for any reason. "Did you get Dad's latest letter?"

Zora seemed lost in thought for a moment. "The part about his trip to the Ruined Town got me thinking. He was looking for information about a scientist named Maxwell Doran. Does that ring a bell?"

"Nevan McBrain discovered a letter meant for him." *To Maxwell Doran, Professor of Atmospheric and Etheric Sciences,* its author had written on the eve of the Great Wakening. *Last month, you visited our fine county to investigate its legendary ghost-lights.* "Doran was studying the first warning signs of the spirits."

"And he taught at the old college in the Ruined Town." Zora's voice went high-pitched with excitement. "What if he figured out how the harbinger opened the rift?"

"I wonder if Mr. McBrain found anything else from back then."

"We could ask Dad to dig through what's left of his notes."

Quinn suppressed rebellious thoughts. "I'll do that the next time I write him."

The road snaked by a creek with a sign on its bank: *WARNING—WELKIES IN THE WATER.* Paige had once made the mistake of stepping on one of those things. She liked to show off the marks it had left on the sole of her foot.

"I wonder why the Judges didn't invite Dad," said Quinn. "He made it as far as the Dead Hollows and back without your inventions to help him." Quinn had to give him credit for that.

"Maybe they thought he smelled too much of hemp." Zora shrugged. "Or they wanted to make sure my mom would come. She can hold a grudge like nobody else."

"Except maybe her daughter."

Zora gave him a gentle punch on the arm. "Fair enough, but I've *almost* forgiven Dad. And even that ferret-faced Spiritist sneak we saved—"

"You mean Lurana."

"Right, her, but I'll never forgive Evelyn Fontaine."

They passed another Ranger sentinel camouflaged in the trees. Captain Flores was taking no chances on anyone sabotaging their mission. "How was your winter in Lightning Bug Hollow?" Quinn asked.

"Dull without you and my friends," said Zora. "My old classmates begged me to come to their parties, but there's still no one back home on my wavelength."

"Wavelength," he repeated. "You could take that radio operator under your wing." Zora loved explaining her theories, and Abigail might be a receptive student.

Zora hunched her shoulders. "I'll have plenty of time to teach her how my banishers work."

"I wish you were coming with us." Quinn felt rotten to be leaving his sister behind, but he couldn't see any way around it.

The woods opened into the flat white expanse of an airfield. The *Reynardine* hung overhead like a brown and tan patchwork cloud, squat engines sticking out from its keel and long ribs showing through its skin. The symbol of the Hollows was painted on its fins: a sun flanked by two hills. The zeppelin was moored to a skeletal mast as tall as a Ranger watchtower.

Quinn steered the horses toward a sprawling red barn by the edge of the field. Beside him, Zora was gazing up at the ship with her mouth partway open. The instant the wagon halted, she swung down from the seat and made for the mast.

He hitched the horses and followed her toward the airship. Everyone but Signe had already arrived. Paige and Mr. Epps were unloading brass telescopes and theodolites from a cart. One wagon over, Zora's mother was packing her pneumatic tools. Abigail had a crystal set under each arm, and Doctor Caudill held a stack of thick leather-bound tomes. Captain Flores and Mr. Vandy stood at the rail of a platform, looking down over them all.

When Ranger Tate walked by with a crate labeled *FRAGILE*, Zora fell in step with him and called out instructions. As Quinn watched her go, a line from a Carson van Patten mystery sprang into his mind. *The bigger the haystack,* the detective had said, *the easier it is to hide a needle inside it.*

He had the start of a plan to bring Zora along. A long shot, but the best he could hatch on the fly.

Soft footfalls came up behind him. Then Signe spun him around and shaded them both with her black parasol. "I've finally caught you alone," she said.

Quinn kissed her, and she kissed him back until her glasses misted.

♈

Stepping inside Signe's wagon was like walking through a portal to a fairyland. Magenta lights dangled from the ceiling; filmy curtains hung over the windows; the walls were lilac with gossamer hangings. Wind chimes clinked by the doorway, and the scent of lavender filled the air.

On a small table lay a book with a library tag and ribbon markers spilling out from its pages. The strange beast on its cover had the head of a deer but the wings and claws of an eagle. Quinn read the title embossed on the book's spine: *Revelations from the Veiled Realm.*

"Now I have you all to myself." Signe ran a fingertip down the back of his neck. "Unless some enchantress who hunts spirit-hunters charmed you while I was away."

Quinn turned around to meet her eyes. Her lenses made her pupils and irises look huge. "I'm already under your spell," he said.

They kissed again and then both started laughing. "It's nice to be back with someone who appreciates my weird notions," said Signe. "Everyone else in my family can be so hardheaded, though I think my siblings are coming around to my way of thinking."

"What about your parents?" Quinn asked.

"They didn't want me to come here. Not on account of you—in fact, they offered to help us set up our own school for spirit-chasers." Signe twisted a strand of her hair around her finger. "My father told me something I never knew. He and Mamma had a strange encounter the year before I was born. An indigo light swept over them during a solar eclipse and made them feel, well, *otherworldly.*"

Quinn was perplexed. "Indigo? Not green or yellow?"

"I've never heard of anything like it," said Signe. "I think it was the source of my spirit-sight."

"Did this light show up anywhere else?" Maybe there were other spirit-seers in the Hollows, ones who hadn't discovered their talents. Or who had but were keeping them hidden.

She nodded. "A farmer in Sodium Lick ran into it during the same eclipse."

"And did he have any children later on?"

"I don't know." Signe let go of her hair. "I'd like to find out when we get back. My siblings also put me on track of this." She picked up the book from the table. "It's by a writer named Ulysses Bell."

"I take it that's not another occult detective novel," said Quinn. "What sort of revelations did he receive?"

"Signals from a radio station called Peryton One." She opened the book to one of the marked pages and read aloud. "'We followed the glowing path to the eyrie.' And so on about red stars and whistlers and dawn choruses. The messages are all rather cryptic, but they might be a Spiritist code. Some of them talk about stags, does, and harts." She flipped to the back of the book. "And a loom. That may signify something to Zora."

"About her," said Quinn. "Do you think she belongs on the mission?"

Signe pulled off her gloves and set them down on her black lacquer dresser. "I was for it, but Captain Flores overruled us."

"We could help Zora stow away. That airship is enormous. She could find some corner to hide in and come out once it's too late to turn back."

Signe bit her fingernails and nodded slowly. "I'm on board with your plan, and I'm sure Paige will be, too. But Ms. Coldiron will be furious."

That was what worried Quinn the most. Give or take them dying in a crash or a titan's blazing corona. "Captain Flores won't be thrilled, either."

"I hope they'll understand," said Signe. "I'm sure they took their own chances when they were younger."

"Ms. Coldiron ran away at sixteen to work as a riverboat mechanic." He and Zora had learned that from their father. "And Captain Flores is old friends with our daredevil skipper. Maybe she took a joyride on one of his hot air balloons. Maybe she even had a fling with him back in the day." Quinn glanced at the filigreed clock on the dresser: half past four already. "We should tell Zora and Paige the plan when we meet at the ship."

Signe sat down on her bed. Its quilt was purple and white with a cobwebby pattern. "How do you feel about what we're getting ourselves into?"

"Scared," he admitted. "But I've always dreamed of seeing the world outside the Hollows."

"I know." She kicked off one of her shoes and then the other. "It's exciting to think we're no longer alone." She hesitated. "I had my fortune told on the way here. I'm sure Zora would side-eye me if she heard."

Probably so, but Quinn kept that thought to himself. "What did your clairvoyant say?"

"The cards told her I'd see my—see *you* soon and go on a swift voyage. That much was clear, but she dealt me other signs, too. A pair of identical birds and a wheel in the sky and a train hauling a coffin." Signe sighed. "Those last two sound ominous."

"I was part of your fortune?" Quinn's face went a bit warmer.

Signe took his hand and pulled him down onto the bed. Her smile made her look even more elfin. "So, do you realize this may be our last day alone together?"

Despite himself, Quinn shivered. She'd said almost the same words last summer, right before a spire had appeared outside her window.

But this time, no spirit interrupted them.

♈

Quinn found his sister at the helm in the *Reynardine*'s gondola. Abigail was hovering beside her, all bright-eyed and bouncing on her heels. The two young women watched, spellbound, as Mr. Vandy explained the controls. "Drop ballast to go up. Vent gas for a rapid descent. But don't touch those toggles—helium's a bear to distill."

"How do you navigate?" asked Abigail.

"Dead reckoning with the compass and drift indicator. We use the rudder wheel"—Mr. Vandy gestured toward Zora—"to adjust the heading. The elevator wheel over there controls the pitch." He tapped an instrument panel. "Inclination, altitude, air pressure."

Zora eyed the barometer. "What happens if you run into bad weather?"

"Good question." He launched into a monologue that Quinn only half understood. The gist seemed to be that airships should steer clear of thunderstorms.

"At least lightning bolts can't blow you up," said Zora.

Mr. Vandy chortled. "Now it's your turn, Putnam. Let's hear how your radio works."

As Abigail hopped to obey, Quinn dragged his sister away from the wheel. Paige and Signe were waiting for them at the rear of the gondola. Nobody else was aboard. The crew had left to rest up for the voyage, and the Rangers were pacing the field with their rifles. Over by the hangar, Ms. Coldiron and Mr. Epps chatted and drank from mugs.

"Check this out." Zora patted a glass tube as big as an old Sylvanian oil-pipe. "My new and improved banisher-cannon. Though I hope you won't need to field-test it."

Quinn swiveled the barrel. "This looks like it could take down a hount." He dropped his voice to a whisper. "We want to help you stow away. When the crew boards in the morning, Paige can raise a ruckus to distract them. She's good at that sort of thing."

Paige shot him a look of mock annoyance. "Pine-Box can scout out a hidey-hole and lead you there."

"I'll be the lookout," Signe added. "Not the best job for the nearsighted person, but I'm the only one free to do it."

"I'm touched," Zora said with a bittersweet air. "But I'm not stowing away."

Quinn goggled at her. "What about your plan to take back the Wastes? You've been talking about that since I met you. You deserve to come with us."

"We'd be easy prey without your inventions," said Paige. "It's not fair for us to ditch you."

"I swore I'd follow Mom's rules, and I mean to stick to my promise." Zora wiped her forehead, leaving a grease stain above one eyebrow. "Then I'll do things my own way, with no hiding or sneaking around. Besides, Mom would see through your scheme in a second."

Her answer left Quinn crestfallen. They'd spent six moons separated, only to be parting again. And yet he did feel a twinge of relief. His sister would be safe in the Hollows, and none of them would be landing in trouble.

"You're certain?" asked Signe.

"I've made up my mind." Zora opened a crate of beehive-shaped devices inset with hexagonal prisms. "I still have these bombs left to charge, plus the cannon."

"I'll help you." Paige nudged Quinn and Signe away. "Y'all take a moment to enjoy the view."

Quinn gave in and wandered over to the starboard porthole. The sun had set behind the hills, leaving dark purple clouds in its wake. Far below, Ranger Tate was sweeping a blue beam across the snow-covered field.

Signe leaned her head on Quinn's shoulder and entwined her arm in his. They stood there for a while, watching the last of the daylight dwindle away. When the sky had faded to black, she pulled him by the hand to the other side of the gondola.

"Maybe we can see the aurora from up here," she said. "It's particularly dramatic above the Lost Gorges."

Quinn peered through the thick glass. A shimmering blanket of light lay over the southern range—the auras of countless spirits, from tiny coblynaus to gigantic elementals. All of them corpse-candles for the people who'd died in the Wakenings.

"What do you see when you look at the aurora?" he asked.

"It's like an oil painting in the sky, with colors so vivid they don't even seem real. I can only bear to look at it for so long." Signe squeezed her eyes shut and reopened them. "The brightest part marks the way to Moonbow Falls. The wavy patch between those two hills—" She leaned closer and touched the porthole. "That's odd."

Quinn saw it, too: one swath of aurora that rippled more than the rest. As he stared at the wrinkle in the sky, it grew larger and even more brilliant.

"It's coming closer," said Signe.

A muffled thump echoed behind them. Then another, and then a third. Quinn tried to place where he'd heard that sound before. On the Big Lake, when Zora's spirit-mine had gone off underwater? In Deadfall Wood, when they'd blown up a cluster of orbs?

No, at the All Hollows celebrations. Those thumps came from black powder rockets firing into the air.

Quinn turned around just in time to see scarlet fireworks blossom in the sky. A few seconds later, three booms shook the gondola's sides.

"What in the Festering Barrens was that?" said Mr. Vandy.

More pyrotechnics lit up the hills, each bloom as red as Evelyn Fontaine's spirit-lures. "Strontium carbonate, I think," Zora said through the ship's speaking tube.

"Are we under attack?" Abigail squeaked. As if in reply, another blast rattled the ship.

Down on the ground, Ranger Tate and the young sentry in camouflage dashed toward the source of the rockets. A cobalt searchlight raked over the woods. Ms. Coldiron and Mr. Epps dropped their mugs and ducked into the hangar.

"It's here," said Signe. Quinn looked over her shoulder at the spirit striding silently toward them. Its long streamers curled down to the treetops, and the haze from its aura distorted the hills.

A spire had strayed here from the Wastes. It was taller than the one that had left Signe in a coma. Taller than the mast. Taller than the top of the ship.

"On our left!" Quinn shouted. "Spire!"

Paige swore a relic hunter's curse. The Rangers stopped in mid-charge and spun to face the oncoming spirit. The trees parted before it like hay in the path of a scythe.

"I'm charging the cannon," said Zora.

When the spire reached the head of the hollow, Signe's breathing abruptly sped up. Then her whole body started shaking. Quinn had never seen her react to a spirit like this.

Another rocket exploded overhead as the Rangers scurried for cover. The young sentry hid behind a mud-wagon, while Ranger Tate crouched under a pig hut. Quinn balled his fists in frustration. He couldn't help anyone from up here.

Abigail flicked a switch, and static hissed from a speaker. "Radio on, sir."

"*Reynardine* to Ground Base." Mr. Vandy was deathly serious now. "Can you hear me?"

"Captain Flores here," said a flat voice. "I reckon you see the roamer."

Ms. Coldiron ran back out of the hangar with a double-barreled banisher in her hands. Mr. Epps trailed close behind her, now hatless and toting a pouch. The trees swayed as the spire drew nearer, but it made no noise at all—not the roar of a hount or the wail of a pharos or so much as the buzz of a wisp.

"It's too powerful for me to stare down." Signe's forehead was damp with sweat.

"We'll find some way to stop it." Quinn took her gloved hand in his. He could feel the blood pulsing in his ears. "I'm going down there."

"You'd never make it in time." Mr. Vandy flipped a lever. "We need to launch before that monster wrecks the ship."

"We're leaving?" Abigail sounded thunderstruck.

"Just for a jaunt over the South Hollows." The propellers started to hum. "We'll loop around and dock when it's safe."

"Who's on board?" Captain Flores asked through the speaker.

"None of my crew, but all five of the youngsters."

There was a long pause on the other end. "Take care of them," the captain said at last. "And yourself."

"Sylvia, what are you—"

"No time to talk. I'm coming to unmoor the ship."

"Clear out when you're done," Mr. Vandy tried to tell her, but the signal was already dead.

Signe gripped Quinn's fingers so hard they hurt. The young sentry fired her rifle too soon, and its ray fell short of the spire. Quinn had made that mistake on one of his first spirit-hunts. Farther back, Ms. Coldiron and Mr. Epps were loading glass cartridges into her weapon.

"HERETICS!" cried a loud voice. "I'VE BECKONED YOUR DOOM FROM THE RADIANT LANDS!" At the far end of the field stood a figure in a long, billowing coat: a woman holding a megaphone. Quinn grabbed a spyglass and raised it to his eye. The Spiritist he'd passed on the road glowered back at him through the lens.

"That's Evelyn Fontaine's messenger," Quinn told the others. "She summoned the spire to attack us." But how had she known where to find them?

Mr. Vandy pounded the console. "Coldiron, take the helm. I'll handle the pitch. Putnam, stand by your radio and listen for incoming signals. Zhu, you're our Spotter—tell us what's happening below. Prosser, you're the gunner—fire the cannon when ready. Janasdottir"—his voice softened when he saw her distress—"I need you to watch the instruments for me."

Signe drew a long, shuddering breath. "I can do this," she told Quinn. He squeezed her hand and made for the cannon while Zora tromped by on her way to the bridge.

"The spire's closing in on the field," Paige called out from the porthole. "Ranger Tate is opening fire." As Quinn took his seat at the cannon, he glimpsed a flash of amethyst light.

"YOUR WEAPONS ARE NOTHING TO THE SHINING ONES," screamed the voice from the megaphone.

"She's a copperhead, but she's right," said Paige. "That was a spitball to the spire. Cap's halfway up the stairs. Zora's mom is—take that, you glowstick!"

Quinn craned his neck for a better view of the action. Ms. Coldiron's gun was spraying violet bolts at the spirit. With each direct hit, its aura flickered like a bulb about to burn out.

"It felt *that*." Paige sounded ecstatic, but only for a moment. "Watch out. It's still coming."

The spire lashed its streamers in the air and lumbered out of the forest. Quinn checked the battery gauge: almost ready to shoot.

"YOU CAN'T STOP THE HORNED CROWN'S REVENGE." The Spiritist raised a fist to the sky.

"Where'd she come from?" Mr. Vandy's words echoed through the pipes. "And how did she slip past the Ranger patrols?"

The spire ripped the mud-wagon in half, and the young sentry scrambled toward the hangar. Ms. Coldiron blasted away with both barrels while Ranger Tate took potshots from the hut, but the spirit ignored their attacks. In a few heartbeats, it would reach the airship.

"Cap made it to the top of the mast," Paige said. "She's releasing the cable." The *Reynardine*'s snout tilted up in the air, sending a landslide of loose parts toward Quinn. Bolts and screws bounced past his feet.

"Twenty degrees starboard," said Mr. Vandy. "Steer us away from the spirit."

The airship lurched to the right, and Quinn clung to the cannon to keep from falling. Someone—Abigail?—yelped from the bridge. One of Zora's spirit-bombs rolled across the floor and struck a bulkhead with a thud.

"Run, Captain," Paige hollered. "It's right on top of you!"

As the ship pulled away from its mooring, Quinn lined up the spire in his sights. Before he could pull the trigger, the spirit yanked a girder away from the mast. With a loud metallic groan, the rest of the structure collapsed.

"Did Sylvia . . ." Mr. Vandy didn't finish his question. The *Reynardine* yawed toward the hills, leaving the spire to thrash in its slipstream.

"NONE OF YOU CAN ESCAPE THE WRATH OF THE SPIRITS." The Spiritist broke into amplified laughter.

Quinn felt tempted to shoot her with the cannon—not that it would do anything to her. Then he spotted the shape looming behind her: another spire stalking up from the mouth of the hollow. This one he recognized from the worst night of his life. He'd watched it stab Signe in the chest.

"YOUR DEATH AWAITS YOU IN THE CLOUDS." The Spiritist hadn't noticed the second spire's aura, nor had she heard its quiet approach. She must not have figured on summoning more than one giant roamer.

No time to worry about her. The first spire had pulled itself free of the girders, and two people still stood in its path: Ms. Coldiron and Mr. Epps.

Paige and Zora cried out at the same time. With his heart in his throat, Quinn took aim at the spire. One squeeze of the trigger, and violet energy flowed through the barrel. The beam struck the spirit dead center, knocking it flat on the ground. Ms. Coldiron and Mr. Epps fled to the hangar but stopped in the doorway to look back at the ship.

"THE AIRBOUNDS WILL BURN YOU TO—" The Spiritist let out a shriek as green streamers coiled around her. The second spire snatched her up by the coat and flung her into its translucent maw. Her silhouette was visible for an instant before she dissolved into ribbons. The megaphone landed in the snow, narrow end pointing up toward the stars.

Quinn tasted sour liquid on the back of his tongue. If the Spiritist had any people to mourn her, they'd be burying an empty coffin.

Gears rumbled overhead, and the *Reynardine* wallowed

toward the clouds. The first spire rose from the earth to follow the ship, while the second gave chase from another direction.

"I'm glad my boss and Zora's mom are safe," said Paige. "But this would be a good time to start firing again."

Quinn picked up the mouthpiece by the cannon. "I drained the battery dry." His stomach fluttered as they sailed through a notch between two mountaintops. Behind them, the spires shone like torches against the black crowns of the trees.

"The cannon's an energy hog," said Zora. "We'll only get one shot every few minutes."

"Why are those spires so keen to catch us?" asked Mr. Vandy.

"And why'd they show up in the first place?" Abigail wanted to know.

"I've been thinking about that." Signe sounded calmer now, though her voice still carried a tremor. "The first spire was already coming toward us when the fireworks started."

Which could only mean one thing. "Something else drew it here," Quinn said. "Something on this ship." *The bigger the haystack, the easier it is to hide a needle inside it.* "There must be a spirit-lure on board. We need to find it—and fast."

"In the meantime, let's lead those things away from the Hollows before they hurt anyone else," said Mr. Vandy. "Coldiron, set a course for the Wastes."

The *Reynardine* turned toward the aurora, with the spires close on its tail.

PART TWO

THE LONESOME SCENES OF WINTER

6

THE SKY UP AHEAD BLAZED IN NEON GREEN AND FLUORESCENT yellow. Beneath the aurora, the halos of a thousand elementals speckled the hills. Signe couldn't see the twin spires behind the ship, and that, at least, was a mercy. She still felt pins and needles in her fingertips and a phantom pain in her chest, but her hands had finally stopped shaking.

Mr. Vandy shouted something at her.

Signe shook away the fog in her head. "Could you kindly repeat that?"

"Tell me our heading." He studied a bubble level and turned his wheel to the right.

"How, exactly?" She should've stuck around earlier for the lesson on flying the ship.

"Read the gadget on the navigator's desk."

She inspected a compass set in a trio of concentric brass rings. "One hundred and sixty-six degrees." Judging from the map, they were headed straight for Ram's Horn.

"You're doing great, Janasdottir. Helm, hold this course."

"Aye, aye, skipper." Zora looked the part of a seasoned

sky-dog with her goggles and fingerless gloves. If she was frightened, it didn't show on her face.

"I'm sorry for freezing up when the first spire appeared." Signe hung her head, and her glasses slipped down her nose. She'd panicked at the sight of the spirit instead of helping her friends. But it was petty to nurse her own pride after what had befallen Captain Flores.

"Belay that talk," said Mr. Vandy. "The first time I rode a hot air balloon, I was so nervous I puked over the—" He broke off in mid-sentence. Abigail had turned green in the gills. "I was distinctly unsettled," he finished.

"More trouble ahead," said Zora.

Signe pushed her glasses back into place. A river of foxfire was surging up a hill in their path. A hount, no doubt drawn by the lure on the ship. The spirit reared like a rattlesnake about to strike.

Zora steered the ship to the left, and the hount lunged into empty air. Its momentum sent it streaming over the edge of a cliff. The spirit crashed on the rocks below and flowed out of sight down the slope.

"The spires are matching our pace," Paige called out from her post at the porthole. "Can this ship go any faster?"

"Or higher?" Abigail gulped for air and covered her mouth with her hand.

"We don't want to lose them till we're out of the Hollows," said Mr. Vandy. "Unless we can vaporize them first. Prosser, how's the cannon?"

"Ready to fire." Quinn must be scared, too—Signe had faced enough spirits with him to know that—but his soft baritone sounded steady and reassuring.

Zora leaned toward the voice-pipe by the helm. "This time, let the charge build up before you shoot."

"And aim for the spire that attacked us last summer," Signe couldn't help adding. She held her breath as the cannon started to buzz. The gondola vibrated in rhythm with the coil, but Quinn held his fire for what seemed like an eon.

"Now!" said Zora.

Signe rushed to an aft-facing window. The buzz turned into a blare, and the cannon's ray cleaved the spire from its crown to the tips of its spurs. Each half of the spirit disintegrated without a sound, leaving clouds of green cinders that swiftly faded away.

"Great shooting, Pine-Box!" Paige crowed.

Signe exhaled, and the ghost-splinter in her chest melted. She usually favored a less violent approach, but this case warranted an exception. Maybe now she'd be free of the night terrors that had started with her spirit-sickness. Once a moon or so, she would wake up in the dead of night, unable to speak or move a muscle. An invisible force would press down on her ribs, and unseen things would hiss in the shadows. Then the spell would suddenly break.

"We just crossed the Border Hollows," said Mr. Vandy. "Time to drop ballast." He pulled a lever, and the *Reynardine* soared toward the heavens.

"Try and catch us now, glowstick." Paige made a rude gesture toward the remaining spire. Quinn cheered, and Zora hooted, but Abigail only grunted. Then the radio operator threw up in her tin dinner pail.

Signe held out one of her handkerchiefs. "I know just how you feel. The same thing happened to me on a boat." This must be a rough initiation for a novice at meddling with spirits.

"Thanks." Abigail took the handkerchief and wiped flecks of vomit from her striped coveralls.

"Don't celebrate yet," said Mr. Vandy. "Airbounds like to hunt at this altitude. Janasdottir, do you see any out there?"

Signe made her way forward and squinted through the glass. Above the aurora, the sky was black except for the stars. "Clear so far."

"Ground Base to *Reynardine*," Ranger Tate drawled through the radio speaker. "What's your situation?"

"All hands safe. We took down one spire and drew the other away to the Wastes." Mr. Vandy cleared his throat. "Any word on Captain Flores?"

"She broke both her legs," said the Ranger, "but Doc Caudill thinks she'll recover." Mr. Vandy exhaled, and Signe did, too. The captain might be gruff, but she'd saved Signe and her friends three times and counting.

"Are my mom and Mr. Epps okay?" Zora asked.

"They're fine but worried about you," said Ranger Tate. "You're coming back now?"

Mr. Vandy unfurled a schematic. "We think the Spiritist hid a beacon somewhere on board. No clue how she did it, but we can't risk leading more roamers back to the Hollows."

"A shame we can't interrogate her." The Ranger didn't sound terribly sad about that. Signe tried and failed to dredge up a shred of pity for the cultist who'd tried to kill them.

"I should look for the lure," Zora said. "I have a knack for finding those things."

"Can't spare you from the helm." Mr. Vandy rubbed his mustache. "Nor Prosser from the cannon. This ship's built to fly with a dozen more hands aboard, so we're already a skeleton crew. Not literally, I hope."

"I'll do it," Abigail said, though she looked ready to throw up again.

"I need you here to tend the throttle." He gave Paige the schematic. "Zhu, search inside the hull. It's a big space to cover, but your boss says you're the best scout he's ever trained. Janasdottir, keep watch from the top of the ship." He glanced down at Signe's black poplin dress. "Better grab warmer gear before you go aloft."

Signe found a fur-lined parka in the gondola's locker. She'd sworn off wearing dead animals, but she could wrestle with her conscience later. Putting on the parka, she trailed Paige up the ladder that led to the hull.

As Signe climbed into the open air, a wave of vertigo swept over her. The wind stung her cheeks and made her eyes water. Spirit-shine from the aurora splashed in green waves across the ship's envelope.

The *Reynardine* listed to the left, and Signe's heels slid along the rung beneath her. She swallowed her fear and kept going. All the while, the void howled in her ears.

When she reached the hull, she hoisted herself through the hatch and plonked down on the keel. "I just need a moment for my bones to turn solid again," she said.

Paige slammed the hatch shut. "Looks like this is where we split up. Keep those fairy eyes of yours peeled."

"Good luck sniffing out the lure." Signe tried to think of a nickname. "Pixie, um, Nose."

Paige laughed and started along the keel, poking her

snout into crannies as she went. Signe followed the corridor in the other direction until she came to the base of another ladder. This one disappeared upward into the darkness between two enormous gas cells. On a nearby hook hung a miner's hat. She put it on, lit its lamp, and set to climbing the cold metal rungs.

The ladder seemed to go on forever. She passed narrow catwalks and wire cat's cradles, sharp shadows against the soft skin of the cells. Her arms ached, and her lungs burned, and her long dress kept trying to trip her.

The last time she'd climbed so high, she'd still been wearing short pants. But only on cloudy days or after dusk; her skin had always burned in the sun. One hot summer night, she'd chased a boge to a silo on a neighboring farm. The little spirit had led her up to the dome and then jolted her with a spark. She'd almost lost her grip on the roof.

That had taught her to mind even the smallest of spirits. Sharing a world with their kind was a delicate balance.

The trapdoor at the top of the ladder opened onto a crow's nest—a lookout roost the size and shape of a bourbon barrel. Banishers pointed fore and aft from its railing, and a pennant fluttered from the tip of its mast.

The aurora scintillated around Signe in every direction. To the north, the Ruined Town was a glowing wound on the earth. At her back, the Hollows lay dark save for a smattering of earthbounds and electric lights.

The gusts were back and stronger than ever. *You'll travel like the wind,* her fortune had said. And here she was, alone with the zephyrs.

No, not alone. Far behind them, a line of thunderheads

stretched the length of the sky. Green lightning flickered within the anvil-shaped clouds.

She picked up the speaking tube. "A front of derechos is following us."

"We see them, too," said Mr. Vandy. "No turning around for us so long as those cloudbusters are on our tail. The only silver lining is that they're too slow to catch us. Stay up there and holler if you spot anything else."

"Aye, aye." Signe pulled on her hood and settled in for a long, chilly vigil.

♈

They flew on through the witching hour, over dead lunar valleys and lakes alive with turquoise luminescence, past mountains taller than any in the Hollows. No Spotter or relic hunter had ventured this far from home and returned to tell the tale.

Signe ducked as a flock of sylphs broke harmlessly across the *Reynardine*'s bow. When she raised her head again, the gauzy spirits were roiling behind the ship. The turbulence quickly scattered them into the night.

"Are you okay?" Quinn's voice was muffled and distant.

"Safe and sound," she said. "Though there's an icicle forming on my nose. Will you thaw it for me when we land?"

"I promise," said Quinn. "What's it like on top of the ship?"

"Sublime but solitary." Signe wrapped her arms around herself. After this trip, she and Quinn should lie low in their secret dell. On one of their autumn hunts, they'd found a forgotten hollow and made it their own sanctuary. It had a glade for their wagons, a barn for their horses, and an old cemetery for atmosphere. No Spiritist spy would ever trouble them there. "I missed you while you were away."

"I missed you showing me your favorite junk shops and flea markets. I missed cooking dinner together at odd hours. I missed coming back from our spirit-chases and reading in bed beside you."

Zora coughed through the pipes. "Just so you know, we can hear you."

"Let them have their moment." Mr. Vandy laughed wistfully. "Romance can thrive in the harshest circumstances. One time my balloon crashed in a—"

"No sign of the lure," Paige broke in. "I've searched up and down the hull."

"What about the engine nacelles?" asked Abigail.

Paige huffed and puffed. "Nope. How do I get out to them?"

"Walkways from the keel," said Mr. Vandy. "Just watch your step. It's a long way down."

"Peachy," Paige grumbled. "I'll report back once I've walked the plank." Signe felt dizzy just thinking about it. The crow's nest might be precarious, but at least she could crouch down inside it if spirits attacked.

She took off her glasses and extended her telescope. The thunderheads were still tailing the ship, and so were the airbounds they concealed. Derechos always stayed hidden inside their cloudbanks; nobody knew what they looked like.

If fate favored Signe and her friends, none of them would find out tonight.

She pointed the telescope up toward the constellations. The Crawdad and the Hound were as they should be, but the

Catamount gazed down at her with one extra eye—a pulsing green point among the stars.

"There's a spirit at eleven o'clock," she said.

"What kind?" Quinn asked.

The point split into seven green fireballs. "Bolides," Signe said. The hex cards hadn't shown her this. Nor the derechos, nor the spires. Just twin birds, a starry whorl, and a black funeral train.

"Hang on tight," said Mr. Vandy. "Putnam, give us more speed. Coldiron, take evasive action."

The propellers whined, and the *Reynardine* angled toward the right. The bolides shifted course and fanned out as they swooped toward the ship. Six moons ago, Signe had watched one of their kin snatch up a man and burn him to dust. He'd tried to sacrifice Quinn to the spirits, but they'd turned on their own worshipper.

"They're too fast to outrun," said Abigail.

"I know that." Mr. Vandy's laugh was grim now. "But Zhu needs time to search the engines. Turn hard to port."

Their auras blazing, the bolides mirrored the maneuver. They were gaining on the *Reynardine*.

"Still out of range," said Quinn.

"I missed out on last year's bolide-shooting party," said Zora. "Not tonight, I guess. Try firing short bursts at these things."

Two of the spirits peeled off to the right, two curved away to the left, and two dove into a mist-covered valley. The lead bolide plowed into a bolt from the cannon.

"One down," said Quinn. "Paige is outside the rear starboard engine."

A bolide streaked up from the fog. "Five o'clock," Signe said. A blast rocked her perch and knocked her spyglass askew.

Quinn gasped. "Paige got it with one pistol shot, but she almost lost her balance. Keep the ship steady, or she'll fall."

A second bolide zoomed past the ship and looped around toward the bow. "Look out ahead," Signe shouted. The ship veered away from the spirit's path, but not in time. Green flames punctured the hull, and Signe braced for a fiery death.

The explosion never came. *I guarantee my ship won't catch fire,* Mr. Vandy had said. *I've filled the* Reynardine *with helium gas.* Thank the stars he hadn't used hydrogen.

The bolide burst out of the ship and wheeled toward the tail fins. A ray from the cannon extinguished it.

"One of the gas bags is leaking," said Abigail.

Signe's stomach plunged as the *Reynardine* lost altitude. Would they sink through the fog and run aground on the reefs of the mountains?

With a jerk, the ship leveled out. Signe grabbed the rail with both of her mittened hands.

"Snuff the rest of those overgrown sparklers," Zora said. "I don't want my last words to come out all squeaky from helium."

Signe leaned over the side of the crow's nest. Four bolides left to go. One far off to the left in the aurora, one high overhead on the Milky Way, and one down in the layer of mist. But where was the final spirit?

Hurtling straight toward her, of course. And toward the muzzle of the aft banisher. She tore off her mittens and pressed a bare finger to the trigger.

But no. She'd never fired a gun, and this one felt wrong in her hands. Shooting spirits wasn't part of her calling. The universe had blessed her eyes for a reason.

Signe flipped her goggles on and gazed through their indigo lenses. The bolide slowed down but kept coming. Now it was only a stone's throw away.

"Let us pass in peace," Signe said.

The spirit orbited her, drawing closer with each revolution. Its glare dazzled her eyes, and its whirring hammered in her ears.

Signe's nose began to drip. "Leave us alone."

The bolide's aura filled her field of vision. Everything was a blur of bright light, dark veins, and transparent specks.

"Go away!"

The glare vanished, leaving only a mauve afterimage. Signe blinked away tears and pulled off her goggles. She'd stared the spirit away, but her eyes needed time to recover. Her pupils must look like pinpoints.

Somebody screamed. That had to be Abigail. The ship shuddered as metal creaked and then snapped. A crash echoed from the forest below.

"A bolide sheared off the rear starboard engine," said Quinn. Nobody spoke for a long moment.

Zora broke the silence. "Was—was Paige still in it?"

"I don't know," Quinn whispered.

Signe's windpipe constricted, and she covered her eyes with her palms. Did the final hex card signify Paige's death? She'd taken a train to the meeting, and the fallen engine might be her coffin.

Too late to warn her now.

The last three bolides had formed a flying wedge behind the ship. "Here they come," Signe said.

The spirits careened toward the keel. For once, Quinn's aim

went astray; his bolt passed under one bolide and over the others. He and Zora barked the same curse at the same time.

"I found the lure!" Paige yelled. "Snakes alive, that was close. What should I do with it?" Signe had never been so happy to hear her voice. Or misread an omen.

"Stick it in a spirit bomb," Zora said. "And throw them both overboard."

As the bolides closed in on the ship, a flashing red light fell toward the earth. The spirits swerved to follow the lure and flew right into the side of a mountain. Green and violet plasma spewed from its slope.

The bolides did not rise again.

"Well done, crew," Mr. Vandy said. "Now we have a choice. We could turn around and make for the Hollows. Without the lure to give us away, maybe—just maybe—we'll slip past the cloudbusters."

Signe grimaced at the wall of emerald-tinged clouds. Derechos left trails of dead eagles and hawks in their wake. The zeppelin would make for a much larger target.

"Or?" said Zora.

"Or we press on to Ram's Horn and rescue whoever's there."

"But we lost a gas cell and an engine," Quinn pointed out.

"We can still fly with the ones we have left," said Mr. Vandy. "So long as we don't take too much more damage. And we could repair the ship before heading home. What do y'all say?"

Signe pictured the hex cards in her mind. Two songbirds, one inverted: the Distelfinks. A spiral galaxy: the Skywheel. A coffin on a railcar: the Black Train. They told her nothing about what to do next. She had to rely on her own intuition.

"We should keep going," she said. "Our destiny lies in Ram's Horn."

"I agree." Abigail sounded skittish, and Signe understood that all too well: they'd come a long way to this desolate place.

Paige and Zora voted to continue, too. "This all feels familiar somehow," said Quinn. "Like I've been here before in a dream. But those folks need our help. I say we finish the mission."

"You're a fine crew," Mr. Vandy said. "Putnam, get on your radio and tell the Rangers we're pushing ahead. Coldiron, set us back on course for the Sounding Gap."

♈

At first light, Signe climbed back down to the gondola. The aurora had dissipated, and the elementals lay dormant under the soil. A landscape of ash and dead trees stretched out before her.

Quinn had dark circles beneath his eyes. She warmed her nose against his shoulder while he rested his forehead on her tangled hair.

"I suppose it's too much to ask for a hot bath when we arrive," she mumbled into his jacket.

Zora stifled a yawn. "See that notch in the mountains? Ram's Horn should be on the other side."

Everyone stared blearily at the gap. Ruined houses littered the valley; jagged stumps dotted the slopes. Nothing stirred against the gray dust. Signe couldn't imagine how anyone had survived in this place.

Paige pointed at a mountaintop. "There's the radio transmitter."

No wonder the signal had stopped. Some great force had

bent the antenna in half so that its tip almost grazed the ground. Knots of cables dangled from the girders.

"I hope we don't run into whatever did that," said Abigail.

The ship descended into the gap and glided on past the antenna. Beyond stood a log fort with its back to a cliff. A pair of watchtowers flanked the stockade, and a wooden keep rose from its center. The front gate was shut.

"Cut speed," said Mr. Vandy. "Steer us in slowly."

As they drew near the fort, Signe spotted signs of a recent battle. Shattered timbers lay strewn outside the walls, and a deep furrow in the dirt marked the trail of a hount.

Make that three hounts. A trio of gouges converged on the fort.

Quinn ran his fingers through his hair, like he always did when he was thinking. "Did we come too late?"

Before anyone could reply, the low note of a hunting horn echoed across the gap. The sound was coming from a copper cone on the roof of the keep.

"Well, I'll be hexed," said Mr. Vandy.

The horn blasted again, and a head peeked above the left tower. The watcher's eyes looked out from behind a blue mask.

The radio spat bursts of feedback, and Abigail adjusted a knob. "Ram's Horn, can you hear me?"

"Who are you?" asked a high-pitched, halting voice. Not the one from the distress signal. "And what in the Name of the Syzygy is that flying monster?"

A small face with a bluish tint popped up in one of the tower windows. Did the fort's sentries use cobalt glass in their panes?

Mr. Vandy put on a grandiose tone. "I'm the skipper of the

Reynardine, and this here's a zeppelin of my own devising. I got the idea for it while hanging by my fingernails from a—"

"A what?" The voice's owner sounded bewildered.

"An airship. Or a dirigible, if you prefer."

"We received your message," Signe cut in.

A sharp intake of breath from the radio's speaker. "You're here to save us from the spirits?"

"That's right," Quinn said soothingly. "We're from a place called the Hollows. We can take you there with us."

"But first," said Mr. Vandy, "we need your assistance to anchor our ship."

"I'll talk to Cousin Nova and Cousin Nick." The radio went silent.

"We did it." Signe kissed Quinn on the neck. They'd made the right choice; this voyage was part of fate's grand design.

The gate swung open, revealing two figures. Tattered clothes hung loose on their skinny frames. In the shadow of the keep, their faces seemed strangely discolored.

Signe watched them through her spyglass. From their looks, they might be around Zora's age. One was a girl with hollow cheeks and a pointed nose. Horns curled out from a crown on her head. The boy beside her bore the same angular features. He wore a tool belt around his waist and a violin case over his shoulder.

As the pair strode through the gate, the sun caught their faces.

Their odd complexion was no trick of the light. They both had pale bluish skin, and so did the children in the towers.

7

"MY NAME IS NOVALYNE MARTIN," SAID THE GIRL WITH THE CROWN. "And this is my brother Nicholas." She stared at Zora and the others as though they'd flown down from the moon on luna moth wings.

Not that Zora blamed her. Their ship had dropped out of the sky without any warning and delivered an odd rescue party: a silver-haired skipper and five teenagers, all of them grungy and sleepy-eyed.

Though their hosts seemed out of the ordinary, too. The blue skin, for starters. And one of the pair had set off a sensor on Zora's wrist-watcher, like Signe always did with her eyes. Whatever mutation caused spirit-vision, either the sister or the brother had it.

"You must have undertaken a dangerous voyage." Novalyne spoke with a twangy, old-fashioned accent. "We welcome you to Ram's Horn."

Mr. Vandy tipped his hat and presented his crew. "Thank you for helping us moor the *Reynardine*." They'd wrangled wires for an hour to anchor the ship. Now it sat rooted in the gap like a gigantic cloth watermelon.

Nicholas smiled lopsidedly. His hair looked as if he'd cut it himself without a mirror. "I can't believe you heard my message. We'd given up hope on anyone coming." He had the same lilting intonation as his sister.

"That was me," said Abigail. "I found your signal with my shortwave receiver."

Zora felt a flash of annoyance. Then again, she would've bragged, too.

Nicholas's eyes lit up. "I can't wait to learn about your technology. Your airship. Those glass guns you have." He glanced at Zora's wrist-watcher. "And whatever that device is."

A rush of pride warmed her cheeks. The boy just might make for a worthy lab partner.

"Allow us to show you our home." Novalyne led them through the gate. "Though this fort is all that remains. Generations ago, the Folk of the Ram lived throughout the Sounding Gap." Her voice rose in anger. "Then the spirits ravaged our towns and turned our pastures to ash."

"Nevertheless, we've endured," said Nicholas.

They walked past shriveled gardens and an enclosure that held a few scrawny lambs. The inside of the fort was eerily quiet. Cabins with empty windows and boarded-up doors huddled against the palisades.

"What happened to everyone else?" Zora knew in her bones, but she still had to ask.

"Our elders sacrificed themselves to protect us." Novalyne bowed her horned head. "The last one was our grandmother. Her heart gave out during the first hount attack, the night after the fall equinox."

Guilt knotted Zora's stomach. She'd spent that evening

celebrating with her family and friends. They'd seized the Fontaine family mansion and toasted to peace in the Hollows. Meanwhile, the people here had been holding a funeral.

Paige started to hug Novalyne, stopped short, and then went on ahead. The girl flinched but didn't pull away.

"You two are the oldest ones here?" asked Mr. Vandy.

"Yes, we're both sixteen," said Novalyne. "Nicholas is my twin. The children are twelve, ten, and nine."

"Are they your siblings, too?" asked Quinn.

"Not strictly speaking," said Nicholas. "But we're all cousins one way or another."

An iron lattice barred the way to the keep. Novalyne pulled a rope, and chains clanked behind the portcullis. It rose to reveal a dim, windowless room with thick wooden columns and beams. Painted constellations shone down from the ceiling. Zora recognized a pair of bright stars as the Horns of the Ram.

Nicholas struck a match and lit a betty lamp. Its glow illuminated a set of wool tapestries along the chamber's eight walls. The one to Zora's left showed green meteors raining down from the sky. The one on her right showed a girl with a fiddle standing up to a spire.

"No spirit has breached this keep in a hundred and forty-four years." Novalyne's expression was flinty. "The hounts broke through the palisades in their last attack, but we drove them back to the mountains."

"How did you stop them?" asked Zora. She hadn't seen any weapons on display.

Nicholas pantomimed sawing a fiddle. "With my playing, amplified through the cone on the roof."

Zora eyed his battered instrument case. Had he figured out

how to fight spirits with sonic vibrations? That puzzle had stumped her all winter long. She'd tried strings of gut and of steel, at every frequency on the scale, but nothing had worked on the wisps in Lightning Bug Hollow.

"And I bear the Mark of the Syzygy." Novalyne touched the band of her crown.

"I heard that phrase in your brother's message," said Abigail. "What does it mean?"

"Our grandparents had a visit from an . . ." Novalyne said a name Zora didn't know. Eye-something. Eidolon? "They passed its mark down to our mother, and she passed the gift along to me. I always know when the spirits are coming."

Signe blinked behind her blue lenses. "You mean you have spectral sight?"

"Not sight." Novalyne lifted her chin. "I can sense their presence with my mind. You could call it claircognizance."

"Unlike my twin, I was born without any preternatural talents," Nicholas added wryly. "But I learned how to fiddle and tinker to make myself useful."

"Do any of your people bear the Mark?" asked Novalyne.

Signe seemed dazed, so Zora answered for her. "My friend here has spirit-vision."

"What's a" —Paige tripped over the word— "syzygy?"

"A configuration of celestial objects," Zora said. "An eclipse, for example. But I have no clue what an eidolon is."

Novalyne pointed to the tapestry on the far wall. It showed a man and a woman surrounded by indigo flames. "A bane of the spirits. When the sun and moon align with the earth, the eidolons manifest to bestow their gifts."

Signe found her voice again. "Do they speak to you?"

"Not that I've ever heard," said Novalyne. "Their ways are unfathomable."

Zora weighed the girl's explanation. Were these eidolons real? If so, where did they come from, and how did their powers work?

She should find time for a long conversation with Signe.

A bulb on her wrist-watcher flickered, as if it had a loose wire. After a moment, it stopped. Two others shone on: one for Signe and one for Novalyne.

Feet pattered on the floor above, and three children ran down a staircase. The oldest was a boy; the middle and youngest were girls. They had the same blue complexion as the twins.

"It's time for our breakfast." Nicholas steered them to a table under the radium stars. "We'd be honored if you joined us."

"We don't have much food to offer, but we're happy to share." Novalyne took off her crown. Beneath it, her hair was as ragged as her brother's. Without the horns, she looked less like a druid priest and more like an apprentice sheepherder. "Fetch what's left in the cellar," she told the children.

Zora collapsed into a chair. She'd stayed awake for twenty-four hours straight. When the children came back and Nicholas introduced them, she instantly forgot their names.

The twins handed out plates of blotchy apples, soggy corn-bread, and dollops of some mashed root vegetable. "We're out of mutton," Nicholas said. "The hounts butchered our flock."

Zora snuck a peek at the other plates. The twins had given their guests and the children the biggest portions, leaving only scraps for themselves. Zora would've offered them hers, but she didn't want to offend their pride. Besides, the airship was loaded with barrels of food. Soon they'd be dining on venison jerky and strawberry jam.

The youngest child gaped at Signe. "You're so white," she blurted. "Are you a ghost? Or a cave-goblin?"

Signe winced but then smiled. "Perhaps I'm a young woman with albinism." She arched her eyebrows. "Or perhaps I'm the Queen of the Fair Folk."

Novalyne scowled at the girl who'd asked the question. "We should treat our guests hospitably."

"Forgive us," said Nicholas. "We've never seen anyone from beyond the gap."

"Except in old books," said the middle child. "Y'all look like the folks in the pictures. I thought the artists colored them that way as a style, but I guess no one has blue skin but us."

Zora took a bite of the mash. It tasted like moldy rutabaga.

Mr. Vandy pushed back his empty plate. "The *Reynardine* needs fixing up. We should leave straightaway if those hounts are still out there."

"They always come back," said Novalyne. "I fear they'll attack again soon."

"We're abandoning Ram's Horn?" asked the oldest child in a faltering voice. "Forever?"

"There are only five of us left." Nicholas put a hand on the boy's shoulder. "We can't survive here anymore."

Novalyne gazed at a tapestry of two women: an old one wearing a crown just like hers and a younger one rocking a matched pair of cradles. "Our home is finished."

Zora had never heard anyone sound so bitter. Her own grudge against the spirits suddenly seemed petty. They'd terrorized her and split up her family, but they hadn't slaughtered her people or blighted her hollow. "We'll reclaim this pass someday," she promised.

"Bring all the records you have," said Quinn. "Any letters or diaries. We can preserve your knowledge and history."

Nicholas stood up. "Gather your things," he told the children. "And pack the journals in the study."

"I should rest while it's light out," said Novalyne. "I guard the fort from sundown to dawn. We have beds to spare if anyone needs them."

Mr. Vandy gestured at Quinn, Paige, and Signe. "You three get some sleep so you can watch over the ship tonight. Coldiron and Putnam, you're with me."

"I'd like to help, too." Nicholas radiated excitement. Mr. Vandy waved him over, and the four of them set out from the keep.

♈

Zora's boots squelched in the mud as she walked by the silent cabins. Daffodils had sprouted through the snow, and the noon sun was melting the ice on the eaves. Maybe winter had finally broken.

Nicholas frowned at the mast on the mountain. "We worked on that for a year, and the hounts wrecked it in a night."

"How did you build it?" asked Abigail.

"The children scavenged pieces of scrap, and I welded them into a tower. We raised it with ropes, and Nova scaled the side to wire the antenna." His face clouded. "I couldn't do that."

When they arrived at the ship, Mr. Vandy and Abigail climbed up to patch the holes in the hull. Zora and Nicholas stayed below to replace the missing engine. Good thing they'd stowed enough parts for a new one.

Zora soldered wires while her new helper tightened bolts and fired off questions. "What fuel do these engines use? Where did you find so much helium? And how do you keep it from escaping?"

"Hemp diesel. Thermal springs. Membranes made from goldbeater's skin." Tired as she was, she still got a kick out of explaining things to him. But she also had questions of her own. "How'd you find a way to stop spirits with music?"

He brushed a bead of sweat from the tip of his nose. "My grandfather taught me a set of uncanny cross-tunings. He learned them from his great-grandmother, and she learned them from a wayfarer—the one who named all the spirits."

Zora pulled off her hat and mopped her forehead. "A girl with a fiddle?"

"That's what Grandpa told me. She came to Ram's Horn, stuck around a few moons, and then rambled on. Her name was Jessamine."

Zora smiled to herself. More proof the legends were true. Wait until she told Quinn; the fiddler girl was his hero. "What types of spirits have you serenaded?"

"A dwayyo and a tailypo." Nicholas ticked off his fingers. "Two roperites and one pack of herns. Along with the occasional boge"—he pronounced it *bogey*, like Zora's grandparents did—"and other sorts of little roamers."

"I've never bagged a tailypo," she said. Those things smashed their way into lonely shanties and left nothing behind but scorched bones. "I'm a little green-eyed about that."

He looked bashful. "It was tricky. I started with Black

Mountain Rag, switched over to Old-Timey D, and finished in Dead Man's Tuning. But the hounts are too strong to dispel. It's all I can do to ward them away." He turned toward the cannon. "And how do your weapons work?"

"Ah, my turn to rivet," she said without thinking.

"Say what?"

Zora grabbed the pneumatic hammer and ducked behind the propeller. "I fill the glass barrels with purified argon. The coil ionizes the gas and generates ectospectral radiation."

"Ectospectral?" Nicholas sounded intrigued.

"Like electromagnetic, but spookier. In a quantum mechanical sense. A beam at the right amplitude can disrupt a kirlian field. Kaboom: no more spirits."

"Does it destroy them?"

Zora drew two circles in the ash with the end of her crutch. "I think the explosion creates a dimensional rift." She added a squiggle connecting the circles. "The spirits flow through it back to their own universe."

"That's phenomenal." His eyes flicked down to her crutches. "I hope you weren't injured on our account."

Zora swallowed her irritation. He'd grown up out here in the back of beyond; she couldn't expect him to know any better. And he'd given her an excuse to pry, too. "I'm not hurt at all. I was born with a tether at the tip of my spinal cord." She erased her drawing. "Why couldn't you scale the mast?"

"I apologize for assuming." His face went from bluish to purple. "Climbing that high would strain my heart. If it beats too fast, I start to get woozy and muddled. Nova calls it my woolgathering."

Zora wished she'd studied more biology. "We left our doctor

back home—long story—but we did pack a medical kit. Stay right there." She marched over to the gondola, found Doc Caudill's bag, and carried it back. "Could you undo your coat?"

Nicholas fumbled with his buttons. "What exactly do you have in mind?"

"I want to take a listen." Zora pulled out a stethoscope. "I'll try myself first." Her own heartbeat was steady, if faster than she'd expected. "Now yours." When she pressed the silver diaphragm to his chest, she heard a double thump and a whoosh. "Your heart makes extra sounds. Is that connected to your"—she'd almost said *weird*—"distinctive complexion?"

"I'm not sure. Nova never gets dizzy spells." He rebuttoned his moth-eaten coat. "The children don't, either. But my grandparents did."

She tucked the stethoscope into the bag. "What about your parents?"

"Not that I recall. Nova and I lost them the night a titan swept down through the gap. They went to draw it away. Mom had the Mark, and Dad had his fiddle." He looked off toward the powdered hills. "They tried to double back, but the titan caught them in sight of the walls. I watched them face it together."

"Nicholas, I'm sorry." That sounded empty. Quinn would've known what to say, but she didn't. "How old were you?"

"We'd just turned eight." Nicholas wiped his eyes. "You can call me Nick, by the way. Only my sister calls me by my full name."

Zora did the math: that would've been the year the harbinger baited her into the woods and told her to run for her life. The year Dad had gone away so the spirits would leave her alone. His plan hadn't worked in the end—but then again, neither had the harbinger's.

"Our doctor can check out your heart with an etherscope," she said. "Once we get you to the Hollows."

"What's your home like?"

"I always thought it was boring." Zora pictured her own hollow covered in dust, her own house vacant and ruined. "Now it seems like Fiddler's Green from the foragers' stories or Big Rock Candy Mountain from that old song."

Nicholas—no, make that Nick—gave her a crooked grin. "I know that tune. I could play it for you sometime, minus a verse or so."

"How about on my birthday?" she said. "I'm turning sixteen in—wait, I've lost track of the date."

"Tomorrow's the spring equinox."

"Six days after that." Zora tightened a screw on the engine. "I just hope we make it back before then."

♈

They finished their work as the sun grazed the mountaintops. Nick and Mr. Vandy started for the fort, but Abigail pulled Zora aside. "I've hailed the Ranger station. Would you like a turn on the horn?"

Zora nodded and followed her into the gondola. Ruddy light gleamed from the burnished face of the crystal set. Abigail turned a knob, and the speaker warbled. "*Reynardine* to Ground Base," said the girl. Then she handed Zora the microphone.

"This is Ground Base," said a voice from far, far away.

"Hi, Mom." A lump formed in Zora's throat. "Sorry I missed my curfew."

Her mother took a moment to reply. "You're okay?"

"Bone-tired but without a scratch. How are you?"

"Anxious for you to come home."

"That makes two of us." Zora blinked back her tears. She couldn't cry with Abigail watching. "Have any more Spiritists popped up from their holes?"

The signal crackled and buzzed. "No, nor Evelyn Fontaine herself. Ranger Tate sent out patrols, but they've found no clues as to where she's hiding."

"Maybe she's still somewhere in the Wastes." That problem could wait, anyhow. "We found five survivors. I've been talking shop with the boy who sent the message."

"He's an engineer, too?"

Abigail occupied herself with the map. The sunset had tinted her face pinkish red.

"A halfway decent one," Zora allowed. "Though he's sort of an odd bird." His wild hair and pointy nose put her in mind of a fledgling heron.

"You can introduce me." Her mother sounded weary. "Once you're back in the Hollows. You shouldn't be out there at all."

"Don't blame me. I never had a chance to get off the ship." Zora looked to Abigail for support, but the girl was busy plotting a route with pencil and string.

"I know." Zora's mother sighed through the static. "I just wish I were the one risking my skin."

Zora almost broke down, but Abigail came to her rescue. *You should go now,* the girl mouthed silently.

"It's getting dark," Zora said. "I need to head back to the fort."

"Don't stay out too late." Her mother's laugh rang hollow. "My little fox kit."

"Good night, Mom."

Abigail switched off the microphone. "It's tough to worry and wait." Her mood had turned pensive.

It struck Zora that she knew next to nothing about her new comrade. "Did you get a chance to talk to your folks?"

Abigail studied a thermometer. The mercury had fallen past freezing again. "They're no longer around. My mother was a relic hunter. She used to leave me at home while she rode out to the Border Hollows. One night she didn't come back. The Rangers found her the next day with this in her hand." The girl parted her collar to reveal a pendant: a platinum goat inside a circle engraved with symbols.

Zora tried to make sense of the markings, but she didn't recognize them.

"I went to live with my father," Abigail went on. "He spent his days fixing radios and his nights listening for a station named Peryton One." She tuned the dial toward the far end of the band. "Every so often, he'd hear strange signals from it."

"What kind of signals?" asked Zora.

"Garble about red stars and green galaxies. I couldn't make heads or tails of it, but Dad said it was a cipher. He thought if he could crack the code, he'd solve all the mysteries of the Hollows. Like where the spirits came from and why the Wakenings happened. He even wrote a book about his theories: *Revelations from the Veiled Realm*."

Zora had never heard the title. "What happened to him?"

"Two years ago, he set out to track down the source of the signals. He'd used a loop antenna to fix their direction."

Abigail traced a finger along the map. "Dad packed his copy of Clementine Geller's *Atlas* and trekked off into the Wastes. That was the last I ever saw of him."

Zora's heart thawed a few degrees. "So you kept on scanning the airwaves for him. Except you found Nick's signal instead."

Abigail nodded. "My father's all the family I have left. I'd do anything to find him, though I wonder if I made a mistake coming on this expedition. Y'all tangle with spirits like it's nothing, but for me, it's terrifying."

"Let me tell you a secret," Zora said. "When those bolides attacked, I almost peed my overalls." Not really, but she had as a child, encircled by roamers in the woods the night before her own father's disappearance. "What's your dad's name?"

"Ulysses Bell." Abigail breathed out a puff of steam. "You go on ahead. I'll catch up after I run a few tests."

Zora passed the night watch on her way to the fort. Her brother and Paige had blue goggles on their brows and twin-barreled banishers in their holsters. Signe was twirling her parasol and conferring with Novalyne.

"Sleep tight," said Quinn. "Don't let the bed-boges bite."

Zora bumped him with her shoulder. "Wake me up if you get in trouble, and try not to break my inventions." Paige laughed and Signe smiled, but Novalyne only glowered.

Cobalt lanterns shone down from the towers, lighting Zora's path through the gate. The faulty sensor on her wrist flickered again. One of the children—the oldest, the soft-spoken boy—slammed the door shut behind her, and a crossbar slid into place with a heavy thunk.

Zora slogged to the keep and flumped down on an empty cot. She left on her boots and braces, never mind her sore ankles. If the hounts showed up tonight, she'd be ready for them.

Nick wheezed from his bunk, and Mr. Vandy snored like a bear with hay fever. The painted zodiac stayed frozen in place. Zora tossed and turned on her lumpy straw mattress, too wound up to sleep and too bushed to think. But this was Ram's Horn, so why not try counting sheep?

She made it all the way to fifteen.

♈

The wail of the horn echoed through the darkness. Zora's wrist-watcher beeped, and three orange dots appeared on its face. The fort was under siege.

Nick jumped out of bed and snatched his fiddle case. Mr. Vandy was already on his feet, too. As the horn blasted another note, Zora pulled on a bandolier and stuffed a remote control in her pocket.

These spirits were in for a surprise.

8

NIGHTFALL HAD ROUSED THE EARTHBOUNDS OF THE GAP. RIFLE in hand, Quinn wove around spirits steaming from fissures and bubbling in sinkholes. One wrong step, and he'd lose a toe.

"The hounts are behind those mountains," said Novalyne. "I can sense them coming toward us."

Quinn flashed a warning to the watchtowers—four blue pulses for the letter H—and swept his beam toward a black mound. No spirits there. "We'd have a good view from up yonder," he told the others.

"Good thinking, Pine-Box," said Paige.

Novalyne cocked her head like a sparrow. "Why do you call him that?"

"He used to bury folks for a living. You know, in wood coffins . . ." She trailed off as they passed a pair of headstones, each engraved with an epitaph.

Quinn paused to read one of the inscriptions. *Hazel Martin, 98-135 AW. Bearer of the Mark and Sentinel of the Gap.* Beneath his sternum, a swell of regret ached. He'd spent less than a day with his mom before rushing off on this journey.

"Just you wait." Signe walked on, oblivious to the graves. "Paige will coin a new name for you, too."

"The one my parents chose will do fine." An uncertain look crossed Novalyne's face. Talking with outlanders must be strange for her.

"I think 'Nova' sounds nifty." Paige fidgeted with her rifle's coil and set off through the patches of glimmering light.

A roar came from the mountains, still far away but rising in pitch: the call of a hount tracking its prey. Two deeper roars answered in counterpoint. Quinn checked his spirit-sensors, but every bulb was already lit.

Paige scrambled up the mound. "Y'all should hustle," she hollered.

Quinn and the others joined her at the top. Ahead stretched a meadow of mildew green blooms and fungal yellow rings. Behind lay the airship and the beacons of the fort.

"Can you see them yet?" he asked Signe.

She chewed her lip. "Three faint auras approaching."

Quinn knew Nevan McBrain's entry for *HOUNT* by heart. *Huge. Solitary. Lethal.* "I thought they always roamed alone."

"These ones hunt as a pack," said Novalyne. "The first night they struck, they cut me off from the fort. I had to crawl back through a hidden tunnel, on my belly in the dark and the dirt, while my grandmother lay dying without me." She stared longingly at Paige's rifle. "May I borrow one of your guns?"

"But you have your gift," Signe said.

"I can't fight spirits with it. I want to hurt them back for a change."

"The backwash from our weapons might" —Quinn searched

for the right words—"disrupt your equilibrium." He'd watched Signe retch and faint from a spirit-bomb's blast.

"I'll make sure to aim carefully," said Novalyne.

Paige gave her a big-bore pistol and a pair of honeycombed grenades. "Pine-Box and Fairy Eyes work together, so stick behind me when the shooting starts. I hope your brother puts on a good show."

Novalyne smiled for the first time since they'd met her. "The Stars of the Ram favor us tonight."

Three auras flared beneath the horns of the crescent moon. The hounts roared again, closer now. If waterfalls spoke to each other, they might sound something like that. Quinn's gut clenched, and for a moment, he was back on Clack Mountain, running for his life as the trees crashed around him.

The cry of the horn echoed from the keep. Their nine-year-old sentry had sighted the auras.

Novalyne closed her eyes and stretched out her arms. With her straw-wild hair and raggedy clothes, she could've passed for a scarecrow. "They're splitting up. One toward the ship and one toward the fort. The third one is coming for us."

Quinn fought the urge to rush back to his sister. He'd set her snare, and she knew how to catch spirits in it. "We need to guard the ship. I don't want a hount carving our pumpkin carriage into a jack-o-lantern."

Signe pointed her parasol toward the *Reynardine.* "Yes, I'd much rather fly home than walk."

Home. If they made it back there alive, he and Signe could take a few moons to write down their adventures. Call part one *The Sinister Cult of the Eldritch Nemesis* and part two *A Perilous*

Odyssey to the Harrowing Hills. Steal a page from Dad and play up the drama. Leave out the embarrassing bits, like when they mistook a septic tank leak for a new type of waterbound. Or the time a roamer caught them napping and soaked them to the skin in rancid slime.

They'd spent an hour in a creek scrubbing themselves clean after that one.

"You two go ahead," said Paige. "We'll hold the high ground here."

Signe dashed down the mound, stirring up dust in her tracks. Quinn followed her through the gloom and the glow. He couldn't believe he was running straight toward a hount. Not again.

And there it was on the mountain above them: a wingless dragon of churning phosphorescence. It whipped its feelers at the sky and trumpeted to its kin. Two more hounts rose from behind the peaks.

"I preferred watching these things"—Signe gasped for breath—"from the air."

The hounts cascaded down the rim of the gap. When they reached the bottom, they snaked toward their targets: the fort, the mound, and the *Reynardine.* Quinn halted to take aim—

An eerie chord rolled through the gap, and the spirits curled back on themselves. Fiddle notes crystallized into a goblin melody—snail-paced at first but then picking up steam. Even as he ran, Quinn couldn't help humming along. The music conjured up caverns with gypsum flowers and pipe organ formations, endless chasms and whispering galleries, troll kings and gnome courtiers . . .

Nicholas was bewitching the spirits.

The hounts chased their own tails as the earthbounds around them gyrated. From the top of the keep, the notes swarmed toward a frantic crescendo.

Signe ducked under the hull with Quinn on her heels. Just in time, too. The hounts had stopped circling in place and turned back toward their prey. They surged ahead—

Nicholas switched to a lullaby in a minor key. The shining fumaroles ceased spraying; the glowing mudpots slowed to a simmer. The hounts swayed in place as if mesmerized.

Go to sleep, the fiddle murmured to Quinn. *Daddy ran away and left nobody with the baby.*

He pictured river-sirens with muskellunge tails singing under a waterfall, lulling him over its edge. The current dragged him through the teeth of the rapids and into the whirlpool below . . .

Way down yonder in the hollow.

Raising her parasol like a scepter, Signe strode out from beneath the ship. Quinn stepped up beside her, banisher raised.

Buzzards and flies picking out his eyes.

The hounts gave ear-splitting snuffles, tossed their feelers, and twined onward—

Nicholas played a new tune, one with spectral harmonics and wraithlike undertones. The hounts froze in mid-strike; the earthbounds shivered and stilled. Quinn envisioned the ghosts of Ram's Horn rising from their graves, gossamer apparitions with sheep-skull tiaras, as lyrics stirred in the vault of his memory.

The myrtle so bright with an emerald hue.

He pointed his banisher's beam at the crest of the hount above him. Was that its most vulnerable spot?

The pale cornflower with eyes of bright blue.

"Wait." Signe pulled on her goggles. "If it breaks the spell, I'll try to stare it down."

I'll charm every heart.

The fiddle wailed a new measure of unearthly chords. The lanterns blinked from the watchtowers, throwing cobalt light on the hount at the gate.

And the crowd I will sway.

The hount at the foot of the mound twitched its feelers. Paige knelt to draw a bead on it, but Novalyne charged ahead and brandished her pistol.

I woke from my dreaming . . .

With a plunk, a fiddle string snapped. The melody turned dissonant; the earthbounds of the gap spurted and seethed. The hounts by the mound and the fort lunged on forward.

Yet the third stayed pinned in the crosshairs of Quinn's rifle scope. Beside him, Signe stood rigid with her fingers splayed.

The spirit outside the fort flowed along the wall, probing with its feelers for a breach. When it came to a tower, it wrapped itself around the ramparts—only to recoil from the lantern in the window.

Novalyne shouted and fired at the hount below her, cutting a gouge in its flank. The spirit raised itself to its full height, snout level with the young woman. She stood her ground and blasted away.

Brave, but reckless. And possibly fatal.

Its aura coruscating, the spirit coiled back to strike. Novalyne tried to fire her pistol again, but she'd drained its battery. The three-stringed fiddle keened helplessly from the keep.

He neglected the frail wildwood flower.

Paige plugged the hount with both barrels, flipping it onto its side. Bellowing with fury, it thrashed in the dust.

The hount by the fort slammed into the gate and twisted its way up the wall. At the top, it stretched over the sharp points of the logs—and smack into Zora's trap. Violet sparks danced on the wire between the watchtowers, lopping the snout from the spirit. The hount collapsed into a heap of fizzling embers.

"Score one for little sis," Quinn said under his breath. She'd gloat about this for days, just like old times.

Paige and Novalyne hurled amethyst-flecked grenades at the hount below them. The first explosion tore holes in its aura, dark eddies in a river of light. The second caught both its target and Novalyne.

With a parting hiss, the spirit writhed back toward the mountains. Then Novalyne covered her mouth and doubled over.

As Paige sprinted down toward her, Quinn looked back through his scope at the final hount. It still hung suspended in the act of striking, transfixed by Signe's gaze. What had drawn the spirit to this pass, night after night? An alien will, mindless hunger, or nothing at all?

Signe's fingers curled into claws, and her lips formed unspoken words. The hount let out a growl that rattled Quinn's spine.

"I can't drive it away," Signe said. "Or hold it much longer. You'll need to shoot it."

Wielding his twin rays like scalpels, he sliced through the hount's crest and into its gullet. The spirit wriggled but couldn't break free from Signe's enchantment. At last, it moaned and unraveled into the ether.

Signe ripped off her goggles. Blood was trickling from the

corners of her eyes. No, not red—indigo. With his fingertip, Quinn wiped an inky tear from her cheek and held it up for her to see.

"It blinked first," she said.

Quinn touched his forehead to hers. Burst vessels showed as purple blots in the whites of her eyes.

"Slick work dissecting that overgrown glowworm," Paige shouted from the base of the mound. She helped Novalyne up, and the two of them staggered toward the ship.

"My brain hurts," said Novalyne. She'd turned a paler shade of blue. "As if nightcrawlers burrowed through it."

"The shock from the second grenade hit you." Quinn scanned her with his banisher, and one of its sensors pinged. "Zora says her weapons interfere with spooky energy fields. Which I guess includes your spirit-sense."

She pressed a hand to her temple. "You did try to warn me."

"I promise you'll recover," said Signe. "But you should lie down for a spell."

"I'll help her back," Paige volunteered. Arm in arm, she and Novalyne trudged toward the fort. The children whooped from the watchtowers, and the fiddle sang out a three-note jig.

"I believe the stars brought you here," Novalyne called over her shoulder.

Signe dabbed her face with a lace handkerchief and dropped her voice. "Think she'd make a good match for our apprentice Spotter?"

Quinn thought of the glances he'd stolen at Paige in school. Of the days they'd played hooky in caves; of the night they'd slow-danced by a fire. And then he closed that book forever.

"I do," he said. "Let's make sure they survive to find out."

♈

The first day of spring arrived with a gale and a gray horizon. Quinn checked the ship's barometer: low pressure and dropping fast.

"No launching in this mess," said Mr. Vandy. "Not with a lean crew and no one to stay on the ground. But we'll load the cargo while we wait for the weather to clear and any cloud-busters up there to blow over." He gave Quinn and Signe a jaunty salute. "Go get some rest. Y'all deserve it."

Quinn grabbed a pair of books from the locker as Signe stocked up on provisions. They found everyone else bundled up and gathered around a bonfire. Nicholas had restrung his fiddle, and Novalyne was wearing her crown again. The children—Jay, Holly, and Iris—clutched straw dolls tied with scarlet ribbons. Paige and Abigail wore befuddled expressions.

"Congratulations," Zora said. "You finally heard how the fiddler girl played her songs."

Nicholas bobbed his head sheepishly. "I hit a few sour notes on the last tune."

"It was spellbinding," Quinn said.

Motioning for quiet, Novalyne approached the fire. She sprinkled a handful of powder, and the flames burned aquamarine.

"Copper chloride," Zora whispered to Quinn.

"We welcome the vernal equinox," Novalyne intoned. "The day of our greatest woe, but also our deliverance. For seven score and four years, we've guarded this pass from the spirits."

She fell silent, and the whistle of the wind filled the gap. What would happen next? The people of the Hollows didn't practice this custom.

"We thank our ancestors for their sacrifices." Holly walked clockwise around the fire and tossed her doll into the flames.

"We thank the eidolons for their gifts." Jay circled the blaze widdershins and laid his doll on the logs.

"We thank the wanderer for her music." Iris flung her doll onto the flames and jumped over the fire.

As the straw figures blackened, Nicholas played a dirge on his fiddle. "When the pyre has burned," the children sang in harmony, "we won't forget you."

"We will never forget you," Novalyne echoed in a husky soprano.

After the ceremony, Signe shared out pickled beans and canned tomatoes. The children wolfed down their food and filled a cart with their belongings. Patched clothes and dog-eared books, threadbare blankets and stuffed animals. The last remains of Ram's Horn.

Novalyne slouched away, her face a mask of grief. Quinn knew that look from the mourners who walked into Mom's parlor.

"Come on," Nicholas told the children. "I'll show you the airship's control car." He herded his cousins toward the gate, and Abigail tagged along to hail the Rangers. Quinn and the others retreated to the warmth of the keep.

"I've been bursting to ask," Paige said. "What's with the blue skin?"

Signe assumed an innocent air. "Some might say it flatters the twins."

Zora fussed with her wrist-watcher as Paige inspected the hangings on the walls. Neither of them took the bait.

"Let's see what Doc Caudill's book says." Quinn leafed

through the medical encyclopedia he'd retrieved. "Any chance they have colloidal silver poisoning?"

"Unlikely," said Zora. "Unless they found Filson Swift's lost treasure mine."

"So not agyria." Quinn skimmed the description. "Just as well. It's irreversible." He turned to another entry. "How about meth—um, methemoglobinemia?"

His companions stared blankly at him.

"'A condition in which the blood turns brown from high levels of ferric iron,'" he read aloud. "Whatever that is."

"Three electrons instead of two," Zora said. "Otherwise, it would be ferrous."

"'This gives the skin a bluish appearance,'" Quinn continued. "'Sometimes hereditary.'" He studied the figures in the tapestries. Sentinels, oracles, and musicians: all of them had azure faces. "'Resulting oxygen loss can cause shortness of breath, palpitations, and fainting.'"

His sister looked thoughtful. "Those symptoms match what Nick told me."

"According to the book, there's a treatment called methylene blue."

"That's a chemical dye," Zora said.

"Whoa, whoa." Paige held up her palms. "You mean the antidote for blue skin is blue dye?"

Quinn read further. "In small doses. It also turns your pee blue."

Zora snickered. "I'm sure I can brew up a batch once we're back in the Hollows."

"I'll go tell Nova." Paige had one foot out the door. "I should check on her, anyhow. We're taking the first watch tonight."

"I'm off to take a bath." Signe glided toward the stairs. "In a tub of cold water, I fear."

Quinn lingered by the hearth with Zora. They hadn't talked sibling-to-sibling since they'd left the Hollows. The last two days felt more like two moons.

She pointed to the stars on the ceiling. "There's the sign for the start of spring. And me, too, I suppose."

"I thought you didn't believe in astrology," he said.

"I don't. We choose our own destiny, never mind what the zodiac says." She puffed out her cheeks. "No such thing as premonitions."

Quinn remembered her saying that once before. "And yet?"

"It's nothing."

"You can tell me, no matter what."

"I feel silly even talking about it." Zora looked up at the false constellations. "I've been dreaming the same dream over and over. I'm all alone in the Wastes on a freezing night as a titan stalks me through the mountains. I always wake up right before I see it."

Quinn pondered that. "Since the fall equinox?"

She nodded.

"What we went through back then would leave its mark on anyone. Not the kind Novalyne talks about, either."

"If I were tougher," Zora said, "none of that would bother me."

He rested his hand on her wrist. "It's okay to be scared. We're not steel automatons."

"Maybe not." She made a sound that was almost a laugh. "But I *am* a Coldiron. I read that book of fairy tales you gave me for the solstice. Turns out my family namesake repels monsters."

♈

"I've found a new calling for you." Signe was huddled in bed, wet hair draped over her shoulders. "Thawing my toes."

Quinn sat down beside her and pulled up the quilts. "How's that?"

"Toastier." She took off her glasses and rolled onto her side. "Can you read to me? It might help calm my shivers."

He opened the Carson van Patten mystery he'd brought. They'd reached the climax of the story. The detective had tracked down her quarry—the possessed geologist—but could she cast out the evil coal baron's soul?

"Chapter 18," Quinn began. As always, Carson had a plan; she'd drawn mystic symbols to spin an invisible web. But for once, she'd miscalculated: her adversary was too strong to dispel. The geologist swung a pick at the detective . . .

Signe snored softly.

The next chapter beckoned to Quinn, but he bookmarked the page. Next time, he'd revisit the part Signe had missed. He might've overlooked a few clues, anyhow.

Something scratched along the outer wall—a squirrel or maybe a flitterick. Dark clouds drifted past the bare window as Signe mumbled into her pillow.

Quinn snuffed out the candles and spooned her. She kept on snoring, so he told her the words he wasn't ready to say to her face.

When sleep stole up on him, he dreamed of a buzzard with broken wings stitched from canvas and bone.

I found a way back, said a voice. Not human, nor of this world. But familiar, nevertheless.

He dreamed of a dead rabbit walking on its hind legs through a circle of standing stones.

You cannot untangle yourself from me, taunted the harbinger.

He dreamed of a marionette girl with spiral pupils.

The threads that connect can also bind.

Quinn tried to wake up, but he couldn't. The marionette opened its mouth, and darkness poured forth.

9

BLACK TRAIN A-COMING, CROONED THE PHONOGRAPH UNDER THE floor. *It may be here tonight.*

Signe lay trapped under a cocoon of quilts, fully conscious but frozen in place. Stale air burned in her lungs, and damp cloth pressed against her lips. As she struggled to breathe, a shadow rose from the foot of the bed.

A poor young girl in darkness, she hears the whistle cry.

She was suffocating. The silhouette floated above her, weighing her down with its presence. Lapis lazuli eyes glinted in the void of its face.

Death's black train is coming. Prepare to take a ride.

Her tongue came unglued from the roof of her mouth. "Leave me alone," she rasped.

The shadow blinked out of existence, and Signe shoved away the covers. Silver moonlight bathed everything in the room. The plank floors. The log beams. The arch of Quinn's neck and the curve of his cheek.

She'd slept through the day. And drooled on her pillow, it seemed.

Her mouth tasted sour; her heart was racing. She'd never

believed in the Old Hag who crept up on sleepers and sat on their chests, but these nocturnal trances did make her wonder. Perhaps they came from the eidolons. Or perhaps from her night owl habits.

Beside her, Quinn twitched his fingers. "Mockingbird," he babbled. "Her grave. Weeping willows." His eyes darted under their lids. He looked so fragile now, not at all like a crack shot spirit-sniper.

A shapeless murk passed over the cusps of the moon. Downstairs, two of the children bickered, their words deadened by a layer of wood.

"In the valley." Quinn kicked beneath the covers and whimpered. "Where she lies forsaken."

Signe stroked his neck. "Never forsaken, sleepybones."

He bolted upright and grabbed his banisher. "Is it here?"

"You had a nightmare." She brushed a stray lock from his face. "What was it about?"

"A spooky puppet on strings." His voice was scratchy from sleep. "And the harbinger buzzing in my head. It said it found a way back."

A cold draft raised bumps on her arms. She wrapped a quilt around herself and glanced at the empty window. "It's gone till the next Wakening." Sealed away in its world for a lifetime or so. That's what Zora said, and Mr. Epps thought she was right. "When the stars align again."

"It seemed so real." He rubbed his eyes and flopped back on his pillow. "I feel all muzzy."

Surely it was a dream. Not a voice from another world but an echo from six moons ago. From the night when green comets had rained down from the ether and a spinning spirit had sundered the heavens.

The Skywheel, the fortuneteller had said. *Its presence in this sequence is an enigma.*

"I'll take a look around, just to be safe." Signe tucked her quilt around Quinn. "I'm wide awake now, anyway. You go back to sleep." She waited for him to drift off again and changed into her dress with the raven feather pattern (for good luck on the journey home and for its thick lining). Then she padded, boots in hand, down the stairs to the tapestried chamber.

The hangings were gone, but the painted stars still shone from the ceiling. The air smelled of pepper and garlic and onions. The children were slurping burgoo by candlelight.

"What did I miss?" Signe asked them.

"We stowed everything we could pack on the ship." Jay spoke fast and soft in a voice that hadn't yet broken. "Even the tapestries."

"Commodore Vandy says we fly at dawn so long as the weather plays fair." Holly's mouth was full of cornbread. She'd braided her tawny hair into a half-crown.

"Commodore?" Signe must've missed their skipper's promotion.

"He talks like a river-fleet boss from a Coal Age melodrama," Holly explained.

The candles flickered, and the children's shadows wavered on the walls. Iris looked down at her lap. "Ms. Janasdottir, I'm sorry I asked if you were a ghost or a—"

"Don't fret about that," Signe said. "I know you're just a kid." Oh, that must sound so condescending. She fumed every time her siblings talked down to her, but she slipped into the same pattern with anyone younger. Including Zora. When they'd first met, Signe had called her *just a kid*, too.

Also, an *arrogant brat*. With provocation, but still.

"A kid who helped repel a spirit siege," Signe amended.

"You talk highfalutin like Cousin Nova." Iris scrunched her face into a pout. "She blessed me out for sassing you. Says she'll educate me to mind my mouth."

Novalyne had taken on a big challenge, for certain. "I suspect you'll get along well with Paige," Signe said.

"What will become of us when we leave Ram's Horn?" Jay tapped his foot beneath his chair. He'd barely touched his bowl of stew.

A forlorn bleat carried from the barn. "I'm sure the Judges will find you and your lambs a nice place to stay," Signe reassured the boy. "I expect you'll go to school once you're settled. Some of my sisters and brothers are teachers, so maybe you'll meet them in the classroom."

"Are you a teacher, too?" Holly asked.

Signe did her best to sound unassuming. "No, just a shepherd of troublesome spirits."

"I'd rather do that than be trapped in some stuffy school," said Iris.

"I'm sick of watching a flock," Holly snapped back. "Helping folks learn sounds better to me."

"Teaching is a noble profession," Signe said. There, Mamma and Pabbi should be proud of her now. "Though I prefer guiding spirits away from my people."

Jay furrowed his brow. "Why shoo them when you can shoot them?"

Iris stuck out her pointer finger and thumb. "Cousin Nova says you should snuff all the glowies with your guns." She blew out a candle, leaving the room a shade darker. "Like that."

Zora might've agreed, but Signe thought otherwise. "Ever stumble across a snake den?" she asked. The children nodded. "Walk on by, and you'll escape without a bite. Stick your foot in, and you might end up full of venom."

"You could also torch the den," Iris said.

"But most snakes aren't dangerous," Signe pointed out. "Even rattlers and copperheads mostly leave us alone."

Iris looked dubious. "It wasn't snakes that took our elders."

"I'm all for defending ourselves from the spirits." Signe wiped her glasses on her sleeve. "But they outnumber us a million to one. We need to live in harmony with them."

"Can you tame them with your devices?" Holly asked. "Train them to obey you?"

That had been Evelyn Fontaine's plan all along: to bend the spirits to her own will. And with them, the Hollows. "I don't think that's wise," Signe said. "Could we summon the eidolons to protect us?"

In the fireplace, a burning brand popped and collapsed. "We've never seen them ourselves," Iris said.

"They're rarer than a blue moon," Holly added.

Biting his lip in concentration, Jay lined up a bowl, cup, and candle. "Our ancestors charted their visits." He clinked his spoon against the shadow on the bowl. "Where the shade of the moon falls, an eidolon will call."

Signe watched, fascinated. "In the form of an indigo haze?"

"Exactly." The boy slid the cup away from the candle, and the shadow on the bowl vanished. "When the eclipse passes, the eidolon disappears. Those it visits don't receive its gifts themselves, but some of their descendants will. Like Cousin Nova. Or you. Or—"

"She says your gift is different than hers," Holly interjected.

"That's true," Signe said. "How many gifts are there?"

Jay counted with his fingers. "Claircognizance for Cousin Nova. Clairaudience or clairsentience for others—hearing or feeling the spirits from far away. Clairvoyance for you, I gather." He gave her an odd look. "How old were you when your gift manifested?"

"Twelve." Signe abruptly remembered her task. "Where's everyone else?"

"The commodore and Ms. Putnam hit the hay," Holly said. "Cousin Nick's by the horn, and Ms. Coldiron went to the east tower. Cousin Nova and Ms. Zhu are on patrol."

Signe laced up her boots. "I should visit the tower." And compare notes with Zora.

"Take some sassafras tea." Jay fetched a steaming kettle from the hearth.

Beyond the keep, the cabins of the fort sat derelict. Every window was black; every chimney lay dormant. Signe skulked along the palisades, on guard for a telltale noise, but neither whisper nor hum broke the silence.

"Voice of the Spirits?" she called. "Are you out here?"

Nothing answered, so she crossed the yard to the east tower. *WILDFIRE FLY AWAY*, read the letters carved above the door. A twisting staircase led past slits in the walls and chalk doodles of humans with horns. As she cleared the final landing, a cobalt glare seared her retinas.

"Can you kindly lower the light?" she asked.

"How's that?" The lantern dimmed, and an auburn-tipped smudge resolved into Zora. She sat on a stool beside a three-legged telescope. Her open logbook lay against the sill.

"Gentler on the eyes." Signe poured one mug of tea for Zora and another for herself. It tasted like root beer with a dash of licorice. "All quiet in the eastern gap?"

"A few dinky roamers gallivanted by." Zora warmed her hands on her mug. "But the hount that got away learned its lesson. Even the earthbounds seem drowsy tonight."

Signe joined her by the window. From up here, she could see the dark bulk of the ship above a carpet of radiant splotches. "Any sign of a spiral-shaped spirit?"

Zora spat a mouthful of tea back into her mug. "What makes you ask?"

"Tonight's a new equinox. And Quinn told me about a dream—"

"What did he say?"

The edge in her voice mystified Signe. "He had a nightmare about the harbinger."

"Oh." Zora leaned back on her stool, apparently mollified. "That's just his brain replaying things it's already seen and heard, connecting them in random ways." She picked up a pencil and gnawed it. "Strange, it feels like I've said that before."

"You're probably right—I mean, about the dream." Yet Signe didn't quite believe it.

Zora gestured toward the telescope. "Take a look for yourself if you're worried."

Signe stooped to the eyepiece, and a grove of dead trees came into focus. Glistening sap oozed from their trunks as tongues of witch-fire licked at their roots. Hardly an inviting place for a midnight stroll, but no roamers were prowling up there.

She swiveled the telescope until she found Paige and Novalyne. They stood in the lee of the ship, their backs to the fort.

Zora snorted. "Spying on those two?"

"Making sure they're safe," Signe said with as much loftiness as she could muster. None of the earthbounds out tonight were anchored within striking distance.

Down below, Paige touched her companion's arm and pointed away from Ram's Horn. All around them, the earthbounds thrummed in a ragged symphony.

"I wonder why they got noisy," said Zora.

Novalyne looked back at the tower. As the earthbounds of the gap pulsed in unison, she put her palms on the spots where the horns of her crown would've been. Then she buried her face in her hands.

Signe's eyes burned, and her vision blurred. The spirits had stolen so much from Novalyne. Her home, her parents, her childhood—what else was left to take? At least now she and Signe could learn from each other. They both bore the Mark of the Syzygy. They were two of a kind, a pair of tulips in a deck of rosettes.

But wasn't one of them already half of a matched set? *My name is Novalyne Martin*, she'd said, and purple martins were songbirds. *Nicholas is my twin*. Two songbirds on the third hex card. *The Distelfinks*. One right-side up, one upside down. *They'll bring you luck, but also danger.*

What sort of danger?

When Paige offered her arm, Novalyne took it. The earthbounds around them skipped a beat and fell into discord.

"Synchronous spirits." Zora clicked the barrel-release of her pistol. "That's a new one on me, though I've heard of lightning bugs that can pull the same trick. Did you pick up any gossip to share with my brother?"

"I doubt we'll have time for a quilting bee," Signe said. "But I am curious about Novalyne's gift."

"I'll bring her to my lab, hook electrodes to her noggin, and see what I find. My hypothesis is that these eidolons—and your vision—come from another reality. Not ours, or the spirit world, but a third universe. Between that and Nick's acoustics, I'll have plenty to study back home."

If they made it back without catching a ride on the Black Train, Signe added to herself. She turned the telescope to the fallen radio mast. "Ever heard of a transmitter called Peryton One?"

"Funny you should ask." Zora spoke slowly, as if choosing her words with care. "Abigail talked about it yesterday. Her father went searching for it and never came back." Her tone softened. "I hope she finds him. Her description of him kind of reminds me of Dad."

"Was—is—her father Ulysses Bell, by any chance?"

Zora sucked in her breath. "How in the Wastes did you guess that?"

"I've read his book. It was . . . peculiar." Signe aimed the telescope at the head of the gap. Pale green light fringed the farthest range, as if a jade moon lay just below the horizon. An imposter satellite, waiting to catch and devour the crescent above it.

"She figured the signals were a code," Zora said. "But who— your mug!"

Hot liquid soaked through Signe's glove and ran down her

fingers. She'd spilled her tea. "Can you tell me what I'm see-ing?" she asked, though she already knew the answer.

Zora took a turn at the eyepiece. "That thing wasn't there the last time I checked." She unfolded a map and drew a line from Ram's Horn to a chain of black triangles. "It's somewhere past these peaks. To be visible from so far away . . . there's only one roamer that big. It's a titan."

The insides of Signe's mouth had gone cottony. "How soon?"

Zora jotted calculations until her pencil lead snapped. "We need to leave tomorrow."

♈

But the skies were against them.

Signe stamped her feet and sipped from her fourth mug of tea. She didn't dare open her parasol for fear of it tearing. The gale had returned at dawn to snarl her hair and whip the fort's banners.

"Let's hold off a bit longer." Mr. Vandy motioned for his crew to halt at the gate. "This squall could crash the *Reynardine*."

"If your ship's still here tonight, the titan will squash it." Nicholas slung his fiddle case over his shoulder and paced away toward the zeppelin.

The children were antsy to leave, too. They'd led their flock of lambs into the meadow and started a game of roamer-in-the-middle. Novalyne watched them play, her ex-pression unreadable.

Signe consulted her pocket-watch: half past eleven. Already too late to reach the Hollows before darkness fell. They were caught between the spirits and the wild gray yonder.

"My boss told me about the time Clementine Geller spotted a titan," Paige said. "On the night of the Lesser Wakening. She's tramping down the Pass from Sylvania when she stops at a tavern. Everyone's drinking white lightning to celebrate the summer solstice. All of a sudden, the radio sings lower, and the lamps shift from orange to red."

"The Wakenings altered the laws of nature," Zora put in. Signe had heard this theory before. It involved spooky physics, universal constants, and a hypothetical fiend who fought entropy. Neither she nor Quinn fully understood it.

Paige waggled her fingers. "She hears a boom that busts her eardrums. The floor pitches, and she falls with everyone else, upchucking her supper as she tumbles, but she's the first one on her feet and out the door. All she sees is green, bright as noon."

Abigail shuddered, as if a boge had drifted over her grave.

"Once her eyes adjust, she looks up," Paige said. "The titan's blocking the sky. She reckons she's finished, but she's trained to watch spirits, so she makes like a statue and collects her impressions. The smell of electricity and the heaviness in the air. The prickly heat as the hair on her arms singes. The gonging inside her ears."

"Impressively detailed for a thirdhand account," remarked Mr. Vandy.

"It's what we Spotters do." Paige put her hands on her hips. "She braces for the spirit to crush her—only it doesn't. Could be she's too small for it to notice. Could be she's got the stars on her side. Either way, the folks inside aren't so lucky. One moment the tavern's there, lit up in neon; the next, all that's left is a smoking cellar."

Quinn's hand strayed toward his holster, and Signe followed

his gaze up the gap. Beyond a saddleback ridge, the high mountains loomed brown and barren. Somewhere up there, the titan lay sleeping, waiting for the night to come.

"Her nerves scream at her to run, but she stays put." Paige spoke in a hush. "The spirit lumbers off toward Sylvania, withering the woods in its path. She watches till it's out of sight, and then she skedaddles. It takes her three days to reach the Hollows. Three nights of hiding from the roamers flooding into the Pass. She never sees her Sylvanian kin again, but she makes it home to tell her mentor—and, years later, her own apprentice, who passes the story along to me."

The wind died down, and the sky turned cerulean.

"Time to fly," Mr. Vandy said.

"Aye, aye, Commodore," Signe told him. Preening like a kinglet, he swaggered away from the fort. His crew trailed after him, but Novalyne hung back at the gate.

"I'm sorry you have to leave your home," Signe said.

Novalyne's eyes gleamed. "I'm ready for a new start in a wider world." She traced a circle around her heart and set off with her sharp nose pointed slightly upward.

Signe looked back at the sun-bleached walls of the fort. If she didn't know otherwise, she would've sworn nobody had lived there for years. Ram's Horn was an abode for spirits now. And revenants, too.

She hurried to catch up with Novalyne.

By the time they arrived at the ship, the children were herding the lambs aboard, and Paige was climbing the ladder to the hull. Signe sidestepped a sheep pellet and made for the bridge. She found Zora at one wheel, Mr. Vandy at the other, and Abigail by the radio.

"The cannon is tuned and fully charged," Quinn reported from the aft deck.

"The Rangers repaired their mooring mast," Abigail said. "They're standing by to help us dock."

"All hands, prepare for launch," Mr. Vandy announced into his speaking tube. "Zhu, cast off when ready."

The ship jerked as Paige released the first wire from the bow. When the second wire dropped, Signe's intestines wobbled. The scarred earth receded, and the *Reynardine* floated toward the mouth of the gap.

"More graceful than our first departure." Mr. Vandy loosened his vintage silk scarf and turned the elevator wheel. "Coldiron, steer us five degrees west once we clear those knobs."

Signe spent the afternoon with her nose pressed against the glass of a porthole. The landscape rolled by below her, patchy forests alternating with swaths of devastation. At the other windows, the children shouted out each new sight that came into view. They passed deserted farms choked with kudzu vines and ghost towns of tumbledown shacks. Phantom roads and train tracks overrun by laurel and rhododendron. Blisters on the hills where elementals had consumed every living thing in their sway.

Every so often, Mr. Vandy told Zora to adjust course, always toward the setting sun.

As Signe ate apple slaw and biscuits slathered with pepper jelly, the ship flew over a massive crater. Downed trees radiated out from the pit at the center. A monstrous bolide must have struck there.

The lambs let out disgruntled baas. They didn't seem to appreciate flying, but Signe thought it was splendid. So much faster—and softer on her tail—than traveling by wagon.

"If you could take this ship for a joyride, where would you go?" she asked Quinn.

"The ocean," he said straightaway. "A golden shore with palmettos."

Signe considered the prospect. "Sunny beaches don't appeal to me, but I'd love to hear the waves and smell the salt air. From beneath a pavilion, that is."

"I'd visit the Bluegrass," Zora called back from the bridge. "To follow a lead from Dad about the first Wakening. And to see what's left of the cities."

What had Quinn said about that first letter from his and Zora's father? Something about a key and a castle and a goat.

"Be careful not to jinx us," Nicholas said.

Zora laughed uncertainly. "You're kidding me. Jinxes aren't real."

"That's what Granny Martin used to say." Iris soothed a jumpy lamb. "But she let a bird fly in through a window the morning before the hounts came."

"That wasn't her fault," Holly snarled. "Don't go blaming her for what happened."

Nicholas stepped between the girls. "My grandmother knew her time was near. She'd be at peace knowing these folks came to save us."

The conversation dwindled, and so did the daylight. The shadows of the hills enveloped the valleys. Nicholas went forward to chat with Zora, while Holly and Iris curled up in opposite corners. Jay stretched out among the lambs, and Novalyne dozed at the navigator's desk, but Signe stayed on her feet and kept her aching eyes open. The most dangerous part of the journey still lay ahead.

At the break of dusk, Novalyne stretched her arms and rose from her seat. Outside the porthole, a green ray flashed where the sun had sunk.

"That's a mirage," said Holly. "I read about it in an old Juliette Verne novel. The atmosphere acts like a prism."

Signe felt a new kinship with the girl. "My family runs a printing press. If you like books, I can find you enough to fill a shelf."

The lambs pricked up their ears, and Jay craned his head. "Did you catch that?" he asked.

Signe listened, but all she heard was the propellers.

"There it is again." The boy beat a rhythm on his knee. "A sound like distant thunder."

"I don't sense any spirits," said Novalyne.

Signe checked the portholes on the right and then the ones on the left. The aurora had formed on the horizon, and the waxing moon hung low in the sky. "No airbounds in sight."

"Janasdottir," said Mr. Vandy. "Care to go aloft with me? We need your eyes in the crow's nest, and I need to check the rudder. The wind's light, but we're drifting east. Helm, keep us steady while I'm away." He scuttled up the ladder.

With an inward groan, Signe donned her parka and followed. "I'm jumping straight into the Bubbling Cauldron once we make it back to Hot Springs Hollow," she said to nobody in particular as she climbed into the frigid night.

When they reached the hull, they split up—Mr. Vandy toward the tail and Signe for the top. She felt tiny among the *Reynardine*'s metal bones and quilted lungs. Like a cricket in the Mastodon Caverns or a mouse in the Hoary Library stacks.

The rungs shook as a rumble swelled above the whir of the engines. An earthquake in the ether? Or bad spirit weather?

Signe pulled herself through the trapdoor and into the crow's nest. She didn't need her spyglass to see the trouble. A wall of anvil-shaped clouds barred the way, green thunderbolts lighting them from within.

The rumbling rolled to Signe's left and then her right. The wind picked up, and lightning arced across the ship's path.

The cloudbusters had lain in wait for them.

10

ZORA SPUN THE WHEEL, AND THE *REYNARDINE* SWUNG PARALLEL to the storm front. The thunderheads were veiling the northern constellations one by one. The long, skinny Dragon. The Lake King, with its garnet jewels. The Big Dipper, upside down and pointing to the star that marked the way home.

"Derechos at nine o'clock," she warned the crew. Maybe jinxes were real, after all.

The ship shot upward as Abigail overcorrected its pitch. The lambs squealed in terror, and Nick hissed a few strange-sounding curses. The Folk of the Ram must've coined their own batch of swear words. Those might be entertaining to learn.

"Steady as she goes." Zora tried to channel their skipper's hearty manner. "And easy on the elevators."

Abigail set her jaw and leveled the ship's inclination. On their port side, streaks of green lightning reflected in the ribbon of black glass below. That river flowed through the Lost Gorges and on over Moonbow Falls. They'd planned on following its path to the Hollows.

"I'm taking us north by northeast," Zora said. "We'll loop around the squall line." But more clouds had gathered up ahead, dark masses bristling with spirit energy. The power inside them could strike down a million starlings—or one zeppelin.

"They're hemming us in." The rising gale almost drowned out Abigail's voice. "Forming a cyclone."

Waves of turbulence buffeted the ship, pushing it farther off course. Zora steered into the wind, but the wheel fought back against her. Mr. Vandy still hadn't repaired the rudder. Until he took the conn, it was up to her to play captain.

She switched on the speaking tube to the bomb bay. "What do you know about derechos?"

"They hunt under cover of electrical storms," said Paige. "They drop glowy hailstones as they pass over. Besides that . . . truth is, I haven't boned up on my airbounds yet. We Spotters tend to stick to the earth and the water, so watching the sky comes last in our training."

The mercury sank, and the barometer plunged. Zora's ears popped from the change in atmosphere. The ring of clouds was closing around them; soon they'd be trapped in its low-pressure cell. And when its eye blinked . . .

She needed information—and fast. "Nick . . ." She deepened her voice. "Mr. Martin, hail the Rangers."

He fiddled with the radio. "*Reynardine* to the Hollows. Can you hear me?"

The speaker fizzed, and Zora gnawed the insides of her cheeks. Then the static cleared. "Ground Base here," replied Emerson Tate. "Who—say, you're the young man from the distress call. What's your status?"

Nick floundered for words, so she interrupted. "We have a cloudbuster situation. Can you find our spirit expert?"

"Hang on." With the thump of a dropped microphone, the speaker went silent.

Zora flew the ship in a tightening circle as the chronometer ticked away the seconds. No use trying to escape the storm; all she could do was choose where they hit it.

"My erudition is at your disposal," boomed the receiver.

"Hey, Mr. Epps," Zora said. "Any pointers on how to slip through a spirit-cyclone?"

"An intriguing dilemma, though I fear for your safety. Back in Year Zero, the last squadron of Sylvanian biplanes encountered a lone derecho. The Fearless Flying Squirrels, they called themselves. They tried to elude it, but all of them crashed except one."

Well, that was dismal news. "So, what did the pilot who *didn't* crash do?"

Mr. Epps hemmed and hawed. "According to his log, he performed a series of aerial maneuvers. Wingovers, barrel rolls, and so on."

Zora flinched at a discharge of lightning above her. "No way I'm flipping this zeppelin."

"A wise decision, I'm certain." Mr. Epps's tone brightened. "I do recall another detail—the aviator who weathered the derecho wrote of evading updrafts and downbursts."

Just grand. In the unlikely event she dodged the cloudbusters, the squall itself could shear the hull to pieces. On the plus side, they wouldn't explode.

"Fox-Kit," said her mother.

Zora's grip on the wheel eased a little. "I promise I'll make it home for my birthday." If only Mom and Mr. Epps were here to be the grown-ups for her. But then they'd be in danger, too. Watching them fight the spires had been awful; she couldn't stand the thought of seeing them hurt.

"Tell me your location and heading," said her mother.

Zora read their bearing from the gyrocompass and took a wild guess at their coordinates. "I can't wait to open my presents," she added. Last year, Mom had bought her a mercury arc rectifier and three pairs of overalls. The year before that, an electrostatic generator and a party dress she'd never worn. Right now, she'd settle for new pajamas and a crate of caffeinated ginger ale.

"If you can't make it through the storm," said her mother, "take shelter on the ground, and we'll find you."

The sky went brilliant green, and thunder reverberated through the bridge. "That was too close," Zora said. Less than a second between the flash and the bang.

"Are you there?" her mother shouted as the Ranger and the Spotter murmured in the background. Zora shouted back, but none of them seemed to hear her.

"I think that strike fried the transmitter," Nick said.

Zora stewed silently while her mother called out her name. Nick twiddled dials and joggled wires, but Abigail shook her head. The *Reynardine* had lost its voice. They were on their own, with a long way yet to go.

"Turn that off," Zora growled. She couldn't think with Mom crying for her. Simpler to tune out the world and pretend nobody back home would mourn them. Not her mother or Quinn's or Dad.

The hatch clanged, and cold air swirled past Zora. Mr. Vandy clomped down the ladder and onto the bridge. Frost glittered in his mustache, but his expression was gloomy.

Abigail surrendered the elevator wheel to him. "Did you fix the rudder?"

"No such luck. How long till the eye of the storm closes on us?"

"Five minutes," Zora said. "Maybe less." A fork of lightning zagged near their starboard flank, illuminating the ship's underbelly. The fabric of the hull was starting to ripple, and sheens of ice had formed on the wires.

"Why wait around?" He showed his teeth. "Let's headbutt our way through that storm."

An image popped into Zora's head unbidden: the giant sloth she'd seen on her class trip to the Big Bone Museum. Judging by its fossil, the beast could've walloped a pack of wolves with its tail. "We can blaze a path first."

"How? Our stinger's on the wrong side for that."

"Mind if I take your ship for a spin?" Zora figured this would make for a hair-raising ride, but she'd brag about it for years. Assuming they survived, of course.

Mr. Vandy's smile broadened. "Ready with the throttle."

"My family has a saying for moments like this." Nick made a fist with his pointer finger and pinky extended. "In the name of the ram, we salute you."

Zora returned the unfamiliar gesture. "My family has a motto, too: burn in sunfire, spirits." Not so eloquent, but the best she could do on the spot. "You'd better secure the kids and the livestock."

Nick hurried aft with his fiddle case bobbing and his hair sticking every which way. He looked as gawky as the boys she'd met at the Winter Fair dance, yet there was an avian grace to his movements. Plus, he was handy with a wrench and could play a mean tune.

Keep your mind on the wheel, she scolded herself. No time to moon over the boy she was busy saving.

"You fancy him," said Mr. Vandy.

She kept her voice neutral. "I'm impressed with his mechanical know-how. With the right training"—*her* training—"he could apprentice for Coldiron and Prosser Ventures."

"Ah, so that's what you're telling yourself. You're gutsy in a pinch, so why hide from your feelings? When I wrecked my first balloon and a young Ranger named Sylvia found me—"

"You mean *Captain Flores?*" Zora almost choked on her words. "Let's finish this conversation when we're back on the ground." And away from Abigail's rabbit ears. The girl had her eyes on the instruments, but Zora could tell she was listening.

Mr. Vandy sighed and lifted his speaking tube. "All hands, brace yourselves. Prosser, fire on my signal."

"In which direction?" Quinn sounded flummoxed. "They're all around us."

"Straight ahead. You'll see in a minute."

Zora set the ship back on its original heading: north by northwest toward the Hollows. Mr. Vandy lowered their pitch, and Abigail cranked up their speed. The thunderheads towered before them, sparking like colossal Tesla coils.

"Bringing us about." Zora twisted the wheel, and the *Reynardine* turned its tail to the squall line. Jagged arcs from the clouds bracketed the gondola.

"Fire!" Mr. Vandy roared.

The cannon crackled for the space of three breaths, and the children gasped from the mid-deck. As Zora completed the circle, the storm parted to reveal starry sky.

Mr. Vandy cackled. "Full speed ahead."

They sailed into the channel they'd cut, through the fading trails of vaporized spirits. Beyond the cloudbanks, the pole star shone like a beacon. Zora's heart felt as light as the helium carrying them homeward.

But then the Little Dipper vanished behind a shadowy anvil. "Crap," she said.

The thunderheads closed ranks, blockading the passage north. Invisible drums thudded overhead, and streaming white flakes obscured the sky.

"Thundersnow," said Mr. Vandy. Awe and tension mingled in his voice. "A rare sight, and a rarer one to fly through."

Zora could no longer see past the ship's snout. She might as well be flying through a coal mine without a headlamp. Not even a bat could find its way out of this mess.

But what about a spirit-senser?

"Ms. Martin," she said. "We need you on the bridge."

With a soft tread, Novalyne made her way to the front window. Her expression was calm despite the chaos outside. "So, our route lies concealed."

Zora grunted. Such an odd girl, though Signe was, too, and working with her had turned out hunky-dory. "Can you use your gift to guide us?"

Novalyne pressed one palm to her forehead and the other against the glass. "There's a spirit on our right."

Holding her breath, Zora turned hard to port. Dim light flickered by the starboard bow, but the ship sailed onward unscathed. Helming an old-time submarine must've felt something like this. Except she had no periscope for spying on her adversaries.

"Another one up ahead," whispered Novalyne.

"Where?" Zora resisted the instinct to whisper back.

The girl's eyes bulged in their sockets as she pointed toward the roof. "I feel a boundless fury—and beneath it, a ravenous hunger."

Mr. Vandy vented helium, and the *Reynardine* ducked beneath a sheet of lightning. Zora caught herself humming a half-remembered nursery rhyme. *Airbounds, go away. Trouble us some other day.* Now there was a thought. Should she ask Nick to play his spooky music, or would the sonic waves give away their position?

A yelp derailed her train of thought. "I'm getting hailed on," Signe said. "And my hair's standing on end."

A sure sign of an ectostatic field. "Get down!" Zora yelled.

Metal clattered on metal, and boots thumped against ladder rungs. The ship yawed to one side as a splitting sound echoed from the pipes. The compass spun wildly; the dials went haywire; the bulbs on her wrist-watcher blinked out of sequence.

She shook the ringing from her ears. They'd been struck by a spirit-bolt.

"Thank you for the warning," Signe said through a tube from the heart of the hull. "I think the crow's nest is gone."

Abigail tapped on the side window. "Look at those." Blue and purple flames leaped along the ship's spars, painting the hull with ethereal colors. "What are they?"

"Coronal discharges of luminous plasma," Zora told her. "The storm's ionizing the air."

"They're on the propellers, too," Quinn said. "I read somewhere that sailors took them as good omens."

The fires flitted like sprites on an electric arc ladder. "They're pretty," Zora allowed. She wished she had one of Evelyn Fontaine's fancy cameras.

The flames disappeared all at once, as if blown out by a mighty breath. Novalyne raised a warning finger. "There's a spirit directly in our path."

Zora jerked the wheel, Abigail cut the throttle, and Mr. Vandy sent the ship diving. None of them were fast enough. A spirit-bolt smacked the *Reynardine*'s nose, rending canvas flesh from the hull. Abigail cried out, and Novalyne flung herself flat on the deck.

The second bolt shattered the windows. Zora crouched behind the wheel to shield her face, but shards of glass slashed through her sleeves. The cyclone howled and rushed in with a stench of sulfur.

As she dragged herself to her feet, another blast thundered behind her. When it ended, the ship sounded different. *Felt* different, too. No steady drone, no vibrations.

No propellers.

Abigail confirmed her worst fears. "The engines are dead."

Red drops trickled down Zora's arms, but she couldn't spare a hand to stanch the bleeding. "The rudder's stuck in molasses, and my compass is demagnetized."

"So's the one on the navigator's desk," said Abigail.

"All stations report." Mr. Vandy's face had turned pallid. If he was scared, too, then they must be up waterbound creek. No flash of inspiration would fix the *Reynardine* now.

"The tail fins are smoking," Quinn said from the cannon-mount. "The last lightning strike hit them."

Nick shushed his cousins. "We're fine back here. The sheep, too, but they're skittish."

"The ship's frame seems intact." That was Signe, holed up in the hull.

"Same for the keel," added Paige.

Novalyne stuck her head out the window, heedless of the wind and the snow. She had the swept-back hair and impassive face of a figurehead on an ancient schooner. "The skies before us are empty of spirits."

"We lost two gas cells, but the seals on the others are holding." Mr. Vandy brushed snow from his brow and surveyed the storm. "We can glide for a while without the engines. I'll keep us in the air as long as I can and bring us down in one piece."

Dread washed over Zora. Supposing they walked away from the landing, they'd be trekking home through the Wastes on foot.

Mr. Vandy pulled down the brim of his hat, tossed his scarf over his shoulder, and jabbed a thumb at Nick. "Take the kids to the hull. There's a harness in the locker. Zhu, assist from the keel."

"May the eidolons watch over you," Nick said on his way to the ladder. A buckle clicked, and then Iris led the way up, swearing at the storm as she climbed. Jay went second, chanting verses about moon dogs and eclipses.

"What about our lambs?" Holly asked.

"I'll keep an eye on them," Mr. Vandy said. A transparent white lie, but Zora bit her tongue. Holly stamped up the ladder, and Nick followed—without fainting, to Zora's relief.

The ship drifted starboard on a heading away from the Hollows. She struggled with the wheel, but the rudder ignored her. If they didn't land soon, they'd wind up even farther from home.

Novalyne leaned into the blizzard. Her lips and fingers had

turned a deeper shade of blue, but she seemed immune to vertigo. "I sense nothing in this direction."

"Your turn, Prosser." Mr. Vandy flicked toggles on the gas board. "I reckon we're done using the cannon. You, too, Ms. Martin. Go and catch up with your brother."

"Beware what lies below." Novalyne pulled back her head and stalked toward the ladder, dripping on the deck as she went. Abigail looked eager to trail her aloft.

Mr. Vandy took a moment from watching the gauges to read the girl's face. "Putnam, you're next."

"The map showed a wide valley off to the north. You could try steering us there." She twitched her nose and fled for the hull.

That left Zora and Mr. Vandy alone on the bridge. "I'm staying with you," she said.

"No, you're not. When we hit the ground, this gondola will take the brunt of the force." He laughed ruefully. "Besides, I have more practice crash-landing than you."

"But you need me."

"The others will need you more." She started to argue, but he didn't let her get a word in. "When I checked the rudder, it wasn't broken. Somebody had tampered with it. I found a machine welded to the gears—a clockwork device to shunt us off course. It wasn't there when we mended the ship in Ram's Horn."

Zora's gut curdled. Had a Spiritist stowed away with them?

"You'll be the only one who knows." Mr. Vandy dumped water ballast, and the ship caught an air current. "So, you see, you have to stay alive."

What he meant suddenly dawned on her. "I can't abandon you."

"You're still so young. You have gadgets to invent. Hearts to win. Secrets to uncover. You have friends and kin who adore you." On the horizon, black mountains peeked through the snow. "I've followed my own star, and I don't regret coming on this journey. But tell Captain Flores—tell Sylvia—I never stopped falling for her. I've been falling since my first crash."

Zora couldn't find her voice, but she nodded.

"It won't be long now," he said. The mountains up ahead had grown taller. Greenish snow caked their slopes, and elementals stippled their spurs. "You should go."

Fighting back tears, she released the wheel and let the *Reynardine* wander where it wanted. The ship angled eastward, driven by the gale and the sabotaged rudder. When she looked at Mr. Vandy, he gave her a thumbs-up and a grin.

"Good luck, sir," she said.

"Safe voyages to you, Zora."

The deck tilted beneath her as she tromped to the ladder. The lambs were clumped in a corner, bleating frantically. Poor doomed things. If she had magic powers, she'd teleport the whole flock to her barn.

Zora hooked the cuffs of her crutches around her elbows and girded herself with the harness. One pull on the rope, and it went taut. She tamped down her fear and started to climb.

Flurries swarmed into her eyes. Her nose. Her open mouth. A mountainside filled the sliver of sky between the girders. The ship listed harder, and gravity pulled her to the right.

"There's a spirit behind you," cried a voice on the wind.

Zora turned her head. By the ship's tail, a sphere of green lightning was cannonballing toward her. The derechos had taken their parting shot.

Quinn and Paige shouted at her to keep climbing toward them, but she stopped and drew her pistol. Holding the ladder with one hand, she swung around to face the stern. The ball of lightning flared brighter as it darted past the dead engines.

Zora shot once and missed. The world leaned ten degrees sideways, sweeping her feet off the rungs. She took aim again, and her second shot hit the bullseye. The sphere burst with a satisfying explosion.

Then the shock wave hit, and she lost her grip on the ladder.

Zora fell, but the harness caught her, its straps digging into her sides. She hung from the rope like a pendulum weight, rocking side to side and clutching her pistol. From this angle, she had a perfect view of the mountains. They were horrifyingly close.

"I've got you," Quinn called down from the hull.

While he reeled her up, she scanned the ground for landmarks. The river meandered to her left, and the Ruined Town glimmered on her right. Straight ahead, a blue light twinkled in a valley. Or was that her imagination?

Another tug upward, and Zora flopped belly-down on the keel. Everyone crowded around her, but her brother shooed them away. "Good shot."

"Runs in the family." She rolled on her back and coughed. "I feel like a yo-yo."

Abigail leaned over the hatch. "Where's the skipper?"

"He's not coming," Zora said. "He's going down with his ship." And the *Reynardine* was descending quickly; she could feel it in her inner ears.

"I'm aiming for a grassy bald," Mr. Vandy said through the

pipes. "Keep your heads down and clear the wreck as quick as you can." His voice caught. "You've been the best crew I could ever hope to fly with."

Across the corridor, Nick was huddling with Iris and Holly. The older girl let out a sob, and Novalyne stared vacantly at her. Jay had one ear pressed to the floor and a curious look on his face. Abigail was curled up like a possum playing dead. Acetylene lamps swayed overhead among the cables and catwalks.

"What if we land on an elemental?" Iris asked, but nobody answered. Signe interlaced her fingers with Quinn's, and Zora grabbed his free hand.

"I'd make a wish." Paige locked elbows with her. "But I'm not sure it works if we're riding the falling star."

"Whatever happens," Zora said, "I'm glad I had the chance to know you."

Unseen claws raked the envelope, ripping long wounds in its skin. The ship had grazed the treetops.

Quinn squeezed her fingers. "Same here."

With a groan and a crack, a piece of the ship broke away. Let that be a propeller, not the gondola.

"This isn't the end," said Signe. "The universe still has a plan for us."

Zora's pistol slid down the corridor. Against her will, she imagined earthbounds rising from below, their auras aglow and their tendrils grasping skyward.

"For I'm bound to ride the northern current," Mr. Vandy sang in a resonant bass. "Perhaps I'll—"

Girders buckled, and gas cells ruptured. The lamps went

out. Something struck Zora on the crown of her head, and an abyss opened beneath her.

I am free to roam your world again, said a voice from the pit. *You cannot escape from my web.*

PART THREE

THE LAND OF CONSTANT SORROW

11

THE WORLD WAS ASKEW. COLD METAL PRESSED AGAINST QUINN'S cheek, and a soft but solid weight was pinning him down. At the bottom of the sloped corridor, a carbide lamp flickered in the gloom, its gold halo pierced by jutting girders. High above, ripped cloth flapped rampant against a field of stars.

The ship had stopped shaking, and the engines no longer thrummed.

Along the deck, dark figures stirred and rose. As Quinn tried to sit up, the pressure across his chest lifted. "Sorry for landing on you," said Signe. "I hope I didn't crack your ribs."

He patted his sides. "I'm tender everywhere, but nothing's broken, I think." He could make out Paige and Abigail, but not his sister. A sudden panic seized him. "Where's—"

"Behind you." Zora crawled past him to collect an errant crutch. "I'm okay except for all the bruises."

He spotted her pistol and clambered down the deck to fetch it. Not his preferred weapon, but better than nothing until he could find his rifle. He checked the battery—good for another four shots—and rejoined his companions.

"Holly bumped her head." Nicholas used his sleeve to

dab the blood oozing from the girl's temple. She sat slumped against a mangled truss, staring up at the gaping rent in the ship's envelope.

"I feel groggy," she slurred.

"Will she be all right?" Jay and Iris asked in unison.

Nicholas tied a strip of cloth around Holly's head. "I can help her walk."

"Then let's get a move on," Quinn said. "We need to find Mr. Vandy"—if he was still alive—"and hole up for the night. The commotion from the crash is bound to draw roamers."

"They're already approaching." Novalyne was sitting cross-legged with her hands on her knees. "Little ones so far, but worse may come."

As Nicholas pulled Holly to her feet and Signe retrieved her parasol, Quinn and Zora searched the corridor for more weapons. She found a grenade stowed in a toolbox, and he snagged a cobalt lantern from the bulkhead. "Try the hatch," he said.

Paige tugged on the handle, but it was stuck. She took the lantern from Quinn, switched it on, and set off toward the bow. "Cover me, Pine-Box."

Quinn followed her, and the others followed him, ducking beneath snapped cables and fallen catwalks until they came to a gash in the canvas along the keel. Pistol at the ready, Quinn slipped through the tear and stepped onto a grassy expanse. His boots squished in the soggy earth.

Mr. Vandy had brought them down on the edge of a flat, treeless summit. A bald, he'd called it. The moonlight revealed scrub and, in the middle distance, fingerlike rocks. Green fires raged in the valleys below, but the mountaintop was quiet and dark.

Hats off to their skipper's flying skills. He'd found the safest landing spot in this stretch of the Wastes.

Paige dashed along the hull, her lantern bobbing, and Quinn had to run full tilt to keep pace. She stopped when she reached the gondola. It lay buried beneath bent struts and wrinkled sailcloth, its sides bowed and its windows smashed. The cannon at the rear had broken into a thousand glass splinters. Zora would be sore about that.

"Mr. Vandy?" Quinn's voice echoed in the black beyond the paneless windows. "Can you hear me?"

Paige lifted her lamp, and its light rendered her face a cadaverous blue. "I don't see him."

When Quinn tested the door, the hinges creaked and then popped. Pushing back memories of past death tableaus (the bandits who'd suffocated in a miasma; the family who'd drunk from a spirit-tainted well), he stepped inside the gondola. The navigator's desk was flipped on its side, and the ship's wheels had gone off kilter. On the floor lay a human-sized shadow.

Quinn knelt next to Mr. Vandy. From the looks of his forehead, he'd taken a heavy blow to the skull. His eyes were partway open, and so was his mouth. Quinn checked the carotid artery, but there was no pulse.

Paige came over and crouched behind him. "Is he . . ."

"Shh." Quinn didn't have a mirror to check for fogging, so he leaned forward and listened. Not a breath. "Bring the lantern closer." He pulled back an eyelid. No sign of dilation.

"He sacrificed himself for us." Paige's voice was husky.

Quinn closed Mr. Vandy's eyes and set silver coins on their lids. *We preserve the peace of those departed*, Mom always said. "Can you hand me that scarf?" he asked.

Paige gave him the strip of white silk, and he tied it beneath Mr. Vandy's chin. *We prepare them for their journey onward.*

Footsteps scuffed outside the gondola. The others had caught up; now they stood clustered around the windows. "Did you find him?" asked Zora.

"We've lost our skipper." Quinn stifled his own sorrow. Survive first, lament later. "We can come back at dawn, but we should hide out till then." They had the pistol and the grenade, plus Signe's eyes and Novalyne's spirit-sense. That would have to do for tonight.

"He's really gone?" Abigail sounded stunned. "Are you sure?"

"I know a corpse when I see one." Urgency sharpened Quinn's tone. "But feel free to look for yourself." Abigail's face crumpled, and he felt a stab of guilt. Mom would never say such a thing to a mourner. "He'd want us to take this chance to get away."

As Quinn made for the door, a pale flash cut across the summit. Was that a barnstorming soul on its way toward a new horizon?

No, just a lamb fleeing toward the rocks. Another second, and it was gone.

"One of our sheep!" Iris had seen it, too. "Where are the others?"

Quinn looked back at the mid-deck. White shapes lay strewn among the wreckage, bloodied and still—a sad little flock of carcasses. At least they'd escaped a crueler fate in the Wastes. "We lost them, too. But your stray has the right idea. Let's make for those rocks."

Paige led the way with her lantern raised. Iris started to run on ahead, but Jay called her back with a whisper. Holly shuffled behind them, gripping Nicholas by the arm for support. Zora checked her wrist-watcher every few steps, and Abigail glanced around like a squirrel in an open meadow, but Novalyne radiated an aura of calm.

Quinn hung back to guard their rear, and Signe fell in step beside him. "You took command of that situation," she said.

"I did?" He hadn't meant to. "I'm sorry."

She opened her parasol and shaded her eyes from the lantern. "No need to apologize. You made the right call. See?"

Behind them, a yellowy kitelike thing fluttered into view, croaking faintly and threshing its spiny tail. A jarmara, out for prey small or wounded enough to snare. It lingered by the ship, as if to savor the last breaths of the flock.

Quinn took aim but then lowered his pistol. He'd save his fire unless the spirit gave chase.

"Take a gander at this," Paige said from the front of the pack. "It doesn't seem natural."

The rocks turned out to be standing stones arrayed in a circle. Just like in his dream from last night. The coincidence unsettled him, and the altar-like slab in the center disquieted him even more. Still, he and his companions could keep watch in every direction from here.

The stray lamb ran over to Iris, and she coaxed it into lying down by her feet. "Stay close to me, little woolly."

"What is this place?" asked Nicholas.

"The Olden World folk would've called it a cromlech." Quinn touched one of the stones. "And each of these is a menhir."

"Must've been a shrine for some weird sort of cult," said Zora. "Loads of them sprang up after the Great Wakening.

The Spiritists, of course"—Nicholas blinked at that—"but also the Tremblors. The Children of the Goat. The Celestial Lodge. And dozens more, each with its own absurd superstitions." She paused, and Quinn could almost hear the gears in her head grinding backward. "No offense to the Folk of the Ram," she said as Novalyne watched her intently.

"None taken," said Nicholas. "But why a circle of rocks?"

"Could be for astrology." Zora gestured toward the slab. "Could be for human sacrifices."

"Whatever the ring builders did," Signe said, "perhaps it succeeded. There aren't any earthbounds on this summit, and that jarmara hasn't come any closer."

"Maybe you've mixed up your cause and effect," Zora said. "Suppose the folks who raised these rocks picked a spirit-free site for their shrine. Anyway, their hooey didn't save them in the end." She scooped up a blade from the grass: a boning knife, corroded to rust. "Nobody's chanted a charm or slit a throat up here for ages."

"At least they left behind a place to defend," Quinn said. He sat against a menhir facing the ship—the ground was less spongy here—and Signe nestled beside him. Two to a stone, the others hunkered down to wait out the long, frigid night.

♈

The dawn found Quinn stiff and exhausted. He paced the ring to set his blood flowing, and by the gray light, he noticed patterns carved into the menhirs. Five parallel lines on each stone, inscribed with ovals and curves.

"They're notes," Nicholas said. "A melody without a key."

The *Reynardine* was beyond repair, its hull deflated and its ribs puncturing its skin. As Quinn and Paige rigged up a stretcher for Mr. Vandy's body, the others sifted through the flotsam. Soon they'd salvaged as much gear as they could carry. Banisher-rifles and pistols. Twelve spirit-grenades and one scuffed fiddle case. Quilts and tarps folded into packs. A medical kit, a map, and a compass.

Jay also found a bundle of wood and a jug of hemp diesel.

"Bring those to the circle," Quinn said. "We don't have time to dig a grave."

They left behind crates of old photos and journals and tapestries. Holly cried over that, and Quinn could have, too. So much knowledge and history lost.

The funeral party processed solemnly to the altar, laid out the wood, and set the corpse on the pyre. Then everyone gathered around and looked straight at Quinn. Right, the eulogy. He'd watched this part a hundred times, but he'd never done it himself. Best keep things short; they'd burned too much daylight already.

"Walter Vandy fell as he lived," Quinn said. "Flying into the wild unknown yonder. We honor him as a hero of the Hollows."

The stones watched impassively, their long shadows draping the altar. Mr. Vandy had died in a lonesome place, but his monument would be a grand one.

"He was a daring aviator," said Paige.

"And a crafty shipwright," added Zora.

Signe dipped her parasol. "May he be one with the universe."

The grass rippled in the wind, and the *Reynardine* shivered like a sleeping bear. Abigail tried to speak, but her voice failed her.

"He answered our call for help," said Jay. "Even though we were strangers to him."

With a heart of lead, Quinn took the jug and doused the pyre with engine fuel. Then Zora struck a match and threw it on the bier. The diesel ignited in a plume of yellow fire.

"Farewell, Commodore." Iris flung a fistful of powder that turned the flames lilac and purple.

"Potassium?" Zora asked.

"Chloride and sulfate with a dash of saltpeter," Iris said.

Abigail sniffled, and Novalyne looked away toward the mountains.

As the pyre blazed, Jay and Holly traded verses about a poor wayfarer. Afterward, Nicholas raised his fiddle and walked in a circle, pausing at each stone to play the notes carved upon it. The melody came out oddly toneless, as if sung by a violin drunk on moonlight.

"So," Quinn said once the final note had faded. "Which direction should we go?"

Zora faced the rising sun. "The equinox was two days ago, which makes this due east." She raised her arm at an angle. "That was our last heading, but we'd gone off course." She swung her arm sixty degrees. "That's my best guess for the way to the Hollows. Bear west, and we'll hit the river. Bear north, and we'll pass the Ruined Town. Or we could go straight through the valley. Last night, I thought I saw a blue light down there, but it might've been a mirage."

"I vote for west," said Paige. "We can't get lost if we follow the river."

Signe shook her head. "The gorges are teeming with spirits. The northern route would be safer."

"What's in the Ruined Town?" asked Novalyne.

"It was a county seat before the Great Wakening," said Signe. "It had a thousand people and a college with an observatory. Now it's full of earthbounds and shines in the night."

Novalyne consulted the compass. "I'd rather go there than chance dangerous waters."

"If that's how everyone feels." Paige shrugged, but Quinn could read the chagrin on her face.

"I think we should make for the blue light," piped up Abigail. "Maybe somebody was signaling to us."

"You mean someone like—" Zora broke off. "Like Ulysses Bell. We could check it out."

Ulysses Bell. Quinn recognized the name: he'd seen it on a book cover, under a picture of a deer with eagle wings. What was that mythical beast called? A harpy? A hippogriff?

No, a peryton.

"I agree with Zora," Nicholas said as his twin narrowed her eyes. Signe looked contemplative and then nodded, too.

"The blue light it is." Shouldering his rifle and pack, Quinn marched past the pyre and on toward the valley. The others trailed him in silence, all bearing their own heavy loads. With a plaintive baa, the lamb cut short its grazing and stuck to Iris like a white shadow.

The scrub of the bald gave way to trees overhead and ferns underfoot, blighted here and there by elementals. No birds called from the barren branches, and no creatures rustled in the fallen leaves. The deeper Quinn went, the more he felt as if he'd stepped into a painting. And not some cozy pastoral scene, but one of those vast, brooding landscapes in the Fontaine family mansion.

"I almost miss Ram's Horn," Paige muttered to him.

The ten of them plodded along all morning, scratched by briars and staggered by roots. They stopped now and then so Holly could lie down and Zora could rest and Nicholas could catch his breath. Around noon, they found a swift creek and filled their canteens with clear, bracing meltwater.

"Look at this rock," Iris said as she munched on a soda biscuit. "It's got bugs inside it."

Quinn inspected the fossil. "Those are trilobites. They ruled the world in the Deep Time, but now they're extinct. Wiped out by an ancient cataclysm."

"Like a Wakening," said Iris.

"Maybe," Quinn allowed. "I don't know what caused it. The paleontologists never learned, either." He held out his arms. "It happened back when all this was ocean bottom."

She seemed unimpressed, but Holly perked up. "I thought the hills had been here forever."

"They're old as dirt," he said. "But they were mud half an eon ago. The Appalachians formed—"

"I hate to end my brother's lecture," Zora cut in, "but I need his help with this." She brandished a crossbow-shaped device and nudged him toward a stand of bamboo.

Quinn was confused, but he went along. "What's wrong with your illuminator?"

"Nothing," Zora whispered. "We have a bigger problem. Before we crashed, Mr. Vandy told me that someone had tampered with the rudder."

"Wait, is that what"—Quinn realized he was shouting and lowered his voice—"made us crash?"

"No, the cloudbusters did that. But our saboteur steered us off course."

A phantom centipede crawled down his spine. "Why? And who? And when?"

"After we repaired the ship but before we left for home. The wheel was fighting me from the get-go." Zora scowled. "I bet it's part of Evelyn Fontaine's revenge."

"I wouldn't put it past her," Quinn said. "She's set a couple traps for us already. But Ram's Horn would be a long stretch, even for her."

"I have three theories about what happened. Number one: a spy followed us from the Hollows."

And across the Wastes. "Seems unlikely," Quinn said.

"Unless that snake built her own airship. But I think we would have seen it. So, on to number two: a Spiritist stowed away on the *Reynardine*, like you said I should. We assumed Ms. Spire-Bait planted the lure, but maybe she had a partner aboard."

"Paige searched the ship the night we left," he pointed out. "And y'all spent a whole day fixing it up."

"Right, but the hull had lots of good hiding spots."

So did this forest, with its thickets of cane and laurel. "If your stowaway caught a ride back and survived the crash, then we should start watching our tail." Quinn had dropped his guard, but now he was all eyes again. "We brought weapons for fighting spirits, not people."

"The third theory worries me the most," Zora said. "Maybe one of our passengers meddled with the rudder."

Quinn cast a backward glance at the Folk of the Ram. Iris was feeding her lamb a carrot, and Jay was changing Holly's bandage. Novalyne had spread out the map on a flat hunk of shale and set down pebbles to mark out locations. Her twin leaned against a gnarled tree, his chin in his hand and his fiddle case by his feet. None of them had the air of a Spiritist mole. Then again, neither had Lurana Underwood, and she'd spied on Quinn and Zora last summer.

"Would any of them know how to do it?" he asked.

"Nick, for one," Zora said, with obvious reluctance. "He helped me build a new engine. The rest? I couldn't say. We don't really know them at all."

Over by the creek, Abigail fussed with something inside her pack. "I could say the same about our new recruit," Quinn said. "And she has mechanical skills, too. So, who should we tell about this?"

"Just Signe and Paige, for now."

A bleak mood fell over him. They'd struggled so hard just to end up here, shipwrecked in the Wastes with a hidden enemy. "How well do you even know them? Or me? You met us less than a year ago."

"Don't be silly, big brother. I know you'll always stick by me." Zora smiled. "Let's go back before anyone gets suspicious."

♈

The flurries began at the crack of dusk. A few specks of white at first but then a steady fall. Some landed on Quinn's face and melted. Others landed on the branches and stuck.

"Spring's late this year," he said.

Zora brushed flakes from her tasseled hat. "Blame the derechos."

A dull peal drifted down from the clouds—the angry growl of a thwarted predator. The snow came down even harder, lodging in the lamb's wool and leaving wet tracks on Signe's glasses.

"Can they hurt us down here?" Jay asked.

"Not directly," Paige said. "But they could make our walk home unpleasant."

Within minutes, the woods had the look of a powdered sugar cake. Quinn could barely see ahead, and the children were straggling behind. They needed a shelter from the storm: a cabin, a barn, or—or that.

In a grove of gray, scaly birches stood the ruin of a school-house. Its door and windows were missing, but its mossy roof was intact. The epitaph on its lintel read *GARDINEL ELEMENTARY*.

"Let's stop here," Quinn said. "We can't spend another night in the open."

They filed out of the snow and into the schoolhouse. It had a blackboard in front, a tub sink in back, and a cast iron stove in the center. Iris sat down at a wooden desk, and the lamb put its head on her lap.

Holly's giggle sounded out of place in the sepulchral room. "Sorry. It's just—Iris has a little lamb, and it followed her to school today."

"So long as no roamers sit down beside me while I'm eating my curds and whey," Iris said darkly.

Quinn went to the sink and twisted the spigot, but nothing came out except for a dribble of slime. It smelled of silt and tarnished plumbing.

A crash startled him, and he spun around with his banisher drawn. Paige had broken a desk into pieces. "For firewood," she explained.

Signe pulled a book from the dusty shelves and held it close to her nose. "*Sixth Eclectic Reader*." She flipped to a page in the middle. "'The Snow-Shower' by Willa Cullen Bryant. 'See how in a living swarm they come from chambers beyond that misty veil.' It's a shame to burn this, but we do need the kindling." She tore leaves from the book and added them to the stove.

While Zora lit the fire, Quinn wandered over to study the blackboard. The upper part was covered with numbers written neatly in faded yellow chalk. Along the bottom ran a scrawl in a different hand:

THE* **ME *ROM **E PI

Some of the letters were smudged, and the *I* trailed down to the edge of the slate.

"Pi," said Zora. "The students must've been studying circles."

That didn't seem right to Quinn; why spell it out instead of writing the symbol? "Or playing a word-guessing game," he said, though he couldn't think of an answer that fit.

Abigail fished an object from her pack: a chrome-plated box with a telescopic antenna. "Let's see if I can raise a signal." As she turned a knob, the device squeaked and sputtered. "Nope, but these portable two-way sets have a limited range. I brought a couple spares, just in case." She dug out another box and placed it on a desk. "Who wants to keep this?"

"I can," said Nicholas. "I know a few things about radios myself."

Novalyne took it first. "You already have an instrument to lug around."

"I'll carry one, too," Paige volunteered. She poked Novalyne's bicep. "Maybe we can work out our own secret code."

Abigail gave her the third radio. "Quick messages only or you'll run down the battery."

Behind them, Iris snuffled loudly. She'd nodded off with her face on her desk, so Quinn wrapped a wool blanket around her. He'd snoozed in school, too, but without such a good excuse.

"I call first shift as monitor." Paige pulled up a chair and propped her boots on the teacher's desk. "I always wondered how it would feel to sit at the head of the class."

Quinn plunked himself down by the stove, and Signe ruffled his hair. "At least we're in this together," she whispered.

He had so much to tell her—about the saboteur, the standing stones in his dream, and more besides—but he felt too worn down to find the words. "We should talk tomorrow morning," he said through a yawn. "When we have a moment alone."

Beyond the doorway, the swirling flakes seemed to trace patterns in the air. Quinn imagined them forming mystic runes and mathematical equations. Hex signs and alchemical symbols. If he watched and waited, they might reveal the missing chalk letters.

THEN HOME FROM THE PIT? No, that was nonsense.

His companions fell asleep one by one, but Quinn kept his eyes on the doorway. Just a little longer, and the answer would come.

Then Signe was shaking him by the shoulders. "Jay heard a strange noise," she said.

The room was dark and full of soft breathing. "What time is it?" Quinn asked. His mouth tasted dry, and his eyes felt crusty.

Signe checked her pocket-watch. "Half an hour till morning."

He picked up his rifle and crept to the doorway. Drifts of snow had blown across the porch and into the schoolhouse. Past the threshold, the blizzard raged on.

"No spirits this way," Paige called from the far side of the room.

Quinn aimed a blue beam into the whiteness outside. "Nothing over here, either."

The others were waking up and scrabbling for their gear. "Quiet!" Jay said, his mild voice suddenly harsh. "There it is again."

A soft drone emanated from below the schoolhouse. Not the hypnotic buzz of the harbinger or the earth-rending rumble of an elemental; more like those cicadas that only came out of the ground every seventeen years.

"It reminds me of electrical interference," said Abigail.

Orange dots appeared on Quinn's banisher. The droning flowed under the floorboards, swelling with every pulsation.

"I sense spirits" — Novalyne paused — "*everywhere.*"

Signe's skirt swished as she pivoted left and right. "I don't see them at all."

A scent of decay and corrosion drifted past Quinn. He'd smelled that before, and recently, but he couldn't place it. Then he looked back at the writing on the board, and his mind filled in the missing letters.

THEY CAME FROM THE PIPES

Before he could shout a warning, a green fountain burst from the sink.

12

THE SPIRITS CORKSCREWED TOWARD SIGNE, TOO SWIFTLY TO FIX with her gaze. They had the stench of stagnant water and the color of copper patina. There must be thousands of them.

"Get down!" yelled Quinn.

She threw herself flat, and the spirits hummed past, close enough to singe the ends of her hair. Violet strobes lit the room, but the swarm spiraled away along the ceiling. As Zora swore and Abigail squawked, the children dove under desks.

"Gwyllion," Paige said from behind an overturned bookshelf.

Signe's skin crawled at the nape of her neck. She'd read about these things in the *Field Guide*, but part of her wished she hadn't. *GWYLLION are hornet-sized roamers with spiky wings and a verdigris hue*, Nevan McBrain had written. *They make their hives in sinkholes, old sewers, and other dank places, hibernating for decades on end. In sufficient numbers, they can skeletonize a human in less than a minute. Fortunately, they only dwell in the Wastes . . .*

The spirits whirled through the schoolhouse, always in the corner of her vision. As if they were avoiding her line of sight.

As if they knew what her eyes could do.

Nicholas plucked a string, and the droning stopped for

a heartbeat. Then it started back up beneath the planks, louder and hollower now. Signe focused her gaze on the back of the room.

The pipes clanged, and more gwyllion poured up from the drain. And poured and poured in an endless stream of metallic green. Too many for her to stare away. Too many for her friends to blast.

This school wasn't a haven; it was a slaughterhouse. The writing on the board had been someone's last words.

Zora threw a grenade, and Signe scrunched her eyes shut in the nick of time. "Everybody, run!" Quinn shouted as the flow of spirits became a geyser.

Signe grabbed her pack and her parasol on the way to the door. Out of the schoolhouse and into the snowstorm. To her left, the children dashed through the grove with the swarm on their heels. It would chase them down and feed in a frenzy.

Unless she decoyed it away, like she'd done with the spire last summer. On the night she'd nearly died.

Signe traced an arc in the snow with the tip of her parasol. "I see you," she called out to the spirits.

The swarm looped around, scattering the flakes in its path. The children ran on ahead, and the blizzard devoured them. Now if only she could vanish in a puff of smoke like a stage magician—or, better yet, a real enchanter.

Take three steps back, whispered a liquid voice as the gwyllion spun in a helix. She'd caught them in her gaze, but not for much longer.

Trust me, said the voice. *If you want to live.*

Keeping her eyes on the swarm, Signe stepped backward three paces. The snow gave way beneath her, pitching her belly-up in a shallow pit. The force of the fall knocked the breath from her lungs.

Stay down.

The spirits buzzed overhead and disappeared from her field of vision.

Go the other way—and quickly.

Signe was lying in a sunken grave, covered in twigs and dead leaves. She scrambled out of the hole and into the woods, spurred on by desperation. Pushing through hazel and thorns, she came to the edge of a glade. Or possibly the lair of a dormant earthbound.

Stop here.

Signe ducked under a tree and wiped the flakes from her glasses. The smear of night turned into a black crystal ball. Ghostly trunks loomed above her, and pallid bracken swayed by her feet, but the world beyond was a blank. She was lost, and her fairy eyes couldn't see through this blizzard.

Keep still, and you'll be safe.

The voice sounded like the one from the well in her dream. *Save me from this abyss*, it had begged her. Now it was here in her waking life. "What are you?" she asked.

Nnn, the voice glugged, as if it were coming from underwater.

"An eidolon?" Signe persevered. "Or something else?"

Nnn . . . nnn . . . nnn . . .

"Where are my friends?"

No answer. Jinx it—she couldn't wait here while they were in danger. She'd take her chances searching for them.

As Signe opened her parasol, a shadowy figure stepped into the clearing. The newcomer stood still for the space of a breath, shining a flashlight at Signe. Then it turned the beam on its face.

"I thought I'd find you here." Novalyne looked haggard but uninjured. "I felt your gift calling to me. It's different from when I sense spirits."

"I'm glad you're okay," Signe told her. "What happened to everyone else?"

"They split up when the swarm attacked. Abigail ran off toward the valley, shouting about a beacon. My brother and Zora followed her. Quinn and Paige went after the children."

Signe's heart lightened, and so did the blizzard. "I saw your cousins escape from the gwyllion."

"I know." Novalyne regarded her solemnly. "I watched you risk your life to save them. I won't forget what you've done."

"All part of my calling." Did that sound humble or conceited? Not that it mattered at the moment. "Which way should we go?"

"I have a plan to gather our flock." Novalyne aimed her light at the murk and loped away through the forest.

"Where are you—hey, wait up!" Signe tried to keep pace without snagging her parasol on the branches. She'd left her only spare in the wreck of the *Reynardine*.

The snow tapered off into flurries, and the sky went from black to dark gray. They passed decrepit houses and barns. The sagging remains of a two-story tavern. A little brick ruin with a sign that read *GARDINEL POST OFFICE*.

Signe felt like a trespasser here. And now the buzz of the swarm was rising again.

Novalyne stopped abruptly. "Do you see it?"

Ahead of them stood a hulking shape with a hazy green aura. Signe's head swam, and her throat sealed itself shut. The thing was as tall as a spire, with five long limbs stretching down from its crest.

But it wasn't moving, just droning in place. She was looking up at a water tower wreathed in spirit-shine.

"That's where the gwyllion came from," Novalyne said. "They've returned to their hive ahead of the dawn."

All at once, the buzzing ceased, and the aura dissipated.

Signe approached the tower, still a bit warily. "They must have followed the pipes to the school." The tangies had pulled the same trick at the fish farm. "But why did you bring us here?"

"For better reception when I signal the others." Novalyne set to climbing a rickety ladder. "Want to come along?"

"The crow's nest was enough for me," Signe said. "This reminds me too much of my neighbor's silo. I nearly fell off it when I was nine." From below, the ladder looked to be more rust than iron. "Are you certain that's safe?"

Novalyne banged a fist against the tower. "This is nothing compared to the mast in Ram's Horn."

While she scaled the side of the tank, Signe ruminated on the mysterious voice. Was it just an echo of her dream or a visitant from another plane? If it was real, why had it helped her? And where had it gone afterward?

"Here goes," Novalyne shouted from the top of the ladder. Hanging on with one hand, she raised her radio, called out Paige's name, and held the set to her ear. An inaudible conversation followed.

As the minutes dragged on, Signe shuffled her feet in the snow. She should've gone up herself; she could be talking with her friends instead of waiting down here.

More muffled words from Novalyne; more drawn-out pauses as she listened. What was taking so long? Signe's mind spun one grim scenario after another. Her friends had crossed paths with a lichender. Or stumbled into a dwayyo's nest. Or fallen prey to some new sort of horror.

After what felt like forever, Novalyne climbed down the ladder. "I spoke with Paige and Abigail. Nobody's hurt—not even the lamb—and they saved most of the gear, but we decided on a new plan. Paige spotted too many spirits in the valley, so we're switching to the northern route."

"Away from the blue light?"

"Abigail still favored the valley." Novalyne sounded regretful. "But Paige and I overruled her." She pointed to a molar-shaped rock on a distant mountain. "We'll rendezvous at that pinnacle. It's the biggest landmark around."

"Well, I've always wanted to see the Ruined Town." Signe set off with her parasol high and springs in her heels. They'd spent a night in the Wastes and come through unscathed. The derechos had dispersed, and the swarm was hibernating again. Come afternoon, she'd be back with Quinn and Zora and Paige.

And yet a formless worry tugged at the back of her brain. Not the fear of the dangers ahead, but a sense of wrongness she couldn't shake.

♈

From afar, their new route had a stark sort of beauty. Up close, it was a soggy mess. Signe's feet sank in the slush with every step, and her stockings were soaked to the skin. The sun's rays felt warm on her back—one bright side of wearing dark clothes— but the glare from the snow cut straight through her lenses.

Novalyne seemed immune to it all. She kept right on walking, seldom speaking, always fixed on the path ahead.

"You must be anxious about your brother and cousins," Signe ventured.

But Novalyne's face remained set. "Our elders taught us how to fend for ourselves. I trust my kin to find their own way."

Signe wished she felt so certain. "I wonder if we're in the lead or behind them."

"Oh, I'm sure we'll reach the meeting place first. Nicholas and the children are slower than me." Novalyne perused the map. "This next part's a bog, so watch yourself."

As they skirted the mire, a strident honk made Signe start. Then a flock of black-necked geese took wing and flapped away north.

A pity she couldn't fly away, too. And a shame they'd lost Mr. Vandy.

"Where do they go?" asked Novalyne. "What's become of the world beyond these mountains?"

"Nobody knows," Signe said. "In the Coal Age, visitors still graced the Hollows. Sylvanians trekked down the Pass, and paddleboats steamed up from the Delta. The Tidelanders couldn't cross the high mountains, but they hailed our people by radio." She'd read stacks of novels set in that era. With its bold wayfarers and far-flung courtships, it held such a romantic allure. "Then, in Year Seven-Seven, the Lesser Wakening came. The rivers ran green, and the outside world fell silent."

Novalyne jabbed her walking stick in the sludge. "That was a dark night for the Folk of the Ram. The spirits cut off the ends of the gap and took most of our people."

"We lost everyone in the Pass and the Outer Hollows, but the worst of the roamers stopped at our borders. Legend has it the fiddler girl left a circle of protective wards—a sort of musical fence." Red-tipped sumac brushed against Signe's skirt, and cinnamon ferns crackled under her boots. "We may be the last people alive from here to the ocean."

"And the land to the west, with the rich farms and fancy houses?"

"The Bluegrass?" Long ago, its bourbon monarchs and tobacco dukes had lorded over the Hollows. "Laid to waste back in Year Zero on the night of the Great Wakening."

The tall brown sedge parted onto a wide-open field. Here, no blade of grass broke through the white. With a few sweeps of her stick, Novalyne cleared a patch of snow. Beneath lay dust so gray and fine it might've come from a sea on the moon.

"This is the domain of an elemental," Signe said. "The largest I've ever seen from up close."

"So? It can't hurt us."

"In the Hollows, it's considered bad luck to cross one, even by day."

"In Ram's Horn, we weren't so fainthearted." Novalyne walked on ahead, leaving a straight path of footprints behind her.

Signe followed, taking care to step in her companion's tracks. *A silly superstition,* Zora had said on the solstice. *Hogwash for the rubes. Elementals can't hunt you down.* But that hadn't stopped her from sweating on a cold winter's noon at the sight of Old Smoky.

"You and Paige seem to get along well," Signe said. Why not pass the time by playing matchmaker?

"She's a fierce fighter." Novalyne's tone mellowed. "But soft beneath her guard."

"That's perceptive of you." Now they were getting somewhere: halfway across the field and deeper into the realm of the heart. "I took her the wrong way at first—you know, with all the nicknames and hijinks—but she's a keen Spotter and a loyal friend."

Novalyne laughed dryly. "I catch your drift." She stopped in her tracks but didn't turn around. "I suppose folks as smitten as you want the whole world to share in the feeling. So, have you told Quinn you love him?"

Signe halted, too. "I—we've both been rather busy," she stammered. "Tracking spirits, traversing wastelands, that sort of thing." Besides, he hadn't told her yet, either.

"My parents pledged their love to each other with every goodbye, in case one of them didn't return. And a final time before they faced the titan." The young woman kept her back to Signe. "If you have children, they may bear the Mark of the Syzygy, too. That means your kids could have your eyes."

The same notion had crossed Signe's mind, but she wasn't champing to become a parent. Not like Mamma and Pabbi, who'd gone and had a child at twenty. And twenty-two, and twenty-four, and so on.

A new thought occurred to her. "You could pass down your spirit-sense, too."

The snow in their tracks was melting, exposing the ash below. The rushes up ahead stood unbowed, and the muddy pools lay becalmed. Higher and farther onward, the pinnacle cast its eyeless gaze toward them.

Novalyne drew an X in the snow with her stick. "I've never expected to have the chance."

Signe had no idea what to say to that. "About the eidolons," she said instead. "You're certain they've never talked to your people?"

"Why do you ask?" Novalyne finally turned around. "Have they spoken to you?"

"Not spoken, exactly, but something—*communed* with me in the blizzard. Right after the gwyllion attacked."

"That's remarkable." Novalyne's eyes widened, and Signe noticed for the first time that they were hazel. "What did it say?"

"It told me how to escape the swarm, but nothing about itself."

"Was this the first time the . . . presence communed with you?"

"I thought I dreamed it, but I'm not so sure anymore. Before I left the Hollows, it asked me to save it from a well."

"Did it tell you where?"

In Signe's trance, the frozen fishponds had risen to form a quadrangle. "It showed me a vision of the Ruined Town."

And now they were headed there. Happenstance or a secret design? Of the five cards in her fortune, she'd seen three play out on this journey: the Wilkhommen, the Zephyr, and the Distelfinks. Perhaps the Black Train as well—the airship had turned out to be a funeral car. Yet one card remained in destiny's hand: the Skywheel.

Her companion seemed fascinated. "Maybe your Mark is special. Maybe the eidolons chose you for something grand."

After yesterday's storm, the noon sun felt almost balmy. Signe undid the buttons of her coat. "Or my fancies are running free, like my parents used to tell me."

"I feel blessed that we've met." Novalyne smiled for once. "Those of us with the Mark should stick together. You and I have so much to learn from each other."

"I think so, too." Signe would've beamed if not for the spirit underfoot. "Should we finish crossing this place?"

But Novalyne stood facing the way they'd come, her expression wild, her chin raised defiantly. "You're still afraid, aren't you?"

"Yes," Signe admitted. "An elemental attacked me last summer. It came up from below where I was standing."

"This one won't. Watch, I'll poke it with my stick."

"You don't need to do that." Novalyne was starting to scare her. "I'll grant that you're braver than me."

"Spirit, show yourself if you dare!"

The shout crashed against the white silence. Signe tensed, but the stillness prevailed. They might as well be the only two souls on the planet.

"Can we please go now?" she asked in a shaky voice.

Novalyne broke her stick in half and dropped the pieces. "After you."

Signe hurried on ahead, unnerved by her companion's outburst. And nettled at her own groundless fears. No spirit could rise before nightfall. That law had bound their kind from the beginning.

♈

Novalyne's prediction came true: the two of them reached the pinnacle first. The hunk of rock stood balanced on a narrow base, as if poised to somersault down the mountain. In its path slumped a shack with a tree sprouting up through its roof. Whoever built a home there had enjoyed tempting fate.

"Should we explore it?" Signe asked. "We'll need a place to sleep tonight. With no rude surprises this time, I hope."

They hopscotched across the worm-eaten porch, and Signe tried the door. It didn't budge.

"Allow me." Novalyne kicked the door. It swung in with a groan, and fetid air drifted out.

The floor was dirt and full of roots. The tree in the center rose like a chimney, and creeping vines papered the walls. Fungi had overrun the furniture: yellow witch's butter on the table and orange velvet foot on the bed.

In the lone chair sat a skeleton with a spiderweb eyepatch.

Signe screamed, just a little. Then she collected herself. "Sorry about that."

"How long do you suppose it's been here?" asked Novalyne.

Quinn's mom would know—she'd seen more bones than she could shake a shovel at—but Signe could only guess. "Years, I think? There's no flesh on it." She crouched face-to-face with the skull. "All four wisdom teeth and wisps of gray beard on the chin."

"So, a grown man."

Signe sized up an ulna and examined the fingers. "A head taller than me, I'd estimate. He's holding a pencil and journal."

Novalyne pulled out her flashlight. In its beam, the bones took on a greenish tinge. "Infected by spirits," she pronounced.

Signe touched her own sternum reflexively, then pried the journal from the skeleton's hands and unsealed the clasps on the vermillion cover. No name on the first page. Instead, it began with a penciled entry from two years ago.

Feeling like a storybook sleuth—like Carson van Patten

herself—she took out her magnifying glass to read the spidery writing.

Spring 33, 142. My journey through the veil has begun. I took the forager trails into the Border Hollows, but soon I'll blaze a path of my own. I made camp in a cleft beneath a painted hex sign: an eye inside a triangle. No signals this evening; tomorrow I'll search again.

Novalyne picked up what looked like a metal kite frame. Each side was as long as her arm and strung with strands of copper wire. "Is this some sort of dowsing tool?"

"An antenna," Signe said absently. Who was the journal's author, and what signals had lured him to the Wastes? She turned to the next entry.

Spring 34, 142. I'm in the observatory above the Ruined Town. The spirits appear to leave this place alone. Tonight, I heard a new message—the longest and clearest yet. "The professor went west to the land of the goat. The fiddler went down by the river to play. The loom has a shuttle but no warp or weft. The doe will wear the starry crown and show you the way." The signal came from the south, and I will follow. I miss my little operator, but the voice in the ether is calling to me.

The professor, the fiddler, and the loom—*Revelations from the Veiled Realm* had mentioned all three.

Spring 35, 142. A pack of herns skulked through the woods near my campsite. Yet luck travels with me—the spirits passed by, and I caught a new message from Peryton One. "Hang the red stars and summon the herd—the doe is returning." One more signal, and I'll find the source.

Signe had crossed paths with a pack of herns: skittering, razor-barbed roamers that howled as they hunted their quarry. She'd made them blink, but just barely.

Spring 36, 142. No more messages. The herns are stalking me. They struck tonight—I got away, but one of them scratched me. Something is guiding the pack—a spinning, humming spirit.

That had to be the harbinger. Quinn's dad and Nevan McBrain had tracked it for years through the Wastes and Hollows.

"Don't keep me in suspense." Novalyne leaned over her shoulder. "What does it say?"

"He was searching for a transmitter, but something found him instead." Signe read the final entry out loud. "'I don't know what day it is. My wound turned green, and the poison spread, and now I'm too sick to go on. The siren signals have led me to my doom. Here, at the end, I wish I'd stayed with my daughter. If you find this journal, tell her she was dear to me. Yours truly . . .'"

The name stuck in Signe's throat, and a weight descended on her shoulders.

Novalyne motioned for her to go on. "Who?"

"Ulysses Bell." Signe closed the journal. "Abigail's father."

♈

They took turns digging a grave by the shack. "We'll hold a funeral for him," Signe said. "Once everyone gets here."

"I wonder who sent those signals." Novalyne marked the grave with the kite-shaped antenna. "We never heard tell of survivors out here."

Raw-palmed and clammy with perspiration, they sat beneath the rock to watch for the rest of their party. Through her telescope, Signe spied out the bog and the water tower. No trace of life anywhere.

"I never asked you," Novalyne said. "Do you have any siblings yourself?"

Signe had to laugh. "I'm a seventh child, like my mother before me. I used to think that's how I came by my gift." Her cheeks smarted from the sun on the snow. "Just a myth I made for myself."

"Who knows why the eidolons chose you? I'm a twin; you're the seventh child of a seventh child. We were both born under fortunate stars."

"I suppose." Signe didn't feel lucky right now. Only tired and forlorn and frightened. The damp on her brow was already cold.

They waited and waited as the shade from the rock fell over the shack, but the others never arrived.

13

ZORA STOMPED THROUGH THE SNOW WITH ONE THOUGHT RATTLING inside her head. *Don't look back, don't look back, don't look back.*

She looked back. The spirit was gaining, of course, a tide of radium dye spreading over the forest floor. It was the creeping death of the Wastes: a lichender.

"Almost . . . dawn," Nick said between ragged breaths. "A little longer . . . and we'll be safe."

Zora's feet felt as heavy as meteor rocks. "I'm running out of steam." Or diesel. Or whatever. "Can you lull it to sleep?"

"Not without . . . an amplifier. Can you . . . blow it to pieces?"

"Too big." She'd used her last grenade, and her pistol wouldn't slow down the spirit. *Spirits,* she could hear Mr. Epps lecture her. *A lichender is a symbiosis of two roamer species.*

More to the point, it was unstoppable.

And nobody was coming to save her. When she'd told Quinn and Paige to go help the children, they'd hesitated but followed the gwyllion. Abigail was somewhere up ahead, invisible in the chaos of the whiteout. Signe and Novalyne had pulled vanishing acts.

The lichender crawled onward inexorably, withering the

woods with its touch. Ferns and ivy to dust. Saplings and holly to cinders.

Zora was starting to count herself . . . not jinxed. Call it snake-bit instead. She and Nick had run from the swarm, straight into the path of the lichender.

They passed a derelict tractor, a listing barn, a burned-out farmhouse. No refuge here, there, or anywhere. On past a shed, and the ground sloped away into snow-hidden depths. As Zora slipped and slid, Nick windmilled his arms to keep from falling over.

Too steep for feet and crutches; they needed a different way down. "Fetch part of that roof," she told Nick. "Yea big or so." Looking baffled, he made for the shed.

All at once, her sinuses swelled with etheric pressure. The lichender scuttled over the tractor and coursed through the barn. Willows shriveled, and winterberry crumbled.

Hurry up, Fiddler Boy. Death is coming.

Nick staggered back with a sheet of corrugated tin. "Set that down," Zora said. He obeyed, and she plonked herself on it.

"I get the plan now." Nick dithered at the edge of the slope. "But we don't know what's at the bottom."

Behind them, spectral fire lit the gutted house from within. Gnawing sounds filled the woods, and a carrion smell floated on the wind.

"Can't be worse than that creeping carpet." Zora gripped the sides of the icy tin roof. "Sit behind me and hold on—"

Nick pushed the sled, jumped aboard, and wrapped his arms around her. She felt a moment's warmth before gravity seized them. Then her insides went weightless as they plunged through the blizzard.

"Try and catch us now!" Zora shouted back at the lichender.

A tree rushed toward them—she leaned to the left, and they missed it. Nick held her tighter, his breath in her ear. The ground dipped, and they gathered momentum. Let it be toward a gentle slowdown, with no earthbounds or sudden drop-offs.

The sled hit a bump and started to spin. No way to steer, no way to brake, no way off this Winter Fair ride.

They flipped over in a tangle of limbs. Zora caught a mouthful of snow and a knock on the tailbone. Nick wound up beneath her, flat on his back.

"Still in one piece?" she asked him.

"Just a jab in the kidneys." He winced and patted his fiddle case. "From landing on this."

Her pulse was racing, and Nick's heart sounded ready to burst from his chest. "We did a lot of running," she said, placing her palm on his breastbone. "I can feel your double thump."

"My heart is—" He looked past her, and she turned around.

"Good morning," said Abigail. Her cheeks were rosy from the cold. "You two chose the scary way down."

As Zora stood, Nick brushed the snow from his clothes. "A mossmantle is chasing us," he said.

Mossmantle? He must mean the lichender. The Folk of the Ram called a hount a hount and a titan a titan, but they had their own names for some types of spirits. The Spotters would have a field day cataloging those.

"Not anymore." Abigail showed them her chipmunk grin. "It's daybreak. I've been waiting for you."

Because she'd run on ahead, like Zora's old classmates at recess. *We're playing tag—see you later.* "You ditched us at the schoolhouse."

Abigail looked taken aback. "What did you want me to do? You're the spirit-fighters. I don't even have one of your weapons." Her face turned sunny again. "But I have a radio, and so do Paige and Novalyne. Let's hail the rest of our team."

"If they're in range," Zora said. "If the swarm didn't catch them." The adrenaline was gone from her veins, and a fresh wave of fear had rushed into the vacuum.

Abigail moseyed along the base of the slope. "The snow's tailing off—that'll help. Now we need some elevation." She stopped by the trunk of a sycamore. "This tree should work. Who wants to climb it?"

Zora would rather face the lichender again. "That's a job for our radio expert."

"Oh." Abigail's chipperness dimmed, but she grabbed a branch and pulled herself up. Then she scrabbled from limb to limb like a raccoon. Despite her foul mood, Zora was impressed.

"That girl missed her calling as a steeplejack," she told Nick.

High in the treetop, Abigail took out her radio and raised its antenna. Her lips moved, but her words didn't carry.

"Any news?" Zora shouted.

"All hands accounted for!" Abigail shouted back down from her perch.

Zora shared a glance with Nick, and the relief on his face mirrored her own. "Our toboggan ride was kind of hair-raising," he said. "But also fun."

"There's a sledding hill near my house in Lightning Bug Hollow." Zora gathered her nerve and forged ahead. "When we make it back, I'll take you there." She could've said more, but maybe she'd said too much already.

Nick twisted the strap of his case. "I'd like to see that. Along with the lab where you build your inventions."

She kept her voice light, but inside, she was basking. "I'll give you a few demonstrations." Preferably while Mom was away. "Then we'll go to Hildy's Inn for corn cakes with honey butter."

"Sounds grand." He scratched the fuzz on his chin and started to speak, but a hail of sycamore pods cut him off.

"Sorry!" Abigail shinnied on down the tree. When she reached the lowest branch, she jumped to the ground between Zora and Nick.

"Nova—" he began.

"I spoke to her," Abigail said. "She's with Signe."

That pairing equaled spookiness squared. "What about everyone else?" Zora asked.

"Outside my range, but Novalyne raised them. She says they're fine—the lamb included." The girl rubbed her hands together. "Ready to go?"

By now, the storm was a ghost of itself. Farther downhill, the valley's mouth had reappeared: a flat stretch between two sharp ridges. The gateway home stood open, and the spirits lay sleeping again.

Zora sat on a stump to tighten her braces. She wasn't snake-bit after all. "We're sticking to our original route?"

"That's right." Picking sycamore fluff from her coat, Abigail started off toward the valley. "Novalyne said this way looked clear. We'll meet our team at the blue beacon."

Zora fell in step behind her. What would they find when they reached it? Abigail's missing father? The cryptic Peryton One? More lost survivors of the Wastes?

Or a trap?

♈

A platinum sun rose above the valley, flanked by twin patches of prismatic light. Lucky portents to the fortunetellers, but Zora knew they were ice crystal halos. *They're called sun dogs,* Dad had told her when she was seven. *They'll watch over you and your new puppy.*

A sudden longing snuck up on her. If Static were here, he'd sniff out a path to the Hollows. In all his years, he'd only left her behind twice. The first time, he'd chased a noise in the night and then run from its source—a spirit weaving a hypnotic spiral. She didn't blame him for that; she'd fled from it, too. The second time, he'd gone ahead where she couldn't follow.

Best not to stare at the sun dogs. Her eyes were already damp.

While Nick panted softy and Abigail prattled, Zora went over her mental list of potential moles. She crossed off her brother, Paige, and Signe right away. They'd faced death beside her, and she trusted them with her life. They were hopeless engineers, anyway.

Unlike present company. Abigail could've rigged the rudder, and Nick had the know-how, too, but why would either of them sabotage their mission? He was the one who'd sent the call for help, and she was the one who'd found it. On top of that, she was so bushy-tailed, and he was so dewy-eyed. Right now, she was gushing about a radio play—*The Dark Old House with One Lit Window* or something like that—as he listened with a rapt expression.

Novalyne was a tougher read, and her crown made her look

like a sinister priest. Counterpoint: she hated spirits, and Paige fancied her. Plus, she wore horns instead of antlers.

Then there were the children. Zora was building pneumatic motors at Iris's age, but the girl didn't strike her as a mechanic—or a spy. Maybe a future apprentice spirit-hunter. Holly? Harmlessly bookish. Jay? Too meek, though he had an odd knack for anticipating roamers.

Everything pointed to one conclusion: none of them had a motive to steer the airship off course. They all wanted out of the Wastes.

That brought her back to the stowaway theory. Unlikely, and yet more plausible than the alternatives. What if a Spiritist was stalking her and her companions? They'd be easy to track through the snow and easier to watch from the heights.

Down here in the valley, Zora felt like a hunted fox—a red-tagged target against a white background. Even the landscape around her had taken on a more ominous aspect. On one side, a yawning pit; on the other, a hill pared down to its stony core.

"Did a herd of behemoths tear through this valley?" asked Abigail.

"Not spirits," Zora said. "That's the work of humans."

Nick frowned at the beheaded hill. "Why would anyone do such a thing?"

"The coal mines ran out of seams back in the Between Times—"

"The what?"

"Between the Wakenings. That's when the barons who owned the mines shifted to harsher methods. Like digging pits and blasting mountaintops." The sight would've outraged her rock-loving brother. "They stained the streams cadmium yellow and laced the soil with arsenic dust, but their dynamite freed worse than that from the bedrock: land-wights and lares and elementals. Then the next Wakening put an end to it all."

Farther on, they found the thing that had dug the pit: a steel dinosaur on bulldozer treads. Kudzu and corrosion had claimed it.

"It's a bucket-wheel excavator," Zora said.

Abigail scaled the treads and peered into the cabin. She returned with an ashen complexion. "The driver's still there," she mumbled. "Partly. We're coming up on a village."

Nick dusted snow from a fallen sign. "Thirteen Point," he read. "Property of the Something Mining Company."

"Something?" Zora looked for herself, but deep scratches had scored out the name. They might've come from a knife or a claw; she couldn't tell which.

Leaving the steam shovel to its eternal rust, the three of them walked on to the village. It was a picture of order gone wild. Dead weeds ran riot in neatly laid streets; rows of cookie-cutter shacks had fallen to shambles.

"This must've been a company town," Zora said. "The barons would've owned all the houses and paid their workers in scrip." They passed a store with shattered windows and empty shelves. "Worthless paper except in there."

Abigail checked a mailbox and found a rat's nest inside. "Where would the owners live?"

"On higher ground, to look down on their subjects." Zora's great-grandfather had told her stories about working the mines. He'd survived the whitedamp, the stinkdamp, and a pair of cave-ins, but black lung had caught him in the end. "When the miners went on strike, the barons stayed snug in their mansions and sent in their mercenaries."

Had the Coal Wars swept through Thirteen Point? The houses showed traces of an ancient battle. Burn marks on a porch, bullet holes in a wall.

Nobody fought spirits with fire or lead.

"I know some songs from those times," Nick said. "Striker anthems and dirges for lost miners." His tone turned reverent. "The wayfaring fiddler taught them to my ancestors."

"I wonder if she made any phonograph records." Zora would've paid her last bit to get her hands on one of those. For research first, then for Quinn's next birthday present.

"She never came back to Ram's Horn. Where did she wander afterward?"

"Down to the Delta. Up to Sylvania. West to the Bluegrass and east to the high mountains. She was searching for something—just what, the songs never say—but she died before she could find it, saving a backwoods hollow from a spirit-tempest."

A shadow fell over Nick's face. "I should've known—not many old ballads have happy endings." He sat on the nearest porch, wheezing hard. "Should we rest here a bit?"

Abigail walked a few paces farther. "We're probably behind the others."

"I need a break, too." Zora parked herself next to Nick, and he flashed her a grateful look.

Abigail pursed her lips but then shrugged and took a place on the porch. "This town reminds me of a tale I heard from my father." The girl put on a campfire voice. "Years ago, there was a coal baron whose miners kept disappearing. She gave a different reason each time around. They'd moved back to their farms or struck out for silver or started moonshining. Then she'd hire a fresh batch of replacements. Soon enough, they'd go missing, too. The neighbors got suspicious and talked to the Judges."

Nick wrinkled his brow but held his peace.

"The Rangers paid the mine a visit," Abigail went on. "First, they went to the shacks. No miners, just unopened mail for folks named Reece and Travis and Gunning. Once the Rangers were done searching there, they called on the baron. She wasn't home, so they broke down the door. Nobody on the first floor and nobody upstairs. That left the cellar."

"It's always the cellar," Zora said, fishing a jar of strawberry jam from her pack.

But Abigail startled her by snatching the jar. "Pistols drawn and flashlights in hand, the Rangers climbed down the ladder. At the bottom, they found shelves lined with" —she held up the jam— "*jars*, but of what, they couldn't tell. Something deep red and pulpy. 'Canned cherries?' said one Ranger. 'Rhubarb preserves?' said another. Then their captain picked up a jar and read the label."

In the silence that followed, an icicle cracked and fell from the roof.

Abigail lowered her voice to a whisper. "It said *REECE*. The next one said *TRAVIS*, and the third was *GUNNING*." Another pause, to let that sink in. "When the captain saw an eyeball staring back at him, he dropped the jar. It broke on the cellar floor in a crimson splatter."

Nick made a face, but Zora laughed. She never would've guessed the girl had it in her.

"After the Rangers finished losing their lunches," Abigail resumed in her normal voice, "they found a trapdoor leading down to the mines. No one ever saw the baron again. For all we know, she's still out there." She handed the jar back to Zora.

"That's a good one, though I don't believe a word of it." Zora spread the jam on a chunk of bread and took a bite. It tasted delicious.

Abigail held out her palms. "Dad swore it was true."

A cardinal landed on the railing, and Zora threw it her crumbs. "Who are the Judges?" Nick asked.

"Our all-knowing leaders," she said, though her sarcasm seemed lost on him. "Seven magistrates, one for each circuit. We elect them." Not her, personally; she wasn't voting age yet. "How do your people choose who's in charge?"

"The eldest Mark-Bearer wears the Ram's Crown."

"Doesn't seem too democratic."

"We're more of a clan than a"—he fumbled for the word—"commonwealth. Do your Judges rule fairly?"

Abigail tapped her foot on a rotting step. "I don't follow politics."

Zora hadn't either, until she'd left her narrow hollow to go spirit-hunting. "They muddle by," she allowed. "But I know a person who wants to overthrow them."

Nick raised his eyebrows. "Would your . . . friend do better?"

"She'd do much, much worse. And she's not my *friend*." Zora hadn't intended to shout, but the cardinal darted away—a red streak in a world of alabaster.

Abigail stood and eyed the zenith. "I hate to be pushy, but we need to beat the sunset."

♈

They almost did.

Under a bloody sky, they came to a swath of woods that lay flattened. Not in one direction, but every which way. The trees were scattered like jackstraws, and the undergrowth was a trampled mess.

Zora heaved herself over a fallen log. "A tornado?"

"Or a titan," said Nick.

Whatever it had been, it had struck moons ago. Mushroom caps were poking through the snow on the dead trunks.

"We should've used this as an airfield," Abigail said. "We could've drifted down here and made a soft landing. Mr. Vandy might have survived."

Slivers of doubt needled Zora. What if she'd climbed back down to tell him about the blue light instead of saving her own skin? Was it her fault he'd died?

At the heart of the toppled forest, one thing still stood unscratched: a stone tower with a pointed roof and a high balcony. Its glassed-in top story was full of dusk.

"It's a lighthouse." Zora had seen photographs of its long-lost kin on the Tidelands. "But the lantern is missing."

"We're nowhere near the ocean," said Nick. "Why build this here?"

Abigail opened the thick iron door. "Let's find out." She charged up the spiral staircase, and Zora followed the sound of her footfalls. Nick brought up the rear, stopping once a flight to peek out the windows. The steps wound past the keeper's quarters (an austere room with a tidy bunk) and then the lens apparatus (an elegant carousel of polished brass).

No dust on the floors, no grime on the clockworks. Someone had visited recently.

The lantern room was a metal cage with bottle-thick leaded panes—the kind that could keep out a bolide. The platform in the middle sat empty.

"The beacon I saw was here," Zora said. "Where did it go?" She stepped out of the cage and circled the balcony—first to the side in twilight, then to the side that faced the sinking sun.

Abigail raised her flashlight. "Maybe someone will see us." She flicked out three short blinks—then three longer bursts— then three blinks again. An SOS in telegraph code.

No reply from the gloom in the valley. Her face taut, Abigail signaled again.

"We could stop here for the night," Nick said. "This tower's sturdier than our wooden fort was. Strong enough to withstand whatever did"—he leaned over the railing—"that. Should we call the others and tell them where we are?"

Zora spat at the ground and watched her saliva fall. Why weren't they already here? If they'd come and gone, they would've left her a message. Had they run into a Spiritist spy? A menhir-raising, human-sacrificing druid? A subterranean coal baron cannibal?

Unless they'd never gone this way at all.

Who'd told her and Nick where the others were headed? A girl with the skills to sabotage an airship. A girl whose father had gone to the Wastes and never returned.

"Are you sure they were coming here?" Zora asked slowly.

Abigail looked . . . wounded? Or irked? Or something else? "That's what Paige and Novalyne told me. Why would they want to trick us?"

Nick huffed. "My sister would never do that."

"I didn't say—"

When Zora quick-drew her pistol, both of her companions flinched. "Easy there," she told them. Then she flashed the pistol's beam at the valley.

From a nearby hilltop, a cobalt light winked back at her. Dash-dot-dash-dot. Three dashes. Two dashes. One dot. A pause and then more.

"Come now," Abigail translated. "While the path is clear."

The light on the hill went dark. Combing her brain for the code, Zora flashed another three-letter message: *Who?*

The beacon flickered like her own hollow's namesake. *Hurry,* and nothing else.

Abigail was already partway down the stairs. "We can make it," she shouted.

Zora kept one hand on the railing as Nick walked beside her. Even on this second, slower pass, the small, round rooms gave no clues as to the lighthouse keeper's identity. Blank white walls and bare wooden floors. An unset table and a vacant chair. A stove with no kettle and a desk with no pictures.

Abigail was stamping on the doorstep, all fired up to go, but the sun hadn't waited with her. The hill up ahead was a dark, forbidding mass. On its crest, the blue light pulsed steadily.

"I'll lead the way," said Abigail.

For Zora, the slog to the top was a fever dream. Roamers with dragonfly wings floated by her, and peridot earthbounds glowed under the snow. All the while, fatigue tugged on her limbs and scrambled her thoughts. *It was called* Revelations from the Veiled Realm. In front of her, Abigail's flashlight bobbed through the trees. *Is her father Ulysses Bell, by any chance?* Nick tripped over a root but pushed himself up. *Listening for a station named Peryton One.*

The house at the summit was three stories tall, not counting the turret and the beacon above it. Every window was black except one: an octagon set with emerald stained glass. The stone masonry had a greenish tinge, too. Serpentine, Quinn would've called it. Quarried up north and hauled through the Pass generations ago.

A horrible certainty gripped Zora.

Abigail stopped and turned her beam backward. "Now that we're here, I need to make a confession." The flashlight wavered. "I know who signaled us."

"You sold us out," Zora snarled.

Nick goggled at her and then Abigail. "It's not like that," said the girl. "She's a friend. This past fall, I heard her calling and hailed her back. When I told her about my dad, she promised to help me find him. But her enemies are hunting her, and she needs a way to slip past them. At first, I couldn't think of a way to smuggle her into the Hollows—"

"Until you discovered Nick's message," Zora finished. Was the girl a spirit-worshipping cultist or just another dupe?

"That's right. She came up with a plan to divert the airship on its flight home from Ram's Horn. She even told me how to build a gyroscopic autopilot and hook it up to the rudder. But then things went wrong, and we had to . . . improvise."

Fury and pity warred within Zora, but fury won. "You trusted her and lied to us."

Nick snapped his fingers to get their attention. "Who in the Green Abyss are y'all talking about?"

"She calls herself Peryton One," said Abigail. "My dad was

tracking her signals when he disappeared. And I never lied, though I'll own that I kept secrets from you."

The light in the window went out. The house's inhabitant must know they were here.

Zora could've run and dragged Nick along with her. They could've barricaded themselves in the lighthouse—not really a lighthouse but something much darker—and tried to wait for a rescue. But it was night, and she was spent, and neither of them had a radio. Signe would've said this reunion had been in the cards all along, and she would've been right. Zora could feel it at the base of her spine.

Plus, she had to know what her onetime client was up to now.

She walked past Abigail to the house and slammed down the cast-iron knocker. After a second that dilated to forever, the double doors swung open to the rumble of gears.

The woman in the foyer was tall. On the autumn equinox, she'd had salt and pepper hair, but now it was completely white. She wore a mink cloak over her riding clothes and an antlered pendant around her neck. She held her gold revolver at a casual angle.

Zora weighed how to address her. Hierophant of the Spiritists? Revelator of the Veiled Realm? Scion of the Nameless Mining Company?

"Good evening, Ms. Coldiron," said Evelyn Fontaine. "I gather you received my invitation. Welcome to my ancestral home and current lodgings. I'm so pleased you decided to join me."

Zora made a mocking bow. "Hey, copperhead."

14

THE FOOTPRINTS WERE VANISHING BENEATH THE FALLING SNOW. One set veered to the right, but three more ran straight ahead: the small, the smaller, and the smallest. First side by side, and then helter-skelter with shortening strides.

Quinn followed them by the light of his rifle. "The kids slowed down here. Did they lose the swarm?"

"They found something else." Paige aimed her banisher at a fourth set of tracks—not boots but little hooves. "The lamb."

Squinting past the wet streaks on his goggles, Quinn swept his beam through the woods. The prints led toward a row of pale humps that looked like burial mounds. *Across the sea and far to the north, the huldufolk dwell in their mossy houses,* Signe had told him on the first night of frost, her long hair canopying his face. *They cast their glamours on those who dare cross them, just as I've cast mine over you.*

The strides lengthened again on the far side of the mounds, now joined by a new set of prints. These were too big and deep to be human or lamb. They weren't foot-shaped or hoof-shaped, either.

Quinn ran faster. As his banisher pinged, a note blasted out from the blizzard. It sounded . . . yellowish green?

"It's a trow," Paige said. "Hang on to yourself. This is going to get weird."

The prints stretched out toward a tall, boxy shape. A house? A barn? No, a covered bridge. A putrid flash split the darkness within it, and a dissonant stench filled the air.

Quinn stumbled to a halt, and Paige stopped beside him. "Try to tune out the spirit," she said. "It's one of the types that cause synesthesia."

Sourness crawled along his skin, but he shook away the sensation. "You go left, and I'll go right?"

Paige pumped a fist and counted down with her fingers. Three, two, one . . . She angled off to one side, and he dashed toward the other. Thunder-colored bulbs lit up on his rifle.

With a chartreuse howl and a vinegar flare, the trow stormed across the bridge and divided in two. One half lumbered toward Quinn, emanating a prickly odor. He fired a ray of sonorous light, and the spirit's aura turned rancid . . . turned mushy . . . turned green. Then it was gone, and his senses were back to normal.

Paige's target was dissolving, too. Hand on her hip, she saluted him with her weapon. "Smoother than our Harvest Festival dance."

"I thought my footwork was graceful that evening." Stepping onto the bridge, he shone his beam at the shadows. No children, but no corpses, either. Just squeaky planks and the trickle of running water. Beneath the bridge's span, clots of fluorescent foam drifted: harmless creek spirits floating on toward the Hollows.

"My toes would disagree." Paige's voice bounced off the wooden walls.

"I recollect following your lead." Their familiar teasing felt reassuring out here in the Wastes. "The tracks don't pick up on the other side, so where are the kids?"

A knocking came from below. "Down here," someone whispered. Through a gap in the slats, a pair of blue eyes—Iris's— looked up at Quinn.

"Stay put." He slithered under the bridge while Paige guarded his backside. The children had squeezed into a space between the beams and the stones on the bank. Jay and Holly were holding each other, and Iris was cuddling her lamb.

"Y'all were smart to keep out of sight," Quinn said. Three of ten hiding down here, three more running off toward the valley. "Did anyone else come this way?"

"Cousin Nova was right behind us," said Holly. "But she zigged when we zagged."

That accounted for the other footprints—but not for everybody. "What about Signe?"

"She saved our lives," said Jay. "She drew the swarm off our tail."

"That sounds like her." Quinn's jugular throbbed in his neck, right where Mom would've made her incision. "And?"

The boy touched his temples, as if to summon the memory. "I thought I heard a voice—not her, someone else, something *damp*—but I couldn't tell what it said. Did you hear it, too?"

"No," said Holly and Iris.

"Maybe I hallucinated it," Jay said. "But I'm sure I saw what happened next: Ms. Janasdottir stepped backward, and the earth swallowed her whole. Then the swarm flew on by and out of sight." He laughed nervously. "I know it sounds strange. Almost like witchcraft."

Quinn chewed over that. Had the voice belonged to a water-warlock's familiar—like in *Addie the Urchin versus the Hydraulic Hexer*—or a Spiritist shadow in a secret tunnel?

"I'm sure Signe pulled off some clever trick," Paige told him. But she'd said *Signe*, not *Fairy Eyes*, so she must be worried, too. "Should we go look for her?"

"Let's wait till it's light." Signe had gambled her life to keep these kids safe; now it was his and Paige's turn to protect them. The waterbounds were still gliding downstream, and deadlier roamers might be on the prowl.

"I feel like the troll in *The Three Woolly Rams Gruff*," Holly said.

"You mean the three billy goats?" asked Paige.

"No, I'm sure they were rams."

Paige gave Holly the side-eye. "In the Hollows, there's a creature that lives under an old railroad trestle. It's half-goat, half-sheep, and half-human."

"That's three halves," the girl objected. "And you can't cross a sheep with a goat, let alone a—"

"This thing doesn't care about fractions. Nor the laws of biology, neither. It's been around since the Coal Age, and it gobbles up anybody who treads on its trestle. Some folks say a rogue sawbones stitched it together. Others say it escaped from a traveling circus. Still others say necromancers conjured it up from the nether. But all of them agree on one point: gaze into the monster's red eyes, and it'll mesmerize you to your doom."

Holly looked alarmed, so Quinn butted in. "It's a myth," he told her.

"Ranger Tate swore he saw it," said Paige.

"Ranger Tate was pulling your leg, just like you're pulling hers."

Holly relaxed visibly, but Iris seemed disappointed. Jay wasn't paying attention; instead, he'd leaned over the edge of the bank.

The waterbounds sank into the creek, leaving trails of bubbles behind. Where did those spirits go when they reached the sea? Were the oceans covered with shining foam? And what leviathans lurked in their depths?

"Cock-a-doodle-doo, little glow-slicks," Paige said with a showy motion. Then she took out her radio and twisted its knob. "Hey, can anyone hear me?"

The device made a medley of hisses and hums.

"It might work better without this"—Quinn rapped on a beam—"in the way."

"A brilliant observation. I detect your sister's influence." Paige pulled herself up the side of the bridge until only her boots were in sight. "Here's *my* footwork, Pine-Box." After one final kick, her heels disappeared.

Quinn and the children scurried out from under the planks to watch her climb. The blizzard had stopped, and the sky had brightened. Downhill, the creek flowed on out of view, an onyx path between two powdered banks.

When Paige reached the roof, she raised her antenna. A faint, tinny garble came from her speaker. "Nova! Is that you?"

The radio buzzed in reply.

"Tell Fairy Eyes I said hello." Paige flashed Quinn the okay sign. "We caught up with the kids and Little Woolly—they're all safe. Foxtails and your brother went to . . ." More garble.

"Oh, you spoke with her?" A long series of fuzzy noises. "I'm on board with that. See you soon!"

"What's going on?" Iris shouted.

Paige tried to lower herself from the roof but lost her grip and fell into a snowdrift. As Quinn helped her up, she grabbed his arms and twirled him around, her face glowing with pride. "Your sis and your honey-pie are fine. Radio Girl and Fiddler Boy, too. Nova thanked me—thanked *us*—for finding her cousins. And she convinced the others to go with my plan. Forget the valley and the Ruined Town—we're meeting down by the river."

♈

They followed the creek's bends all morning, past ice-rimmed pools and tea-stained rapids, past rocky shelves with frozen glazing. Between the lamb's nibbling and Holly's concussion, their little band moved glacially. And yet Quinn took heart from the schools of minnows swimming downstream. From a woodpecker drumming against a tree. From an otter den and a beaver dam.

Even in the Wastes, life endured.

When the five of them stopped for a meal of stale biscuits and dried apple rings, he drew Paige aside and shared Mr. Vandy's final warning. "Someone tried to send the airship astray. Maybe Jay overheard the saboteur tracking us. We'd be sitting ducks for an ambush. We've got no hunting rifle, no shotgun, no pneumatic pistol."

"I don't need a popgun—I'll fight this Spiritist with my fists." Paige showed off her shadowboxing skills. "I've done it before."

"Didn't you break your hand with your first punch?"

"Yeah, but I won." Abruptly, she was as grave as a Prosser family reunion. "Let's watch our backs without scaring the youngsters. They've been through too much already."

Iris sidled up to them, her lips purple with raspberry jelly. "What are you whispering about?"

"Romance," said Paige. "He wants my thoughts on a ballad he wrote for his fair elven lady. There's lots of lines about smooching."

"Ugh." The girl beat a swift retreat.

"Keep a lookout for the others," Quinn called after her. Then he spoke in a hush. "How did we wind up babysitting three kids and a lamb?"

Paige slapped his back. "Good practice for your destiny."

"Don't you start." First his mom, then his sister, and now his oldest friend. "Or I'll bring up how you've gone googly-eyed for a certain spirit-senser."

Her expression turned broody. "I can't tell if she feels the same way." She smiled ruefully. "But in case she does . . . what's it like having a spooky girlfriend?"

"My only complaint is that fate keeps splitting us up." He gave Paige a light punch on the shoulder, the way she always did to him. "For what it's worth, I think Novalyne would be lucky to have you. You're the bravest apprentice Spotter in the Hollows."

"That's mighty kind of you." Paige stuck her fingers in her mouth and whistled to the children. "Pack up, y'all. Let's try to beat your cousins there."

Taking point, she regaled them with a stream of half-truths (she might've seen an altie in Triplet Creek, but she hadn't ridden it like a water horse) and blatant lies (she'd never dueled a mermaid, Zora wasn't a werefox, and Quinn didn't sleep in a coffin). Meanwhile, he kept an eye on their tail. Around noon, a bobcat slunk past them; soon after, a deer stalked through the trees.

Quinn heard the river before he saw it: a steady rushing sound beyond the next curve in the creek. Iris tore on ahead, and he caught up with her on the bank. Below them, brown water eddied and churned. She threw in a stick, and it swirled away.

"What now?" he asked.

Paige walked along the edge of the bank, waving for them to come. "Nova said to keep going till we found a likely-looking shelter."

"The river's rising," he said. "I hope the thaw doesn't stir up anything on the bottom."

"Don't worry—waterbounds are my specialty." She turned back to the children. "But don't stand too close once the sun sets. One time, Pine-Box and Fairy Eyes went nightswimming in this very river—without his banisher—and a merrow nearly stole him away."

Iris giggled, while Holly looked scandalized. "That didn't happen," Quinn said. Not all of it, anyhow.

The river widened and slowed as it ran through a line of timber pilings. On the bank stood a staved-in tollhouse. *TWO BITS TO CROSS*, read the sign on the gate, but the bridge beyond ended in midair.

Paige trooped on through the snow, and the rest of them trailed after her.

"Have you noticed there aren't any footprints?" Jay asked. "No one's passed through here today."

"We had a head start on the others," said Paige. "They ran farther north when the swarm attacked." But she sounded fretful, and Quinn understood why. Signe and Novalyne should've outpaced them. Maybe Zora and her companions, too.

A pall fell over their journey. Holly's head drooped, Iris's stride faltered, and Paige's wellspring of chatter ran dry. Scanning the map in his mind's eye, Quinn tried to chart their progress so far. If they all met back up without any complications, a two-day voyage still lay ahead. And their new route led through the Lost Gorges—a gauntlet of roamer-haunted cliffs and waterbound maelstroms.

As his mood ebbed to its lowest point, he saw a slate-roofed building among the willows. It was set back from the river's edge on a stagnant canal. Two wooden doors faced the water: one wide, one narrow. Painted-over windows hid the interior.

"Howdy there!" Paige hollered. When no one answered, she trotted along the overgrown towpath and up to the smaller door. It opened on her first try.

Quinn peered past her into a lightless room. It smelled like a tomb no one had opened for a hundred years. Inside sat a hearse-sized thing draped with a canvas shroud.

At his elbow, Iris switched on her carbide lamp. The light from its flame washed over coils of rope and stacks of lumber. Metal bins, wooden barrels, and ceramic jugs. A windup crow with agate eyes. Oars, nets, fishing poles, and machetes.

Paige yanked away the canvas, unveiling a paddlewheel steamer raised up on blocks. The boat had a pilot house in the stern, two benches in the bow, and a smokestack in between. The hull was maroon with white trim, as were the sunburst paddleboxes on either side. Cursive letters on the prow spelled out *MUSKELLUNGE*.

"I think we've struck gold," Paige said. "We can steam homeward tomorrow morning."

"Is it river-worthy?" The last time Quinn had traveled by boat, he'd wound up in the drink—and Nevan McBrain had met a watery end.

Paige inspected the hull. "I'll patch it up. You *do* realize I spent all last summer on rivers and lakes with my boss." She stroked the silver boiler. "This here's a walking beam engine in tip-top condition. Foxtails can fix any snags—question is, what do we burn?"

The children rummaged through the boathouse. "There's something funny-smelling in the jugs," Iris reported. "And coal in the bins. Would it still be good?"

"It's lasted a few hundred million years already," Quinn said. "It'll be fine. I bet we've found the hideaway of a Coal Age bootlegger."

Jay unfurled a piece of dark cloth: a flag emblazoned with a bloody-horned unicorn skull.

"Or we're commandeering a pirate boat," Quinn conceded. The Red Banks Gang or the Cave-in-Rock Outlaws could've absconded upriver from the Rangers.

Paige clapped her hands. "Lamb Chop, fetch a hammer and nails. Rabbit Ears, find me some pitch."

Iris and Jay scampered to follow her orders. "What about me?" Holly asked.

"You should take it easy," Quinn said. "While I check your wound."

The girl sat on a barrel, and he gently removed her bandage.

The gash on her forehead hadn't closed. "This needs stitching up," he told her.

Holly bit her lip but then nodded. "The medical kit's in my pack."

He found the black bag tucked beneath a collection of books and journals. "What are these?"

"I salvaged them from the airship. I couldn't bear to leave everything behind. Most of them are chronicles of my people." Her voice cracked. "But I also brought my favorite novel."

Quinn held up a book titled *Alice of Blue Gables*. "This one, I'm guessing. I always liked it myself." He grabbed a jug, sat next to Holly, and threaded a needle. "Signe and I started reading a book on this trip, but we haven't finished it yet."

"What's it about?"

"A mystery involving a ghostly possession." He swabbed the girl's forehead with pirate moonshine.

"Have you ever done this before?" she asked anxiously.

"Many times." Quinn lifted the needle to her brow. "Just not on a living person," he couldn't resist adding.

"*What?*"

"I grew up in a funeral home. Try to stay still." She jerked a little as he sewed the first stitch. "Have you read the other books about Blue Gables?"

The girl forgot to flinch. "There are more?"

"I'll find you copies when we reach the Hollows." He bandaged her wound again. Maybe this dreadful journey would still end happily for her and her cousins.

Holly gave him one of the journals. "I hope you finish your book with Ms. Janasdottir soon, but you can read this in the meantime."

He glanced at the cover—*The Diary of Violet Martin*—and then leafed through the pages until a passage jumped out at him. *Fall 67, Year 2: A girl named Jessamine arrived in Ram's Horn with a fiddle case on her shoulder. She played a haunting tune and then asked if we'd ever heard of the spirit rifts . . .*

♈

Twilight came and went with no new arrivals. Holly dozed off in the boat's bow, and Paige started greasing the engine's gears. With Jay and Iris in tow, Quinn set out on patrol along the canal. In its dingy waters, gleaming salamanders wriggled. Beyond the willows, blue-green lights flitted under the river's surface.

Iris tugged on his sleeve. "Can I carry one of your gadgets? Cousin Nova has her gift, and Cousin Nick has his music. You and Ms. Zhu have your glass guns. I've got nothing."

Quinn almost said no—almost said she was too young to fight spirits—but then reconsidered. She'd lived under constant siege, standing sentry at night in the fort's towers. And she put him in mind of a younger Zora. He'd missed out on growing up with his sister, but he knew how much she'd wanted a way to defend herself.

"I'll be careful with it," Iris pleaded.

Quinn plucked a grenade from his bandolier and gave it to her. "Don't use this unless all else is lost. You only get one chance to hit your target, so make it count."

She held the device in her palms as if it were a magical geode. "I will, I promise."

He offered Jay a grenade, too, but the boy shook his head.

"I don't mean to sound ungrateful, but your weapons hurt my eardrums."

Like they hurt Signe's eyes. Like they'd hurt Novalyne's head. "I have a hunch," Quinn said. "I think you bear the Mark of the Syzygy. But you don't see spirits or sense them with your mind; you hear them."

The boy took a deep breath and nodded. "The clairaudience started the night we fought the hounts."

"You never told us that," Iris said.

"At first, I couldn't believe the eidolons chose *me*," Jay said. "But then I heard the derechos outside the airship and the gwyllion under the schoolhouse. Right now, I can hear the little waterbounds fizzing in the canal and the bigger ones moaning in the river."

Iris hugged him. "Two in one generation! Cousin Nova will be thrilled."

"Signe, too," Quinn said, but then a new worry struck him. "You said you heard a voice right before she disappeared?"

"I thought I did. But spirits can't talk, can they?"

"One does." *The harbinger,* Quinn thought but didn't say. *The Voice of the Spirits.* "I'll explain when this all is over." The willows rustled, and the river murmured—wordlessly, thank the stars. Keeping a poker face, he herded his little flock to the boathouse.

Paige was roping the steamer to a winch. "I've filled the hold with coal and cleared the webs from the paddles. Do you reckon the others got lost?"

"Here's what I think," he snapped. "I think we should've stuck with the plan we settled on yesterday. I think we'll be trapped in the gorges if this tub gives up the ghost. I think you've mucked everything up."

No, he shouldn't have said that. She was trying her best to keep them alive.

Surprise and hurt showed on Paige's face. Jay and Iris looked the way Quinn used to feel when his parents argued, and the lamb was gazing at him with its sad eyes.

"You could've shared all that sooner," Paige said stiffly. "Nova told me the whole team favored my idea, but you should try hailing them."

"I'm sorry," Quinn said. "Just nerves. The river it is."

He fetched the radio, and they huddled around him. When he turned on the power, the speaker chirped like a cricket. "Novalyne?" he said. "Abigail?"

"Mr. Prosser," said a crystalline voice: Evelyn Fontaine's. "I'm surprised to hear from you this way—I expected to see you in the flesh. Your sister was kind enough to drop by."

For a moment, Quinn was too astonished to speak. "Where is she?" he said, at last.

"At my home away from home in Thirteen Point Valley." The woman's tone was pleasant—if he hadn't met her before, he would've said friendly. "Are you and your enchanting sweetheart close by? I'd be delighted to give you refuge from the spirits."

His shock gave way to anger. "I'm not falling for that." *Keep her talking,* he told himself; she adored the sound of her voice. "Isn't one of your spies following us?"

She laughed. "Not this time. I didn't need one, thanks to Ms. Putnam."

The children gawked at the radio, bewildered. "Abigail works for you?" Quinn asked numbly.

"For Peryton One, which happens to be my alias. She's even more gullible than you and your sister."

"If you hurt my friends," Paige shouted, "I'll stuff you and mount your antlered head in my boss's lodge!"

"That must be Ms. Zhu," said Evelyn Fontaine. "Still so impetuous, bless your heart. Pardon me for neglecting your invitation."

Quinn caught Paige's eye and drew his thumb across his throat. "Is Nicholas there, too?"

"The sheep's in the meadow; the cow's in the corn." The woman recited the nursery rhyme with her phony priest intonation. "But where's the boy who looks after the sheep? He's under a haystack, fast asleep."

That wasn't helpful at all. "Can I talk to Zora?" he asked.

"I'm afraid she and her fiddler friend are indisposed. They're so precious together: a redheaded girl and a little boy blue." The woman sighed. "Speaking of puppy love, why hasn't Ms. Janasdottir spoken up yet?"

Quinn said nothing.

"How curious. I gather my arrangements have gone awry. Still, I have a sneaking fondness for you, Mr. Prosser—I'm sentimental that way—so let me offer a word of advice. Don't try to find us; we'll be gone tomorrow. I'll keep an eye on your sister and Mr. Martin, so save yourselves and make for the Hollows." There was a muffled crash in the background. "My duties as a host call. Farewell and good luck."

With a click, the signal went dead.

Quinn pulled at his hair. Everything had gone wrong. The crash. The swarm. The voice in the night, and now this.

"Who was *that*?" asked Iris.

"The worst person in the Hollows," said Quinn. "She'll use any human or spirit to get what she wants." Like the secrets of

Zora's inventions and Signe's talents. Or hostages for bargaining with the Judges. Or a chance to settle old scores.

Paige kicked over a barrel. "She's got a day's lead on us, and we still don't have a clue why Signe and Nova are late."

Quinn reached a decision—likely his most reckless ever, but Zora would've done this for him. *Had* done it for him once before. "Keep trying to hail them tonight and head on downriver in the morning. I'm off to the valley."

Jay raised a finger. "Listen—"

"You can't go running through the Wastes at night by your lonesome." Paige stood in his way. "You'll never make it."

"Then tell Signe I—"

"Shut up, both of you!" shouted Jay. Iris's jaw dropped, and Holly sat up in the boat, but he froze them with a glare. "Don't you hear it?"

Deathwatch beetles tapped in the walls, and an owl hooted in the distance. Quinn traded looks with Paige. "Hear what?" he asked.

"Footsteps. There's one." Jay counted to six under his breath. "And another. Its stride must be as long as a hill."

In a daze, Quinn walked past Paige and cracked open a window. Far upriver, a green dawn was breaking—three hours shy of midnight.

He couldn't leave the kids with that thing coming for them. Ready or not, the steamboat was their only hope.

"It caught up with us," he said. "That's the titan."

15

INVISIBLE ROOTS HAD GROWN WHILE SIGNE SLEPT, BINDING HER to the dirt floor. She couldn't reach for her glasses or turn her face from the tree in the ceiling. She tried to call out, but phantom tendrils had sealed her lips shut.

This had to be a dream—a trance, a night terror—and yet she felt completely lucid. Every detail seemed sharper than mundane reality, from the shaft of moonlight dappling the tree to the scritch of branches scraping the rooftop.

As Signe struggled to lift a finger, a loamy smell overwhelmed her nostrils. The ceiling peeled back, and the walls melted. Grass sprouted around her, green blades frosting in the night air. High above, the pinnacle transformed into an icy hall rimmed with battlements.

Novalyne was supposed to be keeping watch. Where had she gone?

The blackest train I ever saw, sang the radio, *went down the underground line.*

The tree folded up like a parasol and telescoped into the earth, leaving behind a sinkhole. A stray fingerbone tumbled into its depths with a plunk.

In the pines, in the pines, where the sun will never shine.

A heavy weight pushed against Signe's sternum. The Old Hag from the legends had returned to steal her breath.

You'll shiver when the cold wind blows.

She was shivering right now. A sudden dread of the sinkhole gripped her. If she fell in its maw, she'd be lost to the darkness forever, like a prisoner trapped in one of those bottle-shaped dungeons with the deceptively beautiful name. An oubliette?

Your soul will never be found.

That wasn't how the lyrics went. Some versions said, *His body I never could find,* but she and Novalyne had buried Ulysses Bell's skeleton. Other versions said, *Her head was caught in a—*

An unseen force dragged Signe face-first toward the sink-hole. The frost on the grass stung her skin and bled through her clothes. She cried for help, but no words came out—only stifled grunts.

Keep your eyes open, said a watery voice, the same one she'd heard yesterday. The same one she'd heard the night the card-reader had told her fortune.

The sinkhole's gullet was lined with mossy stones. At its bottom, black water spun in a vortex. A few heartbeats more, and she'd plunge headlong into that whirlpool.

Look into the abyss, said the voice.

Signe fixed her gaze on it, and the trance paralyzing her shattered. She clawed at the ground, digging her fingernails into the dirt.

Don't blink, or the watcher will catch you.

Her hair spilled into the hole, and the rest of her almost followed. Below her, the water turned glassy.

Lead it where it can't hurt anybody. Like you did with the swarm.

Lead it away from . . . mm . . . mm . . . the Folk of the Ram and your people.

Signe sucked in lungfuls of air. It tasted stale and dank—but still heavenly, after the Old Hag's suffocating pressure. "Lead what?"

Me.

That left Signe all the more mystified. "Who are you?"

Nnn, the voice gurgled. *Nnn . . .*

"I'll help you if you tell me how."

Twin points broke the surface, and a figure rose through the ripples. Spiral horns crowned its head; waterlogged hair concealed its features. The clothes on its back were tattered and soggy.

Signe's fear flowed away as pity filled her heart. "You're not an eidolon, are you?"

The figure shook its downcast head.

"Are you a ghost?" She had her doubts about the dead returning, but stranger doings had come to pass. What if a past bearer of the Mark was guiding her from beyond the grave?

This time, the figure shrugged, launching new ripples with its shoulders.

How could it not know whether it was a ghost? Perhaps the answer was more complicated than yes or no. "Do you have a name?"

The figure lifted its chin. Behind the mask of damp hair, a pair of blue fires burned. *Nnn.* The sound dripped with frustration and sorrow. *No . . .*

In a flash, Signe understood. Just as abruptly, she realized the danger she was in. She couldn't say the truth out loud. Or dwell on it in her own mind, not while her enemy could read it there. She had to bury the thought until she found a way to save herself—and Novalyne, too.

But first she had to be certain. "Can I see your face?"

The figure raised a sodden glove to push back its hair . . .

Then Signe woke up, off balance and disoriented. She was standing in front of the tree, her arms outstretched and her fingers touching the bark. Everything was back where it belonged. The ceiling and the branches growing through it. The viny walls. The empty chair. And Novalyne, camped by the shack's only window.

The young woman looked on with a curious expression. "You were sleepwalking."

Signe sank into the chair, and only then did she recall that Abigail's father had died where she was sitting. "I had spells of somnambulism as a child." An honest statement, as far as it went. "Especially when I spent the night in unfamiliar places. One time we stayed at an inn, and my parents caught me marching toward the door, sound asleep with a rag bunny under my arm." A room in an inn sounded wonderful right about now. She'd gone to bed with her coat for a quilt and her pack for a pillow. A clawfoot tub and steaming water would be even better—she hadn't taken a warm bath since she'd left Hot Springs Hollow.

"You were talking, too," said Novalyne. "Though none of it made any sense."

Signe tipped the chair back on its hind legs distractedly. Had she given herself away to her hidden listener? "I always had vivid dreams when I walked in my sleep." Also true, if not entirely forthright.

"What was this one about?"

"Falling." Signe looked at her pocket-watch: halfway through the small hours. Time to end this discussion. "It's my turn to stand sentry. You ought to get some sleep."

Novalyne set the radio on the windowsill. "I tried hailing Paige and Abigail. No luck, and the battery is nearly dead. But if I know my kin, they'll turn up eventually."

Signe felt sure no one—no *human*—would be showing up here, but she kept that to herself. "I'll try again later." She brought the chair to the window as Novalyne settled on the floor. The aurora hung low on the horizon, glimmering wanly over the valley but brighter in the river's direction. Which of those paths had her friends taken?

Once Novalyne's breathing slowed, Signe switched on the radio. If she reached Paige—or Quinn or Zora—she'd deliver a coded warning. *I'm caught up in Carson van Patten's story*, she could say. *I need to finish it by myself.*

"Come in," a voice rasped over the airwaves. Too deep and hoarse to be Quinn or Nicholas, let alone any of the others, and yet familiar. Someone she'd met in the Hollows, for certain.

"Can you hear me?" Signe asked quietly. Novalyne stirred but then rolled over.

"Faith!" shouted the voice. "Who's there in the name of—" The signal faded.

"This is Signe Janasdottir. Tell the Rangers we're stranded in the Wastes. Tell them Walter Vandy died bringing us down alive."

"Jinx begone, it's the spirit-seer! I've been chanting hexes for you since Ranger Tate told me—"

"Never mind that. We're searching for you," a second voice broke in, this one high and nasally. Signe had heard it before, too, though she couldn't put a name to it. "We're on the forager trails east of"—static engulfed the signal, but then it came back—"Coldiron and Mr. Epps. Where should we send the rescue parties?"

Signe hedged her bets. "One up the river, one to the Ruined Town, and one toward the valley between. But wait outside the town until you hear from me again."

There was no reply. The radio had died during her final message.

♈

Signe spent her third dawn in the Wastes on guard, watching over the panorama below. A plume of black smoke was rising from the ridge beyond the valley. Had her friends tracked the blue light to those hills?

She quashed a pang of yearning. When the smoke dissipated, she lowered her spyglass and roused her companion.

Novalyne sat up, instantly alert. "Any news of my brother or cousins?"

"No word from your kin." Not quite a lie, in either sense.

"It's inexplicable. We all agreed on this meeting spot—unless our signals got crossed."

"Maybe you'll see something I overlooked." Signe held out the spyglass.

But Novalyne refused it. "I trust you. So, what now? Wait here, push on, or retrace our steps?"

"I believe we're on our own," Signe said. "All we can do is keep walking toward the Ruined Town. Once we reach the Hollows, the Rangers and Spotters can help us find the others."

For now, she'd lead her adversary where it so clearly wanted to go: the old haunts of the long-gone scholars.

But along the way, she'd craft her own plan to defeat it.

"I suppose you're right." Novalyne packed up her banisher and the dead radio. "You seem preoccupied. What's on your mind?"

There was an easy question. "I'm afraid I won't see the people I love again. Just like Mr. Bell never did." She bowed her head toward the antenna outside. "Should we . . ."

Novalyne whistled an all-too-recognizable tune. "In the pines, in the pines," she sang. "Where the sun never shines, we said farewell to Ulysses Bell."

Signe shivered again. "Your girl, your girl," she improvised in her off-key soprano. "We'll tell her where you sleep forever."

Leaving a bouquet of bloodroot flowers and toothwort blooms by the grave, they turned their steps toward the pinnacle. On the far side, they found a road cut through the mountain's face. It led them down to the forest where a pack of herns had stalked Mr. Bell. The trees still bore the long, looping grooves carved by the roamers' tines.

Every hour and hairpin curve brought them closer to the Ruined Town.

"You mentioned a university," said Novalyne as they passed the husk of a flivver with four missing wheels. "Could we learn more about the eidolons there?"

Signe thought fast, but in the back of her mind. "As far as I know, the Spotters never found records of them in the college library or faculty halls." She didn't bring up Maxwell Doran, the etherics professor who'd gone investigating reports of ghost-lights. "The Great Wakening killed everyone in the town. Nobody but relic hunters visits there anymore."

"That's unfortunate." Novalyne pulled off one of her gloves and rubbed a greenish bruise on the back of her hand.

"Ouch," Signe said without thinking.

Her companion rolled up her sleeve to display a constellation of pear-colored marks. "They're all over me. Must be from the crash."

Signe bared her own forearm. "I have a few myself."

"Yours look more indigo."

This conversation had drifted toward treacherous waters. "What did you and Nicholas do for fun in Ram's Horn?" Signe asked. Then she cringed inwardly at her own awkward question.

Novalyne looked as if she were rifling through old boxes in a dark attic. "We'd sit by the fire while we kept watch. He'd build doodads and dream up silly songs for our cousins. I'd practice picking out roamers in the gap with my eyes closed. How about you and your friends?"

Behind them, a branch snapped and fell into the snow. "Quinn and I wander the byways in our wagons. We watch old-timey bands, visit roving booksellers, and take long strolls in the moonlight, searching for spirits. He patches up stuffed animals—the fluffy kind, not Claire Zhu's taxidermied chimeras—for the children we meet, and I scour secondhand shops for dark clothes. Paige is our social moth, always up for hoedowns and hootenannies. Zora spends most of her time with her nose in her gears, but she's started letting her hair down. I don't really know Abigail, though I gather she's fond of radio dramas."

"I can't wait to see how your people live."

"I promise you will." Signe stuck a hand in her cuff and crossed her fingers. Perhaps for luck or perhaps for lying. "At this pace, we'll reach the Border Hollows tomorrow."

As they walked the switchbacks, Signe kept talking to drown out her thoughts and head off any troublesome questions. She began with stories about growing up as the lastborn and least hidebound of seven (what if she'd been a twin herself, she wondered), segued into tales of her school days (she'd had two of her siblings as teachers, but no kindred souls among her classmates), and then moved on to recipes for her favorite vegetable dishes ("You mean you don't eat meat?" Novalyne asked incredulously). But nothing about spirits or her vision or the surprises stashed in the handle of her parasol.

"Did I tell you" — she cast about for another topic — "how I've decorated my wagon? It's like my own little enchanted realm." No, no, that bordered on dangerous ground.

"We've reached the outskirts of town," Novalyne blessedly interrupted. By the side of the road sat crumpled masses that had once been houses — stately ones with eyebrow-like dormers, wraparound porches, and gingerbread woodwork.

Signe averted her gaze from a blank-faced doll peering out through a basement window. "Something monstrous passed this way back in Year Zero."

"A spire," Novalyne said with an air of finality. "Do you know what caused the Great Wakening?"

No point in feigning ignorance. "A spirit that speaks through telepathy and can summon its kind to wreak havoc. It opened a gate from its universe to ours."

That discovery had set the Hollows abuzz, but Novalyne took it in stride. "Jessamine the Fiddler conjectured as much.

She told my ancestors she heard a voice in her head on the Night of Shining Death. But how did this spirit set loose its kin?"

"The stars aligned on a vernal equinox." So Nevan McBrain had told Signe just before the harbinger had beckoned his doom. "And our worlds intersected."

"Why then? Surely the stars have converged a million times over the eons."

Mr. Epps reckoned so as well. "I know a Spotter who thinks other Wakenings took place long ago," said Signe. "One that inundated the lost Olden World cities of Atlantis and Ys and Lyonesse. One that wiped out all the giant mammals—the ground sloths and mammoths, the dire wolves and saber-toothed tigers. And so on back to the dinosaurs and the Deep Time."

Novalyne stepped over the bones of a bike. "If that's true, where did the spirits from those Wakenings go?"

Signe had asked Mr. Epps the same question, but he hadn't hazarded a guess. "Perhaps the eidolons drove them away each time as part of an endless cosmic cycle."

"But that's all in the distant past. What sparked a new Wakening after thousands of years with no spirits?"

"I have no idea." Did Signe's eavesdropper already know the answer, or was that the secret it sought? "Do you?"

"Maybe humans did something to cause it," said Novalyne. "Out of careless greed or worldly pride. Or both."

Cynical, but possibly correct. The final days of the Before Time were lost to history. Could the answer lay buried in the—

Signe pictured black sheep gamboling in meadows and jumping over fences. *Have you any wool? Yes ma'am, yes ma'am, three bags full. One for the hunter, one for the wiz, and one for . . .*

At the next bend, they came to a mansion standing with a precarious lean. The elemental under the foundation had preserved the siding from termites and the gambrel roof from rot. Beside the front door, a brass plate glinted in the afternoon sun.

"Can you read that from here?" Signe asked.

"It says *Fannin Manor*." Novalyne smiled. "Should we peek inside?"

Signe was set to protest—they needed to reach the college by nightfall for her plan to work—but then she relented. She'd bide her time to lull her enemy.

Together, they crossed the lifeless yard to the porch. The knob fell off in Signe's grip, but her gentle push was enough to open the door. She immediately regretted touching it.

In the foyer, three shadowed figures hung from ropes tied to the second-floor railing. A liquid was dripping from their feet and running along the oddly angled floor.

At first, Signe took the shapes for corpses and the fluid for blood or worse. Then she saw that the figures were cloth effigies stuffed with straw and dressed in water-stained finery. Above them, damp splotches showed on the plaster ceiling: snowmelt from a leak in the roof.

"A mother, a father, and a daughter," mused Novalyne. "What does it mean?"

Drip, drip.

"A sort of memorial?" said Signe. "Elementals don't leave any bodies behind."

"I think you're right. Look at that." Beneath the smallest effigy lay a black case garlanded with blue ribbons. Novalyne stepped forward, but Signe reached the case first. The stenciling on its side said *Mildred Fannin*. The ribbons were all first prizes in the Sorghum County Fair Music Competition.

Drip, drip.

Signe undid the case's latches. The red plush inside held a violin with shiny metal strings and a bow with mother-of-pearl inlay. Had they belonged to the Fiddler Girl?

"Aluminum," Novalyne said in answer to Signe's unspoken question. "Violet Martin wrote in her journal that the wayfarer played on strings made from gut. Not metal. This fiddle's owner was nobody special." She turned her back on the effigies and walked out the door.

Drip, drip.

Signe closed the case and followed with a parting glance at the hanging figures. They swayed ever so slightly in the draft from the porch.

She pulled the door shut behind her.

"Why do you suppose the spirits prey on this world?" asked Novalyne.

Because they transcend us, their worshippers claimed. *Because they're monsters*, Zora would've insisted. "I don't believe they're innately evil," Signe said. "Merely driven by instinct. But the one that unleashed them is different. It's animated by malice and cruelty." She ran her finger along the goggles in her pocket. "I generally favor peaceful resolutions, but I'd destroy that thing myself."

"And what if it can't be killed?"

Signe had no answer for her.

Farther down the road, they passed a scattering of bungalows, all as dilapidated as their grander counterparts. Then Novalyne stopped and frowned at a farmhouse the spire had crushed like a robin's egg. In the glare from the setting sun, her hazel eyes almost looked green.

Did Signe see a flash of recognition reflected in them?

"This one." Novalyne strode to the house and ferreted through the wreckage, digging out seemingly random items. A coffin-style radio cabinet. A scrap of floral-patterned wallpaper. A steamer trunk covered with stickers.

"Are you searching for something specific?" Signe asked.

Her companion opened the trunk and scooped out a sheaf of pulp magazines. "These are garbage." With a sniff of disgust, she flung them on the ground.

Signe picked up one of the magazines. *Eerie Tales, Volume 3, 1925.* The lead story was "The Shadow at the Bottom of the Well." In different circumstances, she might've found the title intriguing. Here and now, it struck her as a bad omen.

Novalyne snatched up a book, read its cover, and tossed it away. "More trash." It was *The Viridescent Ray* by Juliette Verne.

"I wonder who lived here," said Signe.

"It doesn't matter." Novalyne's voice was heavy with some dark emotion. "They've been dead and gone for more than a hundred years." She picked her way out of the debris. "Come on. Time's a-wasting."

She'd left the trunk open to the sky and the elements. Signe thought that was a small tragedy—more pages from the past lost forever—but the day was too short for lingering.

♈

The Ruined Town matched its name and dismal reputation. Every house was abandoned and falling apart; every storefront had been smashed and pillaged. The shells of carriages and tin lizzies clogged the streets, testaments to failed escapes. The movie palace marque still advertised a double feature of *The Silver Rush* and *The Apparition of the Operetta*, but the ticket office was empty, and the lobby's carpet had festered to sludge.

Signe made sure not to disturb the snowy lumps along the sidewalks and alleys.

At the gates of a fallow park, Novalyne sat on a bench to study the map. Behind her, a bronze soldier stood at attention on a stone pedestal. He had a bayonet in his hand and a bird's nest on his helmet.

"Which way to campus?" Signe asked.

"This must be the courthouse." Novalyne shook the map at a brick building with a lopped-off tower fit only for bats. "The college should be up that avenue."

Signe took the bench opposite, with her back to the setting sun. "Let's stay here just a while longer." If her gambit failed — or if Ulysses Bell's diary had led her astray about where to take shelter — then this would be her last evening on earth. On balance, she'd had a fair seventeen-year run. She'd been raised by parents who'd done the best they knew how, even if they'd never understood her. She'd received a blessing from fate — a gift for helping others. She'd found friendship and love and a worthy calling.

But she was scared. She wasn't ready. Would never be ready.

"It's almost dark," said Novalyne.

"We can spare a few minutes to talk." Signe gripped her parasol tighter. No more biting her tongue or submerging her thoughts. "So, what did you really tell Paige and Abigail? Did you even hail them at all?"

Her companion's face twisted into a rictus. "Oh, I did. I told them what they wanted to hear. I sent Abigail off to the valley to dig for news of her missing father." A low, hard laugh at that. "And I sent Paige down to the river so she could show off her skills at spotting waterbounds."

A polar chill swept over Signe. Deep down, she'd hoped she was wrong. "They'll still make it home. I have faith in my friends."

"If you put your trust in Abigail, I fear you'll be disappointed. She's the pawn of a queen who lost her castle." A green vein bulged on Novalyne's brow. "They're all doomed, anyway. Death lies in their paths, and I set the titan on their trail."

In spite of her despair, Signe kept fishing for answers. "Why did you bring me here?"

"Partly for information and partly for amusement." Her adversary held out a hand and wriggled its fingers, as if it were pulling on strings. "But mostly to turn you into my marionette."

"Like you've done with that body you're wearing."

They contemplated each other. "Yes, I made her my medium," said the thing speaking through Novalyne. "I discovered how to control her with the chords I use to summon my kin, much like *her* brother sways them with his fiddle-scraping. I stitched the threads of her mind and bound her with her own power. Plundered her memories and locked her inner light in an abyss." The fingers closed into a fist. "And yet you repelled me each time I tried to enthrall you. I suppose because your talent is different, in the eyes instead of the brain." It was gloating—but also stalling for sunset. "So tonight, I'll cut your strings. Maybe I'll find other puppets in your Hollows—other victims cursed with your mark.

And think on this in your last moments: you and your friends led me to my vessel."

Signe felt sick to her stomach. "When did you possess her?"

"The night before we flew from Ram's Horn." Another laugh, cold and inhuman. "I did it right under your watch as my kindred pulsed to a celestial synchronicity. You were spying on her through a telescope, but I clouded your sight for a moment. Then I cracked the crown of her psyche and tuned her mind to my resonances."

"I see now." Signe gave harmony one final chance. "Why not leave us alone? The spirits rule most of our world already."

"You creatures have weapons against me, and my hunger for life is never-ending. Once you're gone, and I take the key to the gate, I'll slay the eidolons while they slumber and find new universes for my kin to devour."

Those words settled Signe's resolve. "What should I call you when I cast you out? The harbinger or the Voice of the Spirits?"

Her adversary reached its hand up a tattered sleeve. "I found a fortuneteller's deck before we left the fort." It pulled out a card depicting a starry spiral. "You can call me the Skywheel, but nothing will save you. The sun is down, and your time is up." Then it stood and hummed—not a melody but a drone.

The ruins burst into green flames, and a chorus of howls swelled from below.

PART FOUR

THE LOOM OF TANGLED THREADS

16

"YOU MUST BE WEARY AND FAMISHED," SAID EVELYN FONTAINE. "Come on in." She stepped aside and made an after-you gesture with her gun.

As Zora walked into the foyer, electric chandeliers winked on overhead. From the paneled walls, portraits of hard-faced, well-dressed folk sneered down at her. Generation after generation of coal barons, each coronated with antlers. Beside her, Nick gandered at the bronze stag's head mounted above the door.

But Abigail only had eyes for the golden revolver. "Ms. Peryton, why do you have that?"

"I find it prudent to arm myself against both humans and spirits." Their host rested her empty hand on a derringer-style banisher at her hip. "I advise my guests to behave wisely, too."

Zora kept her anger in check, though it was a struggle. "Her name's not Peryton," she told her companions. "It's Fontaine." No, call her *Evelyn*—she didn't deserve any deference.

The woman dipped her head in acknowledgment.

"That means nothing to me," said Nick.

"She's the skunk who wants to tame the spirits and bring down the Judges," Zora said. "One of her spies sent a pair of spires after the *Reynardine*. That's why we left the Hollows with a skeleton crew and no doctor." She rounded on Abigail. "And why the two of us wound up coming along for the ride. Was that the plan? Did *you* hide the lure on the ship?"

"I didn't know what it would do." Abigail looked stricken. "Or who she really was."

Evelyn waved dismissively. "No need to act so mortified, my young informant. Your fiery-tongued friend once did my bidding, too."

Zora slid the tip of a crutch—the hollow one—along the plush rug. One quick swing, and she could smash the hand that held the revolver. She'd used the same crutch to crack the ribs of a ferret-faced Spiritist named Lurana—another sap just like Abigail.

"Don't be rash," said Evelyn. "I've never shot anyone before, and I'd rather you not be the first. Especially as I've already cooked you a three-course meal. Onward, please."

Zora shoved her way through a glass double door. The dining room beyond was every bit as opulent as the one in their host's other mansion. Acetylene candles flickered from gilded sconces, and arched windows looked out over green-jeweled hills. Along the inner wall stood a folding screen with three painted panels. The table was clothed in emerald satin; on it sat porcelain tureens, silver-covered dishes, and topaz goblets.

Abigail's breath hissed out, and Nick snorted like a colt with a rattlesnake in its path.

"The soup is a creamy bisque with parsnips and celery root," said Evelyn. "The main course is venison with blackberry sauce."

"Isn't eating deer kind of like cannibalism for you?" asked

Zora. If she couldn't fight her way out of this place, she'd settle for a spot of taunting.

Evelyn flashed her canines. "We gain the strength of that which we consume. A lesson I learned from the spirits. By the way, did you know that *spirit* was once a synonym for *liquor*?" Holstering her revolver, she opened a dust-encrusted bottle labeled *ABSINTHE VERTE—1913*. Then she poured dark yellow liquid into a glass with a bulgy bottom.

"I thought they called that stuff the green fairy," Zora said. "So why does it look like concentrated pee?"

"The color changes as sunlight breaks down the chlorophyll, you uncouth child." Evelyn placed a sugar cube on a slotted spoon and dripped water through it into the glass until the concoction clouded to a milky white. "It was distilled a hundred and fifty-six years ago. I've been saving it for a special occasion. Would you like a snifter?"

Zora curled her lip, and Abigail wrinkled her nose.

"This may be the last bottle of absinthe in existence," said their host.

"I've never tasted liquor before," said Nick. "Now seems like a bad time to start."

"Your loss." Evelyn raised her glass. "To absent friends." She sipped her drink and filled Abigail's goblet with water. "Ms. Putnam, you told me the rest of your party was coming."

The girl quailed under the weight of her handler's regard. "Novalyne said so."

If Abigail wasn't lying, then where was everyone else? Had they taken a slower route or run into trouble? Were they fighting for their lives out there in the darkness?

"Let's go find them," Zora said.

But Evelyn took a seat at the head of the table. "I would welcome Mr. Prosser's sharpshooting, Ms. Janasdottir's vision, and Ms. Martin's sixth sense." She removed the lid from her tureen. "Provided they arrive before our departure tomorrow."

"We're not abandoning my brother and friends," Zora said.

"Or my sister and cousins," Nick added.

"We set out at dawn, with or without them." Evelyn motioned for her guests to sit. "In the meantime, try the appetizer."

Bristling silently, Zora obeyed. Nick and Abigail followed her example.

"With our combined skills, we can overcome the dangers ahead," Evelyn continued. "Four brilliant engineers working together."

"I'm not falling for your sweet talk." Zora stared death rays at Abigail. "Too late for *you*, I guess."

The girl didn't meet Zora's eyes.

"Ms. Putnam, I see you're admiring my triptych," said Evelyn. She must mean the folding screen. "*The Garden of Unearthly Terrors*. Painted in Year Sixteen by an unknown artist. The middle panel depicts the Great Wakening." On the screen's centerpiece, malachite green spirits rose from the grounds of a castle to immolate their screaming victims. "The right panel portrays the aftermath." An empty shell in a cremated meadow, rendered in carbon black and antimony gray. "But the left one is a mystery to me."

Zora scrutinized the image. Its background was a cavern wall with goat horns carved into the rock. Below the stalactite-studded ceiling, figures in white robes—or maybe lab coats—ringed the edge of a circular pit. Five ruby lines bisected the hole, forming an inverted star.

Try as she might, she couldn't decode the painting's meaning.

"I've never pinned down the castle's whereabouts." Evelyn looked around the table, as if gauging their reactions. Then she uncovered her dish and sawed off a hunk of steak. "As a child, I used to stare at those panels while my parents blathered about the glory days of the Coal Age. The red star inspired my beckoners—or lures, as some call them." She raised her bloody knife. "Ms. Coldiron, it was crafty how you and your brother turned my invention against me."

Evelyn Fontaine as a child? Zora's mind recoiled at the notion. "How'd you end up out here?" she asked. "The last we saw on the equinox, you were hightailing it north from Clack Mountain."

"I circled through the Border Hollows, walking by day and hiding by night." Evelyn brushed back a strand of white hair. "A harrowing journey, but I know the safest path. I've been visiting here for years to experiment on—"

Abigail jumped up from her seat and jabbed her fork at the windows. "Spirits!"

Down the slope, sluglike forms slithered into view, phlegm-colored and wagon-wide. Nick reached for his bow, but Evelyn didn't bat a green-shadowed eye.

Off in the valley, crimson lights twinkled. The slug-spirits stopped and raised their pseudopods. Then they shifted course for the lowlands, leaving trails of luminous slime.

"I've laid out three lines of defense," Evelyn boasted. "One red, one blue, and one purple. The first is a beckoner array triggered by etheric sensors. It diverts most of the larger roamers that stray toward the summit. Any that come closer set off a bank of ectospectral floodlights."

"Ripped off from my illuminators," said Zora.

"Refined from them, you mean. And the last barrier is my xenon-beam fence." The woman was smugness personified. "An improvement on your argon-based technology."

Zora could've smacked her. Instead, she ate her last bite of deer meat.

"Why'd you build that lighthouse down in the valley?" asked Nick.

"It was an observation post for testing her lures." Zora wasn't showing off, just stealing her enemy's thunder. "She put them in the lantern room and watched through her spirit-proof leaded glass as the roamers and airbounds came swarming."

"How astute of you," Evelyn said. A buzzer rang from the next room. "Pardon me while I check on dessert."

She left, and the door clicked behind her.

"Life was hard in Ram's Horn, but simpler than this." Nick sounded wary but dogged. "Should we try to get the jump on her?"

"Too risky," Zora said. Antler Woman was plenty cunning, and they'd get no help from Abigail. The girl was slouched in her chair, mouthing noiselessly to herself.

"Then let's scout around." Nick tested the door to the foyer: locked. Zora tried the windows: bolted shut. But hadn't the Clack Mountain mansion been riddled with secret passages?

As she ducked behind the screen to search for a sliding bookcase or false fireplace, her elbow bumped one of the panels. With a crash, the whole thing fell flat. On its back, an inscription was painted in dried-blood maroon: *THE AZURE CASTLE.*

Evelyn swept back through the door, holding a tin plate

swaddled in linen napkins. "Transparent pie, baked from my family's recipe." Pointedly ignoring the toppled screen, she served herself the first piece of pie. It had browned crust and golden filling. "I spoke with your brother and your impudent Spotter friend."

Zora lost her grip on herself. "They're alive?" she blurted.

"And clueless as ever. I also heard the bleating of children and livestock—and beneath that, running water. I presume they're by the river, despite what Ms. Putnam told us. I encouraged them to press on without you."

"Was Nova there?" Nick's voice was as tense as an overwound wire.

"Not that I could tell. Nor did I hear Ms. Janasdottir." Evelyn cut three more pieces of pie. "Your expedition stands divided. I suspect a deeper design is unfolding." She knit her angled brows. "The night I arrived, roamers thronged the highlands between this hill and the Hollows. They've dawdled there ever since—as if to blockade me."

Zora hated to believe her, but the woman's story did fit a pattern. Three hounts in Ram's Horn, hunting as a pack instead of alone. A front of derechos lying in wait for the airship. Something must be guiding the spirits. Something out of Zora's nightmares.

"Now I can return to take my rightful place," Evelyn went on. "With your assistance."

"Are . . . are you"—Abigail had reverted to timidity—"still going to help me find my dad?"

"Your reunion will come in due time," Evelyn said, but Zora knew all her promises were empty.

After dessert, their captor escorted them down a long

mirrored hallway. Zora was shocked at her own reflection: a castaway with filthy overalls and a feral expression.

At the end of the corridor, Evelyn ushered them through a folding door and into a narrow cage. As she turned a chrome-plated crank, a cable groaned from above. The cage sank past the floor and into the earth.

A grudging admiration burned inside Zora. The Hollows could use more contraptions like this.

"I hope you aren't claustrophobic," Evelyn said.

Nick squeezed closer to Zora, which she didn't precisely mind. Abigail looked as if she'd stepped on a bear trap and was waiting for it to snap shut.

Hydraulics squeaked, and the elevator ground to a halt. The barrel of a gun poked between Zora's shoulder blades. With insolent slowness, she stepped out into a mine tunnel braced with wooden beams. Bare bulbs cast harsh incandescence along its crosscuts.

"Forward," Evelyn commanded. "And take the next left."

The side tunnel brought them to a dingy chamber lined with triple bunks. Barracks for the miners who'd worked this seam? If so, then Zora didn't envy them.

"This is where you'll be staying," said the last scion of the Fontaine dynasty. Then she slammed a thick metal door in Zora's face.

♈

Zora couldn't fall asleep—not for lack of trying—so she sat on the floor beside Nick. He was tuning his fiddle strings for the third time tonight.

"Quinn and Paige will lead your cousins to the Hollows," she told him. "And Signe will look out for your sister. I guarantee it." Sweet jinxes, she sounded like Dad peddling his elixirs.

Nick leaned back against the wall. "I hope they have better luck than us."

"I don't trust in luck. I trust my brother and friends."

"This is all my fault," Abigail said from across the room. "I shouldn't have listened to Ms. Peryton—I mean Ms. Fontaine. Can you forgive me?"

"I could." Zora's mouth tasted as bitter as wormwood. She'd given the new girl a chance and landed down here for her troubles: locked in a mine beneath the Wastes. "But I choose not to."

Nick's eyes went big, and Abigail curled up in a ball. For a while, nobody spoke. From outside the cell came the clang of a hammer on metal. Evelyn must be up to no good.

It was Nick who broke the lull. "She left us our packs."

"She stole mine once before," Zora said. "And got a nasty surprise. I'll give her this—she never makes the same mistake twice."

"So," he pushed on, "we have a radio transmitter."

"Under a hill's worth of rock." Abigail's tone was dull.

"Oh." His face fell. "Right."

At some point, Zora drifted off with her head on Nick's shoulder. A steam-boiler's roar blasted her back to consciousness.

The door swung open. Evelyn had donned a cap with goggles perched on its bill. This time, she marched them to a roomy tunnel laid with railroad tracks. At the end of the line sat a locomotive coupled to a tender, boxcar, and caboose. All four were dusted in soot.

"A black train," said Nick. "Like in the song."

"Or a hex-card deck," their captor agreed. "If you happen to be superstitious. This is our ticket out of the Wastes."

Impossible. "You may have a working engine," Zora said, "but the tracks to the Hollows will be rusted down and overgrown."

Evelyn inspected the pipes from the sand-dome. "Thirty years ago, I led a work crew out this way with my brother and my fiancé. My code name was the doe; they were the stag and the hart. We rebuilt the line, but disaster struck in the final tunnel. We thought it was clear, so we used it as our base of operations." Her eyes were hooded. "We didn't have your spirit-sensors."

"What—what happened?" asked Abigail.

"I wasn't with them that night; I'd come here to repair the spike-driver. When I went back, I found the scene of a massacre. Landwights had drained the life from the crew."

Zora had never heard rumor of this. "Your brother and your fiancé?"

"Both dead." Was there a trace of real sorrow in Evelyn's voice?

"The stag and the hart lie slain," Abigail recited. "But the doe lives on to avenge them."

"Yes, your father heard the messages I sent to my underlings at Clack Mountain. I spun a story to cover up the deaths—a mining expedition wiped out by a cave-in. And then I vowed to bring the spirits to heel." She placed her hand on Zora's collarbone. "You and I have that in common, don't we?"

Zora shook off the woman's grip. "We're nothing alike."

"Be that as it may, we need each other now. I can't drive this train alone." Evelyn let her hands drop to her holsters. "All aboard."

Zora climbed a stepstool to the cab and came face-to-face

with a wall of gauges. Boiler pressure—check. Water level—check. Pyrometer—check.

"Ms. Coldiron, you're our engineer." Evelyn patted a chair. "Your job is to mind the regulator. It controls the flow of steam; think of it as a throttle. This lever reverses the train's direction; let's hope we don't need it."

For a moment, Zora was back on the *Reynardine*'s bridge with Mr. Vandy. *You have a steady hand at the helm,* he'd told her. *Are you sure you've never flown one of these before?*

She'd rather be taking orders from him.

"Mr. Martin, you're our stoker." Evelyn gave Nick a shovel and pointed to the firebox. "Keep feeding the boiler with coal. I've loaded the tender with my last batch of anthracite. Ms. Putnam, you're our braker. Go to the caboose and keep watch behind us. If I give the signal, climb up top and turn the brake wheel." She held out a metal club with a hooked end. "Fortunately for you, it's only a backup for the airbrakes. In the Coal Age, brakers died by the scores on the rails, crushed between the cars or under the wheels."

With a trembling hand, Abigail took the club. Then she fled toward the back of the train.

Zora tried not to feel sorry for her. "What about you, my lady of the antlers?"

Evelyn touched the bill of her cap. "I'm in charge, which makes me the conductor. I've fired the engine and filled the boiler, so our locomotive is ready to go. Release that bar and open those valves." Zora did as she was told, and the woman nodded. "Now shift the brake to the left and pull the regulator—just a little at first." The pistons chugged, and the train clacked forward, its headlight scattering the shadows.

The cry of a steam whistle echoed through the tunnel. Evelyn's eyes twitched, and she glared at Nick.

He grinned and let go of the pull-cord. "I've always wanted to do that. Never thought I'd get a chance to ride the rails."

Zora shook her head, but she was smiling, too. "I doubt anyone's listening."

"I know, but maybe Nova and Signe will hear it."

As the train built up a head of steam, it burst from the darkness and into the morning light. The tracks here were buried in snow, but the wheels plowed right on through it, throwing white spouts in the air.

"Faster now," Evelyn said. "We need to reach the far end before sunset. But don't get carried away—derailments can be so untidy. And watch the boiler pressure. When I paid a visit to my family's scrapyard, I saw a locomotive that had exploded. It looked like an eldritch horror, complete with iron tentacles." She tapped the water-glass light. "Mind this, too. I'd rather not be scalded to death."

"I can always dream," Zora muttered.

At first, the journey went swiftly and smoothly, never mind the constant shaking and noise. She had no choice about which way to go—only a line to follow. Sometimes it ran beside creekbanks; sometimes it curved around mountains; sometimes it cut straight through the hillsides. Along the way, she drafted and nixed a dozen schemes to get the drop on their conductor. A sudden stop, a blowback from the furnace, a jet of steam from the valves—every plan she hatched was too chancy.

When the tracks led into the darkness of a tunnel, Zora scanned it for fallen rocks and risen earthbounds. Still high noon, the clock on the console reassured her.

"This isn't the tunnel where it happened," said Evelyn.

The train passed wooden tanks shaped like giant barrels. Semaphore signals on tilted poles. A station platform crowded with pines. Firebox cinders bored holes in Nick's grubby clothes, and gusts of black smoke made Zora's eyes water.

Then they came to a tree downed on the line.

The train screeched to a halt at Evelyn's signal, and she switched on a microphone. "Ms. Putnam, come forward and clear the tracks. Mr. Martin, help her."

The pair of them tried and failed to lift the trunk. "The wood's still green," shouted Nick. His face was smudged with soot. "It must've fallen recently."

"Take an ax to it," said Evelyn.

While they worked, Zora's thoughts wandered back to the three-panel painting. One of Dad's letters had mentioned a note in a book—a message, or maybe a warning, about the sign of the goat and a castle on the Azure Downs. She had a hunch as to the castle's location: deep in the heart of the Bluegrass. But who were the figures in white, and what was the pit with the star?

Nick came back looking pale and huffing for breath. It hurt Zora's heart to watch him go back to stoking the fire. "Get your own hands dirty for once," she growled at Evelyn, but the woman paid her no mind.

They came to another downed tree in mid-afternoon and a third in the early evening. Each took an hour to chop up and drag away.

"If one tree falls in the forest, it's an accident." Evelyn's smile had long since turned brittle. "Two might be a coincidence. Three makes for a conspiracy. Something out there meant to block the tracks. Increase our speed—we're racing what the night will bring."

But sunset caught them in sight of another tunnel. "The final one," Evelyn said. "I'd hoped to pass through it sooner. Stop here; we need to prepare our defenses."

As the train puffed to a halt, honeydew-colored rings blossomed around the tracks. Innocuous little earthbounds; nothing to worry about. The tunnel was another thing altogether—a dark and hungry mouth with icicle fangs.

Evelyn flipped a lever on the console. "You'll appreciate this." She drew her glass derringer and stepped down from the cab. "Come with me, Ms. Coldiron."

Zora followed her to the locomotive's prow. Along its pointed grille, purple arcs flittered and crackled. "Clever," she admitted. "A cowcatcher for spirits."

"This will slice through the ones in our path, but others may strike from behind. I'll drive the engine the rest of the way. I need you to cover our tail. There's a rocket launcher in the caboose."

Up ahead, a bile-tinted glimmer formed in the tunnel. Zora would've preferred electric luminaires, would've settled for solid blackness. She pulled her hat lower and her coat tighter— not that they'd protect her from an onslaught of life-leeching earthbounds.

Nick waved at her from the cab. "See you on the other side."

Should she say something brave? Witty? Heartfelt? She made a false start at a reply, then waved back and rushed to the caboose.

Abigail reached out a hand, but Zora climbed aboard by herself. Opening a crate stenciled *STOVEPIPE*, she found a metal tube packed in hay. Another box yielded a dozen amethyst rockets.

"I need to tell you—" Abigail began, but it was too late. The engine spewed steam, and the black train rolled on toward the tunnel.

17

THE GLOW UPRIVER WAXED BRIGHTER AND BRIGHTER, OUTSHINING the half-moon above it. The titan was wending its way toward the boathouse, stride by unfathomable stride. At this range, Quinn didn't need spooky eardrums to hear it.

"The ramp is clear," he said. The river-raiders who'd built this hideout had left a set of tracks sloping down to the water—weather-beaten but sturdy, knock on wood.

Paige tied the last of the towline knots. "Fire up the engine."

On the steamer's deck, Iris lit the coals while Jay topped off the boiler tank. When they were done, they hopped down and picked up their ropes. "We're ready," said Holly.

Beneath their soles, the planks quaked from the titan's footfalls.

"On you go." Quinn hoisted the lamb up to the stern. Flockless and bereft of its shepherd, the little thing cowered against the railing.

"Pull!" shouted Paige. She tugged her rope, and Quinn tugged his, and the Children of the Ram tugged theirs, but the boat stayed right where it was. Iris groaned and stamped her feet.

Another tremor shook the pirate's roost, hard enough

to rattle the roof. They pulled again, and the *Muskellunge* creaked down the tracks. The instant it hit the canal, Holly jumped aboard and took the pilot wheel. Then Quinn and the others slogged along the towpath, their boots skidding in the muddy slush as they dragged the boat through the dark, brackish water.

At this speed, Zora's mule could've outpaced them all. *He was a good old worker and a good old pal*, Quinn sang in his head. *Met his fate on an eerie canal.*

For every three steps he took, one deep splash resounded upriver. The air itself felt charged with unnatural forces. The titan was closing the distance.

A green shift in the shades of the night galvanized Quinn to pull harder. How had this monster tracked them from Ram's Horn, across air and earth and water? Could it sense the Mark of the Syzygy on Jay? Or had Evelyn Fontaine's spy snuck spirit-lures into their packs?

"The boiler's started to simmer," said Holly. "But it has a ways to go." Quinn champed his molars as she fed the furnace. Without the paddlewheels turning, they'd be at the mercy of the river.

Jay hooted a warning, but Quinn only caught the words *canal* and *spirit*.

Above the lapping of the ripples, a burbling sound rose. Fist-sized globs of light clamped onto the hull, tinging it algae green and pond-lily yellow. Their luster put Quinn in mind of a watercolor nightscape—translucent and blurry and vaguely unreal.

"Small fry," said Paige. "They hitch rides on boats to hunt water bugs and whirligigs. Just keep your fingers away."

The crash of the titan's next step set the willow branches aflutter. The water swelled, and the steamer bobbed.

"Heave!" Paige bellowed. Quinn tugged until his shoulders ached and his fingers burned. Then again. And again. Ahead of him, Iris tripped on a rock and went sprawling. Braying barnyard swears, she scrambled to catch the end of her rope.

"We've got steam," said Holly.

One last tug, and the roiling river stretched out before them. Iris jumped on the deck, followed by Jay and Paige. *Don't fall in*, Quinn told himself. *The Rangers can't save you this time.* He pushed the boat toward the current and took a running leap from the bank. The hull tilted—

He landed in the stern but slipped on the deck, his feet sweeping out from beneath him. Paige caught him by his shoulder holster just as the torrent grabbed hold of the boat. Then the *Muskellunge* floundered downriver, rocking side to side as it went. Iris clutched the spar on the bow, and Jay latched onto the wheelhouse.

In their ornate boxes, the paddlewheels sat stubbornly idle.

Quinn braced himself against the rail as the steamer seesawed beneath him. Capsize now, and the river would beat the titan to the kill. A cold embrace, an icy kiss, and an eternal sleep on a silty bed.

"What's wrong with the engine?" Iris hollered. "Would it help if we tried to row?"

"The pressure needs time to build," said Paige.

Drawing his banisher, Quinn spared a glance at their wake. What he saw made his stomach twist. Astride the river, the titan shone like a pillar of fire fringed by hundreds of molten limbs. Its aura grazed the flanks of the clouds and warped the night sky.

The sensor-bulbs on Quinn's rifle sparked and fused, but he had no room for them in his thoughts. Beside him, Paige gave a low whistle.

The spirit strode onward, radiating a dreadful majesty—a dazzling corona of wrongness. Its presence was a spike in the mind. A burning brand on the soul. An abomination against scale and perspective.

"That's the same one that almost squashed my boss's boss." Paige sounded revolted but also wonderstruck. "She spotted those star-shaped flecks in its aura. How far do you reckon it's wandered since then? To the ends of the earth and back?"

"Can your guns stop it?" Iris had gone as meek as her lamb.

Quinn lowered his banisher. "Even if we had the cannon, it wouldn't faze that." Flee or die—those were their only choices. "We need the paddles running."

"Granny Martin told me a watched kettle never boils." Holly fanned the engine's flames, but the pistons kept their silence. "I should've listened."

"The titan's making a new sort of noise." Jay cupped his ears. "A moan almost too low-pitched to hear. I think . . . I think it's about to attack."

The spirit slammed down its limbs, launching a river-tsunami. Foam-capped and frenzied, the wall of water surged faster than a pike fish. Faster than an eel. Faster than the *Muskellunge*.

The white wave hit, and the steamer yawed to the left. To the right. To the middle. "I can't control where we're going," Holly yelled over the voice of the river. Frigid water sloshed across the deck, drenching Quinn's trousers and dousing the packs.

"The radio," he said.

Paige snagged her sopping pack and fished out the device. When she flipped its switch, nothing happened. Cursing, she banged on the case.

Quinn dabbed river-spray from his eyes. There went their last hope for hailing Zora and Signe. If they met again, it would be in the Hollows or the grave.

Paige stowed the radio in the boat's locker. "We could let it dry out and—"

"Shh," said Jay. Behind them, the titan raised its countless limbs and flared even brighter. "It's fixing to do something different."

With a throat-clearing cough, the engine rattled to life and spat out a puff of smoke. As the crankshaft revolved, the twin paddlewheels set to spinning. The *Muskellunge* straightened its prow and steamed ahead.

"That's more like it," said Iris.

Quinn leaned out from the stern, shading his eyes with one hand. The titan was losing ground, though the sight of it still smote his brain.

"Now it sounds . . ." Jay gnawed on his knuckle. "Wavery?"

Its limbs drooping and its corona dimmed, the titan thundered away from the river. By the time Quinn's pulse had calmed, the spirit was only a haze behind the mountains.

"We're the fish that got away." Paige laughed, a bit shakily. Iris and Holly did, too.

But not Quinn. "It's heading north toward the valley. That's where Zora and Nicholas and Abigail are, if Evelyn Fontaine was telling the truth."

"She also said they'd be gone tomorrow," Jay pointed out. "Maybe the titan won't find anyone home."

Quinn caught a whiff of damp wool, and then the lamb rubbed its head against him. As he petted it, the tightness in his chest subsided. His sister always found a way to survive—and so, it seemed, did Evelyn Fontaine.

The *Muskellunge* swept around a bend in the river. "Tell me, Pirate Girl," said Paige, "how do you fancy steering this tub? I reckon you're a natural pilot."

Holly stood straighter at the wheel. "I'm getting the hang of it." Her smile was white in the gloom. "Straight on to the gorges?"

"Full steam ahead." Quinn found the lantern he'd salvaged from the airship and hung it on the end of the bowsprit. "This'll light our way through the spirits." In the blue halo, sinuous waterbounds spun and darted. Their vile smells wafted up from the surface, and their raucous calls joined in with the river's song.

"Hey, Rabbit Ears," said Paige. "Any big ones under our keel?"

Jay shook his head. "Nothing louder than a paddlefish."

On downriver, the banks gave way to cliffs of layered sandstone. Eons of flooding had sculpted the rock into chimneys and tubes, bridges and flying buttresses. From the fissures and caves, fey torches blazed: the auras of roamers that flapped like bats or hopped like crickets or crawled like centipedes. Their cries and yowls bounced from the overhangs in a head-spinning cacophony.

Quinn kept his finger loose on the trigger. He could blast every spirit in range, but that wouldn't even the odds. Their best bet was to glide on by without making a fuss.

"The Lost Gorges," Paige said, as if this could've been anywhere else.

The river narrowed, and the cliffs leaned closer. The water-bounds below gathered into shoals, writhing and spuming; the roamers above spun astral webs and spectral lariats. And yet none of the spirits troubled the *Muskellunge*.

Quinn looked on, Jay listened, Holly steered, and Iris shushed her lamb. Meanwhile, Paige drew sketches and scribbled notes by the light of the cobalt lantern. "I've spotted six unknown varieties already," she said, pointing to a school of waterbounds that looked like the shaggy manes of undead mermaids. "I think I'll call those shwaygways—that comes from a legend my grandfather told me. I discovered them, so I get to name them. The other apprentices will all be green-eyed." She bit the end of her pencil. "Assuming I make it home to report my findings."

"I miss *our* home," Iris said. "I miss the fort and our flock."

"Same here, but I miss our cousins even more." Jay rested his chin in his hands. At the pilot wheel, Holly nodded and touched her bandaged brow.

"I'm with you on that," Quinn said. "I wish I could talk to my sister." A season and a moon: that was the sum of his time with Zora. He'd missed her first fifteen birthdays, and he might not make it to see her sixteenth. His present for her was back in their wagon, wrapped up safe and snug in a drawer.

The shwaygways parted in front of the steamer, trailing their long strands of ghost-hair. "I miss my sister, too," said Paige.

"Is she another spirit-chaser?" asked Iris.

Paige tucked away her journal. "No, she's more of a homebody. She took a job in our hollow as an apprentice undertaker. We used to butt heads over everything, but now all our scraps seem so petty."

"Claire's always looked up to you," Quinn said. "In her own morbid way." She'd shown him her collection of trinkets and knickknacks: souvenirs from Paige's expeditions, arranged in a glass case with a pair of stuffed raccoons.

"Undertaking sounds all right to me." Holly turned the wheel a spoke to the left. "You felt otherwise, Mr. Prosser?"

Awash with pastel green, a shoal of spirits pinwheeled toward the stern. Quinn traced their path with his rifle's muzzle, priming himself for a fight, but they ricocheted off the boat's double wake. "I did growing up, though I'd trade this river-cruise for a quiet night in my mother's parlor. So long as I'm not the one on the embalming table."

Paige laughed, but the children didn't. "Pardon the mortician humor," he said.

The waterbounds frothed in the eddies and thrashed in the currents. Up on the clifftops, a roamer waved radiant lassoes. Down among the fallen boulders, spider-legged spirits wove nets of silken light.

"I can't figure out why they're hanging back," Quinn said.

"It's as if they're waiting for something." Holly's voice was scarcely audible over the churning of the paddles.

By the wheelhouse, Jay made like a statue. "Below us," he whispered.

All along the cliffs, roamers ducked behind rocks and scuttled into cracks. Bendy waterbounds dove, and bulbous ones ebbed into grottoes. Where a Milky Way of corpse-stars had twinkled, only the blue light of the lantern remained.

Abandoned by its entourage, the *Muskellunge* steamed onward alone.

No, not completely alone. Deep in the water off the starboard bow, a band of aquamarine streaks had appeared. They co-alesced into a shape that was slender and serpentine. And far, far longer than the boat—by just how much, Quinn couldn't tell.

"An altie," said Paige. "That's not good."

A siren song floated up from the river bottom—alien but honey-toned and beguiling. As the notes ascended, so did the spirit. Without a splash, its crest broke the surface—and rose and rose, on an impossibly elongated stalk. Up past the boat's smokestack; up past the gorge's rim.

When the altie reached its full height, it turned a trio of eye-motes down toward the steamer.

Quinn held himself perfectly still. The spirit's motes glistened like pearls in its nebulous crest, and its voice . . . Years ago, at a roadside shack full of curios, he and Paige had come across a treasure from a faraway shore: a pink and white conch shell. He'd heard the ocean inside it, and she'd played a trumpet-blast through its whorl. The altie's call was a choir of those sounds, magnified and bizarrely transformed.

Holly jerked the wheel, and the *Muskellunge* lurched to the right. Twisting its neck, the spirit tracked their course with its eyes-that-weren't-really-eyes. Then, as swiftly as it had risen, the altie submerged. In the depths of the river, the turquoise undertow faded to black.

"I can't hear it anymore," said Jay.

Paige flashed a beam across the water. "It'll be back. Those things are relentless. They'll toy with their prey for a while, but they always go for the kill in the end."

"You told us you rode an altie." Iris sounded unsure but hopeful. "Can you handle this one?"

"I might've embellished that tale a little. Or, rather, a lot.

Pine-Box, you had a point back at the boathouse. I got cocky about my plan."

Quinn waved his friend's apology away. They had bigger spirits to fry and a long way to go until morning.

As he watched to starboard and Paige watched to port, the cliffs dwindled to rocky stubs. Here, the bursts of spirit-shine came fewer and farther between—a pack of roamers prowling, a cluster of earthbounds levitating. The river was as darkly obscure as a spring in a sunless cavern.

"Are we through the Lost Gorges?" asked Holly.

Paige switched out her weapon's battery for their last fresh one. "The first of two, but the second may be trickier. When Clementine Geller paddled down it, a whirlpool flipped her canoe."

Iris backed away from the railing. "Who's that, and what happened to her?"

"She was the greatest Spotter in the history of the Hollows. A waterbound grabbed her foot and dragged her under, but she shucked off her boot and swam away. I was knee-high to a grasshopper when she told me that story—it's what set me on my path to spirit-spotting. Anyhow, the second gorge ends at—"

"The altie's back," said Jay. "Following us, but at a distance."

"Still playing cat and mouse. It'll slip away in a moment."

"And it's gone," the boy confirmed.

The lamb lay down in the bow, but the rest of them stuck to their posts. Ten minutes passed, and then twenty, as Quinn's thoughts drifted with the sticks and leaves washed down by the flood. If he and his companions survived the next gorge, the worst of the Wastes would lie behind them. And if they reached a Ranger tower, they could send for help to find Zora and Signe and the twins. Abigail, too, even if she'd gone astray. Then they'd catch Evelyn Fontaine, and the Judges could try her in court. The Hollows would mourn Walter Vandy, and life would settle down again. Just like after the last equinox.

Knock on wood, knock on wood.

"Here it comes!" shouted Jay.

Behind them, a line of humps breached the surface. Iris fed the boiler, and Holly cranked the throttle lever. Under the frozen moon, the riverbanks rolled by faster and faster.

Not fast enough, though. Weaving like a water snake, the altie coursed ahead of the current. As it neared the steamer, it raised its crest to blare a song fit for sunken lands and undersea catacombs.

Paige opened fire, but her target whipped toward the bow—right into Quinn's line of sight. He tagged the spirit with violet, and it gave an ululating cry. Then it plunged toward the river bottom, lashing up a vortex with its tail.

As Holly maneuvered the boat past the maelstrom, Jay leaned his ear toward the deck. "It's still down there," he said.

Quinn glimpsed a streak of teal on their port side. Another to starboard. Three opal motes off the stern.

"This one's sly," said Paige.

Iris scooched down and cooed a lullaby to her terror-struck lamb. Ahead of them, another gorge yawned, starless and grimoire black. Engine pounding and paddlewheels threshing, the *Muskellunge* raced toward its jaws.

With no warning at all, a blow struck the boat from beneath and launched it clean out of the water. Gravity paused for a moment as Quinn caught the railing, but then the hull slammed into the river. Spray drenched his clothes, and the deck pitched, and a pack slid over the side—not the one with Holly's books and the doctor's kit, thank the stars.

Smacking the wake with its tail, the altie flowed away and dove again.

"I don't think it liked your guns," said Iris.

"Let's hope it's had enough." Paige opened the hatch and grimaced at the bilge. "The hull's sprung a leak." She snatched a pail from the locker. "Lamb Chop, see what you can do."

While Iris bailed water, Quinn took a moment to wring out his hat. His hair was wet, and his feet were chilled, but the second gorge looked spirit-free.

Jinx.

As if a circuit had closed, the cliffs lit up with auras. In every crevice, a green candle; beneath every arch, a green fire. The river came alive with a menagerie of waterbounds—some skinny like gar, some stringy like jellyfish, all hissing or skirling or caterwauling.

Yet the Children of the Ram kept at their tasks. Holly navigated past sandbars and rocks; Iris scooped bucket after bucket from the bilge; Jay eavesdropped on the spirits in the depths.

Quinn felt a ripple of affection for his young crewmates. "Paige and I are lucky to know y'all," he told them.

"You risked your lives for us," said Jay. "For that, we'd follow you through the gates of the Green Abyss." He frowned. "I hear something else—a dull, steady rumble."

"I hear it, too," said Iris. "Another giant waterbound?"

Paige shook her head. "As I was fixing to say before the altie interrupted, this gorge empties out over Moonbow Falls. Cut speed; we need to tie up—and soon."

The paddlewheels slowed to a crawl. From the left clifftop,

roamers dangled phosphorescent hooks. On the right, a spirit wailed like the Weeper of the Lake. "There's no safe mooring place here," Quinn said.

"I reckon not." Paige drew out the words as if they were stuck in her craw. "Take us ahead—but mind the white water."

Holly steered the boat through a flurry of rapids and on around the next bend. Beyond it, the river ran straight for a stretch and then fell away, roaring louder than a herd of hounts. Past the edge, mist billowed in the moon's rays and the aurora's shimmer.

"Reverse the engines!" shouted Paige. "Anything sneaking up on our tail?"

Jay lifted his hands in a helpless gesture. "All I can hear is the falls."

Rifle poised, Quinn surveyed the walls of the gorge. No dock, no beach, not even a rocky shelf. Just two sheer faces spanned by a ramshackle trestle bridge. "The pirates must've had a way around. I hate to backtrack, but maybe we passed a side canal."

"Whatever you do, try to hurry," said Iris. "We're taking on more water than I can bail."

Paige punched the railing and then flexed her hand. It was the same one she'd broken on the fall equinox. "All right. Forward engines and hard about."

But as Holly spun the pilot wheel, the lights all around them blinked out. Upriver, the water gleamed cyan. Iris dropped her pail, and Jay covered his ears. To the sound of a drowned pipe organ, the altie resurfaced, smelling of brine and dead things.

Quinn's heart sank toward the river bottom. Between the spirit and the waterfall, the *Muskellunge* had nowhere to go.

18

THE HARBINGER'S STOLEN EYES GLITTERED WITH TRIUMPH; ITS stolen throat held one steady pitch. All up and down the streets of the Ruined Town, spirits rose to answer its call: spouting geysers of pea-soup ichor, bubbling streams of honeyed slime, swirling clouds of mustard fog.

Signe had waited for this moment. She hoped she hadn't waited too long.

As her adversary stepped forward, she donned her goggles and met its gaze. "Unbind Novalyne," she said. "And then return to your world."

The harbinger paused in its humming. "Your trick won't work on me, little prey. I've dug my roots deep in this mind."

But Signe had expected that. Holding her parasol like a swashbuckler's rapier, she pressed a button on its handle. *I rigged a device inside your fancy umbrella,* Zora had told her. *For you to use in a pinch. Not as precise as a banisher, but it won't hurt your eyes or make you sick. It stuns spirits with kirlian waves — a dose of their own energy. I call it a spectral jammer.*

Only it wasn't working. Signe pushed the button again. Still no blast of spirit-power.

"Your weapon is missing this part." The harbinger reached into its pocket and pulled out a crystal tube. "I took it while you slept. Did you think I'd forget how your tinkering friend used a hidden rocket to"—it crushed the tube and dropped the fragments—"*delay* my ascendance? You can't catch me by surprise; our minds are aligned in the vast tapestry."

Above the chimneys, moonstone shards hovered. Behind the windows, cat's eye orbs congregated.

"I've read the childish fancies in your memories," the harbinger continued. "Your delusions of being blessed. Chosen by fate. Magical." It laughed scornfully. "But what you are is a cosmic mistake. A chimera."

"You're afraid of the eidolons." Signe willed herself not to crack. Not to crumble. "And you're afraid of me and my friends. We've already defeated you once."

Green and gold pandemonium raged in the streets. With a smile on its spirit-stained lips, the harbinger drew even closer. "The eidolons lie dreaming and helpless." Now it was an arm's length away. "Tonight, you'll join them forever."

Panic welled up in Signe's windpipe. Her gaze was parried, her weapon foiled, her every move anticipated. And so she did something neither she nor her enemy had foreseen: she rammed it in the gut with her parasol.

Then she ran.

The spirits in her path slumped like wound-down automatons. Seizing her opening, she zigzagged around them. Farther up the avenue, parapets loomed dark and enigmatic against the aurora's curtain.

A violet shaft flashed by her face, blurring the world with

kaleidoscope daubs. As tears salted her eyes, she stumbled to the closest building and took refuge beneath its portico.

"I kept the banisher your Spotter-snoop gave me," the harbinger said in Novalyne's twang. "You could shoot back, if only you had one."

Signe breathed softly and stayed frozen in place. When the rainbow spots faded from her vision, she saw the name chiseled over her shelter's lintel: *WORRELL AUDITORIUM*. On her left, a sculpted mask laughed; on her right, another one cried. She knew how the second mask felt.

"I wonder what this pistol would do to your precious gift." The harbinger hummed a droning note, and the spirits around it revived. "Come on out, little chimera. You can't hide from a telepath."

Signe tried to keep her mind blank, but psychic tendrils wormed through her brain to her optic nerves.

"I sense your indigo-tainted eyes." The harbinger whistled, and a pair of roamers catapulted forward: a sizzling lightning bolt and a twisting dust-devil. Varc and vorx, rated three skulls apiece in *Tolliver's Pocket Spirit Handbook*. The more skulls, the deadlier.

The lightning bolt went high, leaping from rooftop to rooftop. The dust-devil went low, whisking up dirty snow in its eye. No way for her to focus on both at once. Look down, and she'd risk a lethal jolt from above. Look up, and she'd chance a rending grasp from below.

Do nothing, and she'd die for certain.

Signe gazed at the whirlwind and becalmed it. Its funnel evaporated, and the debris in its eye fell to earth. One attacker gone, but where was the other?

The hairs on her neck stood up, and her nostrils tingled with electricity. The lightning bolt was on the theater's facade, arcing down an iron drainpipe. Three stories up . . . two stories . . . one. A metallic taste filled Signe's mouth, and the steel ribs of her parasol crackled.

She stared the lightning-spirit to oblivion.

The harbinger whistled again, but Signe didn't linger to see what was coming. Assembling her wits, she faced east and set off across a barren field—a stump-lined yard boxed in on four sides by solemn brick halls. A quadrangle.

The quadrangle. She'd seen this place once in a book and once in a trance. She was close to her journey's end—her last hope for a haven from the spirits.

"Little ghost, little ghost, fly away to your tomb," the harbinger sang in a strange double voice. "Your hollow's on fire, and your friends are doomed."

Signe's eyes throbbed in sudden agony, as if they'd been stabbed with red-hot needles. Gasping, she tottered on past deserted classrooms. Empty dining halls. Forsaken dormitories.

Another violet ray lanced past her head. "All except one, and she'll never tell," the harbinger trilled. "I trapped her soul in the well."

Over her shoulder, Signe glimpsed a pack of galloping roamers. They had spindly legs and wasp waists—along with tusks long and sharp enough to skewer a human.

Her, for instance.

She picked a sanctuary at random: a stone citadel with jutting windows. Oriels, her schoolteacher siblings would've called them. An inscription above the front archway read *WILKINS-FREEMAN LIBRARY.*

That boded well. She'd always thought of libraries as hallowed places.

Behind her, the harbinger bayed like a hound from the Wild Hunt. One by one, the roamers added their howls to its cry.

Signe rushed up the steps, two at a time, to the library's threshold. The blackness within stank of moldy wood and mildewed paper. She flicked on the flashlight she'd pilfered last night and followed its beam to an atrium.

Fifteen decades of dust stirred around her as she searched for another exit. All she found in the reading room were collapsed chairs and splintered tables. The first hallway she tried led to a crater in the marble floor, and the second came to a dead end, but the third ran straight to a door labeled *STACKS*. Fate had left it untouched and unopened.

When she crouched at the keyhole, her inner ears twinged. When she touched the knob, her fingertips prickled.

"So thoughtful of you to guide me here," the harbinger called out. "I've been meaning to study your people's history."

Signe's instincts screamed at her to step back from the door. Instead, she turned the knob and pushed ahead.

She stopped just short of an elemental.

The spirit was small for its kind but large enough to cocoon the stacks in iridescent vapors. Its aura coiled along the shelves without scorching their faces and over the books without melting their spines. If she'd taken three more paces forward, she wouldn't have been so lucky.

And yet a narrow route skirted the elemental—a patchy border of tiles outside its sway. As swiftly as she dared, she sidestepped along the checkerboard path. White to black, then back to white, then black again.

Ring around the earthbound, she chanted to herself.

"Long ago, a veil fell between this world and mine." The harbinger's voice rang out from the hallway. "Millennia of exile flowed by me until I found a flaw in the barrier's fabric—a rupture I could pass through. Then I found another, and then more. When the stars aligned on the cusps of the horns, I wove the rifts into a portal for my kindred. That was the night you call the Great Wakening." It hummed a dirge and laughed. "I need to learn who pierced the veil—and how to rip it to shreds."

Signe's tongue turned to leather, and vertigo spun her head. Steadying herself with her parasol, she sprang over a green-shaded square.

Don't step on the cursed ground.

Footfalls sounded on marble. "So much knowledge conserved by my kindred. None of your world's scavengers looted this place—not the Spotters, nor the relic hunters, nor even the deathwatch beetles."

In her dizziness, Signe almost slipped on a tile. The elemental pulsed hungrily, curling its vapors around the shelves.

Ashes, ashes, we all fall down.

"Now that I know how to decipher your ancestors' scribbles," the harbinger said, "these pages will give me my answers."

But it was wrong. If the secrets it sought lay buried somewhere on this campus, they wouldn't be *here*; they'd be in the—

She blotted out the inkling before it could crystallize. White tile, black tile, white. Not far ahead stood another doorway.

"I know you're in there, little quarry. I can sense your growing terror."

Signe wished she had sealing wax to stick in her ears. Would the Voice of the Spirits ever shut up? Yet it hadn't chased her through the stacks—hadn't risked its human host to the elemental's sway.

That would be the key to her escape.

Two more jumps, and Signe was on the far side of the room. She let all conscious thought drain from her mind, and then she passed through the doorway.

"No matter where you run, I'll track you down," the harbinger shouted. "Just as you've hunted my kindred."

Tuning out its threats, Signe scurried around a bend in the corridor. From the gloom up ahead, a pallid face looked back at her. A dead librarian's apparition? Her own ghostly double come to fetch her away?

She approached the face, and it became a glazed moonbeam shining down through a lunette window. She'd found her way out—and if the stars favored her, she'd lose her pursuer in the night beyond.

The back exit opened onto a snow-covered slope. At its top stood a tower with a copper dome and a quartet of gargoyles. Bear, bobcat, swan, and dragon—constellation creatures, all four of them. She'd reached her destination: the observatory from Ulysses Bell's journal. The one place in town the spirits might leave in peace.

The entrance was boarded shut, so Signe climbed in through an open window. Her flashlight's beam revealed the barrel of a majestic telescope, ten times her height or more. The dome's vaulted shutter was open a sliver. Through the gap, she saw green fireballs streak down from the heavens.

Bolides, searching for her at the harbinger's command. She tried to hide her face with her parasol, but its canopy wouldn't open. Curse her eyes, the flashlight—she switched off the beam and waited for the spirit-storm.

But the airbounds flew on aimlessly.

Mr. Bell's journal had guided her true: a force was shielding this place from the spirits. Perhaps the departed astronomers had used arcane starcraft to cloak their observatory. Or perhaps the fiddler girl had warded it with her music; legend said she'd grown up by the Ruined Town.

Taking a page from a Carson van Patten mystery, Signe set forth to investigate. First things first, she peeked through the telescope's eyepiece. Nothing but a black flag on the sky. The lenses must be out of focus or capped.

The nooks along the wall looked more promising. Circling the platform, she found faded star charts pinned to ratty corkboards. An orrery with rusty planets and a tarnished sun. A broken clockwork astrolabe. Stacks of damp-wrinkled essays, forever ungraded.

Signe felt a stitch of grief for the past that was lost and the futures that might have been. In another life, she and Quinn could've studied here with people from faraway places—the Tidelands, Sylvania, and even across the oceans. Zora could've launched a brilliant career in some neon-lit city, and Paige could've spotted polar beasts or tropical birds instead of spirits. Abigail might still have her parents, and the Folk of the Ram might still have their home. Mr. Vandy might be steering the *Reynardine* through the clouds.

The harbinger had snuffed out those tomorrows, but Signe would find a countercharm to break its spell.

As she passed a shadow-filled room, her flashlight's beam caught a shiny surface. She advanced cautiously until she saw what it was: a block of meteoric iron etched with triangular patterns. She recognized the name and title engraved on it, too:

MAXWELL DORAN

PROFESSOR OF ATMOSPHERIC AND ETHERIC SCIENCES

The office wasn't paneled in wood or furnished in leather like the ones she'd read about in *The Vampire Tomes* and *Reavers of the Hexed Crypt*. It reminded her more of a carcass picked clean by vultures. A desk stripped bare except for the nameplate bolted to it. Bleached-bone shelves naked of books. Stark gray walls graced only by spatters of luminescent fungus.

She'd come a century and change too late for digging up clues.

Or had she? On closer inspection, those specks weren't fungus after all, but radium-painted constellations. The Rabbit and the Hunter on the near wall; the Hydra and the Twins on the one opposite; the Fish and the Lake Princess rising over the desk.

And, above her, the Big and Little Dippers. Had Professor Doran marked the spot with the northern star?

Signe hopped up on the desk and followed the Big Dipper's pointers to a glowing dot in the middle of the ceiling. She'd found the polestar—and, with it, a camouflaged panel. When she pried it loose from the plaster, she uncovered a hidden compartment. Inside rested a tin box the size of a bread pan.

The stars *did* favor her tonight.

Sitting on the desk, Signe opened the box and removed its contents: a rolled-up scroll and an envelope addressed to *A WATCHER OF THE SKY*. She started with the scroll, which unwound into a crinkled map of Old Kentucky.

Though her magnifying glass had fractured, she could still

read through its cracks. Blue lines showed the borders of bygone counties, and black print named their former seats. A red X stood for the Ruined Town, tantalizingly close to the Hollows, but what did the yellow lines and green circles mean?

She slit the envelope and unfolded the letter within. It was dated September 23, 1925. Year Zero of the New Calendar, six moons after the Great Wakening. She read on:

Dear follower of the northern star,

If you're holding this letter, I'm most certainly dead. Yet my research may not be in vain: the findings I set down here will help you trace the roots of our catastrophe. Twelve years ago, I heard the first tales of the spinning green spiral that hums in the night. From then on, I crisscrossed our Commonwealth collecting accounts of the phenomenon. Some witnesses called it the spook-light, but I dubbed it the ignis fatuus—*in plainer words, folly's fire.*

It was the Skywheel from Signe's fortune, the Voice to its bloodthirsty cult, the Harbinger of Sorrows for a doomed wayfarer. So many names for one adversary.

Each green dot on the map indicates a sighting.

There were dozens of them, from the Pennyroyal to the Hollows, from the Cumberlands to the Belle River cities, all labeled with dates and numbers.

They cluster along ley lines radiating from a single point.

Signe touched it with her fingertip: a five-cornered star in the heart of the Bluegrass. That must be where the rifts in the veil had begun.

I went seeking the source, but I never reached it. As I drove west on the first night of spring, the sky split asunder above me. I hid in my truck until dawn and then sped home through the devastation. Along the way, I picked up another survivor: a girl with a fiddle and bloodied fingers. She didn't say a word—just sat there tuning her strings. We stopped here, and she played a song that lulled me to sleep. When I awoke, she was gone. I searched high in the hills and deep in the hollows, but I never saw her again. Now, after half a year of watching and waiting, I'm off to find the origin of the spirits. In case I fail, I've left a map for you to follow.

Your fellow stargazer,

Maxwell Doran

Signe branded the star's coordinates on her memory, then lit a match and burned all the papers—the map, the letter, the envelope—so the harbinger would never see them. She couldn't let it sift through her thoughts again, either. Not at any cost.

Stepping out from under the painted constellations, she scanned the real ones with her spyglass. Next to the grand telescope, it was a toy—but it worked, and no bolides crossed its field of view. The town below was as white and serene as a diorama dusted with corn flour.

Sleepy-headed and sore-calved, Signe sat on the platform and hugged her knees. She'd cracked the mystery, and tomorrow—

Beneath her, the platform tilted. As she gripped the rail, it twisted itself into a rope. The astrolabe clanged past her feet, picking up speed as it bounced.

Another vision? Another night terror?

Skyward turned sideways, and sideways turned topsy-turvy. Her hair went cascading upside down, but she swung around to stay head over hem. The orrery's planets spun out of their orbits, and a flock of essays fluttered toward the dome.

"Are you there?" Signe asked the darkness.

The brick walls transmuted to stone, and the stars winked out underfoot. Folding in on itself, the telescope sank through a floor that had become a ceiling. Far below, a deluge poured through the gap in the dome's shutter.

When the world finally stopped turning, Signe was dangling above a cavernous cistern. Hemp fibers dug into her palms, and magnetic winds pulled at her feet.

Hang on just a little while longer, said a clammy voice—the one from her other trances. *Our enemy may be spying on us.*

Signe looked past her billowing skirt to the bottom of the cistern. Black on black. "I think you can come on out."

In the raging deep, twin sapphires sparkled. Then a pale blue hand reached out of the water and grasped the end of the rope.

"I know who you are," Signe said. "I'm sorry I took so long to understand."

A revenant pulled itself from the depths: a dripping scarecrow with a horned crown. Novalyne, in the form of a shadowy wraith.

Signe climbed down toward her lost companion. "It's good to see you, even if we're in a vision."

I would've told you my name, said the specter. *But our enemy sealed my lips when I tried.*

"You said enough." First the *N* by the schoolhouse; then the *No* in the cabin, and Signe had filled in the rest. "How did you slip past the harbinger?"

Novalyne clawed her way higher, just ahead of the rising water. *When it's distracted, I can spin my own psychic threads. It took my gift and my body, but I've stolen its telepathy. Right now, it's calling spirits to hunt down my brother and Zora and someone else with them.*

"Abigail?"

Not her. An antlered woman—the Hierophant.

Signe's hand slipped on the rope, but she caught herself. The Hierophant would be Evelyn Fontaine. "Have you found Quinn or Paige or your cousins?"

Below Novalyne, the water had formed a vortex—an abyss wide enough for a kraken's lair. In its cauldron, green chaos seethed.

I sensed their thoughts last night, but then the threads snapped.

Anxiety gnawed inside Signe's ribcage. "Can't you see the future?" she pleaded. "You spoke to me before I left the Hollows—before the harbinger ever possessed you. At the fish farm, I had a premonition. You asked me to save you."

Time and space weave differently inside the well. Not as single cords but skeins of tangled yarn binding our world to the spirit realm—the present to what's been and what's yet to come.

That sounded like Zora's description of quantum etherics— spooky physics, she'd called it.

I caught a strand leading back to the past and found you in a square of nine ponds; that's how I called out for help. I've tried to trace the strands forward, too, but they twist into knots when I pull them.

"I discovered where—" Signe cut herself off at a warning gesture from her companion.

Our enemy can hear us.

"I'll cast that thing out of you. I promise." Signe stretched out her hand.

As Novalyne clasped it, the water surged up to the tips of her horns. *It's near,* she whispered mouthlessly. *Look after Nicholas and the children.* Then she released her grip, and the whirlpool dragged her down.

Beneath Signe's fingers, the hemp turned to wet shoots of eelgrass. She lost her hold on the rope and fell toward the abyss—only to land on her feet in a world that had flipped right-side up. The floor was below her; the dome was above her; the telescope was back on its mount. Novalyne's specter was nowhere to be seen.

But Signe was not alone.

"Hello, little runaway." The harbinger leaned in through the open window and bared a set of shining teeth. Its face was mottled with emerald blotches, and the whites of its eyes were the color of brimstone. "I followed my prisoner to this tomb."

19

ZORA FELT LIKE A PASSENGER IN THE BACK OF A HEARSE. FROM THE driver's seat of the locomotive, she'd been able to watch where she was going. In the last car, she could only see where she'd been. And now she was all by herself, give or take Traitor Girl. The rocket launcher was her only comfort: a cold, hard security blanket.

Behind the caboose, the surface world slowly receded. The tunnel's dusk-purple mouth shrank to the size of a porthole. To the size of a peephole. Then the tracks curved, and the black train entered a realm of perpetual night.

Zora rubbed her hands together, but streaks of coal dust stuck to her fingers. By the rear window, Abigail scratched at her scalp with filthy nails.

The sound grated on Zora's nerves. "Could you make yourself useful?" she snapped.

"I can try my hand with this." Abigail lifted a sawed-off banisher-shotgun. "But I don't trust my aim, so I'm lucky you're back here with me." She studied her feet. "It's been lonely riding three cars behind everyone else."

Zora let that pass. "The next car up—what's inside it? Did

your boss bring a treasure trove for bribing the Judges?" Evelyn could've loaded the boxcar with chests of silver bits. Casks of vintage bourbon. Cases of polished agates and freshwater pearls. "Or did she build a secret weapon to conquer the Hollows? A freeze ray? An earthquake machine?"

"She's not my—she didn't tell me."

The girl looked so woebegone that Zora had half a mind to absolve her. Quinn and Signe would've. Maybe Paige, too. But the cut was too deep, the wound still too raw.

"I could never stab you in the back like you did to me," Zora said. "Not to save my own father."

The train crawled on, engine huffing, but the tunnel seemed infinite. How long could it be? Any second, the roof might cave in and bury them in this rolling coffin.

"Would you have done it to save your mother?" Abigail asked in a soft voice.

The question brought Zora up short. Truth be told, she might've been tempted then. Did that make her a horrible person? But no, it wasn't the same. Mom had stuck around for every breakthrough and failure, every low point and high-water mark. Not like Dad.

Nor Abigail's father. Ulysses Bell had left his teenage daughter to her own devices.

Zora snatched the girl's banisher and set it to its widest pattern. "Don't bother with aiming. Just fire and you'll hit whatever's in front of your face." She handed the weapon back. "You wanted to tell me something?"

"It's not important now. When we reach the other side, I'll— what's that on the rocks?"

The tunnel walls were so close that Zora could've reached

out and touched them—supposing she wanted to stick her fingers into sulfurous goo. "Ectoplasmic resin from piddly earthbounds, the sort that trap crickets and spiders. No threat to us."

But down below dwelled the landwights. If Evelyn wasn't lying, they'd slaughtered her workers. Her brother. Her fiancé. And after all that, she'd feigned adoration for the spirits. Chanted their praises, fed them offerings. That must've taken an iron spine and a hollow heart.

The brakes screamed, and inertia pushed Zora off balance.

"We're at a spur in the line," Evelyn said through a built-in speaker. "The switch is set to the wrong track. If I hadn't stopped us, we would've gone deeper into the mountain. No doubt the work of the forces conspiring against me."

Served her right, but bad news for her captive crew. And what forces? The spirits were brutes; they wouldn't go blocking tracks or changing switches unless a hidden hand was behind them. Zora knew one thing—and only one thing—that could be.

Yet she'd banished it from this world, if not from her dreams.

Abigail turned a dial beside the speaker. "What now, conductor?"

"We wait for Mr. Martin," said Evelyn. "He went out to throw the switch."

No surprise she'd made Nick do the job. Why take the chance herself when she could risk a pawn instead? She'd sacrificed two bishops and a rook on the fall equinox and sent her last knight on a fatal charge to the airfield. Doe Queen would trade away any piece on her chessboard.

Above their heads, driblets pattered. Maybe water, maybe not. Zora shouldered the rocket launcher.

"The things that murdered my people are coming," said Evelyn.

As Zora's wrist-watcher beeped, fingers of chlorine mist vented up from the holes in the limestone. The air went sour, and a burst of clicks echoed along the tunnel. The sound made her think of giant bats hunting mosquitos—or a lab full of riled-up Geiger counters.

The landwights had woken from their chasms.

"What's taking so long?" she shouted. Had the spirits caught Nick and siphoned his life away? If so, she'd feed Evelyn to them herself.

The receiver picked up an indistinct voice in the background, then rapid footsteps approaching. "I'm back," Nick said breathlessly. "Go!"

The engine chuffed, but the train stayed put. Outside the caboose, the rising mist smoldered arsenic green—the color of toxic wallpaper and poisonous ball gowns. Another barrage of clicks bombarded Zora's ears.

"Open the door," she said. "I need a clear line of fire."

Abigail yanked the handle and then scooted backward. The landwights had caught hold of the car, anchoring it fast to the rock. As Zora knelt and took aim, foggy talons stretched toward her throat. Behind her, Abigail whimpered.

Zora fired, and a lavender shock wave tore through the tunnel. The train jerked forward, shoving her flat and sending her rocket launcher rolling toward the doorway. A landwight clinging to the rear platform reached out a talon and grasped the weapon.

With one blast of her shotgun, Abigail vaporized the spirit. The rocket launcher dropped to the floor, but more landwights fumed up and snared the caboose.

The train shrieked to a halt, and the rocket launcher rolled back to Zora.

"If you can't free us soon," Evelyn said, "I'll have no choice but to unhook the couplers and go on without you."

Afire with wrath, riven with fear, Zora loaded another rocket and squeezed the trigger. When the glare faded, the tunnel behind her was empty, and the wheels were clacking again.

From up ahead, piercing wails erupted. The arc-ladder cowcatcher must be mowing down spirits in the train's path. A handy weapon, jinx its inventor.

Evelyn chuckled. "Well done, Ms. Putnam and Ms. Coldiron. When properly goaded, you make—"

"Please tell me you're all right," Nick cut in.

Zora found the note of concern in his voice gratifying. "Better off than the landwights. Are we almost through?"

"I see the end of the tunnel," Evelyn said. "And our enemies are turning tail."

"We copy that." Abigail killed the microphone's power. "Ms. Fontaine won't hear us now. Can we talk while she's busy gloating?"

Before Zora could nod, the train shuddered and slowed to a funeral pace. She and Abigail exchanged worried glances. Then the train lurched forward, gathered steam, and roared out of the tunnel. Behind the caboose, black mountains rose against the aurora.

How did that ballad about the midnight train go? *Umbrella on her shoulder, piece of paper in her hand. Marched up to the conductor, said take me home from this land. Let the Midnight Special shine its light on me.*

This Hollows-bound train had left the landwights' lair in a

cloud of soot. But wasn't there another verse? *She left me crying, tears rolling down my face . . .*

Zora's wrist-watcher was still showing seven orange portents of danger. Signaling Abigail to hang back, she set down the rocket launcher and crept out to the rear platform.

Click-click-click.

A landwight was up on the roof. It must've grabbed onto the car and ripped loose from its earthly tether. Now its aura was flashing a ghastly shade of fluorine yellow.

Earthbounds went berserk when they lost their grounding.

She caught Abigail's eye and pointed upward. The girl's mouth was ajar, her shotgun slack in her grip. The aura blinked out, and by the time it blinked back, the landwight had unfurled its talons.

Click-click-click, click-click-click.

A misty snare smashed through the roof and caught Abigail by the neck. Raising her weapon, she fired through the doorway. Sulfur sparks rained around Zora: the embers of a second snare.

That shot had spared her from getting strangled.

Abigail dropped her gun and clutched at the snare around her throat. Her eyes were all whites, no irises. As the spirit pulled her toward the ceiling, she kicked her legs in the air.

Zora aimed a crutch—the heavier one—and pressed the button in its handle. A rocket shot out from the shaft and lit up the car with amethyst pyrotechnics.

CLICK-CLICK-SCREE . . .

Flickering wildly, the landwight whipped a talon at Zora. An image froze in her mind: Abigail face-down on the floor, surrounded by the shards of her weapon's barrel. Then everything exploded in pain.

Zora pitched off the back of the caboose, missing the tracks by a head. Blue-hot fire surged up her ankle as she tumbled down a snowy incline. A few more bumps, and she came to rest at the bottom, her crutches still cuffed to her wrists. From light-years above, the Seven Siblings cast their cold eyes on her.

When she tried to stand, her ankle buckled beneath her. A sprain for sure, maybe broken, and the brace on it had split apart. She sagged back down to the earth, her nose running and her eyes watering.

Across a dark plain, the Midnight Special clacked away without her. To her back, the mountains loomed high and desolate.

She was alone.

Biting down hard, Zora pulled off her boot and unstrapped the broken brace. Ice water seeped through her sock, and sleet from a clear sky tattooed her face. No time to improvise a splint, so she dug out a spare tip and fixed it to the charred end of her rocket-crutch. Then she listened for the train, but its clatter had passed out of earshot. Instead, she heard a thunderous footfall.

There's no such thing as premonitions, she wanted to shout, but part of her had known this would happen. The titan had tracked her. The titan had found her. The titan was here.

Another unthinkable footfall rolled down from the mountains. Above the peaks, a brilliant fringe of spirit-shine eclipsed the aurora.

This is a land of constant sorrow, a radio sang in her memory. *We've seen trouble all our days.*

Fighting to control her breathing, Zora scanned the snowscape for a hiding place. The tunnel? She'd never reach it—and if she did, the landwights would be waiting. The other edge of the plain? That might as well be the far side of the moon.

In these Wastes, I'm cursed to ramble.

Behind the mountains, an acid-green sunrise was breaking. The rippling light gave the scene a dreamlike quality, but the tremors underfoot made everything terrifyingly real. Soon, the spirit would come into view. Against it, she'd be one small soul with a banisher-pistol. Rocket launcher gone. Grenades all spent. Spirit-shield lost in the zeppelin's crash.

Yet she could look her fate in the face—or at least where its face might've been. That's what Nick's parents had done. And the fiddler girl, if the legends of her last stand were true.

I have no one to help me now.

As Zora drew her banisher and watched the dawning of the titan's corona, a steam whistle cried out from the west. Twisting her neck, she saw the black train backing up toward her.

Not alone, after all.

When she faced forward again, the spirit was there: a soaring inferno framed by twin summits. A blot of light against the sky, a supernova fallen to earth. The sight of it fused the wires in her brain. The titan's stride shattered the laws of physics; its form imploded the rules of topology. With a hundred arms, it swept the darkness aside.

But Zora's nerve didn't break—not yet, anyway. Soldering her thoughts together, she pocketed her weapon and fled. On one foot and two crutches—now an evenly weighted pair—she followed the tracks toward the idling train. A running figure met her halfway: Nick, bearing his bow and fiddle, a heart-sized metal cube strapped to his chest.

Zora could've kissed him, but she didn't. Because the titan was almost upon them.

Nick put his fiddle to his chin, and a doomed serenity fell

over her. The two of them were bound to fall side by side, re-staging the deaths of his mother and father. Or so she thought, but he confounded her by tapping his chest. From within the metal cube, feedback screeched.

Where had he found a portable amplifier?

Raising his bow, he played the same tune that was stuck in her head. *A land of constant sorrow.* Yet this version sounded different—down-tuned and distorted, with fuzzy reverberations from the amplifier.

"So fare you well, my own true hollow," Nick sang as he sawed the strings. "The place that I have loved so well."

On the range's downward slope, the titan halted and swayed with the music. Its corona flared a little less brightly; its solar-flare arms wilted toward the treetops. Nick's chords were working their magic. Scratch that—they were working their *parasonics.*

But it wasn't enough. The titan ceased oscillating and took a step the length of a mountain.

"I may be a stranger." The cords on Nick's neck stood out. "My face you may never see no more."

Impelled by sudden inspiration, Zora tuned her pistol's coil and cast up a cone of violet—not at the titan but above it. "There's a promise that is given," she sang in her tuneless alto. "Where we'll meet on that farthest shore."

A few gargantuan paces away, the titan paused in midstride. At her side, Nick played on feverishly. She traced patterns in the sky with her spotlight—figure eights and butterfly wings and zodiac symbols, but no spirals—and the spirit resumed its swaying.

Light and music, vision and sound. Together, they'd mesmerized the titan.

The train hissed and backed up closer, adding the beat of its wheels to the fiddle's melody. Evelyn must've spotted the source of the light show. And just in time. Zora's beam was dying; she'd bled her battery dry.

"Get ready to run," she murmured.

Nick bobbed his head and shifted to a minor key. He'd stopped singing, and his breaths had gone shallow.

When the violet cone vanished completely, Zora made for the train as fast as her arms and good ankle could take her. Nick ended his tune with a crash of strings and caught up with her at the locomotive's steps.

"You came back for me," she said. She still couldn't quite believe it: her nightmare had come to pass, and she'd survived it.

"Wouldn't leave you behind." His speech was slurred. "Flew across the Wastes for me and my kin."

Zora climbed up to the engine. "Did Abigail tell you I'd fallen?"

"No, Ms. Fountain—Fontaine—stopped the train when y'all didn't answer. I left her by the caboose with—" Nick missed a step but righted himself and clambered aboard. "I feel a mite woozy."

The locomotive shook, knocking them both off their feet. Seconds later, another tremor rattled the floorplates and sent spasms of pain up Zora's ankle. The titan was on the move again.

But so was the black train. Below the steps, the ground scrolled by and then turned into a blur.

"We need coal in the firebox," Evelyn said from the driver's seat.

Zora sat up, but Nick didn't. With numb fingers, she touched his wrist and felt a pulse. Had he fainted from the strain on his heart?

"Unless you'd rather play an encore for the titan," Evelyn added with a touch of waspishness.

Leaving Nick by the steps, Zora hauled herself to the stoker's seat and started shoveling coal. The flames in the furnace blazed hotter, singeing her eyebrows with cinders.

Evelyn opened the throttle wider. "Is the titan still gaining on us?"

Zora leaned on her shovel and poked her head out a window. The spirit stood astride the tracks, a blazing, thousand-limbed colossus. Around it, space wavered and folded like cellophane.

Then the titan turned and trampled back toward the mountains.

Zora's eyes pulsed in their sockets as she watched its corona diminish. A shovelful of coal—the spirit had passed by the summits. Another shovelful—it was striding down to the nether. One more scoop—out of sight except for a smudge on the horizon.

She sank to the floor and let out a pent-up breath. That's when she noticed Abigail laid out beside her, eyelids shut and lips slightly parted. Her skin was the color of an unripened apple.

Zora stared at her uncomprehendingly.

"I carried Ms. Putnam back here," Evelyn said from what seemed like a vast distance. "But she was dead when I found her."

Zora shook her head back and forth. "She must have spirit-sickness. Like Signe last summer—you thought she'd died, but you were wrong."

"Not this time, I fear." Evelyn's tone was almost tender.

"Take it from one who built and burned a funeral pyre by the mouth of the tunnel behind us."

"*You're wrong.*" Zora slid a pair of fingers under the girl's scarf. "Give me a banisher, and I'll drive out the infection." She checked for a pulse beneath the jaw. On the wrist. At the crook of the elbow. No sign of life anywhere.

The pistons beat, and the chimney wheezed, but Abigail stayed inert. Outside, the green-shadowed plain rolled on by.

Evelyn eased off the throttle. "Do you believe me now?"

"This is your fault," Zora spat. "You tricked her into leading us to your burrow."

"She came of her own free will, but I . . . regret the loss of her talent." A nearly imperceptible sigh. "How is our other crew member?"

Nick's chest was rising and falling in a steady rhythm. "Alive," Zora said. "But he may need a doctor."

Evelyn beckoned her forward. "Take the regulator. I'll tend the boiler for a spell."

Laying down her shovel, Zora hobbled to the driver's seat. She wanted to cry and throw things and devise ways to make Evelyn suffer, but all of that would keep for tomorrow. For now, the smart move was to play along. "Where does this line end?"

"A station hidden in the hills just ahead. It's stocked with supplies and shielded against roamers."

"And what's in the boxcar?"

Evelyn went cagey at that. "Merely a few of my latest creations."

"Like the amplifier you gave to Nick."

"Yes, that was an extra card up my sleeve: an ace of notes, if you will. Ms. Putnam had informed me of his musical gifts."

Abigail must've called Peryton One from Ram's Horn. Zora looked back at the girl. At her *corpse*. If only she'd spilled her secrets that night in the hot spring or at the meeting in the lodge or even on the *Reynardine*.

"So, my adversary set a titan against me," Evelyn mused.

"Against both of us," Zora said. "I know what's behind this." Why was she blabbing to her captor? Maybe because they shared a worse enemy. "The harbinger found a way back."

"I suspected as much. But how?"

"You tell me, copperhead. You're the one who struck a bargain with it last summer—not that you ever stick to your deals."

Evelyn fed more coal to the firebox. "Not for spirits or spirit-lovers or turncoat Spotters. But I meant to honor my promise to Ms. Putnam." She set down her shovel. "We're arriving at the Black Station."

Zora toyed with the idea of derailing the train but chose not to chance it. Instead, she let the engine slow down. Up ahead, the headlight caught a platform in the shadow of an outcrop. Unlit lamps lined the rails, and dark windows looked down from the station house. Neither spirit nor human broke the platform's stillness.

"From here, it's a short trek to the Border Hollows," Evelyn said as the locomotive pulled up to the station. "And now I have a proposal for you."

Zora snorted. "You can stow it and take a running jump into an elemental."

"You may change your mind once you hear what I have to say." Evelyn rested her hand on her golden revolver. "Of course, I could persuade you by other means."

All at once, the lamps lit up in cobalt. From the station house, four figures stormed out. Emerson Tate, wielding a shotgun and looking ferocious. Bela Holcomb, armed with a deer-hunting rifle instead of his banjo. The young Ranger from the airfield, brandishing a six-shooter in each of her hands. And Zora's mother with . . . was that a makeshift *flamethrower*?

"Mom!" Zora shouted. She felt a flood of relief, followed by crushing weariness. Safe at last, but they'd lost Abigail and Mr. Vandy. Nick hadn't woken yet; Quinn and the rest were still missing.

"Step right on out, Ms. Fontaine," said Emerson. "With your hands up if you have a mind to keep on living."

"And let my daughter go." Zora's mom leveled her weapon at the doorway.

Evelyn scowled for a second, then smiled and dropped her gun. "It seems someone alerted the Rangers about our departure this morning. I suppose I made a mistake leaving Ms. Putnam alone in the caboose with a radio transmitter. And here I thought I'd thoroughly cowed her." She dropped her voice to a whisper for Zora's ears only. "This complicates my plans. But come visit my prison, and I'll tell you about the prototype in the boxcar. I call it the Loom."

20

ONCE ON A SLOW SUMMER MOON, QUINN HAD SPENT A MORNING with Paige building little boats out of discarded milk crates and coffin-wood scraps. She'd painted names on their sides—*Pond Witchcraft*, the *Death's Head Raccoon*, and so on—while he'd spun fake histories of their voyages to living islands and floating cities. Over her big sister's half-hearted protests, Claire had tagged along and crewed the decks with doll-like mariners made of sticks, twine, and corncobs. Then they'd carried their sloops and junks to the head of the creek, set them adrift on the current, and raced downstream to watch them skim under the footbridge. Paige had tried to sink his armada with rocks, and he'd done likewise to hers, but both fleets had met the same fate in the end: a plunge over Cascade Hollow's namesake. Afterward, he'd wondered how it would've felt running the gauntlet for such a cruel reward.

Well, now he knew.

"Should we jump the falls?" Holly asked in a small voice.

"We'd splatter on the rocks below," said Paige. "I reckon we're shooting our way past the altie."

But the waterbound looked set to get ornery. As its eye-motes shone, a row of coils split the river and blocked the gorge from wall to wall. The spirit's cry rose over the roar of the falls like a death knell for the *Muskellunge*.

From the bow, Quinn plotted two courses for watery death—ahead toward the spirit or back toward the void—but then his gaze fell on the black outline of the trestle bridge.

Maybe the only way out was above.

He lined up his rifle and squeezed off a shot that nicked one of the altie's three eyespots. Blaring a foghorn note, the spirit twisted its neck and thrust its crest underwater as if the ray had set it on fire.

"Take us around," he told Holly. "Right up to the trestle." He turned to Paige. "Remember lobbing rocks at each other's ships from the bridge on Cascade Creek?"

"I like this plan," said Paige. "Want me to go up first?"

Iris popped her head out of the bilge. "Let me do it. I'm the lightest, and you two can cover me. Look at this." She held up an iron claw.

Quinn recognized what it was from illustrations he'd seen in *Davy Jones's Logbook* and *Tales of the Jolly Roger*: a grappling hook. The river-raiders must've used it for boarding their targets—barges heaped with logs and coal, keelboats loaded with moonshine and pelts. Bad fortune for the pirates' victims but a lucky break for the steamer's new crew.

Far behind the stern, the altie sprayed water like the fountain at the Grand Courthouse. "It's not chasing us yet," reported Jay.

"I bet it's trapped other boats here." Paige took the grappling hook, tied a rope to its eye, and swung it around experimentally. "It's cornered us to play hide-and-seek, but it'll strike when it gets itchy. We need to be up top by then."

Holly steered the *Muskellunge* in choppy bursts to the trestle and set the paddlewheels against the current. Leaning over the railing, Paige moored the boat to a wooden pile. High overhead, the moon peeked through the gaps between the bridge's slats.

As Iris threaded a spare rope through her belt loops, her bedraggled lamb tried to shake itself dry. She knelt and scratched its head. "We'll get you out of here, Little Woolly."

Quinn hoped she was right. Upriver, the altie had raised its neck from the water and bent its crest forward so that it looked like a dragon ship from one of Signe's sagas. If she were here, she could've glared the spirit back down to the muck with the catfish and carp.

"I wish Spotter school taught me how to use this." Paige whirled the grappling hook and flung it up toward the stringers. It thumped against a slat and fell with a thud next to Quinn. A little to the left, and it would've impaled him.

He dislodged the hook and gave it to Paige, who smiled at him grimly. "Just imagine you're casting for welkies," he said.

Tossing back its crest, the altie broke into a wordless lament. Its keening called up Quinn's memories of a bloated cadaver on the embalming table—a drowning victim carted to the parlor by a pair of Rangers with bandanas over their noses. That job had cracked his resolve to follow in his mother's footsteps.

Paige threw the hook again, and this time it caught onto a slat. With a victory yell, she yanked at the rope. "Tauter than a banjo string. Your show, Lamb Chop."

Iris shinnied on up as if she'd been climbing rigging her entire life. Quinn figured she might have a future as an acrobat—assuming she survived tonight's high-wire act.

When the girl reached the halfway mark, the altie spouted an arc of beryl foam. "It's making high-pitched noises," said Jay. "Maybe it has some sort of echo-sense to track its prey."

Iris must've heard him, given how she set to hauling tail. Quinn winced at the sight of her aloft in the shadows. If she lost her grip, she'd end up as a crimson stain on the deck. And if she reached the top, he'd be trailing her with a waterbound nipping at his heels.

As if to contradict him, the altie changed tack and undulated against the current. With one more bass note, it dove like a submarine from an Olden World navy, leaving the channel upriver unbarred.

"Sucker bait," said Paige. "It's trying to snooker us into an ambush."

At the top of the dangling rope, Iris pulled herself onto a stringer and looped the hook around a crossbar. Then she jumped to another plank—which collapsed and fell, almost taking her with it. Yipping a streak of blue words, she heaved herself from the hole as the broken slat bobbed away toward the falls.

"Watch your step!" Holly shouted.

That advice provoked a fresh curse from on high, but the next plank Iris walked held her weight. She unwound the spare rope, tied it off, and dropped the end to the deck.

"Up you go," Quinn told the other children. Jay hopped to the task, but Holly ran back to the wheelhouse for her pack. Strapping it on, she started up at a slower clip than her cousins.

Paige leaned close to Quinn. "That's a tall climb for a kid mending from a concussion."

"She'll make it," he said, but the girl was already struggling. A third of the way up, she stopped and pretzeled herself around her rope.

Nearer to the top, Jay paused and tilted his head. "I hear the altie. It's making pinging noises from the river bottom."

Iris helped him over the railing. "Drop that pack and get your butt up here," she hollered down.

"Shut up!" Holly barked, but she unknotted her limbs and got back to climbing. As Jay reeled her in, she turned around. "There's a streak of light in the water!" she shouted. "It's swimming straight toward the boat."

Quinn set his sights on the river. Up the gorge, an aquamarine wave was cresting. Too far to shoot, too close to outclimb.

Baaing timidly, the lamb flopped down in the wheelhouse. Paige tapped Quinn's shoulder and pointed a thumb at the little beast. "I hate to say it," she whispered, "but a distraction might buy us some time. If we cut the boat loose with a meal for the altie to chase . . ."

He looked up at Iris. Her eyes were wide, her face a pale shade of blue. She'd lost her home and her elders; the stars only knew where her twin cousins were. He couldn't sacrifice the last sheep in her flock.

Besides, he hadn't liked it when he'd been the one on the altar.

"Rope the lamb and follow it up," he said. "I'll hold off the altie."

"You better not stick me with bad news for your mom." Paige stalked off to collar her quarry. From what Quinn could hear—squeals and swears and frantic hoofbeats—it was no easy task, but the scuffle ended with a sigh of triumph.

"Start raising wool," Paige called up to the children.

The lamb's bleats ascended toward the heavens, accompanied by a stream of human grunts. Then the altie breached the water with a harmonic blast, and all other sounds fell away. Three spectral pupils bored into Quinn: two still opaline, the third now dull and cloudy.

In one motion, he harpooned another eye-mote and ducked. A blueish-green whip flicked above him, and a cold gust ruffled his hair—a near miss by the altie's tail. When he lifted his head, the only trace of the spirit was a white whorl on the river's surface.

The end of a rope landed beside him. "We've got Little Woolly," said Paige. "Come on up while the spirit's underwater."

Quinn holstered his rifle, grabbed the rope with one hand, and wobbled across the deck. When he reached the bow, he drew his knife—an old present from Dad—and sawed at the steamer's tether.

"Below you," Jay warned.

Quinn dropped the blade—*Goodbye, lucky knife*—and gripped the rope with both hands just as the altie smashed through the wheelhouse. River-bottom smells assaulted his nostrils, and galvanic waves set his arm hairs to bristling. Underneath him, the deck yawed and bucked.

Eyespot to eyeball, he and the waterbound regarded each other.

From overhead, a pear-sized object plummeted between them: a grenade honeycombed with crystal tiles. It hit the deck, bounced once, and blossomed into a tiny violet sun. At the heart of the explosion, the altie let out an anguished scream that sent vibrations all along Quinn's backbone.

"This ram's got horns!" Iris shouted.

Thrashing its coils, the altie hammered its crest against the smokestack. Then the mooring line snapped, and the *Muskellunge* swept out from below, pulling the waterbound with it. At the end of his rope, Quinn swung back and forth above the dark, rushing river. Let go now, and the current would drag him toward the falls in the wake of the wreck and the spirit.

"Climb!" Paige roared, and the children took up her cry.

As Quinn pulled himself hand over hand, a metallic peal rang out behind him: the smokestack snapping in two. The altie was fighting both the current and its wooden prison, slamming its crest against the deck and lashing its tail at the paddleboxes. He couldn't help thinking of an old picture Signe had shown him: a woodcut of a sea serpent ensnaring a ship, its curves in the masts and a corpse in its jaws.

To the death groan of bursting timbers, the steamer rolled over and showed its underside to the sky. Still stuck partway through the hull, the altie curled around the paddles and wriggled. Coil by coil, it pulled the foundering boat back toward the bridge—and toward Quinn.

Behind the spirit, Moonbow Falls thundered and steamed.

Tightening his knees around the rope, Quinn pulled the last grenade from his bandolier and hurled it sidearm toward the *Muskellunge*. As the device hurtled through the night, amethyst tiles spinning, he clung desperately to his lifeline. The throw was bound to go wide or fall short or sail over its target, leaving him hanging here like a worm on a hook. A hex-chant bubbled up in the depths of his brain: *Stars of the Hunter, guide my shot true.*

The grenade struck the third eye-mote and set off a flare that painted the gorge lilac and teal. Crestless and smoking, the altie's neck twitched and spewed out sparkling jets of ectoplasma. In his shock, Quinn barely noticed the whistles and hoots from above.

"Nice job beheading the glow-eel," said Paige.

With no engine, mooring line, or rampaging spirit to counter the current, the capsized *Muskellunge* drifted on to the falls. As the boat passed over the edge, the altie's coils evanesced into a turquoise rainbow—a misty bridge to eternity.

Awestruck, Quinn watched the spirit-bow for a moment longer and then made his way up the rope. When he cleared the stringers, Paige pulled him onto a plank. He rolled over and lay there, his back to the river and his face to the stars. *Thank you, Hunter of the Sky.*

"Is this the bridge with the creature?" Holly sounded uneasy. "The half-goat, half-sheep, half-human thing?"

Iris's giggle held an undercurrent of wild, scarcely contained emotion. "Ms. Zhu made that up, silly. Remember?"

"There's no monster here," said Paige. "But we should find a snugger place to camp out."

Quinn sat up. To one side, the gap-toothed span stretched away toward a clifftop festooned with shining beard moss and glowing creepers. To the other, the gorge's rim was capped by the silhouette of a modest structure. A cottage or maybe a coal depot?

"It's quiet over there." Jay pried a bar from the railing—a piece of corroded iron the length of a walking stick. Tapping it on the planks in his path, he picked his way toward the structure with Quinn and the others in tow. The lamb balked at first, but Iris shepherded it with one hand on the back of its head and the other under its chin.

"You made your grenade count," Quinn told her. "When this is all over, I'll teach you how to use a banisher-rifle."

She beamed at him. "I'd appreciate that."

Once they reached solid ground, the structure revealed itself to be a sentry box with a brass eagle roosting on its roof. It looked as cramped as a jail cell and stank of animal droppings; still, it was a harbor from the wind and the spirits.

♈

Nobody but the lamb slept, and so the bloodshot sun dawned on five pairs of bloodshot eyes. As a red-breasted robin chirped outside the window, Quinn chugged river water from his canteen—it tasted faintly of tannins—and splashed the dregs on his face.

Holly shared out a few shreds of jerky. "That's all the food in my pack."

"Then why in green blazes did you go back to fetch it?" asked Iris.

"I brought some books and journals from home. *The Diary of Violet Martin*, *The Cumberland Chronicles*, *Wonders of the Astral World*, and—oh, a few others."

"I'd love to read them," said Paige, "but it's a hard day's hike to the Border Hollows." Pulling her cap over her mussed-up hair, she led them from the sentry box into the white-crusted wild.

After a few minutes of tramping through brambles, they found a deer trail winding down to the base of the cliff. From this vantage, the waterfall was a towering veil of primordial chaos. Along the banks below lay the scattered remains of the steamer: plating from the engine and smokestack, slivers from the hull and paddles. No more river-raids for the *Muskellunge*.

As Quinn stood fascinated, the sun cleared the rim of

the falls and cast pink-gold light on a cliff carving in the mist-shadow. Though untold years of spray had softened the lines on the rock, he could make out the shape of a stick-figure girl with a fiddle. He'd seen the same symbol before, as a prisoner under Clack Mountain, but his captors had desecrated that image with antlers; this one was unmarred—and much bigger. Above the figure, rough scratches formed notes on a treble staff. Below, a second row of markings spelled out a message:

FOLLOW ME THROUGH THE RIFTS TO THE
INDIGO TWILIGHT

Looking up at the carving, Quinn felt a kind of transcendence. A sense of standing at the edge of a mystery as old as the Deep Time, a pattern he could unravel if he kept on tugging at the right threads. The fiddler girl, the rifts, the indigo twilight. What did they mean, and how were they linked? Nicholas might know the key to the music; Zora, the way through the rifts; Signe and Novalyne, the secret behind the color.

Iris threw a rock into the river, and the plunk brought Quinn back to the moment. "At least we lived to see this," he said. "Holly, can I borrow a journal and something to write with?"

She gave him a pencil nub and *Alice of Blue Gables*, open to a blank page at the end. He copied the carvings, handed back the book, and nodded to his companions.

Setting a brisk marching tempo, Paige followed the bends of the river. The children filed behind her like possums summoned by a piper, nodding as if to a silent tune. With Quinn at the rear, they trekked around rockfalls. Under stone arches.

Over pebbled sandbars. No one talked, and nothing crossed their path.

Until a tocking sound from downriver brought them to a sudden halt.

Iris bolted ahead—*again*—and Quinn somehow found the reserves to match her pace. At a twist in the bank, he caught sight of the noise's source: a clockwork motor on the stern of a flat-bottomed boat. A girl dressed all in gray was working the gears while a man in a top hat and duster looked out from the bow through a spyglass.

Quinn was too winded to speak, so he held up a hand.

The man lowered his spyglass and returned the gesture. "Mr. Prosser," he boomed. "I'm delighted to spot you."

"Your mom says hi," croaked the girl at the tiller.

Iris gave a little snort of disbelief. "Their faces aren't blue," she said in an undertone. "I'd gotten used to you and Ms. Zhu, but now it's strange all over again."

"I promise they're friendly." Quinn was startled, too, but for the opposite reason: he knew those faces better than a pair of his favorite dust jackets. "Hey, Paige!" he called out. "Your boss and your sister are here!"

As Claire steered the boat toward the bank, Darius Epps doffed his rumpled hat. "I take it my apprentice is with you," he said. "How splendid!"

Paige chose that moment to burst from the forest, skipping and waving her arms like a Winter Fair hoedown champion. Jay and Holly tromped up behind her with bemused expressions, trailed by the wary-eyed lamb.

"Mr. Epps is a spirit-Spotter," Quinn explained to the children. "And Claire is my mother's assistant."

"She's been fretting since the moment you left." Claire cut the motor and let the boat drift toward the bank. "I could tell from the way she kept chewing her braid."

"This morning, we received a radio transmission," said Mr. Epps. "A message from your friend Ms. Putnam. She told us the five of you were traversing the gorges. Fortunately, we'd already procured a vessel and charted a course for the falls." He tossed a towline to Paige. "I recalled my pupil's zeal for this route."

"She's always been a sucker for boat trips," Claire stage-whispered.

"Ms. Putnam also said she, young Ms. Coldiron, and a lad by the name of Martin were taking a train to the Border Hollows under Evelyn Fontaine's command—as improbable as that sounds." Mr. Epps cleaned his spectacles with a handkerchief. "Fiona Coldiron and a Ranger team went to intercept them. I hope they've all arrived safely."

"And I hope they nab Evil-lyn," said Claire, who shared her sister's fondness for appalling nicknames. "I'd like to see Captain Flores grill that charlatan. Anyhow, we've been cruising upriver since dawn. A ways back, we found a life buoy washed up on a sandbar." A hint of mushiness crept into her voice. "We were worried you might've sunk."

Quinn tried to square their story with Ms. Fontaine's. *Don't try to find us; we'll be gone tomorrow.* That tracked, but what about Abigail serving as her mole? Maybe a lie—or maybe the girl had turned against her.

Either way, there were two castaways nobody had mentioned.

"I can guess what you're wondering." Mr. Epps laid out a gangplank. "But we've heard no word of Ms. Janasdottir or her companion."

"I have to find them," Quinn said, though he was so tired he could've keeled over.

"Search parties are scouring the Near Wastes." Claire waved the children aboard. "There were scads of volunteers. Your dad and your old classmates. A team of scrappers. A pair of fish-farmers. And all of Paige's apprentice pals." She held out a hand to her sister. "Let's get these kids to the Hollows. Y'all look like death frozen over, and I speak from experience."

Paige took Claire's hand, but Quinn hesitated at the river's edge. Somewhere over the mountains, Signe was in danger. Or lying dead with snow in her hair and frost on her glasses. Not knowing which was a torment.

"I'll go looking with you, Mr. Prosser," said Jay. "And listening, too."

"I'll come along," said Iris. "I'll blow up any spirits that get in our hair."

Holly nodded. "We owe it to you—and to Cousin Nova and Ms. Janasdottir."

With one last glance toward the hills, Quinn crossed the plank and sat down with the Children of the Ram. To his left, Holly was resting her head on Jay's shoulder. To his right, Iris was snuggling Little Woolly.

Three children and a lamb saved, but at what cost?

Mr. Epps untied the line, and Claire released the motor's catch. To the rhythm of a ticking clock, the boat barreled ahead toward the Hollows.

21

FAR ABOVE THE SLOT IN THE OBSERVATORY DOME, THE SKY WAS falling toward Signe. The harbinger had called down the bolides: seven deadly comets for the seventh child of a seventh child. One she could stare away, like she'd done from the crow's nest of the airship. Six more? Not if her life hung in the balance—which it did.

"I'll admit that you chose a good hiding place," the harbinger said from the open window. "Your thoughts lay concealed till I caught a stray thread leading out of the well—a psychic projection from my stubborn host. Sneaky of her, but it backfired. If she hadn't shown me where you were, you might've survived through the night. My old foe cloaked this dome with a sonic mirage, but now I see through her illusion."

Old foe? Sonic mirage? Signe turned the professor's letter over in her mind. The day after the Great Wakening, he'd brought a lost girl to the Ruined Town, and she'd played him a tune—a charm to mask his observatory from spirits. *Find the fiddler's songbook,* Peryton One had said. Did that belong to the same wayfaring girl who'd taught the people of Ram's Horn her music? *The fiddler went down by the river to play.* From the

Sounding Gap through the Lost Gorges and on past the falls? *Track the professor's trail.* Signe knew where it led—*west to the land of the goat*—but two of Ulysses Bell's revelations still baffled her. *Unravel the loom's pattern,* he'd written. *The loom has a shuttle but no warp or weft.*

Zora would be the person to ask about that; she'd mentioned a loom at the Judges' council. Now all Signe had to do was dodge a bolide-storm and outwit a mind-reading spirit. Easy as pie—if the pie in question were filled with nightshade berries and death cap mushrooms.

At the harbinger's whistle, shapes took form outside the other windows—diaphanous things that tapped and scratched at the glass. Some had lacy claws; others had filigreed stingers.

Signe was surrounded by roamers.

Their summoner watched her with ravenous eyes. "I would rake through your thoughts for any last wishes, but I have a library's worth of books to pore through and a handful of loose ends to sever."

Yet even as the harbinger's smile gleamed in the night, Signe saw that the sky was no longer black. The bolides were green lines on a purple spectrum; the roamers were green oils on a magenta canvas.

She snuck a look at her pocket-watch: a quarter past seven. She would've guessed that her trance had lasted ten minutes. Instead, it had lasted ten *hours*—which meant that the sun would be rising soon. She only needed to stall the harbinger a little while longer.

And in her lost hours lay a deeper truth: time flowed strangely in the spirit world. She could hear Zora's soliloquy. *The theory of spectral relativity implies that if two dimensions resonate at different frequencies, then a clock in one can tick faster than a clock in the other. Kirlian time dilation, in paraphysical terms.*

Then an echo from Grandpabbi's tales of the Fair Folk—not fair as in Signe's complexion but Fair as in fairy. *My own great-great-great-grandmamma lived among the elves for a season. When she came home afterward, seven years had passed in her absence. Or so she told her family.*

Back here in the present, the seconds had turned to molasses, but Signe knew that was a trick of perception—an effect of the adrenaline flooding through her. "Wait," she said. "If you're looking for Evelyn—"

The harbinger snapped with Novalyne's thumbs, and time flew forward again. All around the observatory, windowpanes cracked from phantasmal blows. Overhead, the bolides formed a V pointing at the dome's shutter.

Signe had come so close, only to fall short at the doorstep of the Hollows. It wasn't fair—that word again—but nothing in this land ever was. *There's no justice to be found in the Wastes,* the relic hunters' saying went. Her one consolation was that the professor's secret would perish with her, safe from the harbinger's prying.

Pushing back her hair, she gazed at the meteor shower raining down toward her. All those shooting stars for one lucky girl. By rights, she should get seven wishes. Her first would be for the telescope's lenses to focus her stares like they focused light beams. Or did it have mirrors? She never could tell a refractor from a reflector.

Focus your mind, Signe chided herself.

And then a wonder appeared in the sky: the lead bolide popped like a soap bubble as a violet ray from the hills intersected its path. One moment, the spirit was there, a fireball among the fading constellations; the next, it was gone. Breaking formation, the other airbounds veered away on haphazard routes, but a bolt from a new source cut their number to five.

A pair of spirit-snipers had come to her rescue. Quinn and Paige? Emerson Tate and a fellow Ranger? Two unknown wanderers of the Wastes? Whoever they were, she'd buy them a round of the finest bourbon at the Floating Tavern.

The harbinger's smile dimmed. "A wild card in the deck of fate," it sneered. "Too little, too late for you. *Look at me when I speak, chimera!*"

Signe had turned to face the opposite window. A roamer was snaking its way through a jagged hole in the glass, flailing its cilia and whining like a cloud of gnats. She transfixed it with her gaze. "Scat," she said, and it did.

A third pop sounded from above: the snipers tagging another bolide. Blue skies ahead, but down here on earth, the roamers had crashed through the panes at every point of the compass.

Hunching low to the ground, Signe slipped through a half-open door in the telescope's base. Beyond, a staircase twisted up into shadow. Softly, she padded up the helix of steps. Softly, she crept to the edge of a balcony. From below came the din of spirits ransacking the nooks for their prey.

Before dawn arrived, they'd sniff out her scent or sense the warmth of her breath. Then they'd butcher her while the harbinger laughed. Unless—unless—she'd forgotten something important. *Telescope. Mirrors.*

Zora had tucked a second surprise inside her winter solstice present. Signe hoped the harbinger hadn't smashed it. And that she hadn't cracked it herself; she'd been dealt enough bad luck already.

She flicked a catch on the parasol's shaft and detached the broken canopy. Next, she slid apart the handle, exposing a circular mirror on a swivel mount. When she tugged on the shaft, it telescoped to twice its usual length. Final step: goggles on.

Carefully—oh so carefully—she angled the mirror at the astrolabe—the orrery—a roamer with chiffony pincers. Holding the shaft in place, she gazed, unblinking, at the reflection. The spirit quivered and then poofed away.

A distant pop marked the end of a bolide's flight. The sky had turned a shade paler, and the gloom on the dome had visibly lightened. *Signs of the air, let the sun shine.*

Signe shifted the mirror to catch a new target—this time, a spirit-heap dyed in the colors of gangrene and mucus. It was too much like the Squirrel King from the loggers' legends, a squirming cluster of things with intertwined tails. She almost retched but kept her eyes on the heap until it moldered to nothing.

"There you are," said the harbinger. As it hummed, footfalls skittered up the side of the telescope's base—so many they all blurred together.

Whatever was climbing toward her, she could smell its acrid miasma.

Pivoting the mirror past the balcony's edge, Signe spied a roamer with a maw like a lamprey and more legs than a millipede. The nearer it crawled, the thicker the miasma grew. Fluorescent smog burned her eyes, and against her will, she squeezed them shut tight.

Then the skittering stopped, as if a phonograph had thrown its needle. A draft blew past the balcony, and the air turned from sour to piney. No more thumps on the walls, no more bangs in the nooks. Into that absence of sound, the harbinger screamed a scream no human throat ever should've made.

Signe opened her eyes again. Morning had come to the Ruined Town. The roamers had vanished like ghosts at the cry of a rooster, but their conjurer couldn't pull the same trick. The harbinger needed Novalyne as its medium, so it would be fleeing on foot.

With no weapon but her parasol shaft, Signe rushed down to a window. By the light of dawn, the campus looked peaceful—even pretty, in a bleak sort of way. Across its snowy grounds, a trail of boot tracks led toward the Hollows.

Past brick halls decked in dormant ivy and fishponds choked with lily pads, Signe followed the prints, racking her brain for a plan. Tussling with the harbinger would be a gamble; the one time she'd tried to wrestle, her next-youngest sister had pinned her in seconds.

When she reached the quad, a figure dashed out from behind the library. A young woman, but not Novalyne.

Of all the people in the Hollows, Lurana Underwood was the last savior Signe would've expected. Ferret-Face, Zora called her, which was unkind but understandable. By any name, shouldn't she be planting seeds and pruning trees back at the Reformatory Farm for Wayward Youth?

"Stars and garters, you're alive," said the former Spiritist spy. She had a glass rifle slung over the shoulder of her orange-striped prison jacket. "Hey, Mr. Crouch, she's here!"

A wild-eyed man bounded into the quad. He had a banisher, too, but wore white from toboggan to trousers and blended into the landscape. Rosette tattoos adorned his bare forearms.

Signe had crossed paths with McKinley Crouch twice: once by a spirit-cursed forest on a sweltering summer night and again along a logging road on the eve of the fall equinox. He was a hex-chanter on a self-bestowed quest to atone for some untold transgression. As likely rescuers went, he ranked a few spots above Lurana.

Now Signe could place the voices she'd heard on the radio that night in the cabin—one deep and hoarse, one high and nasally. She'd been talking with this mismatched duo.

"Ms. Janasdottir," rasped the tattooed man. "We've answered your summons for aid. It lifts my soul that a merciful star guided you hither."

Signe had used the delay to refill her lungs. "We need . . . to catch . . . *her*." She pointed at the harbinger's prints. "She's dangerous."

"My old priest, by any chance?" asked Lurana. "I still owe her for throwing me to the spirits."

"Worse," Signe said. "Your old god, possessing a spirit-sensitive human."

That was enough for Lurana and Mr. Crouch to spring into action. Arming themselves with stout sticks, they trailed the harbinger west through the streets and onto the Forbidden Road.

"We reached the Ruined Town by gloaming and set watch from the mountains above it," Mr. Crouch said as they crossed a meadow of thistle and milkweed. "We sighted roamers rambling the campus and airbounds patrolling the heavens, but no token of where you might be—till the spirits converged on the vault of the astrologers."

"Astronomers," corrected Lurana. "Then we plugged the bolides and charged downhill."

"I'm grateful you came looking for me," Signe said. "To what do I owe the honor?"

Mr. Crouch rolled his sleeves higher, displaying a set of sun-wheel tattoos. "The wind whispered to me of folks in peril. Also, I heard a call for volunteers on the Tower Knob station."

Lurana gave a strangled snort but then turned morose. "I begged my warden to let me join the search. You were kind to me even after I sold you out. I'll always carry a weight for bowing down to the Voice of the Spirits, but maybe helping you will lighten the load."

The sun climbed higher, and the day grew warmer. Snow-dazzle seared Signe's eyes and singed her face. Her head grew heavy, and her feet dragged, but the tracks marched on through the melting whiteness. Even when they went muddy and swelled to ogre size, their stride never varied. She'd read an Olden World tale of footprints like these—the work of some never-seen cloven-hoofed runner who'd crossed two counties in a single night.

At the edge of the Hollows, the harbinger's trail disappeared completely.

♈

Quinn's father was waiting beyond the next ridge with a haunted smile on his careworn face. He gave Signe a courtly bow. "It's a pleasure to meet you again. I brought my kids' wagon and horses."

Undine nickered, and Ursula whinnied.

The last stretch of the journey went by in a haze for Signe.

As Quinn's dad drove, he told the tale of the black train's arrival ("The most obscure hex sign," Mr. Crouch mumbled) and Abigail's fate ("Should've been Evelyn Fontaine," Lurana said).

A coffin on a rail car. The fifth card in Signe's fortune had been a death omen, but not for her. With chin on knees, she blubbered out the final message in Ulysses Bell's journal, never to be heard by his daughter. "Abigail's dad wrote to tell her . . . that she was dear to him."

Afterward, she dozed restlessly in Quinn's bunk.

As they pulled into Hot Springs Hollow, a small crowd gathered to greet them. Mamma and Pabbi, relieved and proud and exasperated all at once. Zora with a plaster cast on one foot, and Paige with an anxious expression. Ms. Coldiron and Mr. Epps, who kept glancing at her daughter and his apprentice as if to confirm they were real.

And Quinn, with stubble and windswept hair that gave him the look of a river pirate. He helped Signe down from the wagon, took her in his arms, and kissed her twice—first gently, then fiercely. When he drew away, she grabbed him by the shirt and made it three. So what if her breath tasted stale and her parents were watching?

When she was done—and it took a while—Zora came over to her. "I can't really hug you on my broken ankle, but I'll build you a new parasol."

"Don't you mean umbrella?" Signe asked, and they both tried to laugh.

Paige wrapped an arm around Zora and an arm around Signe. "I missed my spirit-hunting family." After a crushing squeeze, she released them. "Fairy Eyes, your blood kin want a word."

"We set out as soon as we heard about the crash." Pabbi sounded hoarse.

Signe hugged him and let Mamma kiss her sunburnt cheeks. Seeing her parents gave her a hitch in the throat—a tangle of old resentments and longings. "I did promise I'd see you this spring."

"We're happy you found your way back to us," said Mamma.

"Thanks to my sight and Quinn's aim and Zora's inventions. But I'll be leaving again tomorrow. There's still someone I need to rescue." Signe looked her mother straight in the eye. "I know where my spirit-vision came from. An eidolon visited you on the eclipse."

Mamma frowned. "Eidolon?"

"A nemesis of the spirits. Not from our world or theirs, but a third."

"That's extraordinary," said Mr. Epps. "I anticipate a new field of inquiry, neither spectral nor terrestrial. Could you describe this eidolon?"

Ms. Coldiron nudged him. "I'm sure she can brief you later."

"I bear their mark," Signe said. "So does Novalyne."

"Jay, too," said Quinn. "Turns out he has spirit-hearing."

Another one of us, Signe thought. And their enemy had overlooked him—so far, at least. "Where are the children now?"

"With Nick." Zora seemed troubled. "He's on bed rest under Doc Caudill's orders—she says his heart had a hiccup. He wanted to go search for his sister, but the doc wouldn't let him."

"I swear we'll find Nova," said Paige.

Zora nodded. "And banish the harbinger. How in the Wastes is it controlling her?"

Signe told them everything.

♈

After a somber feast, with plenty of squash and cabbage for Signe, Quinn gave her his arm. "I drove your wagon here from the airfield," he said. "I reckoned you'd want to catch up with Fylgja."

Tired as she was, she strolled with him to the stable. Digging a leftover apple from her coat pocket, she held it out for Fylgja. The mare chomped it down, licked her lips, and lowered her head contentedly.

"Good night and rest up for tomorrow." Signe stroked the horse's mane and then led Quinn by the hand to her wagon. "I want to sleep in my own bed tonight."

As she pulled him through the door, chimes jangled above their heads. The lights on the ceiling sparkled, and the curtains shut out the world. She was back in her private little fairyland with the boy she'd somehow enchanted. For the first night since they'd left here, she felt at ease.

Almost. Somewhere out there in the darkness, their enemy walked the hills and the hollows.

Signe changed into her owl-feather-pattern pajamas and sprawled on her bed with her face in her pillow. From a cabinet, her radio played a song of undertakers and unbroken circles. She listened until the final chords gave way to the wail of a stray signal.

"Whenever I hear that sound," she said, "I'll think of Abigail. And when I hear thunder, I'll think of Mr. Vandy."

Quinn sat on the bed beside her. "My mom's coming in the morning to take care of the preparations. She may keep her funeral face on, but I know she'll be glad to see you."

"And your dad?"

"Leaving at dawn to search for the harbinger on his own. He still has a hard time looking Mom in the face." Quinn shifted his weight. "I won't make the same mistakes he did."

"I believe you." She should've sat up and held him, but her pillow was too soft to resist.

On the radio, Bela Holcomb sang a ballad of trouble down yonder in the Sounding Gap. "He's a fast songwriter," said Quinn. "How was it seeing your folks?"

She thought about it. "Comforting. Infuriating. Confusing. I suppose I should be thankful they didn't take another crack at talking me out of my calling."

"That reminds me—Jay wants your help learning how to listen for spirits. Now, Iris, she's raring to fight them. Kind of like Zora when I first met her. And Holly should have a chat with your sisters and brothers—she fancies being a teacher." His tone grew more animated. "She brought her copy of *Blue Gables* all the way from Ram's Horn."

This side of him was one of Signe's favorites. "Did you enjoy watching over three children?"

Quinn laughed. "They grew on me, but I'm in no rush to have my own."

"You and me both. I prefer playing black sheep to my nieces and nephews." She was an aunt a dozen times over and counting.

"They won't have your gift, will they?"

"No, but other children in the Hollows might. We should investigate that."

Quinn took a book from one of her shelves. "*Carson van Patten and the Case of the Missing Geologist.* I lost my copy of this in the crash. I was worried I'd never get to read how she casts out the ghost."

"We'll have to save that for later," Signe said. "Otherwise, I'll sleep through Chapter 18 again."

"I can wait." Quinn kissed her on the ear and the back of the neck.

"Mm. I could use a hot shower. Or another nighttime dip in the Bubbling Cauldron. Do you remember that?"

"Often."

As he rubbed the knots from her shoulders, she let herself commune with the mattress. The clock on the wall had wound down. Time was standing still in her wagon, or so she could make believe. "That feels magical. Are you sure you're not a sorcerer?"

He ran his knuckles along the sides of her spine, between her shoulder blades. "How's this?"

"You can go a bit lower, though I'm going to drift off any moment." *Night hag,* Signe sang in her head, *go away and trouble my slumber no more.* But perhaps she'd dream of a wraith with ram's horns and shining blue eyes. *Novalyne,* she would say, *where did you wander tonight?*

"I have an idea," said Quinn. "How about we stick together next time?"

Signe rolled over on her side to face him. "I'm all for that."

Then they told each other charmed words they hadn't shared yet.

22

ON HER WAY TO BREAKFAST, ZORA WALKED INTO AN AMBUSH. HER brother and two best friends were waiting in the lodge's dining room, smiles on their faces and newspaper-wrapped things in their hands. Frozen in surprise, she tried to tally dates in her head but lost count at the night of her ride on the black train.

"Happy sixteenth birthday," said Quinn, as Paige pulled out a chair and Signe lit a candle stuck in a pie.

Zora sat down and put on a smile to mirror theirs. "With everything going on, it slipped my mind."

"We can't leave without a celebration," said Signe. She and Quinn both had damp hair, as if they'd just snuck a visit to the hot springs. Zora kept her mouth shut about that; those two deserved their interludes from tangling with spirits.

"Quick, make a wish." Paige drummed her palms on the table. "Before the candle burns out."

Zora huffed and puffed, and the little flame died. In slow motion, drops of bloody wax dribbled down to the pie. Its strawberry filling was deep red and pulpy, like the jarred preserves in Abigail's spooky story.

Quinn gave Zora his present, which she knew was a book before she even ripped off the paper. "*The Cosmos as a Web of Resonating Strings* by Cornelius Mendes," she read from the dented cover. Then she flipped to the title page. "Published in 1923? Hey, this is pre-Wakening!"

"I bought it from a roving bookseller a few moons ago. She said a forager found it in the ruins of a Belle River city. I got lost halfway through the first chapter, but it sounded right up your hollow."

Zora leafed through pages of scientific formulae and musical notation. "This looks grand."

"Exactly what I thought when I saw this. It's Coal Age vintage." Signe held out a flat box. Inside, Zora found a sleeveless fringe dress. Dark red velvet to match her hair; brass embroidery to match her crutches. She never wore dresses, but she'd make an exception for this one—if she could work up the nerve.

"It's striking," she said. A new pair of brass ankle braces would go with the pattern.

"For your next dance," said Signe. "Quinn and I tried to cover both work and pleasure."

"Sure," Zora allowed. "Though we may have different notions of which is which."

"My present's a bit of both." Paige handed her a crudely wrapped object that turned out to be a spring-loaded sleeve holster. "I picked it up from an old Skaggs Gang outlaw—don't ask me how. I figured you could rig it for a banisher-pistol."

Zora tried on the device. "I confiscated a derringer that should fit perfectly."

"Once you're healed up," said Quinn, "we'll get back to

chasing spirits together. Our team needs its brilliant inventor."
His eyes were shiny, yet hers were unaccountably dry.

"I already miss you, too," she said.

♈

Fortified with buttermilk pancakes and hot apple cider, Zora went to say her other farewells. To Dad, who told her he loved her and left her with a crateful of notes on the harbinger. To Emerson Tate, who promised her daily reports on the search. To Mr. Epps, who asked her to catalog every spirit she'd seen in the Wastes—when she felt *sufficiently convalesced*, of course. To Mr. Crouch, who muttered a protective hex-chant over her. Even to Ferret-Face—no, make that Lurana—who gave her a profane message to pass along to the ex-high priest of the Spiritists.

Afterward, Zora found her mom on a wicker couch overlooking the hollow. The snow was long gone except for patches of white in the shade. Down in the valley, two wagons were caravanning away. The first had solar cells on its roof; the second had purple shutters.

Happy hunting, big brother; bright stars to guide you, sister-in-arms. Zora eased herself onto the couch. "I'm sorry I put you through so much worry. Again."

Mom shook her head. "None of it was your fault, Fox-Kit."

"I tried to play the dutiful daughter. I followed your rules, listened to my elders. But everything still went wrong."

"Not everything. You flew away and came back to me."

Zora's waterworks should've flowed, but they didn't. "Was it worth it? Two of my crewmates died, and we set the harbinger loose."

A motley trio marched toward the mouth of the hollow: one in olive, one in white, and one in orange stripes. Emerson, Mr. Crouch, and Lurana, off to sweep the northern passes.

"You rescued those kids and caught the most wanted fugitive in the Hollows, all in time for your birthday." Zora's mom patted her shoulder. "How do you like being of age?"

"I feel older and sadder but not any wiser."

"I agree with the first and the second, but not the third. You did your best to keep your promise to me, so this is my gift to you: your freedom to go where you please and do what you want, with my blessing."

Two stories below them, Paige and Mr. Epps set out from the lodge—her with a bouncy step, him with a stiffer gait.

"Has he ever talked about quitting fieldwork and putting down roots?" Zora asked. As a kid, she'd heard her parents lock horns over Dad's gallivanting ways. With an empty den, Mom might want steadier company.

At the crossroads, Paige and Mr. Epps turned around. He tipped his hat, and she waved her cap. Then they took the pike that led toward the meeting hall of the Spotters.

"Maybe when Paige finishes her training, but there's no hurry." Zora's mom put on her nosy tone, just like after the Winter Fair dance. "I'm curious to hear about your new friend—the one who can hypnotize spirits with his playing. How is he?"

"Good question. I should go check on him."

As Zora stood, her mom made a tongue-click. "Just remember that you can always talk to me."

"I know." Zora had too many thoughts orbiting in her brain. Some she could share with Mom, some with her brother and friends the next time she saw them. And then there was the idea she wasn't ready to tell anyone.

The lodge's corridors were longer than she remembered. On her way to the infirmary, she stopped in a bathroom to lean on the sink and inspect her reflection. With clean overalls and a freshly scrubbed face, she no longer looked as if she'd been raised by muskrats. Guided by a whim, she put her hair into pigtails that stuck up like horns. She hadn't worn it this way for ages.

Nick's room was bright and airy, with walls painted robin-egg blue. His cousins had pitched camp around his bed, all three of them dressed in borrowed clothes. Iris was brushing her lamb, Jay was flipping through a spirit guide, and Holly was reading *Alice of Avalon*.

At Zora's knock on the doorframe, Nick sat up against his headboard. He'd combed his hair and put on a new shirt but still looked raccoon-eyed and hollow-cheeked. Not to mention heartbroken. "Did your brother and friends hit the trail?" he asked.

"They'll find Novalyne," she said, though the harbinger had a head start and a thousand hollows to hide in. "You can count on them."

Nick smoothed out a quilt woven with rows of triangles and squares—the pattern they called the Wild Goose Chase. "How's your ankle?"

"Busted in two places, but it should mend if I stay off it till summer. What's the word from Doc Caudill?"

"I have a heart murmur. And an irregular beat, which is mortifying for a musician. She wants me to pace myself." Nick glanced at his cousins. "I'm sure I'll be sledding down hills and climbing up towers before too long."

He'd make a lousy flimflammer, but Zora let that slide for now. "What did the doctor say to y'all?" she asked the children.

"She injected us with some kind of dye," said Holly, who had a wicked scab across her bare forehead.

Zora felt a glimmer of satisfaction at being right. "Methylene blue."

"That's it," said Jay. "The doctor told us it would help our blood carry more oxygen—and, odd as it sounds, turn our skin less blue." He studied his hands. "I'm sad about that, but she says it can't be helped."

"*I'm* more upset that the captain lady won't let us help search for Cousin Nova," said Iris.

"I know it's frustrating," Zora said. "I want to go, too. But there's lots to do while we wait. I can show you how to use all my weapons." She looked at Holly. "And teach you para-physics." She turned to Jay. "And test how your eardrums make my wrist-watcher flicker—you had me thinking its wiring was loose. Then we'll find a way to drive the harbinger out of Novalyne." A banisher-bolt to her brain might do the trick—but at the cost of her spirit-sense or even her life. "What do you say to being my lab assistants?"

Iris put an arm around her lamb. "If Little Woolly comes with me."

"Why not? I'm used to working in a barn full of goats. How about the two of you?"

Jay nodded, but Holly took longer to answer. "Let me think on it," she said. Zora laughed, and the girl scrunched her face. "Did I say something funny?"

"No, you just reminded me of my brother."

"Are you going back to Lightning Bug Hollow?" asked Nick.

So, he remembered the name. "No," Zora said. "I'll need a bigger lab." She'd seen the machine in the boxcar. It was gigantic, but she could ask her merchant friends to transport it—Viola Mack and Kirk Slocum would never say no to her. And she knew the perfect place to tinker with it: the workshop under Evelyn's Clack Mountain mansion. The Judges owed her a favor, and she intended to cash it. "I could also use a"—she tripped over her tongue—"lab partner, someone to handle the sound while I handle the light. If you want to work with me while you recover."

"We did put on a good show for the titan." Nick almost smiled. "When do we leave?"

"As soon as you wrangle your doctor's permission." The moths in Zora's chest stopped flapping their wings and fell to her stomach. "And once Abigail's funeral is over."

♈

It was Paige's sister who answered the door to the icehouse. "The legendary Gadgeteer Girl," said Claire. "I'm thrilled to finally meet you, though I wish the circumstances were better. You can step into our makeshift parlor—we haven't started the embalming yet."

Zora gulped down her misgivings and crossed the threshold. The morgue's walls were bare stone; the air inside was chilly and smelled of pickle juice. Bottles of colorless liquid lined one wooden shelf, and on another sat long silver needles that could've passed for torture instruments. The corpse on the table lay covered by a white sheet.

"I'm so pleased you made it home safely," said Ms. Prosser.

That's Aunt Anne to you, she'd told Zora last summer, though the title was honorary. Quinn's mom seemed as intimidating as ever: a sharp-eyed, taciturn woman with a leather apron over her dress. Yet beneath the frost, her voice had a touch of warmth.

"I'll go mix the fluid." Claire collected an armful of flasks and ducked into a back room.

"Do you use a formaldehyde-ethanol solution?" Zora babbled, keeping her eyes on Ms. Prosser instead of the body under the sheet. "I'm more of an engineer and a physicist than a chemist, but I know there's a science to—to—"

"You came to say goodbye." Ms. Prosser gestured toward the table.

Zora's gaze followed, and then she looked away. "Yes." She'd seen death up close before. When Static had slept in forever one winter morning. When the leviathan had claimed Nevan McBrain for the deep. When Walter Vandy had stayed at the wheel to safeguard his crew. When Evelyn's cutthroats had fallen prey to hount, spire, and elemental. But she'd always known she would outlast her dog. Mr. McBrain and Mr. Vandy had passed on with full lives behind them. And those Spiritists had been terrible people.

This time was different.

"The last thing she did was save me from a spirit," Zora said. "After I'd been so harsh to her. I'll never get to thank her for that. Never get to tell her I forgive her." Abigail had trusted a deceiver and endangered them all, but she'd done it for the sake of her father. A man who'd chased his own doom, who hadn't earned his daughter's devotion.

"You can tell her now."

"She won't hear me say it."

"But *you* will." Ms. Prosser folded her hands. "Did Quinn ever tell you why I followed this calling?"

"He said it was a family tradition."

"True—but when I was your age, I wanted to break with the past myself. My closest friend and I had a scheme to set up a still and use my family's hearse to bootleg moonshine. Before we could launch our plan, she died in a chance encounter with a stray roamer."

"That must have been awful." How many nights had Ms. Prosser sat up wondering whether the same thing would happen to her son?

"My parents asked me if I wanted to help with my friend's preparations. I said yes—and found my own comfort in the task." Ms. Prosser rested her fingers on the table. "Are you ready?"

Zora made a dry, vaguely affirmative noise in her throat, and Ms. Prosser drew back the sheet. Abigail's eyes were still shut, her skin still a vivid green. Her platinum goat pendant lay at the base of her neck. Her lips had been sealed by needle and thread; her face was unreadable. Was she at peace or just hollow? Zora couldn't tell—couldn't reason it out.

She started sobbing and buried her face in Ms. Prosser's shoulder. Her Aunt Anne didn't seem so intimidating now. Just gentle and kind and marked by sorrow herself.

♈

That evening, Zora paid a call on Captain Flores. The Ranger had commandeered a solarium for her headquarters and a wheelchair for her plaster-casted legs. She was busy sticking pins in a map of Old Appalachia. No green ones, which meant no harbinger sightings.

"Ms. Coldiron," she said in her severe way. "Take a load off your feet. Or foot, as the case may be. I appreciate all your work on the expedition. What brings you here?"

Zora sat on the other side of the map, right at the edge of the Bluegrass. "Two things. First, I have a message from Mr. Vandy. I was the last person with him."

The captain's expression softened a fraction. "Go on."

"He said he never stopped falling for you." A radiator clanged, and Zora half expected a swarm of gwyllion to explode from its valve.

"Anything else?"

"Just that he had no regrets."

"Thank you." Captain Flores touched a black pin marking the mountain range where the airship had crashed. "Ms. Coldiron—*Zora*—may I give you a piece of advice?"

"Yes, ma'am."

"Listen to your calling, but don't let it drown out your heart."

"I understand, ma'am." Zora wished she'd heard the rest of Walter Vandy's story about being rescued by a young Ranger named Sylvia Flores. Maybe someday she'd ask the captain what happened next.

"You had another reason for stopping by."

On the map, one red pin was stabbing into Clack Mountain. "Can I speak to Evelyn Fontaine?"

Zora braced herself for a no, but the captain lifted a key ring from her belt. "We have her jailed in the thermal cave behind the bathhouse." She removed a key and gave it to Zora. "This will unlock the gate, but it won't unlock the door to her cell. Do you want me to send an officer with you?"

"No, ma'am. I'd rather do this alone."

Key in pocket, Zora followed the stepping stones to the bathhouse, along the path Abigail had led her. A point of green light drifted across the moon—a high-altitude spirit gliding on the ether-streams. Maybe even the one she'd seen on her last night in Lightning Bug Hollow.

Was that a warning sign? Should she turn around and scurry back to her elders?

No, she could deal with Evelyn. Antler Woman had fallen for a simple ruse on the fall equinox and misjudged her own pawn aboard the black train.

Zora passed by the bathhouse and entered the woods. Another dark forest, but this one didn't scare her. She wasn't a child anymore.

The gate to the cave was solid steel. Last chance to steer clear of the snake den. The plucky young heroes in Quinn's favorite novels—Carson van Patten, Addie the Urchin, and their like— never had to tarnish their souls to defeat the villains. Nor did the naïve blacksmiths and innocent witchlets in Signe's fairy tales.

But this wasn't that kind of story.

Zora turned the key and opened the gate. Beyond, the cave was warm and humid. The farther she went, the hotter it grew. At last, she reached a chamber lit by a solitary lantern.

From behind iron bars, Evelyn smirked. "Hello, my dear." Or did she mean *deer*? "It's so nice to see you up and about. I hope Mr. Martin is feeling fit as a fiddle, too. And I was delighted to hear the news of Mr. Prosser and Ms. Janasdottir's reunion."

Don't let her get your goat, Zora told herself. "Abigail's funeral is tomorrow. Not that you care."

"It was not I who killed that poor girl. As I said, I've never harmed anyone."

Zora reached into a pocket and pulled out a device with a red helix bulb. "Do you recognize this?"

"A beckoner reverse-engineered from my technology."

"If I switched it on, set it down, and walked away, the bars keeping you in wouldn't keep the spirits out."

Between them, a small pool of water rippled and steamed. "We both know you'd never do that," said Evelyn.

"You're like everyone else who ever underestimated me. You don't know what I can do. By your own logic, my hands would be clean."

"Congratulations." Evelyn clapped slowly three times. "You're all grown up. What happens now?"

"I'll keep this in my pocket." Zora put away the spirit-lure. "And you'll tell me what that machine in the boxcar does."

Evelyn's grin was predatory. "I designed the loom to weave a new sort of tapestry, but I need your help to make it work. That's why I invited you to my secret lodgings. Why I arranged for you to come along on the airship mission. Why I went back to save you from the titan." She seated herself on the floor of her cell. "What if you and I could follow the harbinger to its own world and then destroy it forever?"

Zora walked up to the bars and sat cross-legged just beyond Evelyn's reach. "Tell me more."

EPILOGUE

THE MORNING AFTER THE GREAT WAKENING

JESSIE PLAYED ONE LAST NOTE AND LOWERED HER BOW. THE valley below was still flooded with ghost-lights, but the mountaintop was a dark oasis. She'd sawed down all the monsters in her path—the walking water tower, the giant nightcrawler, a hundred more things with no names—and scraped up a wall of echoes behind her. Over yonder ridge, the earthshakers were in retreat from the dawn's approach.

Tucking her fiddle under her arm, she wiped a hand on her shirt. A night of chord changes had worn her fingertips bloody and her nerve endings raw.

High above the hills, shimmering curtains pulled away from an indigo backdrop. Beneath it, the first hints of orange laid bare the town's extinction. Chimneys without smoke, sidewalks without people. Cars and trucks motionless in the streets, trees fallen or burned down to stumps.

Jessie had no earthly idea what to do next. Her bones ached, her feet felt like blocks of ice, and her coat lay entombed in the wreckage of her home. Along with her family. She'd searched all the houses on the way to town—even

Mildred Fannin's—but everybody was missing or dead. She'd thought she'd been lonely before, but that was nothing compared to this.

As the sky grew brighter, the ghost-lights flickered out. Maybe they shunned the sun, like the phantoms in her sister's plays or the vampires in her brother's magazines.

Knowing she'd lost her siblings forever hurt far worse than the bruises on her ribs.

Then a voice whispered in her head—just like after the flash at her window, but now she could make out the words. *What are you, little creature?*

"I'm Jessamine Carter," she said, though there was no one in sight. "Who are you?"

I am the voice and summoner of my kindred.

The whisperer must be a ghoul—a malevolent spirit. "You did that?" Fury rose inside her. "You called up the thing that murdered my family?"

Hush, little prey, while I send you to join them. A low drone rolled over the summit, and a ring of green flame rose around her.

"No." Jessie set her fiddle against her chin. "I beat your monsters, and I'll beat you, too." She'd give it her own kind of fire on the mountain.

The stars are shifting. The voice sounded less certain—more calculating. *I will return when they align again.*

She wondered how long that would take. "I'll be waiting."

You'll be nothing but dust. Once darkness falls, my kindred will hunt you down.

"I have the keys to flatten them." As she drew her bow, the flaming circle sputtered and died. "Want to try your humming against my cross tunings and double stops?"

The voice didn't answer, but its laugh rang in her ears until the sun peeked over the hills.

Blinking away tears, Jessie glanced backward and forward. Behind her lay the hollows she'd shielded with webs of uncanny strings. Ahead of her stretched ravaged forests and blackened slopes. Neither way led anywhere special to her; everyone she loved was gone.

And yet the songs inside her cried out to be played. By daylight, she'd look for a coat, bandages for her fingers, fellow survivors. When dusk came, she'd use her music to ward off the bogeys and monsters—all the spirits wakened from earth, air, water, or shadow. If she lived long enough, she'd set down every note so other folks could read from her songbook.

First, though, she had to choose a path.

Jessie pulled a coin from her pocket—a copper penny stained green with age. "Heads I go onward, tails I go back," she said to herself. When she flipped the penny, it landed face-up.

Fiddle in hand, she wandered on into legend.

ZORA, QUINN & SIGNE WILL RETURN IN

THE
SPIRIT RIFTS

A BRIEF TIMELINE OF THE HOLLOWS
Years AW (After Wakening)

0   *The Great Wakening* (Spring Equinox)
Spirits lay waste to the lands surrounding the Hollows
The cities of the Bluegrass fall into ruin

1–76   *The Between Times*
Wayfarers visit the Hollows from Sylvania
Riverboats steam to and from the Delta
Radio contact with the Tidelands
Airship travel ends after the crash of the *Sheltowee*

77   *The Lesser Wakening* (Summer Solstice)
Spirits overrun the Outer Hollows and the Pass
Last radio contact with lands beyond the Hollows
The Coal Age ends as mines run out or are cut off

125   Solar eclipse in the Hollows

126   Births of Quinn Prosser, Signe Janasdottir, and Paige Zhu

128   Birth of Zora Coldiron

131   Quinn and Zora's father sights the harbinger

135   The harbinger tricks Zora into the woods and terrorizes her

138   Signe's spirit-vision manifests

143   Evelyn Fontaine strikes a bargain with the harbinger
Paige starts her apprenticeship as a Spotter
Zora and Quinn begin hunting spirits together
Signe leaves home to follow her calling as a spirit-seer
Death of Nevan McBrain in a leviathan attack
The Forestalled Wakening (Fall Equinox)

EXCERPTS FROM
TOLLIVER'S POCKET SPIRIT HANDBOOK

To ward off minor spirits, try Tolliver's Anti-Spirit Spray!!!
Two bits per bottle or a dozen bits per case

☠ Innocuous; ☠☠ Troublesome; ☠☠☠ Dangerous; ☠☠☠☠ Deadly;
☠☠☠☠☠ Calamitous; ☠☠☠☠☠☠ Cataclysmic

Altie	☠☠☠☠☠	Giant, serpentine river-dwelling waterbound
Boge	☠	Trilling, ball-shaped roamer; delivers a mild jolt
Bolide	☠☠☠☠	Meteoric airbound; incinerates whatever it seizes
Coblynau	☠	Small earthbound; knocks on walls of caves and pits
Dahoo	☠☠	Keening, ring-shaped roamer; can change its tint
Derecho	☠☠☠☠☠	Thundering airbound; lurks within electrical storms
Dwayyo	☠☠☠☠	Barn-sized, wall-rattling roamer with lethal spurs
Elemental	☠☠☠☠☠	Vaporous earthbound; turns all life in its sway to ash
Flamb	☠☠	Flaming earthbound with prickling touch; dwells in patches
Geist	☠☠☠	Lumpy, cackling roamer; chases its quarry in gaggles
Gize	☠☠	Geyser-like earthbound; sprays up from fissures
Gwyllion	☠☠☠☠	Swarming, metallic roamer; nests in dank places

Name	Threat	Description
Hern	☠☠☠☠	Razor-clawed, howling roamer; hunts in packs
Hount	☠☠☠☠☠	Colossal, roaring roamer; flows after its prey
Indrid	☠	Fluttery, moaning roamer; wanders in flocks
Jarmara	☠☠☠	Kite-shaped, spiny-tailed roamer; drawn to the dying
Kelpie	☠☠☠	Fetid, algae-colored waterbound; inhabits stagnant ponds
Landwight	☠☠☠☠	Chasm-dwelling earthbound; drains life with its talons
Lare	☠☠☠	Poisonous earthbound; lurks in subterranean warrens
Leviathan	☠☠☠☠☠	Massive, tentacled lake-dwelling waterbound
Lichender	☠☠☠☠	Crawling, symbiotic roamer; withers everything in its path
Medusa	☠☠	Floating roamer with long, stinging threads
Mive	☠☠☠	Oozing roamer; resembles effervescent slime
Nimbus	☠☠	Hazy, levitating roamer; makes phlegmy noises
Nixie	☠	Raucous, turbulent waterbound; swims in schools
Orb	☠☠☠	Globular, clustering earthbound; presence evokes panic
Pharos	☠☠☠	Bright, wailing roamer; flickers like a strobe light
Roperite	☠☠☠☠	Yowling roamer; ensnares its victims with lassoes
Shard	☠☠☠	Spiky, crystalline roamer; skewers its prey
Snarlyyow	☠☠☠☠	Undulating, sulfurous roamer; filaments burn like acid
Spire	☠☠☠☠☠	Silent, towering roamer; streamers hang from its crown
Sylph	☠	Gauzy, flocking airbound; drifts on thermal currents

Tailypo	☠☠☠☠	Scorching roamer; smashes its way into lonely houses
Tangie	☠☠	Sinuous, shoaling waterbound; glides in looping patterns
Tangle	☠☠	Snaky, whistling roamer; can exist in two places at once
Titan	☠☠☠☠☠☠	Mightiest of all roamers; leaves devastation in its wake
Trow	☠☠☠	Lumbering roamer; induces synesthesia; can split in half
Umbra	☠	Shy roamer with a dim aura and a haunting cry
Varc	☠☠☠	Crackling, lightning-like roamer; gravitates toward rooftops
Vorx	☠☠☠	Whirlwind roamer; scoops up debris in its eye
Welkie	☠☠	Small, shoaling waterbound; etches marks on bare skin
Wengo	☠☠	Funnel-shaped roamer; touch freezes its target
Whimpus	☠☠	Swift, elusive roamer; scrambles senses with its aura
Wisp	☠	Tiny, swarming earthbound; forms hives in sinkholes
Yallery	☠	Meadow-dwelling earthbound; sprouts in clumps
Zhar	?	Scintillating airbound; sails on the high etherstreams

Annotations by Zora Coldiron:

- *The information in this handbook is transparently plagiarized from the* Field Guide to the Spirits of the Hollows *by Nevan McBrain (RIP).*
- *I discovered the tangle (with Quinn's help, of course).*
- *Do not, under any circumstances, rely on Tolliver's Anti-Spirit Spray.*

ACKNOWLEDGMENTS

I'm grateful to my wife, mom, dad, brother, and kids for their support and feedback during the writing of this novel; without them, Zora, Quinn, and Signe wouldn't exist. I'm thankful to Adrienne, Josh, and Lydia for taking another trip to the Hollows and being my beta readers again. I'm also thankful to James T. Egan of Bookfly Design for creating a cover with an ominous and wintry feel, Sarah Waites of Illustrated Page Design for bringing the Wastes to life with her cartography, Bodie Dykstra of BD Book Design for polishing my manuscript with his editing and typesetting, and Stephanie Garcia for designing the Lockegee Books logo. Finally, I'm grateful to the many folk, bluegrass, and old-time musicians whose songs helped inspire the world of *The Spirit Wastes*.

ABOUT THE AUTHOR

P. R. Brewer grew up on a fish farm in Rowan County, Kentucky, a short hike away from Cave Run Lake and a winding drive away from Clack Mountain (the site of sinister rituals, according to local legend). He currently lives in Delaware with his wife Barbara and their two children. In his day job, he teaches and writes about science and the media. He spends his free time watching horror movies, playing D&D, going to metal concerts, and wandering through spooky forests. His nonfiction work has appeared in *National Geographic*, *Skeptical Inquirer*, and various arcane journals.

To learn more about the Spirit Hollows series, visit P. R. Brewer's website: www.prbrewer.com.